Kate Furnivall was born in Wales and studied English at London University. She worked in publishing and then moved to TV advertising, where she met her husband. She now has two sons and lives with her family by the sea in Devon.

You can discover more about the author at www.katefurnivall.com

THE ITALIAN WIFE

Italy, 1932: Mussolini's Italy is growing from strength to strength, but at what cost? One bright autumn morning, architect Isabella sits in a café in the vibrant centre of Bellina, when a woman she's never met asks her to watch her young daughter, just for a moment. Reluctantly, Isabella agrees — and then watches in horror as the woman climbs to the top of the town's clock tower and steps over the edge. This tragic encounter draws vivid memories to the surface, forcing Isabella to probe further into the secrets of her own past as she tries to protect the young girl from the authorities. Together with charismatic photographer Roberto Falco, Isabella is about to discover that some secrets run deeper, and are more dangerous, than either of them could possibly have imagined . . .

KATE FURNIVALL

THE ITALIAN WIFE

Complete and Unabridged

CHARNWOOD
Leicester

First published in Great Britain in 2014 by
Sphere
An imprint of
Little, Brown Book Group
London

First Charnwood Edition
published 2016
by arrangement with
Little, Brown Book Group
An Hachette UK Company
London

The moral right of the author has been asserted

All characters and events in this publication, other than those clearly in the public domain, are fictitious and any resemblance to real persons, living or dead, is purely coincidental.

A catalogue record for this book is available from the British Library.

ISBN 978–1–4448–2668–5

Published by
F. A. Thorpe (Publishing)
Anstey, Leicestershire

Set by Words & Graphics Ltd.
Anstey, Leicestershire
Printed and bound in Great Britain by
T. J. International Ltd., Padstow, Cornwall

This book is printed on acid-free paper

For a special little boy
with all my love

Acknowledgements

A big thank you to my inspired editors Lucy Malagoni and Catherine Burke for their insight and unfailing enthusiasm for this book, and to all the fantastic team at Little, Brown UK — especially the intrepid Thalia Proctor. Thank you all. I am also grateful to Liz Hatherell for her sharp eye on the manuscript.

I also want to say a special thank you to my wonderful agent Teresa Chris for her support and guidance at all times — I could not ask for better.

Many thanks to Marian Churchward for ploughing through my scribble and for staying calm while sharing Isabella's hectic journey with me.

My warm gratitude to my friends at Brixham Writers for listening to my moans and feeding me tea and biscuits on demand. As always, it's been fun.

Many thanks to Filippo Serra in Latina, one of the towns on the Agro Pontino, for showing me around the beautiful area and for being an invaluable fountain of knowledge about its fascinating history.

My thanks also to Leigh L Klotz Jr. for his generosity in sharing his knowledge of all things Graflex — his passion for the camera is infectious.

Most of all, huge and heartfelt thanks to Norman for giving me the idea of setting my story in the Pontine Marshes in the first place — and for coming to explore them with me.

1

MILAN 1922

I didn't know I was going to die that warm October day in Milan. If I'd known, I'd have done things differently. Of course I would. If I'd known, I wouldn't have died.

But I was nineteen years old and believed I was immortal. I had no idea that life, which seemed so snug and warm in my grasp, could be snatched away at any moment, though I did nothing more than turn my head for a split second to inspect a market stall.

A gunshot rang out. The sound of it ricocheted off the ancient pink stone of the market square, making my ears ring and shoppers scatter in panic across the cobbles. It was market day and I had come to idle away an hour among the stalls, passing the time of day with neighbours and exchanging news with friends. Believing that an hour of life was something I could fritter away without thought.

I picked and prodded at the colourful piles of fruit and vegetables on offer, handling the warm leathery pomegranates as I chose the ripest one and inhaling the musty scent of the skin of deep purple aubergines. All around me stalls overflowed with the vibrant yellows and greens and rich scarlets that are the colours of life.

How could I know I was about to lose mine?

If it had happened in some stinking back alleyway in a rough district of Milan, I'd have understood. I wouldn't have liked it, but I'd have understood. Or on one of Mussolini's fast new *autostrade* where cars race each other as if desperate to leap into the arms of death. There it would make sense. But not here. Not on the lazy warm cobblestones of my home district. Not with my belly swollen with child and a piece of pecorino cheese salty in my mouth.

'Take a bite, Isabella,' Arturo Cribori called out from behind his cheese stall, waggling his black eyebrows at me suggestively.

He sliced off a tiny triangle of pecorino for me to taste. I smiled at him and laughed.

Thinking back on it now, I listen to that carefree laugh and it makes me want to cry. It was the last laugh of the person I was back then. The laugh of a girl who believed she had everything she needed to make her happy for the rest of her life — a handsome husband, a baby growing inside her, a three-room city apartment with a set of silver spoons in pride of place on the sideboard, a future that stretched ahead of her on rails as shiny as Italy's new train tracks. It was the laugh of a person who still believed in goodness. I remember that girl dimly. I touch her lustrous raven's wing hair and my chest aches for her.

The real reason I had come to the street market was to stroll between the rows of stalls alongside Luigi, showing off my fine husband and the *bambino* growing inside me, displaying them proudly for all to admire. I paused to taste the cheese, I remember that. I didn't look out at the houses surrounding the square or spare a glance for the upstairs windows overlooking the stalls. Why should I?

If I had looked up, things might have been different.

I remember looking across at Luigi, seeking him out in the bustling crowd. So many people were milling around the stalls, laughing and arguing, haggling over the price of yellow peppers or the weight of a sack of potatoes, but my husband was easy to spot. He was half a head taller than anyone else and possessed the handsome features of a Roman senator, though in fact he came from generations of farming stock. 'I'm a fine stud bull,' he would laugh as he stroked my swollen belly.

Luigi was a powerful presence in his crisp Blackshirt militia uniform. Men stood back for him and women's eyes followed him like fawns. Not just the young signorinas tossing their dark manes at him, but the black-clad matrons as well and the loud-mouthed peasants on the stalls, with bosoms as large and ripe as their melons. They all let their eyes linger on Luigi Berotti. I was proud of him. So proud it almost choked me at times. Stupid, I know, but that's how it was. Even though he raised a hand to me after he'd taken a grappa too many, I saw no wrong in him.

I know better now.

The first shot came out of nowhere, ripping through the market, The crisp crack of it sent stallholders ducking behind their wares and a tethered dog howled. The second shot sent a wave of pigeons wheeling up from the campanile into the flat blue Italian sky.

I swung round from a salami stall in time to see Luigi's dark head slide from view. It lurched forward as if he'd spotted a five hundred lire note lying on the ground. I screamed. It was a vile sound dragged up from deep inside me and scoured my throat raw.

A man seized my wrist. 'Are you hurt?'

It was my father. I should have thanked him, this father showing concern for his only daughter amid the whirlwind of fear that swept through the market. But I didn't. Wordlessly I dragged my arm free and hurled myself into the huddle of people crouching on the cobbles in front of a stall selling embroidered shawls. Their eyes were huge with panic. Heads whipped back and forth, seeking the hand with the gun. But they didn't run. Those brave people stayed with the limp figure on the ground. Others ran and I couldn't blame them. They had families. They had loved ones. They had lives to live. Why should they stay behind to stop my husband bleeding to death on the cobbles?

Luigi's dark eyes were frozen open like a doll's and gazing blindly up at the sun as if he could outstare it. In that tiny fraction of time before the second shot rang out, I saw the slack hang of his full lips that had always been so muscular in seizing mine, and I knew what it meant. I saw scarlet raindrops sparkling on the small hairs of his eyebrows. I saw his strong hand curled up like a claw. And in the centre of his big bull chest

I saw a hole in his shirt. The blood barely showed against the colour of its material but it made the blackness of the shirt glisten, like the blackness on the back of a fly.

I snatched a shawl from the deserted stall. I would stop the bleeding with it. I would stop it and he would live. He must live. My Luigi. My husband. His child kicked fiercely inside me to urge me on.

'Luigi!'

I called his name to summon him back to me.

'Luigi Berotti!'

I didn't hear the second shot. All I knew was that my sandal had left a perfect imprint in my husband's blood on the ground. I was horrified by it. I saw it as I bent forward to kneel at his side and that was when the backache that had nagged at me all day, where the baby was pressing on a nerve, suddenly flared into a white blinding pain. I thought it was my bones cracking with grief.

Before I hit the ground, I was dead.

★ ★ ★

'Is she breathing?'

I woke. Nothing worked. Not my eyelids. Not my limbs. My tongue lay lifeless on the base of my mouth. I tried to cry out but the silence in my head remained absolute while pain wrapped itself around my body.

'What in God's name is the matter with you, nurse? You're meant to be monitoring her airways.'

'Yes, Dr Cantini, I'm sorry, I was just checking her . . .'

'Sorry? Where will sorry get you when she's dead and cold on the slab? Tell me that, nurse.'

The doctor's voice was loud and curt to the point of rudeness, the voice of a man who believed in the divine right of the medical profession. I knew that tone. He'd used it on me at times. It was the tone he resorted to when trying to hide fear. Dr Cantini is my father. If my father was afraid, I knew I was in trouble.

Help me, Papa. Hold my hand.

But the words remained ice cold inside my head.

'Isabella, can you hear me?'

My father's voice sounded close, as if he were leaning over me. I could picture him, his moustache black and bristling, his blue eyes behind his spectacles abandoning any pretence of professional calm. His daughter was dying.

'Isabella!'

Was he holding my hand? I couldn't tell. I willed him to be holding my hand, but right now my will was a weak and flimsy thing.

'Isabella, hold on. Don't let go.' His tone was fierce. 'You hear me?'

'She's lucky,' the nurse commented quietly.

'Lucky! You call this lucky!'

'Yes, Dottore. She was lucky that you were in the market beside her and you restarted her heart when she was shot. You pumped God's good life-giving air into her lungs. Our blessed Virgin Mary was watching over your daughter today and the good Lord is giving her strength

6

now to stay with us.'

Papa grunted. He was never one to argue against blind faith, though he possessed none himself. He claimed it did more good for his patients than any number of pills and potions.

'So why wasn't your Virgin Mary watching over her dead husband too?' he muttered sourly.

Luigi. Luigi.

The sight of my husband's eyes, blank as a doll's, came into my mind and sucked the breath out of me.

'Oxygen!' my father bellowed. 'Get her oxygen!'

There was a flurry of hospital noises around me and the soft sound of the nurse intoning a prayer for my soul.

'Don't, Isabella.' I could feel Papa's hot anger crushing my chest. 'Don't you dare die on me, *cara mia.*'

Papa, it's all right. Don't grieve for me. I love you, but I want to be with Luigi and my baby. Let me go.

But he didn't listen. Papa never listened. A mask was pressed to my face and oxygen was pumped into my lungs. This was my second chance. A new life. Whether I wanted it or not.

2

BELLINA 1932

Ten Years Later

The air vibrated to the sound of pigeons and the sun streamed down on the newly constructed buildings in the piazza. To Isabella's eye some were a little too grand. Italy's leader, Benito Mussolini, had decreed that this brand new town of Bellina must display the past glories of Ancient Rome in its architecture. He wanted its people to revel in the fact that Italy's Roman eagle had once dominated the world.

But all those arches. And columns. And marble colonnades. All adorning the Fascist Party headquarters. Did they really need to be quite so massive? Or quite so grandiose? Isabella's fingers itched to redesign them. She was an architect, but was only one of the many lowly assistants to Dottore Architetto Martino, the chief architect here in Bellina, so what did she know?

Very little, according to Martino.

She sipped her scalding coffee, stretched her bare legs into a patch of autumn sunlight and looked around at the people crossing the huge piazza. There weren't many of them and they didn't linger. A few were idling outside the cream curved façade of the elegant cinema. The

8

film *L'Armata Azzurra* was showing there today — an Air Force adventure. Mussolini was a great believer in cinemas. Keep the populace entertained and they won't bother you. That was his theory and Isabella wasn't going to argue with it. But she suspected that the people of Bellina weren't quite as docile as Il Duce liked to think they were and that they didn't like the sense of being watched from the Fascist headquarters which was raised up above the piazza by a dozen sweeping steps. She didn't like that feeling herself.

Every year Isabella took this day in October off work. She would sit, sunk in silence, wearing the sleeveless peach dress that Luigi used to like so much, the breeze raising the small hairs on her skin. During the past week, as this day drew nearer she'd started to get jumpy, and by the time this morning dawned, she was wide-eyed and sleepless.

It was ten years to the day. The day that she and Luigi were shot. It had been hot that day and was hot again now. She had taught herself self-control for the rest of the year, but on this one day each October she allowed herself to cry. Not so that anyone could see. Of course not. But deep inside herself. Something split open, she could feel it, and the tears flowed unseen. She cried for Luigi. For her unborn child. For that young easy-going girl she used to be. That October day had ruptured the fabric of her. It was that simple.

She had no idea that a decade later her life was about to be disrupted again.

She was sitting in Gino's café, the only permitted café in the piazza because Fascists didn't like people to gather anywhere in large numbers unless they'd organised it themselves. She was sipping coffee — strong and full of bite, just the way Gino knew she liked it — and all around her she could spy touches of her handiwork in the grand municipal buildings that bordered each side of the square. They sparkled in white marble, interspersed with intricate terracotta brickwork, their arches and their columns and wide spacious steps dwarfing the people who used them. These buildings were designed to impress. To remind each person, who stopped to admire them, of the power of the State.

Isabella found it hard to explain — even to herself — exactly why she loved pouring so much of herself into these buildings. All she knew was that it filled with warmth a place within her that was stark and cold. Sitting here in the sunshine she could laugh at her passion for injecting life and breath into the stone and mortar of this town, knowing it was this passion that always had the power to bring her back from despair. Even on this dark day it made her happy, and she exhaled a string of curling coffee steam with a sense of quiet satisfaction.

The important thing to remember was this: for that moment she was happy and it was that brief sliver of happiness that made her vulnerable. If she had been in her usual rush, her brow creased in a frown of concentration, her mind churning over her next piece of architectural work and her eyes preoccupied with whatever was taking form within her head, the woman with the wild hair who hurried into the piazza dragging a child behind her would have chosen someone else to approach. And if not, Isabella would have said *no, I'm too busy.* Nor would the child have been willing to remain with her, a stranger who had lost her smile somewhere along the way.

So it was that moment of happiness that Isabella blamed for what happened next. But how could she not be happy when she was looking at the tower? It was so beautiful. Of course she was biased because she had designed it herself. It towered the way a tower should, square and tall, surmounted by a great bronze bell, its pale travertino marble shimmering like a shaft of light, sending out a message of dominance to the whole region. It was attached to the Fascist Party headquarters. Oriolo Frezzotti, the architect in charge of the whole project of constructing Mussolini's six new towns, caught sight of Isabella's design on one of his lightning visits from Rome and gave Dottore Martino, her immediate superior, no option. Frezzotti had overruled his objections with an extravagant wave of his hand.

'Don't let it go to your head,' Martino had growled at her.

'No, dottore.'

And to make sure she didn't get ideas above her station he'd stuck her to work on gutterings and facings for the next few months. But Isabella didn't mind. She loved her work as an architect, all aspects of it, and from her office window she watched her tower grow block by block.

'*Scusi*, signora.'

Isabella looked at the woman. She didn't know her or her child. She put her coffee cup down on the table and inspected her, squinting against the sun. The woman was slight and dressed in black shapeless clothes with a face it would be easy to overlook, except there was an urgency about her that made Isabella pay attention. She wore an anxious expression, her eyes darting around her as she stood beside the café table and stretched her hand out to Isabella, palm upwards. For a moment Isabella thought she was begging. But she was mistaken. The woman was offering something. It was a brass crucifix on a chain that was dull and grimy. Isabella shook her head. She didn't want it.

'No, *grazie*, no.'

The woman looked a few years younger than Isabella, maybe no more than twenty-five, and the child, a girl, could have been anywhere between eight or ten. Both possessed unkempt black hair and a nervousness that was unsettling to be close to. Isabella wanted them to go away. She looked over at her tower, hoping they'd be gone when she looked back. She was more at ease with buildings than with people. Ten years ago she'd lost her trust in people, but buildings were solid and dependable. You knew where you were with a building. That's why she'd worked so hard to put herself through architectural college after her recovery from hospital, to give herself something she could depend on.

'Signora,' the woman said, 'I have to go

somewhere for just a few minutes. It is very important. Will you please watch my child for me while I am gone?' Her eyes flicked a secretive glance at her daughter. 'She will be good.'

The child stared at her own feet. She was dressed in a simple blue cotton frock and had sunk her hands deep into its patch pockets. She didn't seem any keener on this idea than Isabella was.

'Well, I'm not sure . . . ' Isabella said uneasily.

She looked for help at the next table but the man seated there with his pipe didn't lift his nose out of his newspaper. If it had been any other day she would have said a firm no, and maybe things would have turned out differently for all three of them. But it had to happen on the one day of the year when she was not her usual self-contained self.

'Please, signora, *per favore?*'

The mother placed the crucifix on the metal table where it clattered noisily.

'I don't want your crucifix,' Isabella said immediately.

'I will be quick. Very quick.'

Isabella saw sudden tears fill the woman's eyes and her pleading face loomed closer as she leaned down to Isabella.

'You are a good person,' the woman told her. 'I see it in your face. You are full of resolve. Be kind to me.'

Isabella opened her mouth to object. She didn't want to be told she was good or full of resolve, not while she was sitting quietly minding her own business over a coffee, but the woman

13

leaned closer and said in a low intimate hiss, 'They know who killed your bastard husband.'

Isabella saw the tremor in her own hand as she put down her cup and heard it rattle in its saucer.

'Who do you mean? Who are 'they'?'

The woman pulled back and jabbed an accusing finger in the direction of the Party headquarters. 'Them.' She spat on the ground in disgust. 'Those Fascist murderers.' Her mouth took on a strange shape that Isabella only recognised as a bitter smile when she heard the laugh that came from it. '*They* will pay for it now.'

'How do you know that my husband died?'

But the black-clad figure was already striding away, almost running down to the far end of the piazza, scattering the pigeons. Isabella stood up, aghast.

'Wait!'

'Mamma won't wait.'

She looked down at the child's mass of dark curls. She was too thin, all elbows and collarbones.

'What do you mean, she won't wait?'

Her narrow shoulders shrugged, her face didn't look up. 'She told me I must wait here with you.'

* * *

Isabella sat down again. She wasn't certain what had just happened. She didn't know anything about children. Since the bullet she couldn't

14

have any *bambini* of her own and she'd gone out of her way to avoid them, though in Italy she couldn't help but be surrounded by them much of the time. She tried to keep them at a distance when she could, but this time she had no choice.

'Please, sit down.' She waved a hand towards the chair opposite.

The girl slid into it, taking up no space.

'I'm Isabella Berotti. What's your name?'

'Rosa.'

'So, Rosa, do you live in Bellina?'

'No.'

'Just visiting?'

'Yes.'

'Where have you come from?'

'Rome.'

Her voice was so slight, Isabella had to prick her ears to hear her.

'Did you come by train with your mother?'

She nodded. Or rather, her curls nodded. She still wasn't looking up. They reached a brief impasse and Isabella finished her coffee to cover the awkward pause. She felt sorry for the child. Stuck with a woman who could find no words for her. In desperation her gaze returned to the figure of the mother racing across the sunlit piazza towards the Fascist Party headquarters. Isabella couldn't bring herself to abandon the child and chase after her, but she was shaken by the woman's words.

'How about something to drink, Rosa, while we wait?'

'No.' But the girl added a polite, '*Grazie*.' It was almost drowned out by the cooing of the

15

pigeons that drifted around the tables.

'An ice cream then?' Isabella called out to Gino before Rosa could refuse again. '*Uno gelato, per favore,* Gino.'

When it arrived at the table with a flourish from Gino, the girl gave Isabella a direct look for the first time. Her deep-set brown eyes were as wild as her hair and in a panic. Isabella felt a jolt of dismay for the pale-skinned face.

'I can go,' the girl said quickly. 'If you want me to.'

'No, Rosa. Of course not. I want you to stay. Your mother has left you in my care.' Isabella smiled at her.

She didn't smile back, but the panic in her young eyes seemed to die down a fraction. Isabella had an urge to hold her small angular body, to tell her not to worry so much. She was too young to worry. Isn't that what Italian mammas do instinctively? Provide hugs and kisses? All Isabella had to offer her was ice cream.

'Eat up,' she encouraged.

The girl took up the spoon and steadily consumed the ice cream with quiet concentration. The warmth of the day was beginning to build and the sun was picking out the *fasces*, the symbol of Fascism that was carved above the entrance of each of the municipal buildings in the piazza, painting them golden. Isabella's gaze shifted back to her tower.

'Rosa, do you have any idea what your mother meant when she said 'They will pay for it now'?'

The child remained silent.

16

Isabella hunted for another topic of conversation, swapping to an easier one. 'Do you like Bellina?'

Rosa frowned and glanced around the beautiful piazza that was the heart of the town. Its pavements were a mosaic of marble, of pinks and greys and unexpected bands of speckled white in geometric designs that gave endless pleasure to the eye of pedestrians. In the centre rose a fountain — not one of Rome's baroque monstrosities, but a simple, yet powerful, vast globe of black granite with a circle of water-jets surrounding it. Bellina had risen from the watery marshes and this was the symbol of the glorious new world that Fascism was creating for the workers of Italy.

'Do you like Bellina?' Isabella asked again.

'No.'

'Why not?'

But the girl was already back at her ice cream, hunched over it, blocking out all else.

Isabella knew that it must be excruciating to be abandoned with a stranger, so if Rosa wanted silence, that was fine with her. The sun was behind her, throwing soft purple shadows over the mosaic flooring, and Isabella sat back in her chair, letting her gaze drift up to her tower with its brass-faced clock that struck the hours.

Immediately she noticed a figure emerge on to the viewing platform at the top of the tower. She felt a rush of pride that someone liked the town well enough to climb the two hundred and sixty steps to gain a wider view of it. Even from here she could see it was a woman. She had

17

wild dark hair. With surprise Isabella realised it was Rosa's mother. Rosa was sitting with her back to the tower, so Isabella opened her mouth to say *Look, there's your mamma. Wave to her, Rosa,* but in the split second it took for the words to travel from her brain to her mouth, she saw the woman in black clamber up on to the parapet.

She teetered there. Her arms spread out sideways, holding her balance on the edge, and a breeze snatched at the folds of her long black dress and tangled the loose strands of her hair. Behind her the empty blue sky seemed to watch and wait in silence. Isabella expected her to shout to Rosa, to cry out across the length of the piazza: *Look at me.* But she didn't. She dipped her head, stared down at the people far beneath her and without any warning leapt off the top. She performed a perfect swallow-dive to the marble steps below.

No sound emerged from Isabella's mouth. How she kept her scream inside, she didn't know, but she couldn't stop herself from jumping to her feet. Rosa looked up, wary of her, but her attention was distracted by a man's shout behind her and a woman's high-pitched scream. The child started to turn towards the group that Isabella could see gathering around the steps.

'A dog has bitten someone,' Isabella said quickly, scooping the crucifix into her pocket. 'Rosa, I've just remembered that I have to collect something from my home.' She reached out, took hold of the girl's skinny arm and pulled her

18

to her feet. 'You can come with me. It's not far. We won't be long.'

She didn't know if it was because the girl was used to being told what to do or because she had finished her ice cream and was ready for other amusement, but she allowed herself to be marched out of the Piazza del Popolo without a murmur.

Neither of them mentioned her mother.

*   *   *

Isabella rushed Rosa along Via Augustus. The street of small shops with apartments above was quiet at this hour but in the dusty heat there lingered the smell of *arancini* and fried onions from someone's kitchen. Everywhere was coated in a pale layer of building dust that didn't want to shift, but hung in the air. It had a habit of getting between teeth and under fingernails.

Isabella was moving so quickly that she felt her limp grow worse. She was aware of people staring, watching her out of the corners of their eyes, and after all these years she thought she'd be used to it but it still stung. It had taken three years' hard sweat and seven operations to get her walking again but right now she was more concerned with getting Rosa as far away from the Piazza del Popolo as she could.

How do you tell a child her mother just died?

Isabella was shaken by a deep anger towards the mysterious dark-haired woman who would do this to her daughter. As they approached her home, she eased up on her pace and gently

19

released Rosa's arm.

'It's not far,' she assured the child, waving a hand towards the elegant apartment blocks that lay ahead. This was the most stylish and expensive part of town. It was the quarter where the streets were widest and where an abundance of young trees had been planted that would one day transform them into leafy avenues. This was where the top government employees lived. There were forty different designs for the houses and apartment buildings in Bellina, the forty designs repeated over and over again in a set order. It gave the town a symmetry and a sense of being part of a greater orderly scheme that Mussolini wanted the people to value.

The layout of Bellina followed the designs of Ancient Rome with a central forum and the town divided into four quadrants. The roads radiated out from the main piazza on a grid system. This made for efficient movement of people and traffic along the ramrod-straight streets, as well as ease of navigation, so that it was hard to get lost in Bellina. Mussolini intended the people of Italy to know exactly where they were going.

'Do you have relatives in Rome, Rosa?'

'No.'

'Your father?'

'He's dead.'

'Oh, Rosa, I'm sorry.'

The girl flicked her head round to look at Isabella, her large almost-black eyes fixing on her with the knife-sharp curiosity that only a child knows how to summon up. 'Why are you sorry?'

'Because it's sad for someone to lose their father?'

'I didn't *lose* him. He died.'

'Do you have brothers or sisters?'

'No.'

'Aunts or uncles?'

The girl shook her head.

'Just you. And your mother.'

'Yes.'

Isabella touched the girl's curls lightly. They felt warm from the sun and springy, far more childish and boisterous than the solemn face turned towards her.

'There's something wrong,' Rosa said warily.

She was quick, this child. Quick to pick up on what Isabella was trying to hide, but Isabella was saved from saying more by the appearance of a pair of tall metal gates that she reached for with relief.

'Here we are,' she told Rosa. 'This is where I live.'

They walked through the gates into a spacious courtyard that was scorched by the sun and surrounded by three very modern four-storey apartment blocks with long curved balconies and silky-smooth stone exteriors. A yellow-tailed lizard was sunning itself on the stone path, too lazy to move, and Isabella could hear music playing in one of the ground floor apartments, an aria from *Tosca*. So Papa was home.

She found herself inspecting the exterior of the apartment through the child's eyes, seeing the Modernist beauty of it, the stark and stylish plainness that was such a contrast to the

21

suffocating fussiness of the old cities. Isabella loved its clean refreshing lines but she wasn't sure what Rosa would make of it. The shutters were half closed against the brilliance of the cobalt autumn sky. The courtyard consisted of stone pathways around a central dolphin fountain but there was not a blade of grass yet to be seen. The seeds had been planted but the town needed time to grow into its own skin. There was just a small olive tree on the left that her father had planted, but its young branches were dry and brittle. It looked no happier here than he was.

'Here we are, Rosa,' she said again cheerily. 'Come on in.'

★ ★ ★

Isabella's father was sitting in his favourite armchair, a large ruby-coloured velvet wing-chair that was so old it wrapped itself around him. In his hands, as always, lay a book. Dark, densely carved furniture cluttered the heavy shadows within the room, while on the table beside him stood an open bottle of red wine and a glass. Next to it the gramophone was playing, *Tosca* spinning hypnotically on the turntable.

'This is Rosa,' Isabella announced.

The girl flashed Dr Marco Cantini a brief glance before fixing her gaze on the terracotta-tiled floor.

'*Buongiorno*, Rosa.' His eyes crinkled into a large smile of welcome under heavy eyebrows. 'To what do we owe this pleasure?'

22

Rosa's mouth remained firmly closed in complete silence, the ultimate weapon of a child.

'Sit down, please, Rosa,' Isabella said, and steered her to a seat at the table. She hoped the girl would know better than to touch the gramophone or she would provoke Papa's wrath. Isabella poured wine into the glass and drank half of it straight down but she was shocked to see the hand holding the glass was shaking.

'Papa, I need a word with you.' She glanced pointedly at the child. 'In private. Outside in the courtyard, please.'

'Send the girl out there if you want to — ' He stopped. Looked at her hand. Without further comment he exchanged his reading spectacles for his distance ones and strode out into the bright sunlight. Isabella was hot from hurrying through the streets and led her father into a cool patch of shade.

Dr Marco Cantini was a big man with a barrel chest and a large important-looking head. He kept his grey hair cropped short but his moustache and eyebrows remained so stubbornly jet-black and luxuriant that he rarely had the heart to trim them. He liked to laugh a lot. Sometimes Isabella suspected that his patients came to him more for his laughter than for his pills and potions.

'What is it?' he demanded.

Isabella wanted to say *Hold my hand*. Like ten years before. But instead she took a mouthful of the wine she had brought out with her to make the words slide over her ash-dry tongue.

'I saw a woman kill herself today, Papa.'

His hooded eyes didn't even widen. Her father had probably seen too many dead people in his time as a doctor.

'She jumped off my tower.' Her voice sounded odd, even to herself.

'Off the top of Party headquarters?'

She nodded. 'Head first.'

'Jesus Christ!'

'The woman came up to me in the Piazza del Popolo and asked me to watch her daughter. It was Rosa, the young girl inside. She promised to return quickly and I believed her but instead she threw herself off the top of the tower and I dragged Rosa away from the square, so she doesn't know about it yet, hasn't realised, and,' her words were breaking up into fragments, 'and I understand that I have to tell her . . . ' She paused. 'But I am so angry at her mother for — '

'There is no point in anger at death, Isabella. I learned that a long time ago.'

'But I can't stop it, Papa.'

They both stared at the bright splash of wine left in the glass in her hand. It was swirling up and around the curved sides as if it had its own private torment.

'I have to take Rosa to the police station . . . ' Isabella started.

But her father took a long stride towards her. He was tall and always held himself upright as if he believed he belonged up there in the more rarefied atmosphere, but he bent down now to peer closely at her face.

'Are you all right, Isabella?'

'Yes. But I'm worried about Rosa.'

She didn't tell him that she kept picturing the mother's dead eyes at the bottom of the tower, wondering if they were like Luigi's. Outstaring the sun. But it wasn't the kind of thing Isabella and her father told each other. There was always a gulf between them, however hard they sought to avert their eyes from it. Her father had never forgiven her for marrying one of Mussolini's Blackshirts. *Thugs*, Dr Cantini called them, the word ugly in his mouth.

Isabella finished off the wine and swung around to return indoors but Dr Cantini put out his hand as though to hold on to her. It only hovered for a moment without touching, then fell to his side. They rarely touched each other, the two of them. They were very un-Italian in that way. He did so much laughing and touching in his work as a doctor that at times it seemed there was none left for his daughter. She understood that. They may not touch often, but they talked. They both liked words.

'Isabella, I am going to telephone Sister Consolata. She will be able to help.'

'I'm not sure that . . . '

His large face thrust even closer. She could see suspicion in the deep lines that ran vertically down his cheeks and she knew he was assessing her, judging her, the way he would a sick patient.

'Do you need a shot of something?' he asked.

She shook her head adamantly. 'No.'

A flush crawled up her cheek to her hairline. They both knew that her father could remember a time not so long ago when she would be begging him for a shot of something to ease the pain. She wanted to say, *I'm all right now, I'm back in control. Rosa is the one with the problem, not me, Papa.* But the words were lost somewhere in the gulf between them, so she hurried out of the courtyard back into the house to find Rosa, and the dimness of the room with its heavy mosquito mesh over the windows washed over her. Rosa was no longer seated on the chair. She was standing on tiptoe in front of Dr Cantini's marble clock that rested on a dark mahogany cabinet. She had prised open its glass face and had moved the hands, so that it was now striking twelve noon. The chimes rang out in the silent room like a death knell for her mother.

At the sound of Isabella's footsteps on the tiles Rosa turned her head and gazed at her with mournful eyes.

'She's not coming back for me, is she?' she said.

3

Roberto Falco had never photographed a dead woman. A dead ox once, yes, before it was spitted and roasted. A dead woman, no. She lay inside his camera, upside down and in miniature — only four inches by five — and he found it impossible to look away. As he stalked around the smashed body on the ground with his Graflex in his hands, winding the shutter cloth on its internal spools and popping up the viewfinder on the back, he was disgusted to find himself relieved that she wouldn't move. He didn't want her to spoil the shot.

It was only when he lowered the camera to change the film sheet and looked at the scene with his naked eye that the horror of it gripped his guts and he felt a wave of sorrow for the dead woman. She was spreadeagled on her front. Her head hung down several steps lower than her feet, as she lay there in her black garments. Limbs snapped in fifty places. Bones poking up through flesh. Yet the fingers of one hand were curled in a tight fist as though she'd made one last desperate attempt to cling on to life before she hit the steps.

There was blood. Of course there was blood. He dragged his eyes from her body, removed the film holder from the camera and replaced it with another from his leather equipment case with practised skill. His fingers worked smoothly

27

despite the shakes. He craned back his head, squinting up at the milky-white tower, assessing the exposure he would need — most likely 1/20 second at f/16 and the Schneider wide angle lens. The tall white building rose sharp and menacing against a backdrop of wind-swept sky, but as he stared at it the tower seemed to lean over the sad little scene at its foot, watching the people in the square below with satisfaction. Roberto took an instant dislike to it.

What made her do it?

A young woman, judging by the skin of her hands. Yet so eager to embrace death. Why would she do such violence to herself?

There must be someone who knew. Someone, somewhere, whose world would be rocked to its core by this supreme act of selfishness. In death he felt the force of her, and it filled the sun-drenched piazza in a way she could never have done in life. Roberto knelt and brushed his fingers against the unknown woman's clenched hand, full of regret for a life thrown away.

'Falco! Get away from there,' a man's voice snapped.

Roberto's hand recoiled. Abruptly he became aware of people and sounds around him. A crowd had gathered on the steps, voices wailing, a woman sobbing quietly, a man on his knees praying and others crossing themselves in the presence of death. The click of rosary beads started up.

'Falco! Give me that camera!'

Roberto turned to see a large fleshy man in a well-cut suit advancing on him, chest first, shoulders back, his broad shadow leaping ahead of him as if it couldn't wait to get its hands on the camera. Signor Antonio Grassi, chairman of the local Fascist Party. Roberto rose to his feet with no intention whatever of giving up his camera. It would be like giving up a limb.

'Chairman Grassi,' he acknowledged with a cool nod of his head. 'A tragic incident here on your own doorstep.'

Grassi's arrogant brown eyes did not even glance at the woman on the steps as he held out his hand.

'Give me that camera,' he ordered again.

'I think not,' Roberto replied softly. This was not the moment for a shouting match over a camera. 'The *carabinieri* need to be informed.'

'I am already here, signor *fotografo*.'

A uniformed figure, thin as a blade, stepped out from behind Grassi, and Roberto had to suppress a shudder at the sight of the distinctive dark blue uniform with silver braid on collar and cuffs, and the distinctive red stripe of the carabinieri police down the side of the trousers. The wide bicorn hat gave his head the look of a cobra as it flares its hood ready to strike.

'Hand over the camera to Chairman Grassi.'

'Colonnello Sepe, it's not necessary. I am just doing my job as official *fotografo* of Bellina — taking photographs.'

Behind him police officers were beginning to push back the crowd to the bottom of the wide steps and take up positions like a dark blue wall around the body.

'Signor Falco, you are employed by me,'

Chairman Grassi pointed out with irritation, 'to record the creation of this new town. Not to take ghoulish pictures of death.' The volume of his voice was rising.

Roberto let his gaze fix once more on the black smear of life that had been ended on the steps of the Fascist headquarters. He was under no illusion as to why Chairman Grassi wanted no photographs of it. He flipped up the catches on his Graflex and, cursing under his breath, removed the film holder from the back of the camera and held it out at arm's length to Grassi. The chairman took it from him and ripped it open, exposing the film on both sides to the light.

At that moment a tall man walked briskly through the crowd. He was dressed in a long winter coat and was carrying a medical bag. The doctor had arrived with that ineffable air of distinction that seemed to stick to members of the medical profession closer than their own shadow, but he was too late to be of the slightest use. Roberto's eyes were drawn to the woman's mane of untidy hair that still seemed to shimmer with life, as the doctor knelt at her side.

He snapped shut his own equipment case and before Chairman Grassi thought to ask for possession of any of the other film holders in there, he moved away. The taste in his mouth was sour and with a sudden change of direction he headed for the door to the tower.

★　★　★

Roberto stood in silence on top of the tower, his heart beating fast from the climb. Before him stretched the long narrow flatlands of the Pontine plain, bare and bleak, all vegetation uprooted. A few kilometres off to the west glinted the silvery ribbon of the Tyrrhenian Sea, while inland to the east of the plain rose the purple ridge of the Lepini mountains with the ancient trade route of the Appian Way.

A sluggish wind from the sea was stirring the air that hung heavy with dust over the town of Bellina. Though only thirty kilometres south of Rome, it was a barren and godforsaken place in Roberto's opinion. Flat and lifeless, as well as too hot and humid in summer. But he had to admire Mussolini's audacity. His gross arrogance. His sheer strength of will in believing that he could succeed where Roman emperors, popes and even Napoleon had failed before him. It was a mammoth task — to drain the malarial swamp that was the Pontine Marshes. The trouble was that the dunes along the coast lay at a higher level than the ground at the foot of the Lepini mountains to the east. This meant that the rivers that drained off the mountains had pooled and stagnated on the plain for centuries and turned it into an unhealthy mosquito-ridden marshland. Not only was Mussolini draining the marshes, but he was also replacing them with the construction of six perfect new towns on the reclaimed land. It took breathtaking hubris and yet Il Duce was succeeding. Against all the odds. Delegations flocked from all over the world to inspect this eighth engineering Wonder of the World and Roberto was obliged to photograph each one of them who came.

Bellina was the first of the new towns to emerge from the swampy ground. God help the thousands of peasants who were being rounded up from the north, from Veneto, Friuli and Ferrara, and shunted on trains down here to be cooped up in the little blue farmsteads like experimental mice in glass cages. They would be watched. Every move they made.

Roberto pictured the woman breathing in the dusty air, drawing it deep into her lungs, trying to calm her nerves as she stood on the tower. What made her jump? Had her spirit been torn out of her, the way the heart of the marshes had been torn from the land?

Not long ago this land had seethed with animal life, with wild boar sharpening their tusks on a dense forest of trees. Dangerous brigands used to hole up here for the winter and shepherds brought their sheep and goats down from the mountains to graze during the winter months, when the mosquitoes were dormant. But for most of the year the swampy plain had been impenetrable because of the vast suffocating clouds of mosquitoes that infested the swamps, as black and vicious as the shadow of death itself.

They were anopheles mosquitoes. One bite and the bastards could pump tertian malaria into your blood and you'd be dead and buried within forty-eight hours. Or if you were really lucky, you'd get one of the slow kinds of malaria that crept up on you as silent and stealthy as a Medici assassin, with bouts of fever and an inexorable poisoning of the liver. The mosquitoes had to go, Mussolini was right about that. Il Duce was intent on dragging Italy to the forefront of modern Europe, hand over fist, whether it wanted it or not, and in his Great Battle for Grain there was no room for this black plague.

The parapet of the tower was chest height and Roberto ran his hand over the warm white marble edge. He pictured it, the woman hauling herself up on top of it, her feet scrabbling to find a toehold. *Will it hurt?* That thought must have stuck in her head, that question pounding against her skull as she balanced on the edge. *Will the fall feel like for ever?*

Who was she? What had driven her to this?

Roberto flipped open his camera case, slipped a new film holder into the Graflex and took his time focusing on the spot on the bare white wall where there were definite scuff marks. Then he looked down over the edge of the parapet and immediately wished he hadn't. The drop was giddying. What kind of desperation did it take to leap off solid stone into nothingness?

An ambulance had pulled up at the base of the steps. Roberto snatched the Leica from his case — it was less unwieldy than the Graflex, though the picture quality was nothing like as sharp — and focused it on the scene below, where the body was being shuffled on to a stretcher. The church bell abruptly started to toll at the far end of the piazza, sounding slow and regretful, as a figure in loose black robes appeared on the steps

33

of the church. It was a priest, standing in front of his plain and angular house of God. Even from this distance Roberto could feel the mood down below change as the priest's shadow spread its arms in the shape of a cross and stretched out into the square.

'What the hell are you doing up here?'

Roberto swung round to find a burly middle-aged policeman behind him on top of the tower. 'Taking photographs, of course. That's what Chairman Grassi commissions me to do.'

'No one is allowed up here, the colonel's orders.'

The officer was beetroot red in the face, sweating and short of breath from the long climb up the tower steps. He glanced round the ten-metre-square space with its bell-house at the centre as if hoping for a chair to sit on. He removed his bicorn to cool his head but the sun slapped straight down on his bald patch, and the hat was rapidly replaced.

'There's nothing here to see,' Roberto told him. 'No sign of the woman. She's left no imprint.'

'That's for Colonnello Sepe to decide, not you.'

Roberto inclined his head. 'Of course.' He had no wish to cause trouble.

'So clear off, *fotografo*.'

'I'm just packing up.'

He started to place the Leica back in his camera box but to his surprise the policeman stumbled over to the far corner and vomited. He remained bent over, his chest heaving. Roberto

34

abandoned his camera box, strode over, and placed a hand on the uniformed shoulder.

'Are you all right?'

A grunt and a spit of sulphurous bile, then the man righted himself and wiped the back of his wrist across his mouth. His eyes looked anguished but he shook off Roberto's hand.

'I'm all right,' he muttered. 'It's just that I've never seen a woman's body damaged like that before. She's no older than my own daughter and the thought of anything like that happening . . .'

'Do they know who she is?'

'No.'

'No identification on her? No purse or . . . ?'

'Nothing.' The policeman shook his head weakly and propped himself against the parapet. 'What the hell makes a person do such a thing?'

The question hung in the air high above the steps below.

'A desire to punish,' Roberto said softly, more to himself than to the police officer. 'To punish herself or to punish someone else.'

'She's beyond pain now.'

Roberto felt a need to get away from this place, so he picked up his camera box, hitching its strap over his shoulder, and headed for the steps.

'One thing,' he said briskly. 'Tell Sepe to look at her right wrist.'

The policeman suddenly became a policeman again. 'Why? What's on it?'

'A scar.'

White. Shiny. The width of a flat knife blade.

'A burn,' he elaborated. 'By the look of it, not recent.'

The policeman snorted. 'Women are always burning themselves on the stove.'

Roberto shrugged and ducked into the cool silence within the tower. But as he hurried down the spiral steps, his left thumb could not keep from sweeping over the smooth shiny bar of skin inside his own right wrist.

4

'What's that?' Rosa asked.

'It's machinery. For the pumping station.'

Two haycarts were rumbling down the street towards Isabella and Rosa, slowing all the traffic, but instead of hay the vehicles were carrying massive machine parts. A great long screw hung out over the rear of one cart like an iron tail.

'It must be heavy,' the girl murmured.

'It is,' Isabella assured her. 'They come by train and are carted out to the pumping station.'

'They must be strong.'

Each cart was hauled by two well-muscled beasts and Rosa was staring at their long curved horns.

'Here they use Maremmana cattle instead of draught horses,' Isabella explained. 'They can pull from dawn to dusk.'

As the hefty grey animals trundled past, their chests glistening with sweat, Isabella continued to lead the way to the police station. Like the Maremmanas, she was in no hurry. She had no wish to get where she was going. The roads were busy here, the noise of cars filling the air as people ambled along the pavements, going about their business at their usual leisurely pace. The houses in this part of town were smaller and more traditional, nudged up tight against each other under terracotta roofs and intended for lowly office workers. Splashes of colour spilled from their windows. An amber rug was hanging out to air and a vibrant amethyst fuchsia trailed its tendrils from an earthenware window box.

Rosa looked around with interest as she walked at Isabella's side, as docile as a well-schooled dog — it made Isabella wonder about the girl's past. It wasn't that she lacked spirit — she could see it in the dark flashes of her watchful round eyes — but Rosa knew how to keep it curbed. Isabella glanced down at her gleaming curls and at her neat profile that had the beginnings of a patrician nose that promised to be somewhat too large for her delicate face.

She would have to be told. Isabella knew that. She couldn't let Rosa skip blithely into the police station with no idea why they were there. The words were prepared. *I'm so sorry, Rosa, but a terrible thing has happened . . .* Yet she could feel a resistance from Rosa, as if she sensed that something bad was about to come out of Isabella's mouth. When the noise and smell of the carts had died away, Isabella tried again.

'Rosa, there's something that you — '

'Why do you limp?'

Isabella sighed. 'My back is damaged.'

'Why?'

Rosa's attention was on a group of barefoot children playing a game with pebbles in the gutter.

'I was shot,' Isabella said.

The dark head whipped round. Now Isabella had her attention.

'Really?'

'Yes, really.'

'Why?'

'My husband and I were both shot. But he died. The week before, he'd been in the March on Rome with Mussolini and . . . ' Isabella shrugged. As if it meant nothing. 'Someone wanted us dead because of that. That's what the police said anyway.'

Their pace slowed. The child's feet in scuffed sandals dragged across the paving stones. She stared up, eyes bright with curiosity. 'Who did it?' she whispered.

'I don't know. No one was ever caught.'

Rosa's face turned away. 'Oh,' was all she said.

'Your mother said something to me, Rosa. Something about my husband.'

Isabella looked for a reaction in the girl's face, but there was none.

'Do you have any idea how your mother knew about my husband?' She asked the question gently, aware that she shouldn't be asking. Not now. But she needed to know, so still she asked it. 'How did she know who I am?'

The girl abruptly stopped walking, her thin blue dress clinging to her legs in the breeze, and stared directly into Isabella's eyes. 'I never know what thoughts are in Mamma's head. She tells me nothing.' She gave a sharp single shake of her head to underline the word. 'Nothing,' she repeated. 'So I don't know.'

A rush of guilt brought a flush to Isabella's cheeks. How could she be having this conversation with the girl just before she told her that her mother was dead?

'Rosa.' She wrapped an arm around the small bony shoulders. The girl stiffened but didn't pull away. 'Take no notice of me, Rosa. I'm not used to talking with children, so I'm no good at it. I say the wrong things.'

Rosa dipped her chin to her chest. The slender pale triangle of the nape of her neck looked vulnerable in the glare of the sun.

'Yes,' she said solemnly. 'You do.'

'We're going to the police station now.' Isabella took Rosa's hand and started pushing herself along faster. 'It's about your mother.'

Rosa's small fingers tightened. 'Don't say it,' she whispered in a voice so soft it was whisked away immediately on the wind. She tipped her head back and gazed up at the carved triangular pediment above the meeting hall that they were passing. 'Tell me more about the architecture instead.'

Isabella understood. The desire to stave off the bad news that was rolling like thunderclouds towards them. She felt the same herself.

'See those,' she said, pointing at the façade of the building. 'They are fluted pilasters copied from the designs of Ancient Rome. But see how Frezzotti has combined them cleverly with soaring straight lines in the verticals and abrupt angles to create a building that is modern and exciting. We are creating a city that all Italy can be proud of.'

Rosa smiled and looked up, eager for more.

★ ★ ★

Isabella was not used to policemen. Or nuns. Or even priests, for that matter. In the airless interview room in the police station, she could see that the blackness of their robes and dark uniforms was crushing Rosa.

Isabella refused to give up her seat next to the girl at the table, despite the fact that Colonnello Sepe clearly wanted her out of the room. The nun was Sister Consolata and she took Rosa's face between her two large hands and beamed God-given comfort into her young soul with a warmth and conviction that Isabella envied. Rosa didn't cry when she was told the truth about her mother. She sat there with lips white as bone, her hands gripping the edge of the table and her shoulders hunched forward as if she'd been punched in the middle of her chest. She said nothing. Not a word. Just a faint rush of air escaped from her lips. Isabella wished the girl would cry.

They had entered the police station and found a waiting-committee of priest, nun and police-men ready. The priest informed Isabella in a low rumble that her father had telephoned them all before hurrying to the suicide scene himself. She thanked him and held tight to Rosa's hand, overtaken by an urge to turn around and drag the girl out of there, to flee from the accusations and complications that she could sense hovered in the air, thick as the cigarette smoke.

They were marched down a polished corridor flanked by dark office doors. Isabella could hear the chatter of typewriters behind them and she glanced to her left when she saw that one of the doors stood open, revealing the figures of two men inside. Part of her hoped that one might be her father, though what he could do to help, she had no idea, but she knew his presence would steady her.

'Did you find out anything? Was she pushed?'

The words came to Isabella clearly from inside the room, though they were not spoken loudly, and she recognised the voice of Signor Grassi, the Party chairman.

'No.' The answer was firm. 'There was no sign of anyone else up there with her.'

The tall figure who replied had his back to her and as she passed she caught the impression that he was a younger man with a pair of strong shoulders and a restlessness that made her think he did not want to be in that room.

Was she pushed?

Isabella looked quickly down at Rosa. Had she heard? Had her fingers tightened? The small face gave no sign but stared straight ahead with eyes that were flat and dull. The policeman opened a door at the end of the corridor. The interview room was painted a soulless beige and contained nothing but a metal table in the centre and a row of chairs. It felt crowded with all five of them in it and smelled of bad drains — a problem that the new drainage pumps were fighting hard to rectify. A raw young police officer marched them into it, and it was plain to see that despite his crisp uniform and the gun holstered on his hip, he was ill at ease when confronted by an orphaned child and the might of God in a cassock and a wimple. Like the coward he was, he went for the easiest target.

'You,' he snapped at Isabella. 'Who are you? What are you doing here?'

'My name is Isabella Berotti. I am a friend of Rosa's.'

That silenced him. Even he realised that the child needed every friend she could get right now. It was Sister Consolata who did most of the talking at this stage and Isabella hoped that her sweet musical voice was bringing comfort to Rosa. The middle-aged nun, her grey eyes cradled in soft folds of freckled flesh, spoke to the girl with a gentle kindness from within the tight jaws of her white linen wimple and her stiff white headdress.

'Sorrow,' she crooned to Rosa, 'is a heavy burden for one so young to carry, but our dear Lord is with you, He is our refuge and our strength at all times, my dear. Blessed are they that mourn, for they shall be comforted. He gives us that promise, Rosa.'

But Rosa said nothing. Her small figure sat silent on the hard chair, her head bowed, her eyes down, cutting them all out of her world. Only her shoulders twitched now and again, a ghost walking cold fingers over her skin. Isabella longed to wrap an arm around her but knew instinctively that the girl wouldn't welcome it, not here, not in front of these people. The priest stood in matching silence, a tall imposing silhouette in flowing robes in front of the window where the light seemed to stream through him. The abrupt arrival of the carabinieri chief of police, Colonnello Sepe, in the interview room altered the atmosphere. It became suddenly more threatening. He took the seat opposite her.

'What's your full name, Rosa?' he demanded. 'What are you doing here in Bellina? Why did your mother go up our tower?'

The child's lips didn't move.

'She's badly shocked, Colonnello. It's too soon to be questioning her like this.'

'That decision is not yours to make, Signora Berotti.'

The police colonel was a man whose voice was as sharp as his features and whose dark hair, glistening with brilliantine, was cropped into a Julius Caesar style as though to remind people where the power lay. To Isabella's surprise it was the priest who stepped forward in her support and she noticed that an odour hung around his cassock, the smell of mothballs and incense. His eyes were the exact colour of the ancient Bible clutched in his hand. His high forehead was deeply lined although he wasn't old, as if the battle for souls had left its mark on his face.

'She's right,' he said. 'Let the girl go with Sister Consolata. You can speak to her tomorrow.'

'I brought her to you, Colonnello,' Isabella added, 'because she needs help, not for her to be treated like a — '

'Silence!' Sepe snapped. 'We have to ascertain whether this is the child of the dead woman. I need names. Rosa,' he leaned across the table, his hand slicing through the air between them as if to cut through to the truth, 'what is your full name and what is your mother's name?'

Even Isabella, who knew nothing at all about children, could have told him he wasn't going to get far with a child using that tone of voice. All it did was make Rosa curl tighter into herself. Her head dropped further down on her chest, her dark hair hiding her face from his inspection and thwarting his intent to intimidate her.

'We need the truth, girl,' he told her. 'Your mother has committed a crime against God. As well as a crime against our town and a crime against Fascism itself. Her blood has tainted us. It defiles the steps of a glorious building that stands as an example to other towns and cities throughout the world. Italy is proud of this town. How dare your mother come here to — '

'Maybe, Colonnello,' Isabella interrupted, 'if you tried being kind to young Rosa you would learn more. Offer her something that she needs right now, instead of insults.'

The police colonel's glance slid across to Isabella. A tense silence spread itself through the room.

'Such as?' he asked coldly.

Rosa's head jerked up and her eyes fixed on Colonnello Sepe with an unblinking stare. 'I want to see Mamma.'

'*Madonna mia!*' The words burst from Sister Consolata. 'But she's dead.'

'I want to see her. Please. Let me see my mamma.'

'Rosa,' Isabella murmured, 'are you sure? It will not be pleasant.'

But Colonnello Sepe had already pushed back his seat and was up on his feet. The faintest of smiles tugged at one corner of his mouth and Isabella wanted to knock it off his face.

'Request granted,' he announced and headed for the door.

Rosa jumped to her feet and was at his heels before he had crossed the room. Father Benedict strode forward and carved the sign of the cross into the air behind her.

★　★　★

It didn't take long, but for Isabella every minute was a minute too long. She was not good at disguising her emotions. The hospital morgue lay in a windowless chamber in which harsh lights picked out the details of the female form stretched out on a metal slab. Fingers at strange angles, the gleam of black hair muted by dried blood, a broken body hidden beneath a coarse brown rubberised sheet. In the foul-smelling silence they approached it warily, alert for the slightest movement.

Isabella tried not to look at the face but it was impossible. It drew all eyes, a brutal mask of blood and bone. Someone had mercifully closed the dead woman's eyes, so there was no doll's empty gaze this time, but her forehead curved the wrong way like a saucer of blood and the raw ends of cheekbones and jawbone protruded through the blackened skin. Isabella took Rosa's hand firmly in hers.

'Enough,' she said. 'You've seen enough.'

Rosa didn't speak. Didn't cry. But she was shaking. Her whole body was shaking so hard that Isabella could hear her teeth rattling in her head. On the other side of her, Sister Consolata was intoning a prayer, but it would take far more than a prayer to repair the damage being done in this room.

'So?' Colonnello Sepe stood on the far side of the slab, his sharp eyes watching every breath Rosa took. 'Is it her?'

It was her all right. Behind the mask of blood, even Isabella could see that it was the woman who had stood in the sunlit piazza earlier and said, *You are a good person.* Why hadn't she invited her to sit down? Why didn't she have the sense to offer this troubled woman a sympathetic ear for her problems? All she had given was ice cream to her daughter.

'So?' Colonnello Sepe demanded again.

'*Si*, she's my mother.' Rosa squeezed out the words between chattering teeth. 'She is Allegra Bianchi. She brought me to Bellina to get rid of me.'

5

Isabella believed that was the end of it.

She honestly tried to put behind her the woman's words — *They know who killed your bastard husband* — and to slot back into her old life, knowing that Rosa was beginning a new one in the care of the nuns. That was what was meant to happen, wasn't it? You just had to get on with things — like learning to walk again and breathing and doing whatever it is you do to fill each day. She'd done it once before ten years ago, she could do it again.

But it wasn't that simple. The day that was meant to be a day of sorrow for Luigi had cracked open and allowed the past to flood in. Isabella lay in bed that night, tossing and turning, her legs fighting the bedsheets and her head pounding. Allegra Bianchi's suicide was a hard thing to live with in the dark. Her words had cut open old wounds.

All night Isabella listened to the wind whipping itself up into a fury and roaring across the flat floodplain from Cisterna to Terracina. It was rattling the shutters, scraping the dry bones of its knuckles over them, making her skin crawl until she could stand it no longer. She kicked off the sheet and gave up on the night.

★ ★ ★

'What are you doing?'

'Scrubbing.' Isabella was on her hands and knees.

Her father looked down at the soapy brush in her hand and at the spotless kitchen flagstones and walls, and sighed with an exaggerated shudder.

'Oh, Isabella.'

He removed her scrubbing brush and tossed it with disdain under the big enamel sink. 'Come, *mia figlia*, sit and drink coffee with your father.'

They sat down at the table. Isabella had already laid it for breakfast with freshly baked rolls, prosciutto and moon-shaped wedges of melon. But her father reached for his favourite, the hard *fette biscottate*, which he proceeded to dip into his coffee. He regarded her over the top of his spectacles with disfavour.

'Let it go, Isabella.'

'Rosa is all alone. I'm worried about her.'

'No, she's not. Sister Consolata and the nuns are taking good care of her because that's what they do. That's why they have the school. They help children who have no parents. It's not your job, it's theirs.'

'I know.'

She drank her coffee and stared mutely into the bottom of the empty cup as if it might hold the answers she needed. She wasn't in the mood for a lecture, not today, not when the image of a sunken forehead had lodged itself behind her eyelids.

'Do you, Isabella?'

'Do I what?'

'Do you know? Do you understand? Do you realise what happened yesterday?'

She glanced up and found him waving his biscuit at her and chewing fiercely on his moustache as if he would bite his way to the truth if it killed him. Dr Cantini was a great upholder of truth at all times. Sometimes, just sometimes, he was so blinded by the glare of truth that he didn't notice who or what his large feet were stumbling over in the dark shadowy world of compromise and half-truths where most people lived. He possessed full heavy features and a high forehead that was clearly needed to accommodate all the knowledge whirring around inside his head, and Isabella loved him. Despite the interminable lectures. Despite the fact that he could see no one else's point of view but his own and had a temper like a firecracker.

She loved him because he had looked after her ever since her mother's death from poliomyelitis when Isabella was six years old. She used to follow him around like a pet dog, leaning against his strong legs and clinging to his laughter as she grew up. But everything changed after the shooting.

It was hard to explain. Even to herself. After the shooting they were both angry at the world or at God or at anyone who even looked at either of them the wrong way, so they took it out on each other for a while. Though he never put it into words, he blamed her for having married what he called 'a filthy Blackshirt' and for a while she could not bring herself to speak to him because he had refused to let her die alongside

Luigi. It was only after her third operation that she came to her senses. So she gave him a smile now, reached behind her for the bottle of grappa that sat ready on the sideboard and poured a slug into his coffee.

'Tell me, Papa, tell me what happened yesterday?'

'Isabella, we live in a Fascist state.'

She rolled her eyes at him. As if she didn't know that.

'In a Fascist state,' he continued, 'the state controls every aspect of our lives. It believes it knows better than we do what is good for us.'

Isabella sighed. She had heard this before.

'Isabella,' her father said more sharply, 'I would remind you that those who oppose Fascism in Italy are punished. Mussolini has bestowed the title 'Il Duce' on himself and has his secret police and his Blackshirts to do his bidding. He needs only to whisper his thoughts and someone will make them happen. That's the kind of power he has.'

'Papa, don't — '

'Listen to me, Isabella. What happened here yesterday was a slap in the face to Fascism and an insult to Mussolini's proud new showcase town. I warn you, they won't let it pass without retaliation.'

'Against the child? No, Papa, you've got it wrong. They won't hurt her.'

He frowned. 'You believe that?'

'Yes, I do. Be reasonable, Papa. It's 1932, a new modern world. Look at this beautiful town. Look how far Italy has come. Only seventy years

51

ago we were just a jumble of warring nation states, trampled over by foreign powers. We didn't even become a united country under one king until 1861.'

Papa smiled. 'I know all that, Isabella.' He pulled his pipe from his pocket, cradling it in his hand. 'Just remember that Benito Mussolini is not a man to overlook a deliberate insult to one of his precious new towns.' He narrowed his eyes at her. 'So you really believe young Rosa is safe?'

Isabella's chest suddenly became tight. 'Don't you?'

'What I think, Isabella, doesn't matter.'

She felt a thud of unease. Her father always believed that what he thought certainly did matter. He was not a man who underestimated the power of his own mind.

'What matters at the moment,' he said, 'is that you steer clear of her.'

'But, Papa, I need to speak to her. To make sure she's all right.'

'No, Isabella.' His cheeks were growing flushed, always the first sign of anger in him. 'Stay away from that girl. If you want to keep your job.'

'What?'

He shook his head impatiently. 'You can't afford to stir up any trouble, so don't go near the child. I insist on it.'

Isabella sat wordless, stunned into silence. She stared at her father but he jabbed his unlit pipe back into the pocket of his crumpled jacket and rose from the table, his heavy frame moving quickly for a big man.

'What do you mean, Papa? I am a respected architect here.'

'This business has not ended and I don't want you involved.'

He snatched up his medical bag from its place beneath the coat hooks and stalked out of the front door. Isabella heard the mosquito screen bang shut behind him.

6

Isabella was standing at her drawing board in the office. She was retracing the section of a building in Via Corelli, busy working alongside the other architects and engineers employed on the Bellina project. But her father's words kept getting in the way of the detailed drawing in front of her.

If you want to keep your job.

Her father wasn't a man to say things he wasn't confident were true. If he said her job was at risk, then that's what he meant. It was Dottore Martino, the chief architect under Frezzotti, who had appointed her to this job; a small energetic man who possessed rigorous standards and a string of medals pinned to his chest by Il Duce. He was the kind of man who made Isabella feel cleverer just by being in the same room with him. But now she was confused and wondering why he had picked her for his team.

Why her?

She was surrounded by some of Italy's most innovative architects. They were all crammed with their drawing boards into the large airy rooms of the architectural offices, where huge windows allowed light to stream in from the piazza. Each of the employees was under constant pressure to get everything right. No, not just right. Perfect. Bellina was the first of the six new towns to be built on the drained marshes and each one had been allocated only two hundred and sixty days from start to finish.

So deadlines were tight. Everyone worked long hours. That suited Isabella. She was happiest when working. There were twenty-two architects and over forty draughtsmen in this group of offices, each with a wary eye on his neighbour's drawing board as they measured and drew, and remeasured and redrew according to Dottore Architetto Martino's pronouncements. Isabella was the only female architect working on the project, surrounded daily by the odour of hair oil and by the casual touch of male hands on her bottom whenever she was foolish enough to allow them too close.

'Signora Berotti!'

Isabella jumped. Everyone in the office jumped when Dottore Martino entered a room in his Milan-crafted suit and black-rimmed spectacles.

'Signora Berotti, there is a job I need you to do.'

He stopped in front of her board, eyeing Isabella's section drawing. She was working on a three-storey building containing six apartments that was already under construction, a fairly straightforward design for the artisan quarter of town. No great challenge. But even so, the pen in her hand itched to improve the lines on the top sheet of tracing paper before his critical eye spotted anything it didn't like. Throughout the large room pens and set squares paused, heads turned. She could sense the half-smiles, the male desire to see soft female flesh torn to shreds.

'Yes, sir?'

'Get yourself down to the stone-yard. A new delivery of stone has come in for the apartments and I want you to check the colour and quality. There have been some questions about it. Be quick. And make sure you're at the rail station by two o'clock for the reception of the new farmers from up north.'

When Dottore Martino said go, you went. She put down her drawing pen and snatched her bag from under her stool, and as she did so, he added casually, 'You're good with stone.'

This was a man who did not often offer praise. It might not have sounded like much, but it meant a great deal to Isabella.

'Get going, then,' he said curtly. 'And get this drawing right.'

'Yes, sir.'

She saw the faces of her colleagues as she strode from the room.

You're good with stone.

That would annoy them.

★   ★   ★

Dottore Martino was right. Isabella *was* good with stone. She reacted to it the way normal people react to pets. She loved to stroke it, to caress it, to feel each ancient layer of history within it. It spoke to her in ways that humans didn't, so it was with a hitch of pleasure in her step that she walked into the stone-yard. It was set way back behind the station and rattled with the sounds of chisels chipping away at slabs and

56

the occasional shriek of an electric saw biting through granite.

The air shimmered with stone dust as Isabella walked past the slabs of pale limestone and richly coloured blocks of marble and headed for the wooden office. She banged on its door and called out, 'Tommaso!'

There was the clatter of a chair inside and the door burst open with a roar.

'Isabella!'

She was grasped in a bear hug and kissed on both cheeks. When her ribs were on the point of cracking, she beat off Tommaso Lombardi and grinned up at him. He looked as though he had been hewn out of one of his own slabs of rock and his grey beard stank of garlic.

'*Buongiorno*, Isabella, come in, come in. Your lovely face makes my old heart sing.'

He drew her into the office by the scruff of her neck. It was always like this. She loved the warmth of his greeting and of the home-made hooch that he kept under the chaos he called a desk.

'How's life treating you, Tommaso? Still breaking women's hearts?'

He laughed, shaking his big belly and the flimsy walls of his office, the laugh of a man who relishes every minute of his life. His skills as a stonemason were much in demand and she reckoned he must have more than fifty men working for him in the yard, but even that number never seemed to be enough. Dottore Martino drove him hard.

'Ah, Isabella, my pretty one, I never break a

woman's heart. I make her happy.' He was already pouring a dark liquid into two grimy glasses and handed one to her. It was only eleven o'clock in the morning but she wasn't planning on arguing.

'*Salute*, Tommaso!'

'*Tanta salute*.'

They took a moment to let the alcohol hit their stomachs with the impact of a train, then set to work. He led her around the yard and together they examined the great slabs of stone. He grumbled deep in his beard over the fact that there had been some complaints about the quality of some of the stone being used in construction and he encouraged her to run her hands over the mottled granite that she needed for the apartment block. As she did so, she asked casually, 'Have you heard anything about the death in the Piazza del Popolo yesterday?'

'A terrible way to die!' His stone-hardened hand marked out a cross on his chest.

'What are people saying?'

'That she was crazy for love. That her husband had run off with another woman.' He tossed his great grey head. 'That's no reason to . . . ' His chest heaved. 'She'd been cutting herself with a knife, they say.'

'What? Where did you hear that?'

'It's the gossip in the wine shops all over town.'

'I hope it's wrong.'

'Why would it be wrong?'

Isabella shrugged. 'Maybe Chairman Grassi wants people to believe that only an insane

58

woman would kill herself in his beautiful town. Does anyone know anything about her or why she chose Bellina?'

Tommaso grimaced and raked his fingers through his beard. 'No, not that I've heard. Bad luck for you that she chose your tower.'

She chose my table for her child. My tower for her death.

'Yes,' she muttered. 'Bad luck for me.'

'Ah, Isabella, don't look like that. It was not your fault.'

She fixed her mind on what she was here for. The stone calmed her. She moved over to a stack of travertine that had just been delivered from up near Rome. Travertine is a calcium carbonate that results from hot spring water penetrating up through underground limestone. She loved the way that when the water evaporated, it left behind magical layers of dissolved limestone. This gave it a rough banded appearance, a beautiful honey-beige with stripes of tan weaving through it like the pelt of a ginger cat. It was so enticing that she stood there stroking it, its pinhole indentations rippling under her skin, and she would have stood there happily all day if she had the time.

'Signora Berotti, I didn't know you would be here.'

Isabella swung around. Before her stood a slightly built man in his late thirties with light brown hair and pale caramel eyes that missed nothing. They were inspecting her with interest. She realised that she must have been standing there longer than she thought because Tommaso

59

was gone and so was the lazy blue sky. In its place hung a thin layer of bruised mist and she could see in the distance an army of storm clouds massing above the Lepini mountains, their dark shadows crawling down on to the plain.

'Signor Francolini,' she said. 'I was sent over by Dottore Martino to check on the granite for the apartments in Via Corelli. There have been complaints.'

Davide Francolini was Dottore Martino's right-hand man. He was the person who made things happen, working with engineers and builders, ensuring that the drawings on Isabella's tracing paper leapt into life as buildings of solid stone and brick. She didn't envy him his job when so many hundreds of buildings had to be constructed at such breakneck speed, often with untried workmen, but he functioned with a calm efficiency and was well respected within the office. He'd never spoken more than two words to her before.

'Complaints?' he asked.

'I only know what I was told by Tommaso,' Isabella explained. 'You should speak to him.'

'But I'm not. I'm speaking to you.'

He said it with a soft smile. He wasn't looking to make trouble for her.

'I just heard from Tommaso,' she said, 'that some of the builders are complaining about the stone quality and that makes him spit nails because he would never provide inferior stone.'

He considered what she'd told him. 'I will look into it.'

His manner was friendly, so when he started to move away towards the iron gates that opened on to the wide thoroughfare where a constant stream of lorries poured in and out of the yard, she moved with him.

'Signor Francolini.'

He glanced at her, surprised that she was still at his elbow.

'What can I do for you, signora?'

'I was wondering whether you had ever discussed with Dottore Martino why he decided to take me on as part of his team.'

She knew the question was risky but she might never get another chance to ask it. To her surprise he laughed easily.

'No, Signora Berotti, I have never discussed that subject with him. But I assume he took you on for the same reason he hires any architect — because you're good at your work.'

His eyes examined hers and he was about to add something more when a sudden barb of lightning ripped open the underbelly of the black clouds that were still jostling above the mountains. It seemed to suck the light out of the sky and a crack of thunder rolled across the wide open plain. Isabella sensed a change in Davide Francolini. He wasn't just staring at the distant storm, he was transfixed.

'Are you all right?' she asked.

'I used to live up there,' he muttered, 'when I was a boy. I know what those storms are like.'

'Violent, I imagine.'

'Yes.'

'It must be interesting for you to see how the

61

plain has changed now.' She smiled at him. 'For the better, I hope.'

He shook himself. The way a dog shakes a rat.

'Come,' he said, reverting to his usual courteous tone, 'and have lunch with me. We don't have to be at the rail station for the grand reception of the new arrivals until two o'clock, so we have plenty of time.'

Isabella's feet took a step away from him before she could stop them. But she had the sense to arrange her face into an expression of regret.

'I'm sorry, but there's somewhere I have to go first.'

'Well, another time perhaps.'

It was vague enough. She said, 'Yes.'

Isabella hurried away down the street. She couldn't tell Davide Francolini that she hadn't had a meal alone with a man for ten years — except her father, of course — because it plunged her back into that time when being alone with a man meant being with Luigi and she would hear the shots and the screams all over again.

She couldn't tell Davide Francolini that just the thought of lunch with him set the bullet hole in her back throbbing.

⋆　⋆　⋆

The convent building bore the distinctive fingerprint of Dottore Martino. Isabella could see it in its use of heavy triglyphs on the stone architraves and on the Roman pilasters. It was

62

the convent of the Suore di Santa Teresa, a newly constructed cruciform building with attractive planes of symmetry and strong vertical lines heading straight up to God.

Isabella felt nervous. There was something about the girl and Chairman Grassi's lies about her mother's madness that tangled together in her head, sharp as strands of wire. She walked up the gravel path to the oak door and lifted her hand to the brass bell-pull. She rang it and waited. They made her wait a long time. She stood on the front step, the air cooling around her as the mist thickened to a leaden cloud, and she watched a flock of crows descend on to the convent's patch of dark earth. They proceeded to rip up the film of grass seed where someone was trying to create a lawn.

'Yes?'

A small hatch in the centre of the door had slid to one side and all she could see was a pair of suspicious blue eyes and the crisp edges of a wimple.

'Can I help you?'

'Yes, I hope so.' Isabella smiled pleasantly at the nun but the suspicious look didn't go away. 'My name is Isabella Berotti and I would like to speak to Sister Consolata, please.'

'She is busy at the moment.'

'I believe you have a girl called Rosa Bianchi here. She's a friend of mine and I'd like to speak to her.'

'That's not possible.'

'When will it be possible?'

'I don't know.'

'When will Sister Consolata be free to see me?'

The blue eyes blinked, as if trying to blink her away. 'I'm not sure.'

'Can I make an appointment to see her?'

'I'm afraid not.'

'Can I make an appointment to see Rosa?'

'I'm afraid not.'

'Is this a convent or a prison?'

'May God's blessing be upon you.'

The hatch banged shut.

*　*　*

'Francesca, are you coming down to the station to welcome the newcomers?'

'You bet I am, Bella. I'm not *stupido*. The Party is one of my best customers, so of course I'll be right there on the platform waving my flag with the rest of them.'

The young woman leaning against the bakery shop window wafted her cigarette through the air at Isabella as a demonstration of her flag-waving prowess. She possessed white-blonde hair inherited from her Norwegian father, and the heavy-boned features of her Sicilian mother; the unusual mix gave her a striking appearance. She had three passions in life — dough-making, Hollywood film stars and cigarettes. Francesca Chitti chain-smoked every day outside her shop, when she wasn't baking bread, and she coughed like a camel. The two women had become friends since Isabella had taken to dropping into Francesca's shop each morning to buy breakfast rolls.

'Busy?' Isabella asked.

'No, not now. I was up all night baking bread for this latest lot of farm newcomers,' she yawned elaborately, 'but it's quiet now.'

'So walk with me to the station.'

A broad smile spread across Francesca's face. 'What's up?'

'Nothing.'

'Well, tell me all about this 'nothing' of yours.'

'I just want to ask you a few things.'

'Bella, cara mia, I am all yours. Just give me half a minute.'

She threw off her apron, locked up the shop, pulled the net off her pale hair so that it cascaded in a snowy river down her back, lit another cigarette and scowled at the sky. 'I hope it doesn't rain. I can't bear all the mud in this blasted town.'

'At least the rain gets rid of the dust.' Isabella removed the cigarette from her friend's fingers and trod it into the pavement. 'The buildings will be all finished soon and the grass will grow in the spring, transforming the place. Wait and see. It will be beautiful.'

'You are an optimist!' Francesca laughed and she rolled her dark eyes in mock despair.

The two friends found the pavements crowded as they walked together along the street, conscious of cars and pedestrians all hurrying in the same direction towards the railway station. Many of the town's workers had been granted a half-day holiday for the occasion.

'So what is it you want to know?' Francesca

asked with curiosity.

'I was wondering whether you've heard anything about the woman who died in the square?'

'Oh, Isabella, you're not fretting over that sad woman, are you? You've got to forget about it. I know it was a grisly shock but . . . '

'Have you picked up any rumours? Allegra Bianchi was her name.'

Francesca was always a source of astonishing amounts of information that she wheedled out of customers or overheard while making deliveries of her bread. She had as good a nose for gossip as she had for dough and made Isabella laugh with her stories of impending disasters or clandestine affairs.

'Why are you so interested in her?' Francesca asked with a lift of a pale eyebrow. She looked closely at her friend.

'Because she knew something about Luigi.'

'No, Allegra Bianchi was new in town. How could she have known anything about your husband? Bella, you're imagining it.'

'No, I'm not. She mentioned him to me before she climbed up the tower.' Isabella saw Francesca shake her head. 'It's true, Francesca, so I need to find out more about who she was and why she came here.'

She tried to make it sound normal. Not like a burning need. Not like something that was churning in her stomach with every breath she took. But Francesca knew her too well and stopped short in the middle of the pavement, ignoring a woman's perambulator that had to make a quick diversion to avoid a collision.

'Bella, don't do this to yourself. You've been through enough.'

'Allegra Bianchi knew something about Luigi's death and I have to find out what it was.'

'Are you sure you can believe her?'

Isabella nodded. 'Help me, Francesca. Please. I've got to speak to her daughter too. I'm worried about her.'

'The girl in the convent?'

'Yes.' Isabella gripped Francesca's arm and set off walking again more briskly. 'Chairman Grassi is involved somehow, according to Rosa's mother. She claimed the Party knows who killed my husband — which means Grassi must know.'

Francesca quickly lit herself a new cigarette. She inhaled harshly. 'Be careful, Bella.' She glanced around nervously as if expecting a *carabiniere* to step out of the shadows. 'It was a long time ago. Let it stay in the past.'

'How can I?' Isabella turned her head and looked with bewilderment at her friend. 'He was my husband. My husband!'

'Oh, Bella, my dearest Bella, don't do this.'

They walked in silence for a whole block, not one of their usual easy silences but an awkward spiky one that made their shoes sound loud on the pavement. As they neared the station Isabella was only dimly aware of the voices around her, of the crowds gathering, of the sense of excitement making people smile at strangers.

'Francesca, listen to me. I know you. If your husband were killed, you'd move heaven and

67

earth to find out who did it. However many years it took.'

'If Piero was killed, my angel, *I* would be the one who did it!'

Isabella could not help but laugh. Her friend's domestic relations were always stormy.

'See what you and that nose of yours can sniff out,' she urged. 'You're good at digging up things.'

Francesca sighed. 'Oh, Isabella, you know I'm hopeless at saying no to you. But don't let me catch you doing anything . . . foolish.' They both were aware that the word 'dangerous' had hovered on the tip of her tongue, but she had not allowed it out. Everyone in Mussolini's Italy knew not to talk out loud about danger. It made daily life feel too fragile.

'Of course I won't.'

Francesca nudged an elbow in Isabella's ribs and dropped her voice to a whisper. 'I've heard one rumour you'll be interested in.'

'What's that?'

'Mussolini is coming to inspect Bellina.'

Isabella's thoughts curled around the name. *Mussolini.* And a door seemed to open to the darkness at the back of her mind.

7

Chairman Grassi had something important to say. That was obvious. The dais on which he stood was a mass of colour, all decked out in the bold green, white and red of the Italian flag, and it seemed that half the town had turned out to listen to him, dressed up in their Sunday best. He cleared his throat, stuck out his chest and his dark eyes scanned the crowd of faces till they fell silent. Only then did he speak.

'People of Bellina, Il Duce is proud of you.'

'*Viva* Il Duce! *Viva* Il Duce!'

The shout surged from the crowd and rang out across the railway station platform, sending the pigeons fleeing up into the grey sky with a resentful clatter. Grassi's large head nodded, satisfied.

Isabella shifted from foot to foot. Standing for a long time always made her back ache and sent what felt like ants in red-hot boots marching up and down the thigh of her right leg, but she fixed an attentive smile on her face. They'd done this before. This waiting. This speech-making. The part she liked best was the brass band but she knew she'd have to be patient before the trombones got their turn to belt out '*Giovinezza*', the official hymn of the Italian Fascist Party. Maybe the train would be early.

That's what they were here for — the train. It

was bringing the newest contingent of incomers selected to become residents of the area, but this time it was to be a collection of farmers, a hundred of them. It was autumn. Time for planting. Isabella couldn't wait to see the barren landscape transformed from black to green when the wheat and maize burst forth in the spring. It was impossible not to be excited for the town and she felt honoured to be chosen as one of the ten representatives of the architectural office to attend this event, but her eyes kept switching from Chairman Grassi on his dais to the skeletal figure of Colonnello Sepe nearby.

What do you know, Colonnello? How much have you discovered about Allegra Bianchi?

The architects were lined up neatly in two rows, alongside groups from the hospital, the shops, the state offices, the fire brigade and many others on the platform. Isabella was tucked away at the back of her group but she noticed Davide Francolini was standing right at the front. He glanced around when she arrived and treated her to a half-smile. That was all. She was surprised she even got that much after turning down his invitation to a bowl of pasta.

'People of Bellina,' Chairman Grassi's deep voice came booming out of the loudspeaker, 'our great leader, Benito Mussolini, is building a powerful new Italy for all his people. Today here in Bellina we are witnessing an important advance in his Battle for Grain and in his Battle for Land. Il Duce is leading us forward in the magnificent economic rebirth of Italy, and he has vowed to make us self-sufficient in food. Here in

70

Bellina we are in the forefront of that great Battle for Grain.'

For a second he stood silent, silhouetted against the oppressive grey sky, his listeners hanging on his every word, and then his right arm shot out in the Fascist straight-arm salute. Instantly Isabella's shot out too, and a forest of arms launched around her.

'Il Duce! Il Duce!' they roared back at him.

'Five thousand new farms will be built.'

'Il Duce! Il Duce!'

'Five more magnificent towns that show the way to the future will be constructed on these plains. Mussolini has promised.'

'*Bravissimo!*'

'Bellina this year, Littoria next year, then . . . '

Isabella's gaze slid inexorably back to Colonnello Sepe in his dark uniform and glittering silver braid, and her ears ceased listening. What kind of man was he, this colonel in the *carabinieri* with the face of a hawk? One who could keep a child imprisoned, even after she had lost her mother in such a terrible manner. One who was willing to let a daughter view her mother's broken body. The convent may be a holy place but it must be a barren prison for Rosa. Grieving and alone in a world of hair shirts she must be confused and frightened. Isabella felt a wave of pity for the lonely child. She remembered only too well what it was like to lose a mother when she was young. She drew a deep breath but her emotions were starting to spiral out of control and she realised that although she needed to learn information from Rosa, it was also important to her to know that the girl wasn't falling apart in the cold corridors of the convent. With an effort Isabella forced herself to look away from the hard lines of the policeman's face.

★ ★ ★

The train was coming. Isabella could see it in the distance, like an iron monster heaving smoke from its lungs as it advanced on Bellina, and the ground shuddered at its approach. The town was new and raw, and somehow she could feel its nervous breath on her neck. Even the sky seemed to lean closer to take a look at the newcomers from Friuli and Veneto.

The band struck up with 'Giovinezza', and the waiting crowd bustled nearer the edge of the platform, so that when the doors of the train finally flew open and the travellers tumbled from the carriages, they had to fight their way through the townspeople shaking their hands and slapping their backs. They looked dazed, the men in flat caps, the women with flowered head-scarves and pale northern cheeks, all of them weighed down by possessions. Cardboard boxes were tucked under their arms, string baskets dangling from their wrists, scuffed suitcases gripped in their anxious fingers as they stared wide-eyed at the new world they were being thrust into.

Isabella stepped forward to one old woman in black who was bent over with a roll of bedding strapped to her back and a pure white chicken struggling under one arm. She had dropped her walking stick, so Isabella picked it up and placed it in her arthritic hand with a smile.

'Welcome,' she said. '*Benvenuta.*'

'*Grazie*, signora.' Tears were rolling down the cobweb lines of the old woman's face as she raised her powdery eyes to the skies. 'And thank you, Lord in Heaven, for bringing me to this grand town before I die.'

A group of boys rushed past, excited and boisterous, jostling them, and Isabella eased the burden from the old woman's back on to her own shoulder.

'Where are you from?' she asked.

'From Veneto, right up north. The cold gets into my old bones sharp as nails in the winter.'

'I'm glad you're pleased to be here. I thought people may not want to come to Bellina. It's a big wrench to uproot like this.'

'A new start for us all,' the woman stated proudly and handed over the chicken, sliding her arm through Isabella's.

'Now, where's your family?' Isabella asked.

The woman nodded towards a wiry, assertive-looking man who was unloading a crate of ducks from the goods van at the back of the train and handing it to his wife and son to carry. Each family had to register at a row of tables set up along the station wall, manned by officials in dark suits, but inside the station itself stood long trestle tables laden with bowls of good rich garlic lamb, *linguini pescadoro* and Francesca's fresh bread for the new arrivals. The women of the local Fascist party were damned if they weren't going to show these northern polenta-eaters what proper food was.

Isabella could feel the excitement shiver through the old woman as she scurried along at her side, uttering fervent promises to her chicken and leaning heavily on Isabella's arm, almost tipping her over on her bad leg. The crush of bodies was intense as more people tumbled on to the platform but Isabella became suddenly aware of a bulky camera pointing straight at her and the old woman. Its big round eye was glaring at them. She heard it click and a head of ruffled chestnut-brown hair lifted above the camera and a pair of eyes the colour of rain focused on her. The stare they gave her would have been too direct, too intrusive, if it hadn't been for the warm smile of welcome on the photographer's lips.

'*Benvenuta*,' he said. 'I hope you'll be happy here in this wonderful new town.' One dark eyebrow shot up in an ironic underlining of the word 'wonderful'. 'There are even wonderful refreshments for you over in the station waiting room.'

Isabella recognised his voice first and then the broad set of his shoulders in his pale jacket. It was the same man who had been at the police station with Chairman Grassi, the one she'd overheard saying that there had been no sign of anyone else up on the tower with Allegra Bianchi. What, she wondered, was his connection with the tragedy?

'You must be hungry after your journey,' he added kindly.

Isabella shook her head. 'But I'm not a — '

The old woman screeched in her ear with delight. '*Andiamo*,' she shouted above the hubbub of voices, 'let's get Alfonso and Maria.'

Isabella was dragged forward and the photographer vanished. She shouldn't have minded, but she did. A ripple of disappointment pricked her skin. All these people were farmers, a hundred of them with their families to occupy the newly blue-painted farmhouses around Bellina. So the photographer and his ironic eyebrow would naturally assume that she was a farmer's wife, of course he would. With a hen under one arm, a roll of bedding slung over her shoulder, she looked all ready to move in. She couldn't blame him. What else was he supposed to think? But she wasn't a farmer's wife. She was an architect. She had fought damn hard to become one and had spent long years training to be the best in Rome after she got out of hospital. Yet now, because of this photographer, she would go down in the picture archive of this historic town as a farmer's wife. She shouldn't have minded. But she did.

She glanced back over her shoulder and spotted him about ten metres away above the bobbing heads — she hadn't realised he was so tall. At that exact moment he looked back. Their eyes caught and she lifted the stupid hen and waggled it at him, meaning *It's not mine*, but he just laughed, misunderstanding. So now she'd go down not only as a farmer's wife, but as a farmer's mad wife. She had to laugh also, and their laughter mingled together above the heads that divided them.

75

A large pack of ragged children suddenly surged forward from the train and the photographer was swept away, so that Isabella lost sight of him in the crowd. But instead she caught a glimpse once more of a dark police uniform and a flash of silver, so she deposited her new companion and chicken with her family, wished her luck, and then headed straight for that silver braid.

★　★　★

'Colonnello Sepe.'

The policeman's head snapped around, fast as a rat. 'What is it, Signora Berotti? I am extremely busy.' He gestured at the crowd of people on the platform.

At least he remembered her name.

'Why am I not allowed to see Rosa Bianchi?' Isabella asked with no preamble. 'You have shut her away. Why?'

A frown stitched its way across his forehead, the skin so tight she feared the bones would push through from beneath. 'It is not your business, signora. You have given your statement about what you saw that day, so now forget it and get on with your work here.' He started to turn away.

'Colonnello Sepe, I am concerned about the girl. Have you found any of her relatives?'

'No need for your concern. We haven't yet traced her relatives but she is being well cared for by the nuns.'

'Let me see her,' she said quietly. 'Just once.'

'Signora,' he said impatiently, 'you were once

76

married to Luigi Berotti, were you not?'

All air seeped out of Isabella's lungs. He had caught her completely off guard. 'I was,' she said.

'Luigi Berotti was a loyal member of the Fascist Party.'

'So am I. That's why I'm here.'

His thin lips spread in what was meant to be a smile but their corners still curled down in tight creases of irritation. 'I'm glad to hear that, signora. As a loyal member of the Fascist Party, I am ordering you to stay away from the girl.'

Isabella's hand shot out and seized his arm. She could feel the tension under his sleeve. 'Whatever it is you want from Rosa Bianchi, you won't get it with your methods. She's just a child, for heaven's sake. If you want information from her, let me speak to her.'

His eyes didn't change but his stiff stalk of a neck inclined a fraction towards her over the collar of his uniform. 'What makes you think that she'll talk to you?'

'Because she knows her mother put her in my care. Let me try.'

The ash-grey eyes considered her coldly. 'How do I know I can trust you?'

'Colonnello, you said it yourself. I was Luigi Berotti's wife. I am a widow to the Fascist cause.' She smiled at him and released his arm, only just managing to stop herself wiping her palm on her skirt. 'I am working hard to help build Il Duce's vision in this corner of Italy. Of course you can trust me.'

He hesitated for a full minute and she thought she had him, but then he shook his head. 'Stick to your bricks and mortar, signora. Leave policework to me.'

He started to move away, examining the immaculate material of his sleeve as if she might have dirtied it.

'Colonnello Sepe.'

He paused reluctantly. 'What is it now, Signora Berotti?'

'This young girl is alone. She has no one. Except me. I'm asking you to give me some time with her, so that she learns to trust me and then I might discover whatever it is that you want to know from her.'

''Might'?' He regarded her scornfully. 'Don't waste my time.'

'She is a lonely child.' Isabella observed the colonel carefully. 'There might be other people out there,' she waved a hand in the vague direction of Rome, 'whom she would want me to get in touch with. Or maybe even take a message to.'

She had him hooked. She saw it in the tightening of his mouth as he bit down on the bait.

'It's possible,' he conceded. 'A message to . . . ' He broke off and exhaled heavily. 'That is possible.'

'So you will arrange it?'

'Very well.'

'Today?'

He nodded mutely, as if he had no words left to waste on her. He strode away along the platform and Isabella felt a drop of rain. The grey sheet of sky had sunk lower, swallowing the smoke of the train, and she heard a man with a

78

shovel on his shoulder exclaim, 'Where's the sun? We were promised sun.' Isabella fought her way through the queues at the registration tables to the spot where the architects had been stationed, but no one was left there now, everyone had scattered. It meant she could leave without anyone noticing, so she headed for the open exit-gate.

She had to leave. Because of the children. They were everywhere, their high-pitched voices buzzing like blasted mosquitoes. She was trying to keep her eyeline above the level of their silky heads, in case the soft curve of a rosy cheek or a flicker of mischief in a bright young eye drew forth a smile from her and reminded her what she'd lost ten years ago.

A hundred farmers. A hundred wives. A sprinkling of aunts and uncles and milky-eyed grandparents. But it was the children that covered the platform like wild flowers that had sprung up out of cracks in the concrete, more than six hundred of them. Of course she didn't count them, but everyone knew that only families with at least six children — some with as many as ten or eleven — had been selected for the honour of coming to Bellina. Italy needed a greater population to increase the workforce and the Fascist Party was making sure it happened. Mussolini had put in place his Battle for Births, alongside his Battle for Grain and Battle for Land, all forming part of the well-orchestrated economic renaissance of Italy.

It worked like this. If a man had six *bambini*, he received tax relief. If he had seven or eight, he received even greater tax relief. And for those macho machines who had produced ten or more infants for the glory of Italy, well, those lucky men paid no tax at all. They just buttoned up their trousers and laughed their way down to the nearest wine shop. Any woman who didn't stay at home and rear her brood alongside her pigs was frowned upon.

So the exit-gate beckoned but when she reached it a child was blocking her path. He was crouched right in the middle of the open gateway, a short-haired urchin in a cut-down shirt. He was clutching a chunk of bread in one grubby paw and trying to coax an alarmingly large black and white rabbit back into its cardboard box with the other. Isabella stopped. How could she possibly *not* stop to round up a rabbit?

Such a trifling thing to do. To help a child whose small hands were too puny for the job. Isabella hunched down beside him. Together they tried to corral the rabbit, both of them laughing at its bad-tempered antics, and she had just made a grab for one of its long satiny ears when she heard a shout. But she was busy so she was slow to look away from her furry captive, far too slow. When she did look up, her heart kicked a hole right through her ribs and she snatched at the child.

A horse was barging its way across the platform straight at her. All she saw was a furious black mane flying, sweat-soaked flanks heaving, flecks of foam around huge yellow teeth and eyes rolling wildly in panic. It took another heartbeat for her to hear the hooves striking the concrete at speed and voices screaming. The animal had been unloaded from the goods van, seen the open gate and charged for it, just as she had.

Time became slippery. It skidded through her grasp as she threw herself sideways, but the rabbit-boy dug his heels in the ground, acting like an anchor on her, unwilling to desert his pet. Isabella wasn't frightened of pain — she had looked that sharp-clawed foe in the face too many times before and won — but she *was* terrified. Terrified of losing the life of yet another child. Instinctively she spun her body at the very last second so that her back was towards the charging wall of horseflesh.

She could hear the rasping sound of the horse's breath but her feet seemed stuck in wet concrete and she gripped the child so tight he squealed. But at the very last second a figure hurled itself forward, seized the halter and yanked it sideways with brute force. The horse was forced to swerve.

It didn't miss them. They weren't that lucky. The massive muscles of the animal's shoulder slammed into Isabella's own shoulder and sent her sprawling on the ground with the boy, but they were still in one piece, not trampled flat for the crows to pick over. A blur of hands lifted her to her feet but she shook them off with thanks and ignored the stab of pain in her arm socket. The child was crying, but more from shock than hurt, and was scooped out of her arms by his mother. Isabella looked around for the horse and caught sight of it just outside the station gate

81

being walked in wide circles to calm it down. It was still up on its toes, snorting through flared nostrils and trying to throw its panicked head around, but the man walking it held the halter tight.

He was leaning in close, murmuring words that only the horse could hear, rhythmically running his hand down its long sweating neck and gradually slowing the animal's pace to his own. It was entrancing, like watching a kind of magic. She had seen men deal with difficult animals before, but there was something about the naked love that this man offered the horse, visible in every curve of his body and in every touch of his hand, that set up a dull ache within her. For a long shaky moment, she wanted to be that horse.

She walked up to him. 'Thank you,' she said.

His head was turned away, his attention focused on the horse, so all she saw were his broad shoulders in a light cambric shirt, and short wavy hair, the same chestnut colour as the horse.

'*Grazie*,' she said again. 'I'd have been trampled to pieces.' She gave a light laugh. It was awkward. She knew she was intruding.

Reluctantly, as if coming back from somewhere far beyond her range of vision, her rescuer twisted his head to look at her directly.

'Oh,' she said, surprised. 'It's you.'

It was the photographer. His mist-grey eyes smiled but his mouth didn't take part in it. 'Are you hurt?' he asked immediately. 'I saw you limping.'

So he *had* known she was there.

'No, that's an old battle-scar. I'm not hurt.'

'Good.' His mouth joined in the smile. 'I'm glad to hear it. That wouldn't be an auspicious way to start your life in Bellina.'

'I'm not one of the newcomers. I was just helping the old lady on the platform. I already live and work here. I'm one of the architects.'

He shook his head. 'My apologies. I should have known.'

'Known what?'

'That you weren't a farmer's wife.'

'I'm from Milan.'

'Well, that explains it.'

'Explains what? Why I don't have straw sticking out of my ears?'

He laughed at that, an easy ready laugh that made the horse utter a throaty rumble in response. They were still walking in slow steady circles and Isabella fell into step beside them.

'Where are you from?' she asked. It was a question everyone in this town asked each other because no one was from Bellina.

'From Sorrento, down south.'

'A farming family, I assume.' She nodded towards the horse.

'Not really. My father was a fisherman but my uncle owned a small farm in the hills. I was always either off on the boat or shovelling out the barns.'

'A far cry from photography,' she commented.

But just then a man wearing a flat cap marched up and clapped the photographer on the shoulder with evident relief.

83

'*Grazie*, young man, for stopping my horse. The bastard gets the very devil in him some days.' He slapped a hand heavily on the animal's rump and a hoof lashed out but caught only air.

'The poor creature was frightened,' the photographer pointed out with an edge of annoyance. 'All that noise — the train and the band.'

'We're all bloody frightened,' the man said scowling at the nervous animal. 'We're all in a sweat about this place.'

He stuck out a hand to take over the halter but the photographer smoothly eased the horse forward and out of reach. 'I'll walk him to the wagon for you.'

Outside the station building — with its frontage curved like the great prow of a liner — stretched a whole row of horse-drawn wagons. They were to transport the peasant farmers with their families and chattels to their allocated new farmsteads, and any extra horses were being tied on behind.

'Come along then,' the man urged. 'You can ride in the wagon with us to keep him quiet if you've nothing better to do.' He hurried off towards one of the wagons that was already piled high with children and packages.

Isabella didn't want to see the photographer go. She wanted him to tell her about Sorrento and what it was like to sail in stormy seas. She wanted him to understand that not for one moment did she underestimate the danger he was in when he stopped that charging horse and above all she wanted to say thank you. *Thank you*. For risking your life. And a voice deep within her was whispering, Where were you ten years ago when I needed you to stop a charging bullet?

'Goodbye, then,' she said politely.

He had started leading the horse towards the row of wagons but he stopped in his tracks, suddenly realising she wasn't coming too. She was aware of a sense of disappointment but wasn't sure if it was his or hers, until she saw an expression of quiet amusement flit across his face.

'*Milanese*, would you be so kind as to retrieve my equipment case for me? I abandoned the poor thing on the platform when I ran for the horse.'

'Of course. I'll fetch it.'

Isabella pushed her way through the crowd and located the camera which lay miraculously undisturbed on the station platform where he had left it. It was a long rectangular leather case with a shoulder strap, and was heavier than she expected when she picked it up. She ran her palm over its smooth surface and wondered just how much it had cost him to desert it the way he did. *The poor thing*, he'd called it. As if it had feelings. By the time she returned the equipment case to him, he had hitched the horse to the back of the wagon and was climbing up over the backboard. His eyes lit up at the sight of the case and he drew it to his side protectively.

'Thank you, *Milanese*.'

Isabella smiled. 'Thank *you*.'

The rain was falling harder now, big fat drops of it that speckled the ground. The horse edged sideways and stamped one foot, impatient to be gone.

'Why don't you jump in the wagon for a ride too?' the photographer suddenly asked with a grin. 'By the way, what's your name?'

'Ah, Signora Berotti,' a man's voice intruded as if in answer to the photographer's request, 'I've been looking for you.'

It was Davide Francolini from her office. *Not now. Please don't talk business to me now.*

Isabella half turned towards him. His hair was flattened by the rain.

Go away. Go away.

He placed a hand on her elbow. 'I have a message from Colonnello Sepe for you. He has telephoned the convent and arranged for you to see the girl right away.' He waved a hand towards a black car parked on the opposite side of the road and tried to draw her away but she hesitated.

'Come now,' he said.

Isabella felt a churning of something cold inside her but this time she let him wheel her away from the wagon. Nevertheless she turned her head.

The cart carrying the man in the flat cap along with his wife and excited children was already rattling off down the street, the horse still skittish behind it in the rain. The photographer was standing up at the back among the bundles of belongings. He moved easily with the sway of it, the way Isabella could imagine him doing on a

86

boat-deck, and all the time he was watching her and her companion. She raised a hand and waved goodbye.

He didn't wave back.

8

Convent living was not hard. Not for Rosa. Yes, it was cold at night; yes, the meals were only scraps to feed a starling; and yes, some of the girls were spiteful. But she had moved around from place to place so many times that she had learned how to make new friends quickly. And how to leave them just as quickly too.

What was hard was the nuns. With their angry eyes and their crepey cheeks and the ruler ever ready in their hands to smack down on soft young knuckles or to clip across the back of calves, stinging like a snake bite. The one good thing Rosa had to say for her own mother was that she never hit her, so these sudden casual physical attacks left her speechless with rage and misery.

Rosa liked mathematics, liked the symmetry of it, and she was in the middle of an arithmetic lesson with Sister Agatha when Sister Consolata stuck her cheery head around the door. Her cheeks were bunched into a smile that was at odds with her sour black habit and stiff white headdress. Sister Consolata was the exception among the nuns, a beam of sunlight in a dark and thwarted world. All the girls wanted to be in her sewing class because there were no rulers there and she would sing to them in her pure soprano voice while they worked.

'May I borrow Rosa Bianchi for a while?

Reverend Mother wishes to speak to her.'

Sister Agatha, a stout woman who preferred cold baths to children, frowned to demonstrate her disapproval but could not gainsay the orders of the Reverend Mother.

'Very well, Rosa. You may be excused.'

'Thank you, Sister Agatha.'

Rosa had learned that much, to thank them for every tiny sliver of mercy if she wanted to keep the skin on her knuckles. She glanced with lowered eyes at her friend, Carmela, sitting next to her, a pale-faced Venetian with unholy Titian curls, legs like stilts, and carrying the stigma of being born out of wedlock. Carmela tried to give her a tiny smile of encouragement but her eyes were huge with concern. Why? What did the Reverend Mother do? Whip you? Make you pay for your sins? Rosa shuddered because she knew she carried around a whole heap of sins.

'Hurry up, girl,' Sister Agatha snapped.

'We don't want to keep Reverend Mother waiting,' Sister Consolata added gently.

Rosa hurried to the door and down the stark corridor, scurrying behind the long black robe that moved surprisingly fast. She yearned to grasp one of its musky folds, to smell it, to let its incense drift into her head, to hold on to it. To hold on to *something*.

'Rosa, dear child, let's tidy you up.'

Sister Consolata had come to a halt in front of a large oak door carved with the image of Christ on the cross. Rosa lowered her eyes and was taken by surprise when the nun started attacking her hair with a hairbrush that appeared like magic from the folds of the black habit.

'You have such lovely curls,' the nun laughed, 'and we don't want Reverend Mother cutting them off, do we?'

'No, Sister,' Rosa whispered, appalled.

She submitted mutely to the tidying process, to being patted and pressed and brushed down, but her fingers managed to creep into one of the black folds where they nestled quietly for a few seconds. When finally satisfied, Sister Consolata rested a blue-veined hand heavily on Rosa's head and closed her eyes in silent prayer. Rosa watched the way the soft layers of her face settled into stillness like ripples in a pond and the way the scarlet flares on her cheeks faded. She stared up at the nun for a long moment and wondered what she'd look like if she were dead.

'Now, little one,' Sister Consolata popped open her eyes, 'the good Lord has brought you a visitor today.'

The nun's words made the world outside — on which Rosa had slammed the doors tight to keep it out of her head — come sweeping back to her, but now it had changed: it was bent and twisted at the edges. Suddenly she felt as if she were drowning, something dark and heavy flooded her chest and she had to squeeze her eyes shut to keep tears away. Once again the stiff and savaged body of her mother on the cold slab flared up inside her head. She started shaking.

'Courage, Rosa. Our dear Lord in Heaven is with you and knows all that is in your heart. Call on Him for strength.'

She patted Rosa's chest right on the spot

90

where her heart was hammering so hard she feared it would crack open her ribs and spill a crimson flood on to the clean scrubbed floor under her feet.

'You're breathing too fast, Rosa. Slow breaths. That's better. Stand up straight now.'

Rosa took slow breaths. She stood up straight. She stared blindly at the door.

Sister Consolata tapped timidly on its oak surface and put her ear to it, her face tense within the tight circle of her wimple. A murmur came from the other side. With a bright smile pinned on her lips, the nun opened the door.

★　★　★

Dislike. It hung in the room, as grey as mist; the air was drenched with it. That's what hit Rosa first when she stepped over the threshold of the large high-ceilinged room. The woman in this room disliked her intensely. And Rosa knew why. Sister Agatha had spelled it out to her. Reverend Mother was pure of heart. She talked to God every day. She read His Word every day. Whereas Rosa was nothing but the tainted offspring of a wicked woman who had condemned her own soul to eternal Damnation in the Fires of Hell. That's what Sister Agatha said. Tainted blood careened through her veins. Did she bear a mark on her forehead too, like the evil Cain in the Bible? One that others could see but Rosa couldn't? That thought tormented her.

'Here's Rosa Bianchi, Reverend Mother.'

When Rosa didn't move, Sister Consolata

placed a firm hand against her back and launched her across the expanse of Persian rug under the critical gaze of the vast oil paintings on the walls, all of them old men decked out in violent red or gaudy purple robes.

'Come here, girl.'

Rosa warily approached the figure in black who was seated near the log fire. The room was far warmer than the corridor or the classrooms. Mother Domenica sat stiff as a poker in a carved chair that looked very old and extremely grand. She wasn't tall but reminded Rosa of a giraffe because of her long skinny neck and pointed face. Her tongue kept flashing across her lips, grey and thin, but otherwise she remained totally still, hands folded like pieces of bleached paper on her lap. But a movement in the chair opposite on the other side of the fire caught Rosa's attention and for a second her feet froze. Paralysed with hope.

'Hello, Rosa. How are you?'

It was the architect.

'I'm well.'

'I'm very glad to hear it.'

Rosa could not take her eyes off her visitor. She was sitting in a smaller carved chair and seemed to glow in the amber light of the fire. Her dark hair hung wet and shiny to her shoulders and her skirt, the soft colour of mushrooms, was speckled like a bird's egg by raindrops.

'Signora Berotti has generously come to visit you, Rosa, to enquire after your welfare.'

Rosa didn't know what to say. She nodded.

'Don't be sullen, girl. Come and sit here.'

Mother Domenica jutted her pointy chin towards a small pine stool placed beside her own chair. Rosa wanted to pick it up and carry it over to place it beside the architect's chair but she didn't want her knuckles skinned in front of her visitor, so she did as she was told and sat on the stool. Sister Consolata backed out of the room and shut the door quietly, leaving Rosa alone with the grey mist of dislike.

Rosa had thought a lot about the architect since she'd been brought to the chill corridors of the convent. Signora Berotti was different. And she had that way of looking at you. Isabella, she'd said her name was. An architect with a dead husband and a bullet hole in her back. Rosa wondered what it looked like. What she did know was that Signora Berotti wasn't like other people. No one else had ever talked to her about 'pilasters' or 'symmetry'. No one else would ever think she would care.

'Tell me about your day, Rosa,' the architect prompted gently. 'Mother Domenica tells me that you had French and mathematics lessons this morning and a good lunch of lasagne.'

Then Mother Domenica is a liar.

Rosa nodded. She could smell the lies in the black material that hung its holy disguise on the woman in the big carved chair. The lies smelled like rotten grapes. Sour in her nostrils. When Rosa lifted her gaze to the pointed face, the Reverend Mother was smiling at her, but Rosa didn't smile back. She stared straight at the nun's sharp black eyes.

93

'Do you enjoy learning French?' the architect asked when the staring had gone on long enough.

'*Oui*,' Rosa muttered.

What else could she say? She thought about saying: No, Signora Berotti. We stand in a row in the French class and Sister Maria fires a word at each of us that we have to shout back in French. If a girl gets it wrong, she has to kneel on the floor and the flat side of Sister Maria's ruler slaps down on her head. She stays there until she gets a word right. I have never learned French. My head is sore. My knees hurt. Is that what you want to know?

Rosa lowered her eyes to the round table that stood at knee height between the two chairs. On it sat two cups of coffee. The Reverend Mother picked one up and raised it to her thin lips, the aroma of it drifting thick and heavy to the back of Rosa's throat, making saliva spurt into her mouth. Beside the other cup stood a small silver jug of milk and a stubby glass of water. She could guess who the water was for. The hard bones of her shoulder blades slumped forward and she sat in silence, listening to the logs crackle in the flames and feeling the coffee torment her empty stomach.

'Rosa.'

The architect drew her attention.

'Rosa, I've brought you something.'

Rosa's gaze jumped to her face. The architect's eyes were blue, not blue like a flower is blue, but blue like the sea, full of greys and purples and greens that threaded their way in and out of the blue. They were smiling at her.

In the large carved chair the black robes rustled and the coffee cup was replaced on the table. 'And what might that be, signora?' Mother Domenica asked.

'I've brought Rosa some *torcetti*.'

'Our girls are not allowed to eat between meals.'

'I'm sure you can make an exception in this case.'

Rosa became aware of the architect changing shape. When she'd first entered the room, Signora Berotti had seemed soft in the chair, her body curved, her head tilted on one side, her mouth rising at the edges in a smile. Now, Rosa could see that the signora's limbs had grown spiky, her fingers straight, her shoulders back. Her eyes were no longer round when she looked at Mother Domenica but had a hard edge to them that had not been there before. From a canvas bag at her side she withdrew a small package wrapped in grease-proof paper and held it out to Rosa, offering it on the palm of her hand, the way you would tempt a nervous foal.

'Enjoy them,' she said.

Rosa's hand was fast. Faster than the Reverend Mother's. She snatched it on to her lap and started to rip open the paper, hunger driving her stomach to lurch and bile to shoot into her throat.

'Just one.'

The Reverend Mother's stern voice barely reached her ears. All she could hear was the tearing of the paper. All she could smell was

95

sugar. On her lap lay a nest of *torcetti*. Baked worms. That's what they looked like, worms with heads crossed over tails, sugar-crusted and crunchy. Rosa lifted one, sank her teeth in, bit it in half and felt the sweetness and crispness explode on her tongue, making her dizzy. Immediately she pushed the rest of the biscuit into her mouth.

Dimly she was aware of the architect talking, moving her hands through the air, laughing and shaking her head, telling a story it seemed. Something about a train. A brass band. A horse and a rabbit. But Rosa only caught snatches of it. She was too busy with the *torcetti*, her golden twisted worms, the crust of sugar gleaming like diamonds catching the firelight. Swiftly she started to cram them whole into her mouth, to fill up the lonely spaces, to stifle the voices inside her, to squeeze more and more down her throat until all the emptiness would be gone and all she would feel was full. Stuffed full. No more pain or —

'Rosa Bianchi, stop that at once!'

The Reverend Mother's hand was reaching for what was left of the package. Vaguely Rosa was conscious of the architect rising to her feet, still narrating her story of people arriving on a train, still trying to distract the Reverend Mother's attention from the appalling and repulsive sight of Rosa cramming food into her mouth.

'Enough!' Mother Domenica shouted.

The nun's veinless hand seized a corner of the greaseproof paper.

'You are disgusting, girl.'

The hand started to remove the package but Rosa clamped both her own hands tight around it. The Reverend Mother's face distorted with disbelief and a shudder ran through her.

'Give it to me, Rosa Bianchi. At once.'

'No.'

A shocked silence made the room suddenly grow smaller but Rosa dug her fingers in tighter.

'Let go, you undeserving child.'

'No.'

Crumbs spilled from her lips. She was suffocating in sugar. Air wouldn't go in and out of her lungs.

'Do as I say, girl!'

'They're mine.'

'Release it at once.'

'No.'

The crucifix that hung around the nun's neck rattled on its chain as the other veinless hand started to swing forward. Rosa was so fixated on the biscuit package that she didn't see it coming. It hit her full across the face, sending slugs of half-chewed biscuit sailing out of her mouth over the table and into the milk jug. For no more than a second a numb silence ricocheted through Rosa's head but then came the bolt of pain and a roaring in her ears. For a moment her mind couldn't recall where she was, but then the architect's hands were lifting her to her feet, softly touching her hair, and it was the architect's voice that hissed, 'How dare you hit her?' at the figure in black.

'Apologise!'

The nun spat the word into the room. She

moved stiffly out of her chair, raising herself to her full height, stretching her skinny white-bound neck to its full extent until she looked to Rosa like a crane on a riverbank preparing to strike a frog in the mud.

'Rosa, apologise to Signora Berotti and to myself. May God forgive you in His mercy. You should be ashamed of yourself. You are no better than your mother.'

That was when the shame came, thick and foul-tasting. It seeped under the door, dripped down the chimney and squeezed under the window frames. Shame that was white-hot when it touched Rosa's skin. It crawled up her legs, beat its way across her chest, drumming on her heart, and burned a path across her cheeks. She was consumed by shame.

She detached herself from the architect's touch and backed away with eyes lowered.

'It's all right, Rosa, there's no need to apologise or — '

'I am sorry, Signora Berotti.' Rosa dragged air into her lungs. 'I am sorry, Reverend Mother.'

'God in Heaven is the One who sees a truly repentant heart,' the nun said in a brittle voice.

'The girl has done nothing to repent. Let me speak with her alone, Reverend Mother. Allow me to take her into the courtyard to — '

'You have done enough, *grazie*, Signora Berotti,' the nun said coldly. 'Please leave now.'

There was a long hard silence in the room. Behind it Rosa's ears could pick up faint whispers, as though the Devil were laughing behind the paintings of the old men. The only movement came from the architect's hands as they clenched and unclenched at her sides, long-fingered and restless, a tangle of fine bones that she was holding in check.

'Do you want me to leave, Rosa?' the architect asked quietly.

Rosa nodded. Shame scorched her throat.

'Very well. I'm sorry, Rosa. The biscuits were meant to bring you pleasure, not anguish.' She picked up her canvas bag. 'Good afternoon to you both.'

'Goodbye, signora,' Mother Domenica said. 'There's no need to come again.'

Still Rosa could not bring herself to look at the architect's face and after a pause Signora Berotti swung away and limped across the Persian rug to the door. There she turned.

'Take care, Rosa. I am sorry about your mother. You know where I live if you need me.'

The door opened, then closed. She was gone. Rosa tried to call her back but there were no words in her throat and no breath in her lungs. The Reverend Mother did not speak but she seized Rosa's wrist with her sinless fingers and hauled her across the room under the accusing eyes of the men in red and purple. She swept her down the corridor until she stopped in front of a door and Rosa stood there, mute and obedient. The nun yanked open the door. It was a cupboard full of mops and buckets.

'Repent!' she commanded.

She thrust the sinner into the cupboard, slammed the door shut and turned the key. Rosa uttered no sound but stood in total silence, shaking in the darkness.

★　★　★

The darkness kept moving. Shifting around her. It was never still. It brushed itself against Rosa's skin, cold and clammy, making her turn her head blindly again and again. It twisted through her hair and whispered in her ear sounds that sent her heart fleeing up into her throat. It crept deep into her lungs, squeezing out the air, while her small fingers clawed at the door. She dropped to her knees on the stone floor and begged. She hammered on the door with her clenched fists. With her head. With her feet. With a bucket.

No one came. Not even God.

The hours ticked past. She made herself lie quietly on the hard floor, curling her body into a tight ball, knees up under her nose, but the blackness grew too heavy. It was bruising her ribs, crushing them, so she groped for one of the buckets, turned it upside down and sat on it instead. She paraded through her head those moments that she'd spent walking through Bellina's streets with the architect, opening her eyes to the buildings, but they were forced out by other images that stalked the darkness. Taking up space. Cracking open her skull. Gnawing at her feet. She cried out once to her mother, but only once.

Don't let me die. Please, don't let me die.

★　★　★

The door was thrown open and light streaked inside, making Rosa screw up her eyes. She was startled to see it was morning. She had been in the cupboard fourteen hours and had peed in one of the buckets with no shame.

But she was not the same Rosa when she emerged from the cupboard. She knew that. She could feel it. A part of her was missing — she'd lost the part that wanted to be with people. It had spilled on to the floor in the cupboard, alongside the stinking mops and the rat poison, and made her feel lonelier than ever before.

Sister Agatha was the one who opened the door and stood there with a black Bible in her hand. She made Rosa kneel in the soulless corridor right outside the cupboard and she prayed over the small sinner's bent head for thirty long minutes. At the end, Rosa asked for forgiveness. But as she trailed behind the shapeless black figure on her way back to her classroom, Rosa knew she had gained something too. She hugged it to herself, as warm and comforting as a kiss.

Rosa knew now that whatever they did to her, these devils in black robes, she would come out of it alive.

Not like her mother.

Rosa had refused to let herself die in the cupboard because she had promised her father that she would keep going. Until he came for her.

* * *

'Where did you live in Rome?'

It was Colonnello Sepe asking the questions this time. He didn't frighten Rosa, not any more. She knew now what it meant to be frightened and Colonnello Sepe didn't come close. She was in the Reverend Mother's high-ceilinged room once more, watched by the secretive eyes on the wall, and the police colonel was trying but failing to make his thin face appear kindly. He was seated behind Mother Domenica's sturdy oak desk and Rosa was perched in front of it on the edge of a hard chair. The room was too warm. The nun was pretending to read the Bible in her carved chair over by the fire but couldn't resist glancing across at Rosa each time she spoke.

'I don't know the addresses where we stayed,' Rosa insisted, fighting to keep herself from snatching the heavy brass inkwell from the leather desktop and hurling it at the Reverend Mother. She had even picked out the spot on her white left temple where she wanted it to land. 'We moved around so often,' she explained. 'Rome, Milan, Padua, Naples.' She shrugged the bony tip of one shoulder. 'We stayed in a shepherd's hut in the mountains one year. I liked it up there.'

Rosa made herself meet his eyes and blink in a childish stupid way. He had to believe her and leave her alone.

'Were you not educated? Didn't you go to school?'

'My mother taught me to read and write.'

'What did she live on?'

Rosa lowered her eyes, her lashes fluttered

with nerves. 'She used to go out in the evening. Sometimes.' Her mouth grew dry.

'To do what?'

'Whoring.'

She heard his intake of breath. Felt the nun's disgust slither across the floor. 'Whoring' was a dirty word. Rosa was ashamed to say it, even though her mother had made her promise to use it if she was interrogated. She flicked her tongue over her lips to clean them.

'Some nights,' she added, staring at the policeman's long brown shoes under the desk, 'she came back smelling of beer and cigarettes.' She felt a flush rise to her cheeks.

'Why did she keep moving from place to place?' the policeman demanded.

'I don't know. She never explained. I think it was because . . . ' She paused and recalled the exact words her mother had made her learn. 'Because she was running away.'

Colonnello Sepe leaned forward, elbows on the desk, eyes sharp with expectation. Rosa could see that he wanted to grab her by the scruff and shake the words out of her, but he was good at control, this man. Almost as good as she was.

'What was she running away from?' He squeezed out half a smile.

'From herself. That's what she told me.'

'And you believed her?'

'Yes.' Rosa looked at him with wide innocent eyes. 'Why wouldn't I?'

9

It was dark and Isabella wasn't good in the dark. At night her thoughts bumped into one another and elbowed each other out of shape and that was why she didn't see it coming, this soft, quiet realisation: *I should have made more fuss*.

She lay in bed and stared relentlessly at the black space that was the ceiling, listening to the rain. It drummed on the shutters so hard that she could picture it churning the oily black water in the drainage canals into a hissing frenzy that could threaten the safety of the town.

The water levels were rising. Six days and nights of unrelenting rain, so that the pumping stations were forced to work overtime to prevent flooding. She was acutely aware that the Agro Pontino fields needed no encouragement, none whatsoever, to transform into a quagmire that would seize any chance to reclaim its land from the controlling fist of Fascism. Isabella lay there wide-eyed among her mangled sheets, certain that she could hear the sucking, squelching, indecent sound of the parched earth drawing in the water, and she was convinced that she felt the house lurch. Actually lurch. Its foundations settling deeper into the mud with a sigh of satisfaction.

But not even the rain could drown out the noise of the slap. The sound of the bloodless hand of the nun making contact with young defenceless skin. It did something bad inside her. The girl's dark eyes reacted with shock, as though the religious hand had reached in and stolen her soul.

Isabella knew she was the one who could have stood her ground in that stiflingly hot room and demanded that the hard-eyed Reverend Mother account for her action. She could have stormed into Chairman Grassi's office at the base of her tower or shouted in the face of Colonnello Sepe and insisted that the girl be removed from the Suore di Santa Teresa convent. As a last resort she could even have begged for help from Father Benedict and his gilded altar. She could have called down the Wrath of God to smite that woman's shaven head.

Suffer little children to come unto me.

That's what the Bible says, isn't it? *Little children*. Rosa was a little child. So Isabella lay on her bed listening to the rain and convincing herself that what she did was right. If she had stormed and shouted, Rosa would have suffered. All of them — Mother Domenica, Chairman Grassi, Colonnello Sepe and even the taciturn Father Benedict — would have taken their anger out on the child. Isabella was sure of that. Rosa would be the one who was chastised, punished in some way that Isabella couldn't imagine, or even removed from the convent completely to somewhere where Isabella couldn't reach her.

And she couldn't risk that.

For Rosa's sake. And if she was honest with herself, for her own sake too. She had to keep Rosa here. Because the child must know things that she wasn't saying, things that Isabella needed to hear. What was the connection between Luigi and Allegra Bianchi? What made the woman say what she said, as Isabella sat minding her own business in the town square?

Yet the voice in her head just wouldn't shut up, the thin whispery one that said over and over till she dragged a pillow over her face, *You should have made more fuss.*

★ ★ ★

'Isabella, no one is talking.'

Francesca had drawn Isabella into the back area of the bakery where the big oven was belching out heat. The air smelled of herbs and freshly baked dough.

'Who isn't talking exactly?'

'The nuns.' Francesca twitched her hairnet with irritation. 'I took a delivery of bread out to the convent and as usual they were happy to stop and chat. They always love to hear what's going on in town, but they were saying nothing. And then when I started to tell the gossips in the wine bars about the abandoned child and her mother, they clammed up.'

'Is that unusual?'

'Very.'

'So you think they're uneasy about discussing Allegra Bianchi and Rosa?'

Francesca nodded. Her dark eyes regarded Isabella with concern, but also there was something guarded behind the concern. She looked away and prodded at a tray of warm rolls,

106

breaking one apart and inhaling the scent of rosemary that rose from it.

'What is it, Francesca? What else?'

Her friend hesitated, sighed and turned back to her. 'I think you are playing with fire, Bella.'

'What makes you say that?'

'The nuns were nervous. Someone is making them bite their tongues.'

'Who?'

'I don't know.'

'But you did glean something, didn't you?'

Reluctantly the baker nodded her head. 'Yes.'

'Tell me.'

'One young novice nun, Sister Bernadetta, who doesn't know the meaning of the word discreet, told me something when she helped me carry the trays back to my van.'

'What was it?'

'That Allegra Bianchi had been in prison.' She pulled an uncomfortable face. 'That she was again on the run from the police when she came to Bellina.' She frowned at Isabella. 'It doesn't sound good, Bella.'

'No, it doesn't. But it would explain why she was so nervous and anxious.'

Isabella tried to imagine what it must have been like to be hunted by the police when you have a child at your side.

'Thank you, Francesca.' She picked at the broken roll. It tasted wonderful. 'One more favour. An easier one this time.'

Francesca looked relieved to change the subject. 'What is it?'

'There is a professional photographer in town.

107

Chestnut hair and broad shoulders. I am interested to know more.'

Francesca grinned at her. 'That's more like it!'

★ ★ ★

'Papa?'

Her father was standing in the living room in his second-best suit, and even though it was not yet seven o'clock on a Sunday morning he was dusting his collection of records, sliding them in and out of their tawny paper sleeves. He liked to handle them almost as much as he liked to listen to them.

'What is it, Isabella?'

His head remained bent over one of the records and he was smiling at it fondly. Probably Beniamino Gigli as Rodolfo in *La Bohème*. He was humming contentedly to himself.

'Do you think I will lose my job?' she asked bluntly.

The humming ceased. He lifted his head and gave an eloquent shrug of his shoulders. 'We're all working here under sufferance, you must realise that, my dear Isabella. If what we do doesn't please the likes of men such as Chairman Grassi in his marble tower at Party headquarters, then he sends in his Blackshirts in Mussolini's name and . . . ' He stopped abruptly and raised his hands, palms upwards, in a gesture of defeat. 'And none of us knows quite what happens then, but men vanish and names are not mentioned again. It happened to my colleague, Dr Pavese. To this day I don't know what he did to enrage them but he walked down the hospital front steps one day and never came back. We were just informed that someone else would be filling his position.'

'Do you have any reason to think Dottore Martino, as head of architecture here, doesn't want me working for him?'

'No.'

Ah, but you betray yourself, Papa.

His eyes sought out the photograph on the heavy oak sideboard as if seeking forgiveness for the lie. They both looked at it and smiled. She was so beautiful, the woman in the photograph — Isabella's mother. Her dark hair was piled on top of her head in a double knot and her bright eyes lit up the room in a way that still had the power to make her daughter sit down in front of her to ask her advice. Isabella had inherited her mother's strong straight nose and high cheekbones, and sometimes when the light was dim she would look in the mirror and see her mamma there. But Isabella had acquired her blue eyes from her father. For the last twenty-one years since her mother's death, he had not even looked at another woman and every week he lovingly polished the heavy oak furniture that his wife had picked out with such care when they were first married. They rarely talked about her but for both of them she remained forever young and fragrant.

Isabella walked over to the window and inspected the sodden courtyard in the gloom, runnels of water zigzagging across it like silver snail-tracks. 'Papa, have you heard anything more about the girl, Rosa Bianchi?'

She felt his mood change. He tucked the records back in their box and flipped the catches shut with a crisp snap.

'No, I've heard nothing. Now do as I say and forget about her.'

'How can I? For the past week I've been going over to the convent every day but they refuse to let me in to see her or Sister Consolata. And I can't get in to see Chairman Grassi either. It's driving me mad. They're hiding something, I'm — '

'Isabella!'

She turned from the rivulets on the window to find he was standing close behind her.

'Do you,' he asked sternly, 'want to lose the job you worked so hard to get?'

'No, of course not.'

'Then forget this girl. She is a troublemaker in this town, just like her mother was.'

'She is all alone, Papa. Her mother died in front of my eyes by leaping off *my* tower. Yet we know nothing about her. I feel a responsibility for the child. I have to talk to Rosa and find out if I can help her.'

His silence was a solid wall between them.

'Listen to me, Papa.' She needed to be honest with her father. 'I know you think it's risky but her mother told me something before she ran off to my tower, something that means I *have* to speak to Rosa. She mentioned Luigi.'

Her father's heavy brow creased in the way that used to frighten her when she was a child. 'Oh, Isabella! That just makes it worse. I'm telling you to forget about that girl. She will bring you nothing but trouble.'

'What I don't understand, Papa, is why they don't just remove her from Bellina to an orphanage in Rome or Turin, if they don't want me speaking to her.'

'Perhaps they already have.'

His words hit her flat in the chest. She hadn't considered that possibility.

'I have to leave now.' He scooped up his medical case, and in the tiled hallway he snatched his hat and scarf from the hat stand.

'Why so early, Papa?'

'Three more workers were caught in an accident yesterday.' His fingers reached for the doorknob. 'That makes six this week.' She saw the muscles of his jaw tighten. 'Two died. These houses that you and Mussolini are building are killing people.' He buttoned up his jacket. 'And I've heard that Sister Consolata is being transferred to another convent.'

'Why? Where is she going?'

'I have no idea.'

He walked out into the dismal morning and his daughter closed the door against whatever it was that was happening out there in this town she loved so fiercely.

* * *

Isabella stood naked in front of the mirror.

Don't do this.

The air hung chill in the bathroom and her skin felt tight, as if it had suddenly grown two

111

sizes too small for her. The staccato beat of her heart betrayed her nerves.

Don't do this.

But she refused to let herself listen to that soft-tongued voice inside her head. For years it had been lulling her into a false state of calm, whispering in her ear, deceiving her. It told her that if she acted normally, spoke normal words and thought normal thoughts, then she would *be* normal. It had been lying to her.

She stared at the person in the mirror and asked herself when that other person had become her. There were similarities, she would admit that. But nothing more. The same shaped face, but this one had unfamiliar shadows wrapped around her eyes and hollows in places where there shouldn't be hollows. The bones of her cheeks were hard, shiny and brittle.

When had she become so thin? Her hair was unbrushed. Lips open as though ready to cry *Stop this.* She didn't let herself look at her pale, tight-skinned body because she knew what she would see — one hip higher than the other, one leg thinner than the other because it was lazy and didn't do its share of the work.

Her mouth was dry. Sadness was seeping up her throat until she could barely swallow. She didn't want to set eyes on herself and her hand reached out for her dressing gown but she turned away before her fingers could grasp its protective folds.

It was three years since she'd stood bare-skinned like this in front of a mirror and dared to turn around to inspect her back. She had become expert at hiding from herself but now she snapped her head round before she could change her mind and made herself look long and hard at her rear view in the mirror.

Dear God, it was ugly. Still there. Purple and glistening, like a big hollowed-out aubergine. The jagged hole — made by the bullet that smashed its way through her muscles and bone, severing nerves, destroying connections — seemed to grin sideways at her, the skin around it puckered and ridged. Each of the seven operations had left scars that snaked in silvery ribbons down her spine and across to the bony line of her hips. As if she were a parcel tied up with strings of scar tissue. She stared at the reflection and refused to look away.

The strange sound she heard in the room was her own breathing.

No man would want her. She was damaged goods. In this boisterously fecund country where a woman was prized by how abundantly she could produce soft-cheeked bouncing children — as easy as shelling peas — Isabella was barren. Marked by the fingerprint of death.

As she stood in the cold bathroom, anger came at her with teeth and claws. It came from the walls, from the bath and the washbasin, from the curved white lights. From the mirror itself. It ripped through her, making her skin burn and her fingers yearn to tear that image off the surface of the mirror.

It had all started with Allegra Bianchi. Why had she spoken of Luigi? What reason could she have? And what secrets was Rosa keeping stored in that wild young head of hers that might lead Isabella to the killer of her husband? No matter how much she cared for the sorrow of the child or worried about the ill-treatment she was receiving now, Isabella needed to pluck those secrets from her head.

Abruptly she closed her eyes, snapping the connection between herself and that other creature in the mirror. She reached again for her dressing gown and as she did so, the question flashed through her mind one more time: why did Allegra Bianchi choose her? Of all the people in the piazza. Why her?

10

Isabella waited an hour outside the house with the green door. It was where the photographer lived, the one who could handle horses. It was small, one of a row of plain terraced cottages that opened straight on to the street. She wondered why he had chosen to live on the upper floor of such a modest house in the manual workers' district of Bellina, when as a government employee he must have had the option of one of the luxury apartments in the centre of town.

Bellina was divided into zones, well organised and strictly segregated by what job a person held. At the heart of the town stood the government administrative buildings in all their splendour, including the magnificent black and white Banca d'Italia, flanking the central piazza. Spreading out from these were the elegant apartment blocks — in one of which Isabella and her father lived in comfort — but behind them the more mundane housing was grouped in zones for the traders, office workers and artisans.

But it was on the outskirts that things changed. The labourers' cottages crowded on top of each other, elbowing the grim *carabinieri* barracks right to the very edge of the barren plain itself. Isabella had heard rumours from Francesca of unrest in the zone, stories of the Blackshirts sweeping through it with their truncheons. Here the dust was thick, at its worst when the wind raced down off the mountains, and this was where any overflow from the canals risked running into the houses if the pumps failed.

Why on earth would he choose to live out here?

Isabella didn't knock on the door. To do so at eight o'clock on a Sunday morning seemed presumptuous. She didn't mind; she spent the time nosing around the street, inspecting the cornices and checking the headers and heels. The sight of the downspout straps already working loose sent a flicker of annoyance through her that set her prowling in search of other signs of premature decay.

But the green door remained stubbornly shut. Upstairs the shutters lay open but no sounds trickled down to street level in the cool breath of morning, though the voices of an elderly couple downstairs could be heard bickering. The rain had decided enough was enough and had drifted up into the mountains, allowing the morning sun to slide gracefully over the terracotta-tiled roofs, bright as a flame on the glass of the windows. Isabella was thinking of her father's Dr Pavese, the one who vanished without trace, and she almost missed the moment when the green door sprang open.

Immediately Isabella sensed a change in the air. It was subtle but it was there, she could feel it. A quick ripple of energy. Even a tan dog that had been lazily scratching its mangy backside against a drainpipe felt it and shook its long ears

116

noisily. Five houses down, a young woman in a red dress stepped out of her doorway and began sweeping her patch of pavement with rapid strokes of her broom, as if she had been watching for the photographer to emerge.

Isabella had forgotten how tall he was. She'd forgotten the way he moved as if every moment was something of value to him, as if each stride of his long legs or swing of his arm had a purpose. His shoulders were broad under his pale jacket, he wore no tie and his camera equipment case swung easily at his side. As he left the house he nodded at the woman with the broom and paused to check the sky, like a hound sniffing out a change in the weather. He wore no hat and the sun glinted on the unruly chestnut waves of his hair as he squinted up at it, but as soon as he caught sight of Isabella on the opposite site of the street he bounded forward.

'Buongiorno, Milanese.' A smile spread slowly over his face, his grey eyes wide with surprise. 'What on earth are you doing here?'

She considered telling him that it was a coincidence, that she was just in the area to inspect the houses and see how people were settling in. But she looked down at the package in her hands and told him the truth.

'I'm looking for you.'

'Well, you've found me.'

'Yes.' The thick paper of the package crackled as she fingered it.

'How did you know where I live?' His gaze was fixed on her face, not on the package.

'It wasn't hard,' she said. 'I asked around. There aren't too many photographers holed up in Bellina.' She smiled up at him. 'I brought you a present.' She held out the package.

For a moment Isabella thought he looked suddenly wary. A flash of something darker darted across the pale grey of his eyes but then it was gone and she wondered if she had imagined it because it was swallowed by the broad grin he gave her.

'What's this for? A bribe?'

She didn't blink, though the word hung hot in the cool morning air. The sky was pale, washed clean by the rain, with only the mountains in the distance looking bruised and misshapen.

'It's a thank you,' she told him. 'For stopping the horse.' She thrust the package at him.

'*Grazie*. But it's not necessary, you know.'

'I know.'

He carefully unwrapped the paper and a smile of real pleasure softened the angles of his face when he saw what lay inside.

'Two red snappers! Excellent. *Fragolino* is one of my favourites.' He lifted the two fat pink fish to his nose and sniffed. 'Caught fresh this morning.'

Any lingering doubt that Isabella had about her choice of gift vanished.

'You certainly know the way to a fisherman's heart,' he laughed.

'But you're not a fisherman. You're a photographer.'

'So I am.'

For an awkward moment Isabella didn't know

where to go next with the conversation, unwilling yet to blurt out exactly why she was here, but she was aware that at any second he could wish her good day and walk off to wherever he was going. He was a person, she realised, who was capable of standing in silence indefinitely, waiting to see how someone else chose to fill it.

'You'd better put the fish somewhere cold for later,' she suggested.

'Or we could cook it and eat it together, you and I.'

'Oh, I didn't bring you two fish for that reason.' She felt colour rise in her cheeks. 'I didn't mean that. They're both for you to eat.'

'Thank you, Signora Berotti, you are generous.'

Isabella saw him glance at her wedding ring then he slipped the strap of his equipment case off his shoulder and placed the leather box at her feet.

'Wait here,' he said and vanished back behind the green door with his fish.

The young woman in red rested her hands and her chin on the end of her broom handle and regarded Isabella with a scowl that switched to a smile the moment the photographer re-emerged into the street.

'Now,' he said, all bustle and business as he swept up the camera case, 'my car is over there.' He waved a car key in the direction of a brand new Fiat Balilla parked in the street. 'I am heading out to one of the farmsteads, so why don't you come along?'

'Why would I do that?'

He rubbed a palm over the rough Sunday stubble on his jaw and laughed, the kind of laugh that warmed her skin.

'So you can tell me,' he said, 'what you've really come to see me about.'

He looped her arm through his and she tried hard not to limp.

* * *

'My name is Roberto.'

Isabella already knew his name. Just like she knew his age — thirty-two. She knew he'd lived and worked down south in Sorrento and Naples, and that he'd opted to spend the summer when he was nineteen on his hands and knees photographing and cataloguing pottery among the ancient ruins of Pompeii. She knew he liked sour cherry *crostata* for breakfast and that as a child he'd had a dog called Vico that had been trampled to death by a bull. And now he was living on the top floor of a modest house with an elderly couple called Russomano living underneath. All these things she'd learned from Francesca, who should have been a spy instead of a baker.

'I am Isabella.'

He gave her a brisk nod of his head as he drove past the barracks and out of town. '*Buongiorno*, Isabella Berotti.'

So he knew her name. That was a start.

'You have your camera case with you.' She gestured at the brown leather case on the back seat, recalling the weight of it when she'd lifted it at the station. 'Does that mean you're working today?'

'That case goes most places with me,' he smiled, the way Luigi used to when talking about his favourite dog. That same affection in the smile.

'It's Sunday,' she pointed out.

'So it is.'

'I thought you wouldn't be working today.'

'Did you?' He glanced across at her and let his eyes linger a moment too long on her face, so that he had to correct the steering wheel with a twitch of his hands. Ahead of them the road ran straight and empty, its dirt surface raised on layers of crushed stone to lift it above the level of the fields, and alongside it ran a murky drainage channel. All the roads across the plain were being constructed on a rigid grid system but at the moment they had nowhere to go because the other towns were not yet built. But every five hundred metres, regular as clockwork, one of the farmsteads popped up on the roadside, like square blue mushrooms sprouting from the sea of black treeless soil that had been tirelessly tilled.

'You don't like it out here, do you?' Roberto commented. 'Among the fields, away from your carefully created buildings.'

No. No, I don't.

'Of course I do. It's the start of what will be a great grain bonanza. We'll become the bread basket of Rome within a year.'

'Ah,' he murmured, running his hand along the clean curve of the steering wheel, 'so I hear.'

'Don't you believe it?'

'No.'

A small gasp escaped her. No one spoke like that. Not against Mussolini's Battle for Grain. Isabella stared at the quiet expression on his face to see if he was joking. He wasn't. She swivelled round in her seat to face him squarely.

'Why do you say that?'

'I've spoken to the farmers here. If others bothered to do so, they'd hear the same.'

'What is it they're saying?'

He gazed straight ahead through the windscreen and for a moment all Isabella could hear, above the growl of the engine and the distant cawing of a flock of crows searching for seeds that had been drilled into the black tilth, was the uneven thump of her pulse in her ears.

Roberto still kept his eyes on the road. 'The farmers who know grain are saying this isn't the soil for wheat. It won't flourish here. Not now. Not ever. Someone has got it all wrong but everyone is frightened to admit it.'

Isabella uttered no sound but her tongue flashed across her teeth as if it could wipe away his words. 'You don't know me,' she said softly. 'Why are you telling me this?'

'So that when you decide to ask me whatever it is you've come out here to ask me, you'll know it is safe to do so.'

He was trusting her. Telling her she could trust him. It felt as if he had slipped a gift into her hands, something fragile, something she could easily break if she had a mind to. A ray of sunlight squeezed into the car and settled between them, drawing a line under Roberto's words, and Isabella watched it for a long moment as it crept up on to his thigh and sat there.

'Stop now,' she said without warning.

Abruptly he swung the wheel and pulled over on the side of the windswept road. He switched off the engine, and as it ticked in the sudden silence he at last looked at her. His eyes fixed on her so intently that she became acutely aware of her own breathing. Of the risk she was taking. She didn't want her words to be trapped like caged birds inside the car, so she seized the chrome handle and opened the door.

11

They stood on the roadside, the wind in their faces coming off the distant sea but smelling of brick dust, and for a while neither spoke. As if the air between them had to settle to allow an understanding to take place, to allow it to put down roots. Out here in the countryside Isabella was conscious of an unfamiliar kind of world taking shape, very different from her own orderly one in Bellina, because in this one not even Il Duce could lay down the rules. This one had the wind and the rain as its heartbeat and the bellow of the Maremmana cattle as its voice. It was a world that Isabella was unfamiliar with, but she could see the way Roberto at her side breathed the country air deep into his lungs.

'So,' he said, gazing out towards the far horizon where two of the gigantic Tosi diggers were excavating a section of the Mussolini canal, 'no one to listen to us here.'

That's why he'd brought her. Away from eavesdroppers. Away from young women in red dresses. Yet Isabella sensed that he was more interested in the digging machines right then than in what she had to say and for the first time she began to doubt him.

'I need your help,' she stated honestly.

He swung round to her with a smile on his face that for a split second robbed her of thought, it was so full of energy, yet softened by an odd kind of relief.

'What is it you need?'

'Just some photographs taken,' she answered.

His expression changed. Disappointment flickered in his grey eyes but was quickly hidden behind politeness. Isabella didn't care for the politeness. She needed more from him than that.

'You are a photographer,' she pointed out, and then it occurred to her why he may be uneasy about it. 'I can pay you, of course.'

The moment she uttered the words she knew they were the wrong ones. He took a small step away from her and she wanted to snatch the words back out of the morning air. He returned his attention to the Tosi diggers in the distance and cocked his head, as though listening for their rumble and their clanking in preference to her words.

'I'll be happy to oblige,' he said with impeccable courtesy. 'What is it that you would like me to photograph?'

'Some schoolchildren. At the Suore di Santa Teresa convent.'

The faintest of sighs escaped him. 'I'm better at animals than children.'

'It's important, Roberto.'

Instantly he forgot the diggers. His eyes fixed on hers. 'When you came with the fish, I expected a request for something more than a few photographs.'

'The fish were a thank you.'

He smiled, a patient smile. He was waiting for more but a donkey and cart were approaching down the road and they did not speak again until it had passed.

'Tell me,' he said. 'What is this about?'

Isabella's heart was racing. She was taking a risk of appearing subversive. She didn't want to sound like someone who needed to be watched or like someone whose touch would mark you out for one of Colonnello Sepe's prison cells. But Roberto had done something rare in these days of informers and suspicion, he had offered her a slender thread of trust and she held on to it tight.

'I'm looking for a girl. Her name is Rosa. She's nine years old and has been put into the convent school by Chairman Grassi because . . . ' she paused and her gaze was drawn back to the town, 'because he wants to keep her away from people like me. From people asking awkward questions.'

The photographer listened. He didn't interrupt but his full lips had set in a hard line and his broad frame stood unnaturally still. Isabella felt her mouth dry because she couldn't make out what it signified, with the sun flaring behind him and throwing his eyes in shadow. The milky sky seemed to press down relentlessly on the long straight road, pinning the pair of them to this spot beside the ditch that ran parallel to the highway.

'So what is it you want from me?'

She spoke lightly, as if it were the simplest thing in the world.

'Roberto, please will you, as the official photographer of Bellina, go to the convent of Suore di Santa Teresa and take photographs of the school, including one of each class of pupils, so that I can see if Rosa is still there? That's all.' She shrugged. 'Not much really.' She found a smile and felt it curve the stiff corners of her lips. 'Worth two red snappers, surely?'

But she wasn't breathing. It had sounded far more reasonable in the confines of her own head than it did here out in the open on the Agro Pontino with the harsh croak of a frog mocking her.

Roberto leaned back against the car and she knew then that he would say no.

'Yes,' he said. 'I'll do it.'

'Thank you.' Isabella held out her hand.

He shook it firmly. A business deal. But it was more than a business deal, they both knew that. It was a collusion. A breaking of the rules. So an awareness of what they were doing passed between them as his skin touched hers and they smiled at each other. She felt the wind lift the weight of her hair off her neck at the same moment as a weight lifted off her mind, and her smile spread into a murmur of relief.

'Thank you,' she said again.

She wanted to place her fingers tightly around his arm and say confidently, *There's no danger. Not for you.* But she couldn't. She might be lying.

'So,' he said, raising one dark eyebrow at her, 'it sounds simple enough. I will arrange with the Mother Superior for a day when I can come into the school. Under the pretext of recording the town's every feature, as set out in Chairman Grassi's orders, I will take pictures of each class.'

The strong angular lines of his face softened and his voice took on an edge of concern. 'Don't look so worried, Isabella. She isn't going to refuse me entry.' He gave a wry smile. 'No one does.'

'That must come in useful.'

The look he gave her said otherwise. Suddenly it dawned on her that he must be regarded by the populace of Bellina as the spy in the camp and she felt a low buzzing at the base of her chest as a flicker of fear took flight.

'That's settled then,' he said.

'Thank you.'

'Now tell me who this Rosa is and why you are going to such lengths to find her.'

She could have said *That's my private business*. But she didn't.

'Rosa is the daughter of Allegra Bianchi, the woman who — '

'I know who Allegra Bianchi is. Everyone in town knows. What is she to you?'

'Before she went up the tower she left her daughter with me in the Piazza del Popolo. She abandoned her at my table, and I want to make certain she's all right. I need to talk with Rosa urgently but I am not allowed to.'

'Why not?'

'I don't know.'

She said it brightly but for a moment she was stricken by the thought that he might change his mind, that he might think she was lying. He took a deep breath, inhaling the earthy scent of the fields, and she watched each muscle of his face slowly relax. A farm truck trundled past, piled high with logs from the forested mountains, and

Roberto called out a cheery '*Buongiorno*' to the driver. The man in flat cap and shirt sleeves waved back and trailed his gaze over Isabella with a delighted grin.

The small incident broke the mood and Roberto's manner became polite and professional.

'I'll let you know which day I will be at the convent school and when the photographs will be ready, I promise you.'

'*Grazie.*'

There was nothing more to say. In the wide open space of the plain Isabella experienced a strange feeling — as though the emptiness of it was draining the words from them both, sucking them into the wet squelching soil, squeezing the life out of them. She felt uneasy. She wasn't sure what had gone wrong, but something had. She wanted to reconnect with him so she rested back against the warm body of the car, feeling its heat on her shoulder blades, and let the wind snatch at her long black curls without brushing them aside.

'Take my picture,' she said with a laugh.

'Isabella Berotti,' he said with a grand flourish of his hand, 'it will be my pleasure.'

He disappeared into the back of his car, knees bent double to fold his long limbs into the small space, but he emerged with his big boxy camera on a strap around his neck and started to fiddle with the back of it, turning knobs and inserting rectangular plates that he told her were film holders. There was something graceful in the way his hands moved and a quiet satisfaction in the set of his mouth as he worked that gave her pleasure to watch.

'Ready, Isabella?' he called softly, and when she parted her lips to ask how he wanted her to stand, she heard the whirr of the shutter curtain and a click.

She laughed. 'I wasn't ready.'

He studied her as intently as if she were a painting, a slight crease drawn across his forehead as he walked around her, eyes focused downward on his viewfinder. She felt foolish.

'You look lovely.'

'Are you talking to me or to this trim little car of yours?'

He laughed, and as he handled the camera he started murmuring whispered words, whether to himself, to her or to the camera, she had no idea. And then he stepped forward and touched her hair, her neck, arranging her — he cupped her chin in his hand and tilted it sideways, his fingers firm in what they wanted. He bent down and lightly clasped her ankle, placing one foot in front of the other, his eyes seeing not her but the photographic image he wanted to create. She wondered what was going on in his head. Do people exist only inside your camera, while all the time you stand on the outside? she wanted to ask him.

But then the moment was over, the bulky camera was back in its box in the Fiat and the sun was caught up in his chestnut hair.

'Coffee?' he asked.

'Out here?'

He laughed and opened the car door for her.

'The farmer where I'm heading doesn't know one end of a cow from another, but his coffee . . . ?' He touched a kiss to the tips of his fingers and tossed it into the air for the crows. '*Perfetto!*'

As they drove along the long straight roads — each one numbered by how many Roman miles it was from Rome — the wind swept in through the open window, wrapping them in the heavy scent of the wet earth. The landscape stretched in all directions, flat and naked, full of hope.

'What made you become a photographer?' she asked.

'I suppose I grew sick of stinking manure and fish.'

She smiled.

But before she could push him further, he asked, 'Tell me, Isabella, is there a Signor Berotti at home?'

'No. I live with my father. He's a doctor. My husband died ten years ago. He was a Blackshirt.'

Roberto's head turned to look at her. 'I'm sorry,' he said. 'Very sorry, Isabella.'

She said nothing. If she started to talk about that day, she might not stop. She waited, expecting him to ask her more, but he didn't.

They drove in silence for a while until they crossed a narrow stone bridge over a sluggish canal and Roberto said quietly, 'Now, tell me about Rosa.'

★ ★ ★

As the car pulled into the farmyard, a shout from a barn a short distance from the house startled Isabella.

'Hold her!'

'Watch out, she'll have you!'

A shriek tore out of the open barn door.

'Grab the rope, for the love of God, and get her to . . . '

Another cry of pain rang out, deeper this time, and was followed by a string of hefty curses. Isabella leapt out of the car, her foot skidding in a patch of slime, but Roberto ran straight past her into the barn, his long legs covering the distance before she could blink. From outside she heard his voice raised in anger against whoever was inside and the sound of it disturbed her in a way she didn't quite understand.

The yard they were in belonged to the farmstead ONC 480. The *Opera Nazionale Combattenti* was the organisation set up by Francesco Nitti and Alberto Beneduce after the Great War to help war veterans to find their place again in Italian society. The veterans were a hotbed of unrest and unemployment in the towns, causing dissent and trouble in city wine shops with their grumbles, so the prominent politician and agronomist Valentino Ursu Cencelli stepped in. He was appointed head of the ONC and suggested granting the veterans land of their own to grow crops and boost agriculture production.

It was an audacious plan. But Mussolini gave Cencelli sweeping powers and he went at it like a tank. The *bonifica* — the reclamation of the

Pontine marshland — alone would cost seven million lire. The Fascist regime moved into action with typical ruthlessness. It promptly expropriated land from wealthy landowners like the Caetani family and empowered the ONC with the task of overseeing the massive operation.

So the ONC stamped its initials on every single farmstead and proceeded to employ agents to check everything. Isabella had seen them all hours of the day and night prowling the area in their cheap suits and black ties. These men poked their noses into every home and farm, clipboard in hand, taking down notes and names. They weighed out every kilo of seed sown and counted each bucketful of milk drawn. And when the first harvest came next year they would be first in the threshing yard to requisition the lion's share of the grain for Il Duce.

This farmstead was a mess. Bits of harness, iron chains and tools lay abandoned in the yard, as well as three buckets of stale water beside the well, which even Isabella knew was the worst mistake in these parts. Uncovered stagnant water attracted mosquitoes to lay eggs. Then you were in real trouble.

A pair of small girls with identical faces and identical filthy smocks came hurtling on bare feet out of the house. They ran squealing towards the barn but Isabella reached it first. The heavy sweaty smell of animal hide hit her and for a second her eyes fought to adjust to the dim interior, but she could make out two hulking Maremmana cows stamping their feet, heads lowered and wielding massive horns like sabres. They were bellowing with rage and snorting a sour-smelling mist into the air.

Isabella seized the two young twins by their wrists but felt out of her depth here. This was a world with different rules, with animal sounds that were rising out of control and a short stocky man who was brandishing an iron bar to ward off the cattle. Blood spurted down his trouser leg from a long gash in his thigh, and he lashed out at the great grey bovine shoulder with the bar and a torrent of curses.

'Gabriele! Stop that at once!' Roberto launched himself at the man and seized his arm. 'You're making them worse. Quieten down, man.'

'That vicious beast went for me.'

'You must have been too rough with her. I told you before,' his voice was full of anger, 'treat these cows like your children.'

Roberto pushed the man to the floor on a heap of soiled straw and seized the rope tether that was dangling to the floor from the larger cow's neck. Isabella had no idea how he did it but she watched him reel in the panicked creature, just as he had done with the horse at the station, guiding its horns quietly away from him and sweeping a calming hand over the cow's thick quivering neck. She saw him flinch when he touched the trickle of scarlet from a gash that had opened up on the grey shoulder where its hide was stained with dark patches of sweat.

'Here, Alessandro, grab this one.' Roberto threw the end of the second Maremmana's

134

tether to a lanky youth whose hands and feet looked far too big for him. 'Bring her head round towards me. She'll settle when this one does.'

The boy dodged a sideswipe from the cow's hoof and turned to edge the animal closer to the one Roberto was handling. Both animals continued to snort and stamp and toss their heads, and each time Isabella was convinced Roberto would be scythed to the bone. But no. Moment by moment he drew them under his control and to Isabella it again felt like a kind of magic. And totally without warning, desire surged through her. An emotion she had not felt for ten years. A stranger to her now. Yet it ran hot in her veins, the desire to touch Roberto, to lay a hand on him, to hold the quietness of him in the centre of her palm. But she didn't move, not even one step across the five metres of straw and dirt that separated them.

She watched Alessandro work alongside him, his lungs pumping nervously but his hands copying Roberto's, soothing the animal in his charge until he could tether it to an iron ring set into the wall by the concrete manger. Isabella took her chance then to dart forward to tend to the man on the floor, clearly the boy's father. Both possessed the same flat nose and big shapeless ears, but Alessandro stood taller already. Even she could see that these people weren't farmers.

'Are you all right, *signore*?'

'*Bastarda!*' he hissed, glaring at the larger of the cows. 'They are monsters.' His hands clutched his leg.

135

Isabella unfastened her scarf from around her neck and tied it tightly around his thigh in an attempt to stem the flow of blood.

'Let me help you up on your feet,' she offered.

With a grunt and a rough clearing of his throat to disguise his cry of pain, Gabriele slid an arm across her shoulders as she raised him to his feet. For several minutes they watched in silence at the way the cow was licking the back of Roberto's hand.

'I don't know how the hell he does it. They won't let me touch them.'

'How long has he been helping you?' Isabella asked.

'Since we first arrived. Roberto is a decent man. He spotted us the moment we got here and has been coming over each day ever since to do the milking and yoke the brutes to the plough.' He ran a hand across his mouth as if to silence his words, an admission of his own weakness, but left a streak of blood smeared there.

'It's dangerous,' she said softly.

They both knew she wasn't talking about the Maremmanas.

⋆　⋆　⋆

They spent the morning at the farm. While Roberto took the boy, Alessandro, out into the fields to teach him to plough, Isabella bathed and bandaged Gabriele's leg. She told him he needed to go to hospital for stitches but he was having none of it.

'Uniforms!' he said and gave her a friendly

136

slap on the bottom as she turned to pick up the scissors. 'I am allergic to uniforms — whatever their colour. But thank you, Isabella, you have the gentle touch of an angel.' He turned to one of the twins and said with a fond smile, 'Now run into the kitchen, *cara mia*, and fetch Papa his medicine.'

The child scampered off, followed by her twin. There were six daughters. Five of them were squeezed between the ages of four and nine years old, including two pairs of twins, and then there was a baby, only two years old and as close as a calf to Alessandro. He carried her strapped to his back even when he ploughed. Their mother had died when giving birth to this last child and the family was struggling without her.

All the children were dirty. All were barefoot and all were thin, the kind of thinness that makes a face seem all eyes. Isabella wanted to help but she didn't know the first thing about planting or ploughing a straight furrow or what on earth you feed a pig. So instead she rolled up her sleeves and showed the eldest girl how to bake a *pane di Maria* with the remnants of the flour in the pantry, then set the younger girls to scrubbing the tiled floors and cleaning up the yard. Afterwards she boiled up pans of water on the range and dipped each child in a tin bath.

'*Mille grazie*,' Gabriele murmured. 'You are a kind person. My wife, my Caterina, was the beat of my heart. Without her I am no good.' He curled his fingers around the thick brown bottle that the twin had handed him, took another swig and closed his eyes with a sigh, as though it brought relief. Isabella wondered what was in it.

'What work did you do before coming here, Signor Caldarone?' She was scrubbing clothes in the sink which was made of cement and crushed marble. 'Obviously not farming.'

He nodded with a wry smile and took one last mouthful of his medicine before ramming the cork back in. 'I owned a bar in Turin. A fine bar it was too. You should have seen my Caterina in it, the way she laughed and flirted so prettily with the customers.' His mouth spread in a smile of pride. 'Men came from far and wide just to be served by her.'

'You must miss her.'

'I do.' He thumped a fist against his chest. 'When she went, the heart went out of me. Things turned bad then. There were no jobs up north. No one had money to spend in bars. Mine had to close.'

'I'm sorry, it must have been hard.'

'I was desperate, Isabella. Desperate to feed my family. Then I heard about this wonderful new town. So I used my last few lire to buy forged papers that said I'd worked on farms after I came out of the army. Crazy, I know.' He tapped the side of his head. 'My last rooms in Turin were smaller than a coffin — no good for *bambini*. Here in this fine house we can make a fresh start. I thought — how hard can farming be?'

'But what about the animals?'

He scowled fiercely, scrunching his flat nose into a ball. 'They are brutes!'

Isabella laughed. 'But Roberto is helping.

138

You'll manage and your son is learning.'

'*Si*, our good Lord gave me Alessandro to help too.' He reached into his pocket and pulled out a few shreds of foul-smelling tobacco which he rolled into a spindly cigarette. 'I only tell you this, Isabella, because you are kind to me. And Roberto says I can trust you.'

'Did he?'

'Yes.' His dark eyes brightened. 'He likes you.'

That pleased her.

⋆   ⋆   ⋆

They were seated at the table in the kitchen, all Gabriele's family gathered together. It was a moment of calm while Isabella and Roberto were enjoying the promised coffee.

'*Bene?*' Gabriele asked with a grin.

'*Si, molto bene,*' Isabella smiled. 'Thank you for . . .'

She paused. She'd caught the sound of a car turning off the road. She could hear its engine growing louder as it carefully crossed the small bridge over the canal in front of the farm and roared into their yard.

'*Merda!*' Gabriele growled. 'What's this?'

They all knew that cars didn't come visiting out here for the fun of it. The older pair of twins were excited at the prospect of visitors and scrambled to the front of the house, but immediately let out a cry of alarm. Roberto was already on his feet, striding to the window. As he looked out, Isabella saw his whole body grow tense and when he turned back to those in the

139

room his voice was sharp and full of warning.

'It's one of the ONC agents. And there are three Blackshirts getting out of the car with him. So it looks like he means business. Let's hope he just wants to take a look around.'

'Get rid of the bastards, Roberto,' Gabriele begged. 'Don't let them in. If he has Blackshirts with him, he's here to make trouble, and, God knows, I have enough of that already.'

'I'll do what I can, Gabriele, but stay calm. Don't let that tongue of yours provoke them or they'll beat you into the ground.'

Roberto's eyes found Isabella and suddenly the air in the room turned dry and unbreathable.

'Get the girls out of here into the bedroom, Isabella, before — '

There was no knock. No warning. The mosquito screen was torn off its hinges and the interior door sprang open with a crash that set the baby whimpering in Alessandro's arms. A man strode into the room wearing a suit that was shiny and ill-cut and a large-brimmed Homburg rammed down tight on his bald head. He wore thick glasses, carried a clipboard that he brandished like a badge of office, and had the look of a man who enjoyed his job.

'I am Signor Fernando de Lauro,' he announced.

'How can we help you?' Roberto asked with studied politeness.

'I have come to raise the question of Signor Caldarone's competence in working the land and with the animals, because it is clear that . . . '

'Get out of my house,' Gabriele interrupted.

'Signor Caldarone.' The man didn't raise his voice. It was obvious that he had done this many times before. 'We have reason to believe that you have lied to the ONC.' He took a step further into the room, bringing him closer to where Gabriele was sitting with his leg propped up on a stool. 'We have reports from our agents that you are incompetent. They state that you are bungling the work required of a farmer and . . .'

Isabella saw the colour drain from Gabriele's face but he shook his head angrily. 'Then your agents are filthy liars.'

'Signore,' Roberto stepped forward, 'please excuse my friend, Signor Caldarone, here. His leg is hurt,' he gestured to the bandaged limb, 'so he is ill-tempered today. I think there is some mistake. As you will see if you care to look, the fields are being ploughed and young Alessandro has been working hard all morning.' He smiled at the man. 'Sit and have coffee with us.'

Isabella wanted to reach out and steal some of his calmness. Her own heart was racing, yet she heard her voice say easily, 'It's true. The only reason Signor Caldarone isn't working today is that his leg is injured.'

De Lauro's gaze skimmed coolly over each person in the room, lingering on every child, the thick lenses of his spectacles distorting the granite grey of his eyes as he continued to move forward until he was standing over Gabriele. The room seemed to grow smaller. The baby ceased whimpering.

'You don't call our agents filthy liars,

Caldarone,' he reprimanded in a cold voice. 'It is not respectful.'

'It is not respectful, Signor de Lauro, to insult my ability to do my job and feed my family.'

'I intend,' de Lauro hissed as he thrust his face right in front of Gabriele's, 'to teach you respect.'

'Get out,' roared Gabriele.

Without warning de Lauro slammed the metal edge of his clipboard down on the bandaged thigh. Gabriele screamed. Instantly the three men who had been waiting outside burst through the doorway and their darkness crowded the light from the room. They were Blackshirts. With heavy shoulders and heavier hands. They needed no orders. They knew before they entered what they were here to do. Their truncheons flashed and the cups on the table shattered, a mirror disintegrated into a thousand fragments of light and a lamp was smashed, drenching the place with the stink of kerosene.

Isabella saw Roberto seize the arm of one of the men but immediately a truncheon was jammed against his throat so that he could barely breathe. She leapt forward and punched the Blackshirt, distracting him, but she was thrown against the wall like a broken doll.

The noise around her was deafening. Objects exploded with every swing of a truncheon, children were screaming, Gabriele was bellowing his fury. Isabella was shocked at the depth of her own desire to wipe these men in black shirts off the face of the earth. The beat of her heart was violent and intense.

But she gathered the children to her and pushed them through the door to the stairs. She touched a cheek, wiped a tear, all the time aware of Roberto who had placed himself between the immobile Gabriele's head and the swinging truncheons. In Roberto's hair glittered diamonds of broken glass and his face was rigid with silent rage. In front of him stood the cheap suit, an expression of contempt twisting the man's mouth as he waited for Roberto to make one false move.

'Roberto,' Isabella called.

He looked like one of the Maremmana bulls, his eyes narrowed, his head thrust forward.

'Don't,' Isabella breathed. 'Don't provoke them.'

She took a step towards him. Her eyes met his and she stopped short. He shook his head. She hesitated. In the midst of all the chaos and brutal noise, the crashing and the screaming, he gave her the faintest of smiles. Not much, little more than a softening in his eyes, but still a smile. She didn't know how he did it. But it altered something inside her. Something broke. She didn't know what it was but she could feel its edges splitting apart, sharp and painful within herself, and she found tears suddenly stifling her throat.

Quickly she turned away to where the baby was wailing in Alessandro's arms against the wall.

'Leave, Alessandro. Go to your sisters upstairs.'

'No.'

His dark eyes were too bright, whether from fear or anger she couldn't tell. But it was clear he regarded himself as part of a man's world now. She took the infant from his arms and walked out of the room.

* * *

How do you mend what is broken?

Isabella stood in the middle of the floor surveying the carnage. Nothing in the room was whole. Nothing undamaged. Not one single plate or cup or glass in the house was unbroken. The Blackshirts had done a thorough job. Chair legs snapped, table top splintered, the photograph of Gabriele's Caterina in pieces.

How do you mend a family that is broken?

A child's face frozen with fear. A young heart shredded. A belief in the rightness of the world in tatters. These things Isabella knew were over for these children and that frightened her, because what kind of world was Italy offering for the future?

'Isabella, you're bleeding.'

'Am I?'

Roberto stood beside her. He lifted her hand and she saw a gash on her wrist from a flying shard of glass. Her blood was trickling across his fingers and down on to the tiled floor like a scattering of scarlet coins.

'It's nothing,' she assured him.

But he didn't release her hand. 'We have to count ourselves lucky that it wasn't worse.'

'Worse? Worse? How could this possibly be worse?'

'They are coming back tomorrow to witness Gabriele ploughing, with or without an injured leg. That means he has twenty-four hours to learn to handle those cows convincingly.'

'That's impossible.'

'Of course it is.'

'So how could it be worse?'

'They could have hauled him into the yard right then and beaten him to death in front of his children.'

'Don't, Roberto. Don't joke. They'd never do such a thing as that. Italy isn't barbaric.'

But she looked at his face, at the bruise on his throat, at the hard set of his mouth and the anger in his eyes. And she knew he wasn't joking.

'Isabella,' he said gently, his thumb brushing the strings of blood from her fingers, 'that's what Blackshirts do. They make sure Mussolini's rules are written in blood.'

'No.'

'You, of all people, should know.'

His meaning shimmered just beneath the quiet surface of his words.

12

'Come, Isabella, and eat my fish with me.'

'No. Thank you, but I'm not hungry.'

At least she spoke. Roberto regarded that as progress. She had been silent in the car as he drove them through the fading light back to town. Too silent. He had seen her shaken by shudders that caught her unawares and made her toss her head like a mare with colic, a pain deep in her gut. Her long hair, which she usually wore tied severely back from her face with a black ribbon, had escaped during the clean-up of the mess at the farmstead and hung loose in a cascade of dark curls around her face and shoulders. It meant she had somewhere to hide. Her cheeks were flushed and she kept her eyes away from him.

Fingers of white mist were dragging themselves across the fields and crawling up on to the road, where they entwined together to create sinkholes that would swallow the car. They were both tired. Isabella and the girls had worked hard all afternoon to remove signs of the attack and to mend what furniture they could, while Roberto had taken Gabriele and Alessandro out in the fields to practise handling the animals. The boy learned fast, thank goodness, but poor Gabriele had no hope of overcoming by tomorrow either his leg-wound or his ingrained fear of any animal larger than a dog.

'Roberto.'

He flicked a glance at Isabella in the passenger seat. He liked the fine high nose of her profile, but there was something about the way she said his name just then that made him certain that whatever was coming was not going to be good.

'Roberto, I want to explain something to you.'

He waited. An owl drifted through his headlights on silent ghostly wings.

'I want to explain,' she continued, 'that when I meet someone new, I have to try hard not to hate them.'

Roberto was stunned into silence, but when she didn't speak again for another half-kilometre he asked, 'Why is that, Isabella?'

'The first reason' — she was staring straight ahead, though he sensed she was seeing nothing — 'is that I have to try not to hate people for being alive. When my Luigi is dead.'

A dull ache set up behind his eyes. As he changed gear in the car he let the back of his hand brush against her skirt where it hung over the seat, aware that her words sounded like a form of goodbye. He didn't wish to say goodbye.

'And the second reason?'

She took a long breath. 'I was crippled once, Roberto. When my husband was shot. I don't want to be crippled again. So I stop people coming too close.'

Roberto applied the brake and halted the car, its headlights pooling on a rat that scuttled across the road.

'Oh, Isabella, I won't cripple you. I promise you that.'

She lifted a hand and lowered her face into it. But made no sound. It took him a full minute to realise she was crying and that she was embarrassed to be doing so in front of him. The wind stirred the dust in the world outside and here in the car Isabella felt more fragile to him as the light seeped away. Her hair hung in a veil between them but he rested his fingers lightly on her shoulder and left them there, wanting the promise he'd made to flow through the cotton of her jacket and into her skin.

'I am afraid, Roberto. Afraid of getting scarred again. The way Gabriele is scarred by the loss of his Caterina. What will happen to him now?'

'He'll be all right. I'll make sure of that.'

She nodded, trusting him. 'You are a generous man, Roberto.' But her face was still hidden. 'It's taken me ten years, but I have made another life. I have my architecture and I am building a new town. I walk and I talk and I eat and drink like any other normal human being. No one can see the scars. Just my limp is a reminder.'

Her voice dropped as she removed her hand from her face and placed it in her lap. 'No one knows, Roberto. I have said these things to no one before. Not even to my father.'

Roberto curled his hand tightly around hers and could feel the tension strung out in its delicate bones. He leaned back in his seat, giving her room to breathe, space to recover some of the certainty of who she was and what kind of place it was that she lived in. The truncheons had robbed her of that today. He had brushed shoulders with the Blackshirts before and knew

148

how effectively they could destroy a person. He'd seen them tear a man's belief in himself right out of his heart with a few viciously aimed blows and he couldn't bear it to happen to her, but he made himself crush the anger that was growling in his gut.

'I will keep your secret safe, Isabella.'

For the first time she turned her head and looked at him directly, a trace of a smile lifting the shadows from her face. '*Grazie*, Roberto.'

'Now, will you come and eat my fish with me?'

She looked down at his large knuckles wrapped around her hand and he felt a pulse of heat under his palm.

'Yes,' she said. 'I'd like that.'

*   *   *

She picked at her food as daintily as a cat. He had grilled the red snappers and dished them up with beefy sliced tomatoes drenched in olive oil and with chunks of rough bread to mop it up. He liked looking at her. She had small hands that moved with unconscious grace and she licked the oil that glistened on her full lips with quick flashes of her tongue. Roberto wanted her to sit there and let him take her picture, but he didn't ask. He wanted to capture the thoughtful way she studied his photographs that were pinned to the walls, but she was still too tense, so he was happy to sit and talk with her and watch the colour return to her cheeks as she sipped her wine.

He was asking her about the design of the new

fountain being constructed in the Piazza della Libertà when Isabella said abruptly, 'Why do you help them?'

'The Fascists?'

'No, the Caldarone family.'

He couldn't tell her the truth. But he could tell her part of the truth.

'Because, as you saw today, the Caldarones are in a bad state right now and need help.' He smiled. 'And to annoy Chairman Grassi, of course.'

Isabella tilted her head back and laughed, setting her hair into a dance as she swung it off her face. Roberto caught a trace of its fragrance, the warm scent of jasmine, and wondered what one of its rich dark curls would feel like between his fingers. He liked the way she laughed. As if she meant it. Really meant it. Too many women laughed politely.

'So, tell me, Isabella.' He leaned forward, elbows on the table, closer to her. 'Why are you hell-bent on helping Rosa?'

The pupils of her dark eyes grew huge for a heartbeat and then she matched him elbow for elbow on the table and leaned forward till her face was only a hand's breadth from his and he could see the creamy perfection of her skin.

'Because,' she said, 'Rosa is in a bad state right now and needs help.' Her eyes were solemn but her mouth took on a quick teasing curve. 'And to annoy Chairman Grassi, of course.'

'Why take such a risk?'

She looked away. 'I am already involved with the girl, Roberto, whether I want to be or not. I

150

saw her mother jump to her death from a tower that I created.' Her gaze settled on one of his photographs, the one of a boy about ten years old with bony elbows and spiky hair carrying a hod piled with bricks up a scaffolding ladder. Five storeys off the ground. A cigarette in his mouth. 'Allegra Bianchi gave her daughter into my care. I don't know why, but I intend to find out. For Rosa's sake . . . and for mine.'

'Take care, Isabella. Don't underestimate the danger of breaking the rules here. You saw what happened today.'

She seemed in no hurry to abandon the black and white image with its world of construction and hard labour, but he saw a frown tighten the corners of her eyes.

'I'm not the one taking risks with Gabriele,' she pointed out. 'Roberto, you can't fool the ONC agents.'

'I know.'

Abruptly she jumped to her feet and limped over to the photograph. She inspected it closely. She pushed her nose so tight to it that it struck him she was trying to climb inside the picture. He liked that about her.

'How do you do it?' she asked.

'Do what?'

'Make it so real.'

'I went up there. Climbed the scaffolding.'

'What? With that great big heavy camera?'

He laughed. 'No, the Graflex is for high quality pictures that are more posed. A cumbersome but superb beast. This one I took with my small Leica using a fifty millimetre lens.

It makes me anonymous. People don't notice it. And I've painted its shiny parts black to make it even less noticeable.'

She nodded and glanced around the walls at the other photographs. 'They're beautiful. So natural. So intimate.'

'That's because I prowl the streets all day, ready to pounce. Stick a big camera in front of people and they freeze, but the Leica lets me sneak up on them.' He shrugged and waved a hand at one of a man trying to pull a folded newspaper from his dog's mouth outside the library. 'I like to trap a moment of life.'

She turned her head, her eyes suddenly darker as if she'd seen or heard something that alarmed her. 'Is that what you're doing now?' she asked. 'With me? Trapping a moment that you will add to a fine collection? To show someone else later, perhaps.'

He had no idea where it came from, this sudden ferocity, as unexpected as summer lightning, but he could feel the heat of it. He pushed back his chair and moved over to the door that led to the stairs down to the street. He opened it and stood back from it, uncertain whether she would stay or run.

'See, Isabella, you are not trapped.'

He could hear her breathing.

The electric lamp on the bookshelf cast shadows in the room but not enough to hide the flush of colour that swept up Isabella's neck and on to the fine bones of her cheeks. She shook her head.

'I'd better leave,' she said awkwardly.

'Coffee first?'

She found something that resembled a smile. It hung crookedly on her face. 'Another time, thank you.'

'I'll drive you home.'

'There's no need. I can walk.'

'Yes, there is. It's dark out there.'

She shook her head again but suddenly seemed too fatigued to argue. He helped her into the jacket she had abandoned on a chair but he was careful not to touch her, aware of the nervous energy coming off her skin and of her acute desire to be away from him. Once outside, a car swept past, throwing its headlights in her face, and he found himself alert to every flicker of her eyelids and every plume of breath from her lips. Though it was only October there was a touch of winter in the air this evening.

'I'm sorry,' she said softly.

'No need to apologise.' He turned up his collar against the wind and against his cold dismay at losing her so soon. 'Today was hard, Isabella. I'm not surprised you feel that the sooner you're out of the hair of this crazy photographer the better. I feel the same myself sometimes.' He added an easy chuckle to convince her that there was no harm done.

'It's not that.'

'What then?'

She lifted a hand, a faint shift of pale skin in the darkness of the street, and she touched his cheek with her fingertips. That was all.

The night sky was clear and thick with stars, but the mist still slunk along the ground. Roberto drove Isabella home through the quiet streets. He parked his car on the roadside and walked her into the elegant courtyard of her apartment block, conscious that her limp was noticeably worse. He could see she had no strength left to fight against the pain and he didn't like to imagine what kind of effort that must take each day.

'*Buonanotte, signora*,' he said to her. 'Sleep well.'

But again her pale hand crept out of the darkness of the doorway and reached for him. This time it attached itself to the lapel of his jacket and didn't let go.

'Roberto, forget about the convent. I've changed my mind. Don't go there. Stay away from it completely. No photographs.'

'But how else will you know whether Rosa is still there?'

'That's my problem. Forget I ever asked you. Please, just don't go near Mother Domenica and her prison-school.'

'Why?'

'I should never have got you involved.'

'Ah, Isabella, don't you realise it's too late for that? I am already involved. We are already involved.'

He heard her breath catch in her throat and felt her fingers tighten on his lapel. 'No photographs,' she repeated, scrutinising his face fiercely. 'It might be dangerous.'

'Don't imagine,' he told her, rubbing the

bruise on his neck, 'that all Blackshirts are like those brutal men today. To be a Blackshirt doesn't mean you have to have a black heart.'

She made an odd sound under her breath and stiffly unlaced her fingers from his lapel. The mist in the courtyard seemed to possess form and weight, like a person standing between them, and Roberto didn't care to put a name to who that person might be. Instead he stepped back and headed for the car.

'*Grazie* for the fish,' he called out, and raised a hand in farewell.

Only when he was out of sight did he check the weight of the gun in his pocket.

★   ★   ★

'Are you ready?'

'We're ready,' Gabriele answered, propped against the doorpost for support.

'Take only what you can carry,' Roberto told him.

The moon had risen, turning the road across the flat plain into a river of polished steel that flowed through the darkness, but still the mist stalked the fields and ditches like smoke in great white drifts that came and went at will, obscuring stretches of the road. It was the mist that would be their friend tonight.

Four old cardboard suitcases tied up with string stood outside the house and beside them lay four bundles wrapped up in tablecloths, looped in a knot to fasten on someone's back. One for each of the younger children to carry.

155

The baby was wrapped up warm in Alessandro's arms and he was pacing back and forth across the yard.

'The animals are in the barn, all fed and watered for the night,' the boy said as soon as Roberto stepped out of the car.

'You've done well,' Roberto told him. 'We'll get you all up into the mountains before the rain comes. It will wash away any tracks.'

'I don't want to leave here.' The boy looked lost in his cap and threadbare coat, both too big for him. He gazed out across the black expanse of fields that seemed to exhale their night-breath into the mist. 'I liked working with the cattle and the land. It was a fine new life for us.'

'No good looking back, Alessandro.' Roberto placed a hand on the boy's shoulder. He could hear the fear smothered in his young voice. 'You have to look to the future now.'

'Roberto is right, son.' Gabriele limped over to them. 'This bloody town is no good to us. It's a place where you can find yourself behind bars or with a cracked skull just for looking at the Fascist flag the wrong way.' He spat viciously on the ground. 'That's what I think of Il Duce.' He clapped a hand hard on his son's back. 'We'll do better down south, won't we?'

'No,' the boy said stubbornly.

A thin wail rose from near the house. Roberto glanced over to where the sisters were lined up against the wall, thin shadows that scarcely registered in the darkness except that one of the twins was crying. He walked over and crouched down. She was shivering.

156

'No need to cry, little one. You'll soon be warm and safe again.' He pulled the blanket that was draped over her small shoulders more firmly around her. 'Make no sound now.'

'Why can't we take Columbine with us?'

Her twin patted her sister's cheek for comfort. 'Columbine is our pig,' she whispered to Roberto.

'No animals, I'm afraid,' he explained gently. 'They all belong to the ONC, so they have to remain here.' He scooped up both children, one on each arm, and carried them to the car. 'In you get. The sooner we leave the better.'

It was a crush, cramming everyone in, small bodies piled on larger ones and cases strapped to the roof, but Roberto worked fast. He had to get the Caldarones out of here quickly. He kept a sharp watch on the veiled landscape, alert for the slightest movement or the flicker of a torch, but all the time there was a harsh pulse of anger at his throat. Finally he checked the sacking covers taped over the headlights to keep them to no more than a dim glow, but before he slid into the driver's seat of the overloaded Fiat, Gabriele hobbled up to him and clasped him to his chest. Tears were streaming down the man's gaunt face and his lips were quivering behind his whiskers.

'*Grazie*, my good friend, *mille grazie*. I was a fool to come to this hell-hole.' He kissed Roberto ferociously on both cheeks. 'You were sent from God to save me and my family. You will always be in my prayers.'

'Thank you, Gabriele.'

Roberto took one final look at the farmstead.

A hell-hole? The pulse quickened in his throat. Right now the whole of Italy was one damned hell-hole.

'*Andiamo*!' he said, and started the car.

13

Rosa did not believe that God was in the convent chapel. It was much too plain for Him. It had no marble statues of the saints with sad faces, no gilded crosses. And it smelled of empty stomachs.

Why would He bother to come here?

All it could offer Him was one measly Madonna of painted plaster. The whitewashed walls were as bare as a shroud and the heavy wooden altar looked no better than someone's dining table. God wouldn't like it here any more than she did. He would be in Rome, only an hour away by train. Right now, if Rosa had to guess, he was probably in the basilica of Santa Maria degli Angeli e dei Matiri in Rome's Piazza della Repubblica listening to the huge pipe organ. That's where Rosa would be. If she had any choice.

So that's why she didn't think it was a sin to release the mouse in the chapel. God wouldn't even notice. She slid the lid off the small bonbon tin she had stolen from behind the refectory curtain where Sister Agatha kept her secret stash of peppermints. Rosa had hidden it under the bib of her grey pinafore dress, aware all through Father Benedict's sermon of the scratching of tiny claws against the metal. She felt sorry for the poor mouse, imprisoned in a dark place. But it wouldn't be for long. She'd caught it yesterday in the outside lavatory with the help of her friend Carmela who, Rosa discovered with surprise, was immensely brave when it came to mice.

She placed the tiny animal on the top of the backrest of the pew in front of her, watching as its black eyes bulged with shock at its sudden freedom and its naked pink feet set off at full speed towards the far end.

Rosa screamed. Jumped to her feet and shouted, 'Mouse!'

★ ★ ★

Screams are catching. Panic is like fire, it leaps from one head to another, its flames igniting fear even when the person doesn't know what they are afraid of. She had seen it before, how easy it is to stampede a herd of empty-headed girls. The pupils bolted out of the pews into the aisles in a jumble of squeals and shrieks, and it could easily have been an accident that Rosa bumped against the wooden box on an iron stand by the wall. It could have been an accident that her elbow nudged open the lid as it fell.

It could have been.

Sister Agatha and Sister Pietra came flapping their black wings down the aisles, voices raised even in the house of God as they ordered the girls back into their seats. But by then Rosa was picking up all the small votive candles that had fallen on to the flagstone floor and was replacing them in the box.

A hand slapped her ear. 'Hurry up, girl. Get to your seat.'

160

She hurried. It was only after she'd taken her place on the pew once more, heart thumping hard, that she looked up towards the altar and saw the priest's gaze fixed on her. She didn't look away. She sat there and stared back. But the four slender candles tucked behind her pinafore bib were burning a hole in her chest.

★　★　★

'Don't, Rosa.'

'I have to.'

'You'll get caught.'

'No, I won't.'

But Carmela didn't look convinced. They were whispering at the far end of the dormitory, crouched down under the casement window in the dark. There were metal bars over the panes of glass, too close together to squeeze between, and the door was locked on the outside, so all sixteen girls inside were secured until morning. But several times a night the door would swing open and a torch beam in the hand of whichever nun was on night duty would swoop on to each bed.

Rosa wrapped an arm around Carmela and drew her closer. Partly to bring her ear nearer so that the other girls wouldn't wake, but mainly because Carmela may be brave with mice but she was terrified that Mother Domenica would cut her hair. It had been threatened. To shave off her long auburn curls. She kept them covered in a white scarf for much of the time to lessen the provocation they caused. She was shivering and

Rosa rubbed her long back vigorously. Her friend was absurdly tall for a nine-year-old and the nuns found her white-skinned face and fiery hair an irresistible magnet for their slaps and smacks.

'Go to bed, Carmela. I can do it on my own.'

'No, I'll stay.'

Rosa kissed her cheek. 'The match?'

Carmela held up a single match that she had sneaked from the priest's coat in the cloakroom while he was closeted in the Mother Superior's office. Rosa had noticed several times that he drew matches from his pocket when he wanted to smoke his vile black cheroots.

'Candle,' she announced.

She drew a short thin candle from the thick knot of her hair at the back of her head and held it out to be lit. Carmela struck the match on the rough floorboards and it flared into life with a hiss. Both girls glanced nervously at the beds but could see no movement among the blankets. Rosa melted the bottom end of the candle first and stood it on a flat stone she had picked up in the yard, then Carmela lit the wick before the match burned out.

The darkness leapt backward. Wisps of yellow light flickered on their faces and scampered up the wall. The candle was the kind worshippers lit in church as a prayer for someone, so Rosa knew it wouldn't last long, any more than people's prayers did, so she stood quickly on bare feet and lifted the flame to the window. Slowly, carefully, she moved it from side to side.

'Can you see anyone?' Carmela whispered.

162

'No.'

'He may not come.'

'He'll come.'

'Tonight?'

'Or tomorrow night. Or some other night. But he'll come.'

'How can you be sure, Rosa?'

Rosa smiled softly as her eyes scoured the blackness in the convent garden beneath them. 'I'm sure.'

'But there's a high wall down there.'

'That won't stop him. Nothing will stop him.'

'Oh, Rosa.'

'Go to sleep. I can do this.'

But Carmela curled up at Rosa's feet, unwilling to leave her, and it took a whole hour for the candle to burn to nothing. Rosa was ice cold by the end, hearing her father's deep voice in her ear and feeling his hand warm on her shoulder, until she no longer knew what was real and what wasn't. The darkness outside seemed to drift closer, to rap on the glass, to seep into her mind and distort her thoughts, twisting them into knots that she couldn't undo. She believed she saw the architect. Sitting on the window sill and offering her hand. But when Rosa reached for it hungrily, the architect vanished and all she clutched was cold brittle emptiness.

When the answering light flashed, she almost missed it. She blinked. She waited for it to come again out of the darkness but the garden remained stubbornly mute, no sound, no light. Did she imagine it? Had the night played a trick?

She waited another hour. No more lights

flashed. The darkness and the cold swallowed everything out there and her chest hurt so bad that it squeezed tears from her eyes. She dashed them away and knelt down to wake Carmela who was still curled like a long-limbed cat at her feet. Gently she patted her shoulder and placed a hand over her mouth, so that she would make no noise.

That was when she heard the sound of a key in the lock and the yellow beam of a torch sprang into the room.

14

It was the silence that hit Roberto first, a silence so solid he could have stood his tripod on it. The high ceilings of the convent of Suore di Santa Teresa echoed with it. He strode down the corridor behind the black robe that billowed beneath the tall white headdress with its ice-hard triangular edges and he inhaled a smell. That's what hit him second. The raw smell. Not the stink of paint and damp plaster and freshly oiled wood that permeated the new buildings throughout Bellina, he was used to that and expected no less. But over it and under it lay a different smell, one he had not expected to find in this house of God.

It was the smell of a bordello.

Not the cheap scent of a whore's perfume, no, not that. The only perfume here was the smoky aroma of incense. No, what caught his nostrils was the unmistakable smell of sex. Musky and muted in the air around him, a femaleness that lingered, as if it were hidden away behind the bricks in the wall and tucked into the mortar that gripped the tiles under his feet. It made him wonder. What thoughts filled the heads of the nuns when they scourged their pale and untouched bodies at the end of each day, and what dreams stalked the nights of the older girls in their care as their young bodies ripened out of their control?

The squat fat figure in front suddenly halted and turned humourless eyes on him. He could see rage within her but he had no idea whether it was directed at him for being a man and a sinner or at the Mother Superior for being the one whose door she was obliged to tap on so meekly.

'Thank you, Sister Agatha,' he said.

But his tone had an edge. And she was sharp enough to pick it up.

'Signor Falco, while under this roof I suggest you learn to practise a little humility.'

'Thank you, I'll make sure I bear that in mind.'

Her shoulder gave an annoyed little hitch before she tapped on the door and walked away, leaving him to it without a word. He opened the door and entered Mother Domenica's inner sanctum. It was a beautiful room, though he could have done without the cardinal portraits. Tall arched windows along one wall allowed sunlight to drift through the fine muslin curtains that robbed it of its glare and gave the room an elegance that he did not associate with convents, but maybe that was because he'd never been inside one before. Certainly this chamber was furnished with a degree of luxury that came as a surprise to him.

'Good morning, Signor Falco.'

So this was the Mother Superior who didn't stint herself. Wasn't there supposed to be something about a vow of poverty? He hid his frown and didn't offer his hand, any more than she did.

'Good morning, Reverend Mother. Thank you

for seeing me so promptly.'

'It's my pleasure. We are proud to be part of this town and the recording of this historic achievement.'

'I will cause as little disruption as possible. As I explained on the telephone, I will need to photograph the buildings and then the pupils in their class groups. With teachers, of course, to indicate the most valuable work that your convent does here in Bellina.'

'Our most valuable work, as you put it, lies in our prayers, young man. Now, sit down, if you please.'

The order was given affably enough but there was that look at the back of her pale eyes; a look he'd seen before in the eyes of those within the church. A look of forgiveness. As if they could see your sins written in black slime on your skin, yet were willing to let you sit with them and drip your filthy stains on their pristine carpet.

Maybe she was right. Maybe he did need forgiveness. But not right now and not by this woman with her narrow disembodied head that looked too cumbersome in its finery for her thin stalk of a neck. He took the seat in front of the large desk and she sat herself behind it opposite him, her hands folded away in her lap. But Roberto wasn't fooled by the serene expression she assumed. Those eyes of hers were sharp enough to skin a rabbit.

'Here,' he said, and placed a folded sheet of paper in front of her. 'My letter of authority. Signed by Chairman Grassi himself.'

The nun examined it thoroughly and returned

167

it with a nod. 'He must think highly of you to give you such access to people's lives.'

'It's my job.'

'A movie camera team arrives in town every now and again, I'm told.'

'Yes, that's L'Unione Cinematografica Educativa. LUCE. They make short showreels to run in cinemas, so that people throughout Italy can see how well the great project is progressing.'

'But they've never come here. Why you?'

She sat forward a fraction and placed both hands quietly on the surface of the desk. Roberto presumed that was as close as she would ever come to expressing aggression. He sat back in his chair and wondered what it was she was nervous of behind the calm passive face.

'I am employed to keep a record of everything in the town,' he explained, 'not just the big cinematic events. And your quiet haven of peace here at the convent of Suore di Santa Teresa is a small but important part of the whole picture.'

The nun's upper eyelids slid down until she was staring at him through no more than narrow slits. 'You mean you are a spy,' she stated. 'You and your camera have come to snoop on us.'

'No, Reverend Mother. Quite the opposite. I have come to show the world what a model of rectitude you have created here.'

'It is not for the world that we do it, Signor Falco.' The tip of her tongue flashed across her lips. 'It is for God that we do it, for our Father in Heaven.'

'Of course.' Roberto inclined his head in a

small gesture of courtesy. 'Now.' He picked up the letter he had extracted from Grassi when he first agreed to undertake the wretched job and replaced it in his pocket. 'Time to take some photographs.'

★ ★ ★

'The smallest ones in the front, the tallest girls at the back.'

Roberto was arranging the class of pupils. These girls were too young, Rosa wouldn't be among them, but still he studied their small faces, seeking clues to their life here. He did not miss the bruises on the backs of their hands or the quick feral way their eyes darted back and forth. They reminded him of a young fox he'd once seen cornered by two hounds in a field. Quivering on its toes, ready to bolt before they ripped its throat out.

He had carried one of the long benches out into the quadrangle that lay at the centre of the convent. He set up his tripod and summoned the classes one by one. He didn't ask any names, but as each group trooped into the courtyard he arranged them, settling the smallest girls in a row cross-legged on the cobbles. The next in height were seated on the bench and behind them in a line stood the tallest ones, stiff as Roman guards.

He noted how they huddled together, shoulders brushing against each other, as though eager to avoid standing out from the grey nervous little flock. He told them to smile. But

169

they didn't. He checked the average age of every class with each of the nuns who came to stand one at a time smiling placidly beside their pupils, hands tucked discreetly into loose black sleeves, so no man could look on them.

'I need an assistant,' he announced.

Twenty-two pairs of eyes fixed on him instantly.

'Sister,' he addressed the nun with old acne scars over her face, 'I would like one of these girls to assist me.'

'Reverend Mother didn't tell me anything about that,' she answered uneasily. She flapped her wings like a nervous crow.

'*I'm* telling you,' he pointed out.

The class was of nine-year-olds, some in pinafore dresses too large for them. None of them spoke.

'I require one of the girls to help me with my camera equipment,' he explained. He made a fuss of unscrewing the film-holder slot, adjusting the tripod and reaching for a new lens in his case all at the same time. 'I do not have three pairs of hands,' he snapped with a frown.

'Well, I suppose Sofia might . . . ' The nun turned to one of the girls with small sharp features.

'I'll have that one.' Roberto pointed to the only girl who possessed a mass of unruly curls, as Isabella had described, and shy dark eyes. 'She looks competent enough.' He didn't wait for the nun to object. 'Come here, girl. *Pronto*!'

The girl scurried forward. He handed her a film holder to keep ready with a warning not to

170

drop it. She looked terrified. When he'd rewound the shutter and the next class started to file into the courtyard, he told her to place the holder into his dark-box.

'What's your name?' he asked casually.

'Gisella.'

His hand paused. Damn it. The wrong girl. Yet there was no other nine-year-old who fitted the description so well. It would seem that the child Rosa had already been removed from Isabella's reach.

'Well, Gisella, don't worry, you'll be good at this. You just have to hold things when I hand them to you. Understand?'

The girl nodded nervously and Roberto had an urge to wrap one of his hands around the long white throat of the Reverend Mother in her overheated study and question why the girls in her school had eyes that looked out through a veil of fear. What kind of spiritual guardianship or pastoral care did she envelop them in?

'Signore.'

'What is it, Gisella?'

She stared at his shoes. 'Thank you for choosing me.'

'You're welcome,' he smiled.

She 'assisted' him through the photographs of the last two classes and stood silent at his side while he set up for shots of the convent building itself. He talked her through what he was doing with the Graflex, popping up the viewfinder, opening the lens F-stop to make it brighter and using a cable release to press the shutter more gently. When he'd finally finished he led her into

171

a small gloomy storeroom at the back of the kitchens, ostensibly to pack up his equipment case in its dim light without damage to the film stock. It led off the quadrangle and was a place where they would not be overheard.

It was there among the strings of onions and sacks of coarse flour that he asked casually, 'Do you know a girl called Rosa Bianchi?'

Gisella was eyeing up a large tin box that was marked *Biscotti*. 'Si, I know her. She is the one with the mother in hell.'

'Is that what the nuns say about her?'

'Yes.'

'Is she still here?'

'Yes.'

'Which class?'

She didn't answer but her fingers crept out and ran along a corner of the tin. Roberto moved over to the shelf, tore off the lid and scooped out a handful of the hazelnut and aniseed biscuits. She gasped as he piled them into her cupped hands.

'Now,' he said, 'which class?'

'Mine.'

He looked at her plain little face and swore at himself for making such a mistake. Rosa had been there all the time. Right under his nose.

'Thank you for your help, Gisella.'

She heard the dismissal in his voice and quickly finished pushing a biscuit into her mouth, regarding the mound in her hand with a panic of indecision. Clearly they were permitted no pockets in their dresses. Roberto removed a

172

clean handkerchief from his jacket.

'Here, use this.'

She wrapped the biscuits in it, tied the corners in a knot and tucked it behind the bib of her dress. She grinned up at him, delighted with herself, and the grin, so unexpected in the solemn face, pulled at Roberto's heart.

'Would you like me to take your photograph?' he offered with a smile.

Her eyes widened with delight and she nodded shyly. This time he used the Leica. He walked Gisella out into the yard and talked to her for a few minutes about the time when he was also nine years old and had stolen his uncle's dinghy for an afternoon because the sea was so blue, sparkling all colours of the rainbow.

'But the wind off the Amalfi coast can be treacherous,' he told her, 'and the boom swung across and knocked me into the sea. I had to tread water with the fishes.'

'What happened?' she whispered, appalled.

'I went to school the next day with a thumping headache and a backside walloped by my father,' he laughed.

She laughed too and that was when he took the picture. 'When it's developed, I'll get it to you,' he promised. 'Somehow.'

She stared at him with such fixation that it embarrassed him.

'Thank you for your help. You should return to your classroom now.'

He stepped back into the storeroom to pick up his case, but to his surprise Gisella followed him into its musty interior.

'Will you kiss me?' She said the words quickly, as if they were burning a hole in her tongue.

Roberto looked with surprise at the nine-year-old girl.

'No.'

'Please.' Her cheeks were beetroot red. 'The older girls will ask me if you did and they'll make fun of me if I say no. They'll say I am too ugly for any man to want to touch me.'

'No, Gisella. You are far too young. Not ugly at all, for God's sake.'

'They kiss the man who delivers the coal.'

'They're lying.'

Tears slithered down the girl's pale cheeks.

'Oh, Gisella, don't listen to them.' With difficulty Roberto kept a grip on the stab of anger towards the girl's tormentors and quickly swung his case over his shoulder.

She was still standing there between him and the door.

He walked right up to her, gently took her face between his hands, surprised by how hot her skin was, and placed a chaste kiss on her forehead. He smiled down at her.

'Thank you,' she whispered.

'Now go to your classroom.'

She nodded.

'Enjoy the biscuits,' he said.

She nodded again.

He drew a small sealed envelope from his jacket pocket. 'And give this to Rosa Bianchi. In private.'

* * *

Carmela was shaking. Eyes huge with distress. Her long bony fingers were welded to Rosa's wrist, above which a sheet of paper was clutched in her hand. With every tremor it rustled through the air that was ripe with the stench of the lavatory block. They were jammed into one of the cubicles and speaking in whispers.

'Get rid of it,' Carmela hissed. 'You'll be in trouble.'

'No. No one knows.'

'They'll make her tell them. You saw them take the biscuits from her.'

Rosa shook her head and tore open the envelope. Her heart was knocking against her ribs and inside her head she could see the bloodless hand pushing her into the pit of darkness again, except this time it would be worse. This time she would be locked in for days. Or weeks. No one would know or care. They would slide food under the door, flat slices of bread. Or maybe they would let her starve. The darkness would suck all life from her soul and her hair would turn as white as the novices' robes.

'Aren't you frightened?' Carmela asked.

'No.'

She was so frightened her eyes could not focus on the words written in black ink on the paper. She blinked to remove the mist but it clung to her eyeballs like oil.

'Is it from your father?'

'Of course.'

'He must have seen the light in the window.'

'I knew he would.'

'You're just like him, Rosa. So brave.'

But Rosa had stopped listening to her friend. She screwed the letter into a tight ball and hurled it into the lavatory bowl with a feral moan that rose from her empty gut. Her eyes cleared but now they had to fight back tears.

'What does he say?' Carmela demanded in a shocked whisper. 'Is he coming for us?'

'No.'

'Why not?'

'It's not from Papa. It's from the photographer.'

'What?'

'The photographer who came today. He says he is a friend of the architect, Signora Berotti.'

'So why is he writing to you? What does he want?'

'She wants to see me. To help me.'

Her friend eyed her warily. 'That's good. Isn't it? You like her.'

'But Mother Domenica won't let her in.'

Rosa bent over the lavatory bowl, plunged in her hands and tore the sodden letter and its envelope to shreds.

'Don't,' Carmela crooned. 'Don't be upset. The architect can help you find him.'

'She doesn't even know he exists.'

'Then you must tell her.'

Rosa's head shot up. 'Yes, you're right.' She stared with relief into her friend's speckled eyes. 'I must tell her.'

'But how? She can't get in here to see you.'

Rosa flushed the lavatory, dragged her wet

hands down her dress to dry them, leaving behind a murky trail, and wrenched open the cubicle door. She looked straight at Carmela.

'Then I must get out,' she told her.

15

The moment Isabella pushed open the huge brass-edged doors of the Fascist Party headquarters and set foot on the coral marble of its reception hall, she knew she was in trouble. A black uniform stepped in front of her. Bull-chested and heavy-booted. She could smell his sweat.

'No entry, signora.'

He stood too close, forcing her to look up. She could see an old scar like a silver brand under his broad chin and feel the blackness of his shirt squeezing out the narrow strip of air between them.

She smiled at him. 'I've come to make an appointment to see Chairman Grassi.' She had unleashed her hair from its usual tight restraint and shook it at him with a light laugh. 'I'm hoping he might be free today.'

She had been coming to the headquarters every day and taken her place in the queue at the desk of Chairman Grassi's deputy, Signor Marchini, but each time she had been turned away with an abrupt 'No appointments today, Signora Berotti.'

'Tomorrow?' she'd asked.

'Not tomorrow.'

'Next week?'

'Chairman Grassi's diary is fully booked next week.'

'Surely not every day.'

'He is a very busy man.'

Today she didn't even get as far as Signor Marchini's desk. She tried to step around the Blackshirt but he moved with her like a black wall. The vast hall echoed with the footsteps of others who were allowed to approach the inner sanctum, as she was edged back towards the entrance.

'At least give him this letter,' she said quickly before she found herself outside on the steps once more. She thrust an envelope under the black wall's nose. 'For Chairman Grassi.'

His fist swallowed the letter and he opened the glass door for her in a way that in anyone else would have seemed polite, but in this man it just seemed threatening.

'Leave now, Signora Berotti.'

He knew her name. Isabella swallowed a hard knot of anger, smiled politely and walked outside into the sunshine. He closed the door after her and stood behind it, arms folded across his chest, watching her every move. She was certain the letter would be tossed straight into the bin. She descended the steps, picking out a path along the edge to avoid stepping on the spot where Allegra Bianchi must have lain.

She ran a hand across her forehead as though it could alleviate the ache. It was time to find another way in.

★ ★ ★

'Where is Signor Francolini, Maria?' Isabella asked.

'He's out on inspection. Why?'

The older woman paused her varnished fingernails above the typewriter keys. She was always more than ready to stop for a chat, at the same time possessing bat-like ears for the first sound of her boss's footstep. Maria was Dottore Martino's secretary, one of the few other women working in the architect's building and prone to mothering Isabella, given half a chance.

'I need to speak to him.'

'Trouble?'

'No. I just need to query something with him.'

'You always were a bad liar,' Maria chuckled and let her gaze drift over her colleague's slim-waisted emerald dress with flared skirt and at her long dark curls that hung loose around her shoulders. 'You're looking extra pretty today. For someone special?'

'Maria, behave yourself! Of course not. Just tell me where he has gone.'

'To check on the Via Corelli apartment block.'

'Really?'

'Yes. Don't worry though. He seemed quite happy. It's his job to make sure construction is going smoothly.'

But Isabella did worry. The Via Corelli apartment block was the one she was working on herself. *'Grazie*, Maria,' she muttered and hurried towards the door.

★ ★ ★

The building vibrated with noise as Isabella entered. Workmen in grubby vests were hammering and sawing, a plumber was slicing through a metal pipe while whistling the Toreador song at full throttle. And the odour of wet cement caught at the back of Isabella's throat. But the moment she entered, her pulse started to pound. It was always the same. Her response was strong and physical to the smell and sound of one of her designs going through the process of being transformed into the reality of bricks and mortar. This would soon be a building where people would live and dream, give birth and die, generations of them, unaware that her breath and her fingerprints were woven into the fabric of each wall and each door frame. She wondered if at night in years to come the occupants would hear her heartbeat as they lay safe in their beds.

'Is Signor Francolini here, Nico?' she called to a workman with a drill in one hand and a cigarette hanging from his mouth.

He gestured upstairs and blew her a smoky kiss. Not how he would treat a male architect. But she smiled, because that's what you did, and she took the stairs faster than usual to work off her irritation. She found Davide Francolini on the third floor. In one of the rear apartments his slender frame was crouched on the floor in a corner, examining a long crack in the wall. It sent a stab of dismay through Isabella.

'Something is wrong there,' she said with concern.

Francolini turned, caught by surprise, but smiled up at her, his cool caramel eyes warming when he realised who it was. He was wearing a dark suit and tie, marred by a streak of cement dust that snaked up one sleeve. She hadn't spoken to him since the day she'd declined his offer of lunch, though she had seen him now and again flit through the office. He struck her as a man not easy to get to know, with an air of privacy that clung to him as stylishly as his clothes. Isabella stepped forward and offered her hand.

'Good afternoon, Signor Francolini.'

He rose to his feet and returned the handshake with a firm grip, brisk and efficient. 'Don't worry about the crack,' he said easily, 'I'll have it taken care of.'

'I'm glad I've run into you.'

'Why's that?'

She noticed his eyes take in her dress and her hair. 'I wanted to congratulate you on how fast the apartments have gone up. Your men must be working around the clock.'

'They are. We use floodlights at night.' He nodded, as though to reassure her. 'They are good men.'

'I'm sure they are. I've just come to check on the positioning of the pipes. We don't want them in the wrong place, so that they have to be torn out. It has happened before. Not all plumbers study the plans correctly.'

'Are you criticising our workmen, Signora Berotti?'

'No.' She shrugged. 'But in haste sometimes mistakes are made.'

For a moment he regarded her coolly and she wondered if she'd gone too far, but what lay heavy in her mind were the deaths that her father had mentioned among the workforce. But

182

Davide Francolini was clearly a man who put the success of his construction first. He ran a hand through his springy brown hair, the first unplanned gesture she'd seen from him, and his expression shifted to one of respect.

'I am pleased,' he said, 'to see you are so thorough in your work, signora.'

'It's my job.'

'So let us go and inspect these pipes of yours.'

It took longer than she expected, but Isabella didn't risk hurrying or skimping on the inspection in each of the six apartments, not in front of Davide Francolini. She had to request some adjustments from the plumber and one of the door architraves didn't sit squarely, so it all took time. Their voices trailed behind them, echoing in the empty building, but she enjoyed talking it all through with Davide.

So she was smiling when she emerged and it was the easiest thing in the world to turn to him and say, 'I have a favour to ask.'

He raised a dusty eyebrow in surprise. 'What is it? You want me to take the plasterers off another project to bring them in on yours?'

'No. It's more personal than that.'

She saw his eyes brighten with interest and the topmost layer of his reserve fell away like an unwanted snake's skin.

'In which case,' he said as he started towards a bar, 'you can tell me over a drink.'

This time she didn't refuse.

★ ★ ★

'What is *she* doing here?'

They were standing in Chairman Grassi's grandiose office, elaborate in its combination of pale marbles and black ebony in modern geometric designs. The hard lines and strong angles left visitors in no doubt as to the power and dynamism of the owner of such an office. It was intended to impress, and it succeeded. Isabella was careful to do as Davide Francolini had told her and kept her mouth shut.

'She's been working alongside me today,' he informed Grassi casually, 'learning my end of the business. Take no notice of her, she's just observing.'

He took the chair in front of the desk as if it was his by right, leaving Isabella stranded in the middle of the gleaming floor. She moved over to stand by the door, hands behind her back like a dumb sentinel. She let her limp show. Let Grassi think she was no threat.

'I don't want her here,' the chairman stated, puffing out his overfed chest but not bothering to rise from his black chair that looked more stylish than comfortable. 'She's been troublesome.'

'Her?'

Francolini glanced over at Isabella dismissively and shrugged, as though she were far too insignificant to cause trouble. Isabella did not care for the gesture but she had to admit it seemed to work because Grassi focused his attention on Francolini with a grimace.

'Be quick,' the chairman ordered curtly, 'I have other meetings to attend.'

But he opened a cedar box on his desk and both men reached for the cigars inside as if it were their custom. They didn't hurry through the ritual of lighting them from the chrome desk-lighter and exhaled with satisfaction as the skeins of smoke twisted together, binding them to each other for that moment. Isabella stood silent and unmoving. She listened carefully to their talk of delivery of greater numbers of roof pantiles from Naples, of progress on the construction of the sports stadium and the need to widen the approach road to it.

Davide Francolini delivered his report clearly and concisely, explaining the problems and being specific as to where the chairman could use his influence to unblock any logjams. It was an impressive performance. It gave her an insight into his complicated world. Yet it told her nothing about him, about the man behind the efficient well-groomed façade, except that he was good at handling people. He blunted the chairman's darts of anger, just as he had blunted her own fears.

'You have regular meetings with Chairman Grassi, don't you?' she'd said to him over a shot of limoncello at the back of the bar he'd chosen. 'To keep him up to date. That's what they say in the office.'

'Yes, it's true.'

'I need to see him urgently, but I can't get an appointment.'

'What is it you want to speak to our respected chairman about?'

'It's a private matter.' She shook her head

apologetically, not wanting to offend him. 'It's nothing to do with architecture or buildings. Something personal.'

He didn't seem to react, yet she sensed a heightened awareness in him on the other side of the table, a brightness at the back of his eyes that hadn't been there before.

'I see.'

She liked his quick mind and the fact she didn't have to say more. He had made a telephone call. It was as simple as that. Now she was here in Grassi's office, impatient for their meeting to end. Francolini was only halfway through his cigar when he stood up and shook Grassi's hand across the wide ebony desk.

'Thank you, chairman, for your time. We have clarified a number of problems and I can push ahead. I'll keep you informed.'

Grassi prowled forward from behind his desk and clapped a fleshy hand on the narrow bones of Francolini's shoulder with such vigour that Isabella realised he enjoyed working with this man. Davide Francolini had the knack of keeping things clear and simple. She must do the same. When Francolini headed for the door and opened it, she moved for the first time, her skirt rustling, an incongruously female murmur in the hard-edged male office. But instead of following Francolini out of the office, Isabella stepped smartly in front of Grassi.

'One moment of your time, *per favore*.'

The chairman's shoulders pulled back but his head jutted forward. 'Get out of my office, signora.'

'I don't intend to disturb your work. Just a couple of quick questions.'

There was a darkness to his heavy features as thick as the smoke that he breathed in her face. At this time of day his jaw glinted with the beginnings of a silvery stubble, but his hair was the dense black of paint.

'Leave now!'

'In the name of my husband, Luigi Berotti, who died for your Fascist Party, listen to me for two minutes. Please.'

Her voice was quiet. Reasonable. Not a trace of the anger that burned in her throat. She had disconnected herself from it and softened the muscles of her face. 'It won't take long. Then I will leave you in peace.'

Whether it was something in her voice or the mention of Luigi's name, she didn't know, but Grassi pulled back his head and drew on his cigar till its tip glowed like a warning. She saw something more of the man as he disguised his arrogance behind a long shrewd stare.

'Luigi Berotti was a loyal member of the Fascist Party. Back in the days before Mussolini came to power and needed every supporter he could get.'

Isabella hid her surprise. She trod warily. 'Did you know him?'

'No.'

'But you heard of his death?'

'Yes.'

'No one was ever charged with his murder.'

'So I believe.'

'That's why I'm here. Ten years ago I was told

by the police that my husband's killer escaped and no one knew who it was. Presumably an insurgent in a random attack.'

'Unfortunate. But it happens sometimes.'

Unfortunate? What kind of word was 'unfortunate' to describe the escape of a killer?

'He shot me in the back,' she stated.

'That too is unfortunate.'

If she pushed his cigar down his throat, would that be unfortunate too?

'I have reason to believe the Party knows more about the gun attack that day than it's telling me.'

He rolled his eyes impatiently and looked at the door. 'Young woman, the Party knows nothing about the incident, I assure you. The death of your husband was a sad loss. But it's over.'

'No. It's not over. Death is never over.'

He started to pace back and forth across his office, his gleaming black shoes marking out a line that she knew better than to cross.

'Who has been filling your head with this nonsense?' he demanded. 'Not the blasted priest.'

'The priest? No, not him.' She paused. 'Allegra Bianchi mentioned it to me.'

It brought him up short. He drew in a quick breath, expanding his broad chest, snorting out smoke, taking up more of the space in the office.

'That woman was mentally deranged,' he declared. 'Don't waste my time with her unhinged ideas. She was a woman hell-bent on

188

creating trouble and she is now where she belongs.'

Yet he crossed himself. Old habits die hard.

'What about her daughter? Is Rosa Bianchi where she belongs?' Isabella asked quietly.

He blinked at the change of direction and his heavy features became leaden. 'She has gone,' he announced.

'Gone?'

'Yes, the girl is being looked after elsewhere.'

'Where?'

'That, Signora Berotti, is none of your business.'

'Allegra Bianchi made it my business.'

His reaction was immediate. He strode straight over to her and for a moment she believed he was going to strike her, but instead he grasped the lapel of her jacket. He yanked her to him, so close she could see the small broken veins on the side of his nose pulsing with fresh blood and smell the tobacco on his hot breath.

'Signora Berotti, I am telling you to stay out of this. That girl is as damned as her whore of a mother.' He released a grunt of anger. 'As damned as her father will be when I . . . '

Instantly he regretted his outburst. She could see it in the hooded caution that now veiled his dark eyes.

'Who is her father?' Isabella asked at once. 'I thought he was dead.'

In answer, Chairman Grassi tightened his grip on her lapel so that it cut into the flesh of her throat.

'Chairman Grassi, I — '

189

At that moment a second hand landed lightly on her other shoulder and Davide Francolini's voice sounded in her ear.

'Come along, signora, don't delay further. I am tired of standing outside waiting for you.' His tone was sharp. 'We need to discuss the points raised in the meeting.' His hand jerked her shoulder, over-stretching its tendons.

In that second she lost all reason to trust either of them. She ducked from under their hands, tearing a seam of her jacket, and hurried out of the room. Out of the building. Out into the clean smoke-free air of the town. She was surprised to find it was raining, a hissing slippery drizzle that pecked at the back of her neck as she limped across the Piazza del Popolo.

The facts kept circling in her head as she dodged the raindrops. That the girl had been spirited somewhere beyond her reach. That Grassi's eyes had rolled away from her when he stated that the Party knew nothing about Luigi's death. A lie. A blatant brazen lie.

'So what is it, Chairman Grassi, that you are so determined I will not find out from Rosa Bianchi?' Isabella flicked a glance back over her shoulder at the Party headquarters, a powerful monolithic building that defended its secrets with a blank marble face. The rain fretted at Isabella's eyelashes. 'Which one of you,' she asked aloud, 'is a murderer?'

16

Isabella stood on the step in front of the green door. She stood there in a jacket that was wet and torn and with hair that had turned unruly in the rain. Her feet had brought her to this spot unerringly.

She needed to tell the photographer to forget about seeing the Reverend Mother. There was no point. Rosa had left the convent. It would be a waste of his time. But that wasn't the real reason she was here. Not all of it. Not really. Her thoughts were sharp and spiky in her head. The meeting with Grassi had opened up a gaping hole inside her, just as efficiently as the bullet had punched a bleeding hole in her back ten years earlier.

She sheltered against the door and touched her forehead to its slick wet surface as her mind struggled to find something solid to hold on to. Around her, drifts of rain turned the street into a shapeless blur as she rapped her knuckles against the green wood. She heard footsteps on the other side, quick and purposeful, and something stirred inside her at the sound. It did not seem like the footsteps of one of the elderly couple downstairs. The door opened and immediately Roberto drew her into the hallway out of the rain. He studied her face, then touched her cheek, her neck, her hair, brushing off the raindrops.

'What's happened?' he asked.

She shook her head. 'Tell me first how the Caldarone family got on this morning. Did Alessandro and Gabriele convince the ONC agents that they were farmers?'

'The family left.'

'What?'

'In the night. It was safer.'

'Poor Alessandro, he loved the animals. Where did they go?'

'South. Any town far from here, any place where they are not known.'

'I'm so sorry. It will be hard for them.'

He nodded. That was all.

'Come on,' he said, 'let's get you dry.'

He led the way to his rooms on the first floor. The house was small and cramped, but it was clean, and the smell of someone cooking a spicy Bolognese downstairs gave way to the odour of chemicals as she followed Roberto to the floor above. His long legs bounded up the stairs two at a time and Isabella had a sense of it being not just his wide shoulders that filled the narrow passage but the energy of him that rebounded off the walls and sat like a solid presence on the top step. She was pleased he was ahead of her rather than behind. She wasn't good with stairs.

He didn't hurry her. He removed her sodden jacket and fetched a towel, and for a moment she thought he was going to dry her wet skin for her as if she were a child. But he handed her the towel and set about pouring her a glass of wine. He didn't pester her with questions but she caught him scrutinising her face once or twice when he thought she wasn't looking. The table where she'd sat last time was pushed against the wall and he seated her instead in one of the two elderly armchairs that gave a view on to the street. Against the opposite wall stood a single bed covered in a severe black blanket and a deep pile of silky scarlet cushions that transformed it into a sofa. Roberto had told her before that his other room was used as his darkroom, hence the odd chemical smell upstairs.

He handed her the wine and settled back in the other chair with his own glass and a grunt of satisfaction.

'I'm glad you came,' he said. 'I have something to show you.'

She sipped her wine. It was rich and smoky and offered up an aroma of dark fruit that removed the taste of anger from her mouth. She dabbed at long swathes of her hair with the towel but knew the curls would go crazy as they dried.

'What is it?' she asked. 'This something you have to show me?'

'It can wait a moment.' His voice was gentle. 'Enjoy your wine.'

They sat together savouring the wine, and a delicate silence took root in the room, a companionable silence that neither felt the need to break. Everything grew still and quiet around them, the photographs on the walls watching them both as Isabella slowly relaxed.

'Better?' Roberto asked after a while.

She opened her eyes. She hadn't realised they were shut. 'Much better,' she murmured. 'Thank you.'

She took another sip. 'I managed to get in to see Chairman Grassi today. He said things about my husband that upset me.' She didn't think her voice changed but he sat forward in his chair and his grey eyes were fixed on her intently. 'I was foolish,' she continued before he could comment, 'to let him rattle me so easily.'

'Is it still so raw? After all these years?'

'It is unfinished, Roberto. How can it heal when it is unfinished? I still wake up in the night in a sweat of panic. Back in that moment. I see it all as if for the first time. The blood, the stalls, the faces bone-white with terror. The embroidered shawl clutched in my hand. My husband's limp body. Roberto, I am tethered to that moment. When I wake at night I think my heart is going to break out of my chest, it is beating so hard and it is all I can do not to . . . '

She stopped. Silenced the words. Appalled at how easily they had all slipped out.

'I'm sorry,' she said, embarrassed.

'Don't be.'

'It's a long time since I have spoken to anyone about . . . ' She took a whole mouthful of wine.

'And you have achieved so much since then, Isabella. Look around you in this town.' He waved a long arm towards the window. 'You should be proud of what you've done out there, the buildings you've created.'

'I am.'

'But not enough?'

'No, not enough.'

'Still tethered to that day.'

She nodded, and it occurred to her that

194

Roberto was as good at calming people as he was at calming horses and cattle.

'What about you?' she asked with a smile of sorts. 'What brought you here?'

He laughed softly at her shift of subject. 'Oh, you know what it's like for us photographers, we have to scrape a living wherever we can get it. I was offered the job, so I took it.'

'It must be satisfying for you. To be recording the creation of a community, knowing people will study your pictures for generations to come.'

'Maybe.'

One word. But it did not sit quite right in the room.

'Well, you won't have to record the convent of Suore di Santa Teresa.'

His dark straight eyebrows lifted in a query. 'Why is that?'

'Chairman Grassi has removed Rosa from there. He told me so himself but wouldn't say where she — '

'No, the bastard is lying to you. She *is* there.'

Isabella felt a flicker of hope. She had an urge to grasp his hand, to rub her skin against his, like a cat imprinting its smell.

'How do you know?' she asked.

'Because I went there today to take pictures.'

'So soon? You arranged it very quickly.'

He smiled, an ironic smile. 'Reverend Mother was most accommodating.'

'And?'

'Rosa's there.'

'Did you speak to her?'

'No.' He stretched his rangy legs and rose

from his chair. 'Come and see.' He held out his hand to her.

Isabella put aside her glass, brushed back the damp tangle of her hair and accepted his hand. As it closed around hers, her skin committed to memory the feeling of strength in its bones, in the hard pads of muscle wrapped around them. Her skin would remember this piece of him.

★　★　★

The small darkroom glowed blood-red. It altered Isabella's perception. The air seemed to pulse with a heartbeat of its own and everyday objects appeared to lose their hard edges, bleeding into each other.

'Over here.'

Roberto indicated a long table on which a number of photographs were laid out alongside several shallow chemical baths. Every surface in the room, except the sink in the corner, was draped with black and white prints of photographs; each wall and each filing cabinet was covered with them. Some were hung out to dry on lines stretched like spider webs across the room, and the air smelled of chemicals that Isabella couldn't even begin to name.

'Look at this picture. It's Rosa's class.' Roberto lifted up a photograph and handed it to her.

She studied it carefully. There were twenty-two children arranged in three rows and a short sturdy nun standing sentinel at their side. Each girl stared straight out at her with a solemn unsmiling face. It occurred to Isabella that they had probably never had their picture taken before, never been frozen in shades of grey. Roberto snapped the switch so that white light flooded the room instead of red, startling her, and he placed a magnifying glass in her hand.

'Can you see her?'

Her eye ran along the rows of girls in pinafore dresses, seeking the face with the watchful eyes that looked out at the world from under a mop of wild dark curls. She frowned.

'No, I can't. Are you sure she's here?'

'That's what Gisella — '

Abruptly Isabella jabbed a finger at a face. 'There.' Through the lens the faces jumped out in expanded detail and her heart was saddened at the sight of the fragile melancholy that clung to Rosa's features. 'Oh, Rosa, what have they done to you?'

Roberto stood close, looking over her shoulder, and she felt his breath warm on her cheek as he exhaled heavily. 'They've scalped the child,' he said.

It was true. Rosa's hair had been chopped to nothing more than a dark stubble all over her head, and her thin shoulders were hunched, her chin on her chest as she tried to hide from the lens.

'The bastards! No wonder you didn't recognise her from my description. I barely recognise her myself.'

'Look at the girl next to her too.' Roberto pointed to a tall girl beside Rosa whose hair had also been savaged and whose eyes were firmly

197

closed, blocking out all trace of the world. 'When I saw them in the courtyard I thought the pair of them had been ill, but this is . . . '

'Barbaric!'

The word hissed out of Isabella. She shook the photograph harshly as if it were Mother Domenica herself she was shaking. 'Roberto, I have to go to her.'

This had nothing to do with Luigi. This was about a child who needed help. She swung round to the door.

'Wait, Isabella. Think first.'

'No, Roberto, I must — '

He placed both hand on her shoulders. 'Listen to me, Isabella. No, don't struggle. Listen first to what I have to say.'

'It had better be good.'

'I gave a girl in her class a note to give to Rosa.'

That took her by surprise. His strong fingers withdrew, but she could feel the imprint of them on her flesh still and her skin pulsed as it refused to discard the memory.

'What did you say in the note?'

'That you wanted to see her.'

'If I go there now, Roberto, and say to the nun on the door that it is absolutely essential that I see Rosa right now, a matter of life and death . . . '

'No, Isabella. You've met Mother Domenica. Nothing you do or say will make that woman relent from her chosen path. For some reason she is working hand in glove with Grassi on this.'

'I could collapse on the convent's front

doorstep. They would have to take me in.'

His lips curved into a smile. But his eyes looked uneasy as if he didn't put it past her.

'Let me show you these, Isabella.'

He led her over to the photographs pegged out to dry like washing and she saw it was a series of pictures of parts of a building. It was obvious which building. The convent of Suore di Santa Teresa, but this was the convent as she'd never seen it. In intimate detail. As well as the chapel, the bare soulless refectory, the meagre kitchens and the classrooms, she was looking at close-ups of doors and door locks. Of windows and window catches. Of drainpipes and high garden walls and sheds and beehives. One photograph taken through a grimy shed window showed a ladder.

'Roberto,' Isabella's voice dropped to a whisper as though someone else might overhear, 'this is a blueprint for a burglary.' She switched her gaze to his face. 'Or an intruder.'

Slowly he started to smile at her. 'Or an escapee.'

17

They talked. Far into the night.

Over a bottle of red wine and a dish of olives from the groves of Gaeta just north of the marshes. Roberto talked Isabella through his day at the convent. She studied the photograph he'd taken of young Gisella and admired the moment of happiness that he'd captured in the girl.

'Thank you,' she said. 'For going to the convent. I'd fallen for Grassi's lie that Rosa had been moved elsewhere.'

'You should never trust that bastard.'

They were sitting in the armchairs, a green-shaded lamp throwing shadows between them, and Isabella sat forward, near enough to lay a finger on his knee. She thought about it. The desire to touch parts of this man was always there in her, like a thirst that wouldn't go away. She jammed her hands under her thighs.

'Tell me, Roberto, why you hate Grassi so much.'

He turned his face away, deeper into the shadow, and for a long while she could hear his breathing. Finally he said in a flat tone, 'Chairman Grassi forced me into this job. I didn't want it.'

'How did he force you?'

He gave an odd laugh and ran a hand through his hair roughly, as though Grassi was hiding in its thick waves and had to be torn out. 'I was in prison. Grassi offered to get me out.' He flicked his head around to stare at her directly. 'Simple as that.'

'Oh, Roberto, nothing is ever simple.'

But the word 'prison' seemed to stand in the middle of the room, as solid as bricks and mortar. Isabella reached out, placed a hand on his knee and let it rest there. He stared at it, his expression lost in the shadows. Was he putting her allegiance to the test?

'What were you in prison for?'

'For corruption. Attempted blackmail.'

'Were you guilty?'

'No, I was innocent of all charges.'

She didn't doubt his word. Not for a moment. 'That must have been terrible for you. How long were you in there?'

'Five years.'

Her hand tightened on his knee. 'Roberto.' She said his name softly and felt a wave of emotion wash from his body into her own. It shook her. The fact that the boundaries between them had become blurred.

'What made Rosa lie to you about her father, I wonder?'

She didn't blink at his sudden change of subject, just took a mouthful more of the rich wine and answered straight out. 'Because she's been told to keep him secret.'

'Is that what you believe?'

'Yes.'

'By whom?'

'By her mamma.'

'Or by her father.'

201

Isabella nodded, setting her dark curls into a dance of their own. She saw him watch them. His eyelids flicked like a camera shutter, as though committing the image to memory.

'So,' she said in a businesslike manner, 'I have to talk to Rosa. How hard will it be to climb the wall and break in?'

He edged forward, coming into the yellow shaft of light, and his eyes had the sheen of grey silk in the lamplight. His mouth was smiling as if it was wrapped around words he knew she was going to like.

'I have a better idea,' he told her.

'What is it?'

'Mussolini is coming to Bellina on Friday.'

'So?'

'So Gisella told me that all the schoolchildren in the town will be marched out with Fascist flags to line the streets and cheer a welcome to our great Il Duce in all his glory. Rosa will be out in the open.'

Isabella felt her pulse quicken. She pounded the flat of her palm on his knee. '*Grazie*, Roberto, *mille grazie!*'

He laughed and touched her cheek, a tender caress down to the corner of her mouth, as if his fingers had been waiting to do it all evening. He trailed a loose lock of her hair through his fingers.

'Isabella.' He didn't take his eyes from hers. 'Let me brush your hair.'

★ ★ ★

Is that how a man speaks his feelings? She could hear Roberto's voice though no word was spoken, feel the beat of his heart though no flesh touched hers. Each stroke of the hairbrush as he sat behind her sent a message spinning along the length of the chosen tress to somewhere deep inside her. Only the other day she had told a man she couldn't have lunch with him. She couldn't even bear to sit across a table with a man alone, for fear it would drag her back to that day in the Milan marketplace. Now look at her.

Look at her.

Sitting peacefully with a man handling her hair as if he owned it. She asked herself how it had happened. How had she reached this exquisite place? Where each touch sent warmth spilling through her body and a rush of happiness was softening the harsh edges of her day.

How long had he been sitting behind her? She didn't know. But the brush had fought its way through the snarls and was flowing smoothly through her curls now. He put it down on the table and came around to admire his handiwork from the front, grinning at her as he patted a few stray strands into place with his hands.

'A work of art,' he told her.

'You certainly know how to wield a brush.'

'I've groomed lots of horses in my time, you know.'

She laughed, a burst of sound that carried away with it the last of the tension from her body, and Roberto joined in with a delicious laugh that filled the room.

'Now,' she said with a smile, 'show me your camera.'

★ ★ ★

'It's a Speed Graphic,' Roberto informed her. 'Manufactured by Graflex. They're an American company.'

Isabella nodded. She stared at the mechanical beast in front of her in the dark room. A wood-bodied folding plate camera, he'd said. She pictured his strong fingers working its metal knobs and levers and she reached out to touch it, seeking the feel of his skin on it.

'It's an amazing piece of equipment,' he enthused. 'The best for a journalist. Fine quality and manoeuvrable on the hoof when you're under pressure.'

'It looks complicated,' she grinned.

He laughed easily, and it struck her that he was good at laughing. Better than she was, and it seemed to her as though the camera had access to a private spot within him where a cache of happiness lay.

'You have to prove your skill every time you use it,' he admitted. 'If you don't pay attention you can double expose or shoot blanks. I have to confess it is not beyond possibility that in the past I have managed to fog exposures or shoot out-of-focus images on occasion.'

'So it *is* complicated.'

He considered her comment with a crooked tilt of his mouth that she found beguiling. 'Yes, a Speed Graphic can be difficult when it wants to be,' he admitted reluctantly, as though betraying an old friend, 'but once you get used to it, it's easy to use. It becomes second nature.' He smiled fondly at the camera and ran a hand over its wooden case, mellowed with age. 'We get along together just fine.'

'I bet you do.'

'What does that mean?'

'It means I can see that you're good with your hands. Whether it's cameras or horses or wayward hair, you make them do your bidding.'

He looked down at his hands in a distant sort of way as if they might belong to someone else. 'Not always.' He paused. They were side by side at the table on which a rectangular stop-bath containing a dilution of acetic acid stood directly under the ceiling light. The liquid dissected the reflected light into glittering fragments and threw them up at Roberto, so that his face looked oddly disjointed, made up of different splinters that didn't quite connect. 'Sometimes,' he continued, 'I want to wring Chairman Grassi's thick stump of a neck, but my hands don't oblige. And at other times,' he lifted an eyebrow and smiled at her, 'I want to stroke the sweet curve of *your* neck, but my hands refuse. So no, not everything does my bidding. Unfortunately.'

A blush swept up Isabella's cheeks and she couldn't tell by the set of his features whether he was teasing her or not. He was too good at keeping a veil over the black centre of his eyes, and she felt an uncertainty that, even as she turned aside from him, was still bubbling away within her.

He gave a low chuckle and stepped closer. 'Isabella.'

The way Roberto said her name, as though dipping it in honey, made her heart expand until it seemed to fill every scrap of space behind her ribs. She started to swing back to him, the fading images of Luigi running through her fingers like water, and she knew she was going to kiss him. That was the point when her gaze was snagged by one of his photographs tacked to a board behind him on the wall, partly overlapped by a picture of her tower. Slowly, inexorably, the black shape in the photograph dug its way into her mind and her hand froze in mid-air halfway on its journey towards Roberto's broad chest in its dark blue shirt. She was aware of the shirt rising and falling, his breath laboured as his gaze followed hers.

'It's her, isn't it? Allegra Bianchi,' Isabella said softly.

'Yes.'

'You didn't tell me that you took pictures of her.'

He stared at the black shape. With no comment he stepped towards it as if it drew him against his will, and Isabella followed. She was the one who pushed aside the image of her tower and put her face close to the broken body on the steps.

'Oh, Allegra,' she whispered, 'why did you come to our town? What madness brought you here?'

The fan of the woman's black hair and the sweep of her black dress, as ragged as a crow's wing on the marble steps, was a shocking sight. Isabella's stomach lurched. She snatched up the magnifying glass that lay on the table and examined the black and white print through it, viewing each twisted limb and shattered bone, her own face chalk-white.

'What's this?' she asked.

'What?'

'That mark.'

One arm was draped at an unnatural angle over the edge of one of the steps like a broken matchstick and it had inverted as it snapped on impact, revealing the soft inside of the woman's right wrist. A white smear on its flesh leapt out at Isabella amid the tones of grey.

'It looks,' she said, 'like a brand.'

Roberto gently but firmly removed the magnifying glass from her hand. 'It *is* a brand. But one that she didn't ask for.'

Isabella could hear the rage that his quiet words left behind in the room.

'Tell me more,' she said.

'It is a method used by interrogators. They lay the flat side of a red-hot knife blade on your skin. Over and over on the same spot on your wrist until you want to rip your hand off.'

She moved to stand in front of him and lifted his right hand in hers, turned it over and pushed back his shirt cuff. The scar was there. White and smooth as ice. Isabella uttered a low groan that resounded through the room and bent her head to his wrist. She kissed the scar.

Shiny as butter beneath her lips.

His hand buried itself in her hair. She lifted her head, expecting him to kiss her, but all he did was smile gently and move away from her, as though he saw something in her that warned him off.

'Take a look at the Speed Graphic,' he said in a voice that gave no indication of the fact that he had felt the softness of her lips on his wrist.

★   ★   ★

Roberto drove her home. As they motored through the dark streets Isabella could hear the sound of hammering as construction workers laboured through the night shift. They drove in silence, a comfortable silence because enough had been said and there was no need for more.

Roberto parked the car outside her apartment building and walked her through the courtyard to her front door. The moon had risen and its bloodless light turned his hair to polished metal and silhouetted his strong nose. Isabella wanted to lay her hand on his chest, to brush her cheek against his cheek, to feel his breath on her lips, but he had not touched her since abruptly disentangling his fingers from her hair in the dark room and withdrawing his hand from hers.

She wanted to ask why. Why? What shutter has fallen in your head? But he had instead led her around the darkroom, pointing out the features of the camera — its two shutters, its peep sights at the top, its Schneider 90mm Angulon lens, its coupled rangefinder and double extension bellows. He explained how the film is soaked in water first to swell the gelatine layer before being placed in the developer and stop-baths. Only then is it dipped in the fixer, a compound of sodium thiosulphate to remove the undeveloped silver halide material from the paper. This is what makes the image permanent.

But Isabella had stopped listening to his words. Instead she heard the passion in his voice. It was a good voice, warm and deep, rising from within that spacious chest of his. And she watched his face. The way each part of it became animated. His eyebrows lifted and crouched, his eyes narrowed when he concentrated, his nostrils flared and his jaw jutted forward to underline a point. Each feature had a life and a language of its own. His mouth she didn't look at. She averted her eyes. If not, she would be tempted to knock aside the words that were tumbling from it and place her lips there instead.

Neither of them looked again at the picture of the broken crow's wing lying on the steps. Neither commented on why she would be bearing that scar.

Now that they were standing on the doorstep of Isabella's apartment, she knew the moment was in danger of passing without her having grasped it.

'I will be working, of course,' Roberto told her, 'when Mussolini comes to visit. Taking pictures of the event. Moving among the crowd.' He smiled at her in the shadows and she saw the whiteness of his teeth. 'I'll find her, I promise.'

She nodded. 'We will find her. I'll mingle with the flag-wavers. Rosa won't be hard to spot. Just look for the nuns, they'll be obvious enough with their big white headdresses rising up to God like — '

He took her face between his hands.

Her breath ceased.

'Leave the searching to me,' he said gently. 'It will be safer. You'd be surprised how easily people fail to see the man behind the camera. You've already crossed Chairman Grassi today and he doesn't take kindly to that, so you should — '

'No, Roberto.'

His sigh reached her lips. 'I thought you might say that, Isabella, but I want you to keep out of it.'

'No, Roberto.'

He kissed her mouth. He tasted of strong coffee and good wine and of something she had never known existed, something that made her mind slow down to a crawl but set her heart pounding. She needed to twine her arms around his neck and breathe in the scent of his skin, but before she could even move a muscle he stepped back from her into the black pit of the courtyard as if he'd been bitten by a snake.

'Good night, Isabella. *Dormire bene.*'

And he was gone. She stood there on the doorstep in the chill wind and listened for the Fiat's engine to start. She stood there long after he had driven away, aware of a heat spreading from where his lips had touched hers. It radiated down her chin and unfurled over her throat, trickling down to where her heart seemed to have stopped beating.

'Roberto,' she said in a murmur that the wind snatched away, 'what is it you are afraid of?'

18

'Holy Mother of Jesus! Look at that!'

'It's the gateway that I told you about, Francesca,' Isabella laughed. 'A monstrous gateway, I admit, but one that I suspect will please Mussolini immensely. The new gateway to Bellina. Dottore Martino designed it.'

'I know, but I didn't realise it was going to be quite so massive.'

It was hard not to laugh, yet impossible not to be impressed. A vast arrogant letter M straddled the road. M for Mussolini. No one could miss the significance — this was Il Duce's town. Ten metres high and constructed of huge concrete blocks, the gateway dominated the landscape on this eastern edge of town where traffic from Rome and the Appian Way would enter. Mussolini himself would shortly be speeding through it with his cavalcade and Isabella could just imagine the triumphant grin that would spread across his fleshy face at the sight of it.

Francesca stuck out her arm in the Fascist salute and shouted, 'Bravo, Il Duce!'

Heads turned. Other around them immediately echoed the shout. Isabella nudged her friend in the ribs. 'Behave, Francesca.'

'I *am* behaving. I am singing praise to our beloved leader.'

But Isabella had no wish to draw attention to herself today. She needed to be anonymous, just another patriotic face in the crowd that was gathering to line the roadside. She had chosen to wear a plain scarf over her hair and a dark coat, but she knew that as long as she was linked with Francesca, she wouldn't go unnoticed because no one could ever pass the baker without turning to admire the sleek river of white-blonde hair that flowed down her back.

'Francesca, wait here for me. I've just got to slip away for a few minutes to find someone. I won't be long.'

She was sure she had spoken with no hint of urgency but she realised she was wrong. Francesca knew her too well. Her eyes widened and she pursed her mouth around her cigarette.

'Oh? And who exactly is this *someone*?'

Isabella smiled innocently, just as a group of men at their elbow, elderly and weighted down with war medals across their chests, suddenly shifted to allow a tall figure to step in between. A familiar camera was slung over his shoulder.

'*Buongiorno*, a fine morning for the town to turn out in force. I hope you are well.'

Roberto's eyes held Isabella's for a moment, then he inclined his head politely to Francesca and treated her to a smile, and it was all Isabella could do to stop herself seizing his chin and switching the direction of his smile to herself.

'Francesca,' she said grudgingly, 'this is Signor Roberto Falco. He is the town's official photographer.'

Francesca exhaled a smoke ring. 'You're going to be a busy man today, signore, but not too busy to buy us a coffee later, I hope.'

213

He laughed outright. 'Of course not, I'd be delighted. The LUCE cameras are here as well today, so they will be doing much of the donkey work.'

'Good. Come round to Francesca's Panificio on Via Aristotele when you're done.'

'I look forward to it, signora.'

He tipped back his head to inspect the gateway against which long ladders had now been propped. Young boys, between ten and fourteen years old, in the Balilla uniform of black shirts and grey-green shorts, were scampering up them as eager as monkeys to line up at attention on the ledges specially built for them, but the smile grew rigid on his face as he watched them. The Balilla was the youth movement of the Fascist Party and each boy carried a functioning scaled-down rifle on his back.

Don't look so sad, Roberto. Not today. When everyone else is smiling. Eyes are watching.

At intervals along both sides of the road stood the full-size Blackshirts, stiff as toy soldiers, keeping people back, issuing reprimands when the crush threatened to surge forward, and always their eyes darting from face to face. Isabella could feel their suspicion. It blew on the wind and brushed against her skin, as brittle as dry leaves.

'Signora Berotti, have you by any chance seen where the Suore di Santa Teresa are stationed along the route?'

So formal. As if he didn't know the taste of her lips.

'No, I haven't yet. They must be further back towards town.' She noticed his gaze settling on the scarf that covered her hair and a faint frown drawing his thick eyebrows together.

'Why an interest in the nuns?' Francesca asked.

'It will create a strong image. To see the Church and the children waving flags for Il Duce. Mussolini relishes pictures of himself with excited young children.' He laughed but Isabella could hear no pleasure in the sound. 'They are the future of Italy, sitting there in the palm of his hand.'

Isabella was tempted to ask, *What about Rosa? Whose palm is she sitting in right now?* Instead she said, 'I'll let you know if I see them.'

'No need. I'll find them. But thank you, signora.' She knew he would have said more if Francesca had not been at her side. 'Enjoy the parade,' he added, and with a polite nod to them both he started to carve a path through the crowd.

'So, Signora Isabella,' Francesca said, hands on hips and a broad smile on her lips, 'that's the 'someone' you were going to sneak off to find.'

'No, Francesca, it isn't.'

'Ah, but he is the Signor Falco you asked me to find out all I could about for you before, isn't he? The photographer from Sorrento whose dog was trampled by a bull.'

'Yes, he is.'

'What's going on between you?'

'Nothing.'

'What kind of nothing? You think these eyes of

215

mine are blind, Bella?' She wrapped an arm around her friend and whispered in her ear, 'I saw the way he looked at you.'

'He looked at me the same way he looked at you. Polite but friendly.'

Francesca laughed, released her and lit another cigarette. 'My sweetest girl, he looked at you as if he were a cat and you were a dish of the finest cream.'

'The trouble with you, Francesca, is that you are an incurable romantic.'

'Aren't you?'

'No. I see straight lines. I see realism. I measure and calculate. That's why I'm an architect.'

The laughter drained from Francesca's face and a look of sadness that Isabella did not care for took its place. She had seen that look before. It always heralded a lecture from her friend.

'Bella, *cara mia*, you can't go on hiding away your heart for ever just because Luigi — '

Isabella kissed her friend's cheek briskly. 'I'll see you later.'

She hurried away in search of a tall white headdress.

★ ★ ★

The sun had come out for Mussolini. Or was it that he carried it around with him in his pocket? Roberto wouldn't put it past him. Not even the stars would want to cross Il Duce and his infernal Blackshirts. In the distance the mountains seemed to melt into a golden fiery haze, while here in the town the marble buildings gleamed and glittered in anticipation, and the patterned pavements drew the eye onwards to the rows of flags that declared the town's allegiance.

The crowds were pressed behind the barrier of uniforms lining the route that the cavalcade would take, but Roberto strode along the road, his Graflex allowing him that privilege. It meant he could move fast, whereas Isabella would have to struggle through the dense throng of people on the roadside. He tried to keep her out of his mind, but it was like trying to keep the sea back with a child's bucket. She flowed and ebbed and swirled through his every thought, whether he wanted her there or not.

His eyes keenly scanned the clusters of hats and caps and brightly coloured headscarves, but could pinpoint no white headdresses towering above the rest.

'*Merda!*'

He didn't have long. Mussolini's parade would start any moment. He tried asking one of the Blackshirts if he'd seen the nuns anywhere along the route but received only a curt shake of the head. He stopped by a woman at the front of the crowd just because she was wearing a scarf the same blackberry colour as Isabella's and repeated his question. She nodded readily.

'Back there.' She pointed. 'Near the fountain.'

'*Grazie*, signora.'

Roberto lengthened his stride. But he couldn't outpace the question that had plagued him all night and it came spinning into his head yet again. Was Isabella aware that when he kissed her, the second his lips touched hers, her whole body became rigid? She'd uttered a muffled rumble at the back of her throat, the way a hound will when it doesn't want to be touched. He had been tempted to stroke her glorious mane of hair, to soothe her hackles, but he was afraid to touch her in case she bit his hand off and ran away back into whatever darkness it was that clouded her blue eyes when he came too close.

So he'd left. Cursing that black-shirted husband of hers to hell, and this morning he'd smiled pleasantly at her and her blonde friend as if he had no memory of that rumble. No memory at all. Of the demon inside her that uttered it.

If you had a bullet smash your spine, you'd have a demon too, he reminded himself.

It was why he was here, thrashing around looking for women who hid themselves away behind black robes and the absurd white crown of Christ, and for a child with hair shorn close as a monk's. Isabella was strong. She was confident. Talented. Beautiful. Ferocious when she chose to be. But still it had her by the throat, that demon.

That's why he was here.

★ ★ ★

'Mother Domenica.'

'You again.'

'Indeed it is.' Roberto gave the woman in black a smile intended to disarm. 'A pleasure to

218

see you and the sisters out in force today. The convent must be deserted.'

The nun narrowed her colourless eyes at him, her lashes as pale as cobwebs, and said very deliberately, 'The convent of Suore di Santa Teresa is never deserted, young man. God is always there.'

'Just as my camera is always here.' He patted its smooth wooden flanks affectionately.

'Don't be facetious, Signor Falco.'

This time he didn't smile. 'I wasn't. We all cling to what matters to us.'

She opened her thin lips to rebuke him once more but he didn't wait to hear it. 'I am here to take pictures of people welcoming Il Duce to Bellina and I am *sure*,' he emphasised the word, 'he will be particularly pleased to see the children and the convent sisters greeting him so warmly. He cares passionately about the children of Italy.' He inclined his head in an offer of truce.

She blinked once at him. 'Take your pictures, signor *fotografo*.'

He slid a new film holder into the camera and immediately started to take a couple from across the road, but then removed the holder without replacing it. He knew he had to save his film for shots of Mussolini himself, but he continued to operate the knobs and shutter, moving further down the line of girls, away from the huddle of nuns. He studied the rows of grey pinafore dresses. Again. And then again. Where was she? Where the hell had they put her? He scanned the thin faces but not one of them matched the sad little picture in his pocket.

'*Buongiorno*, signore.'

'Gisella.' The girl who had acted as his assistant was standing at the far end of the back row. It occurred to him to wonder if she had put herself there on purpose to give her a chance to speak to him if he turned up. He grinned at her. 'Enjoy the *biscotti*?'

'Yes.'

She was lying.

'I have something for you,' he said in a low voice.

Her freckles grew rosy with excitement. 'What is it?'

Roberto glanced around to ensure no nuns were looking and a brass band obliged at that moment by marching past, attracting all attention. He slid from his jacket pocket a photograph no larger than a cigarette pack. Easy to hide.

'Here,' he murmured. 'It's the one I took of you.'

She glanced at it and slipped it smoothly behind the bib of her pinafore with a practised hand. She smiled at him. The tip of her nose was bright pink. 'Thank you.'

He waited, letting the silence between them stretch to ten seconds, so that she was turning to him curiously when he asked, 'Where is Rosa Bianchi?'

Instantly her eyes dodged away. 'She's not here.'

'I can see that,' he said. 'Where is she?'

Gisella cast a quick look at the nuns. 'She's been shut up in the convent for the day with

Sister Bernadetta, one of the novices.'

'Where in the convent?'

'I don't know.'

'Don't lie, Gisella. You have the picture.'

Her small hand touched the front of her chest and she held it there tight, as though feeling for her own heartbeat through the photograph.

'In the refectory.' Scarcely a whisper.

'Thank you, Gisella. I appreciate your help.'

Her helpless eyes leapt to his and for one daunting second he thought she was going to ask for another kiss. 'Go now,' she mouthed at him.

Yet he lingered. He wasn't sure why. He wanted to tell the child to be brave, to keep in mind that this hell would not last for ever. Just get through one day at a time. One breath after another. That's how he had got through five wretched years of solitary in prison. Sometimes he could still smell the stench of it on his skin. On his soul.

'*Arrivederci*,' he murmured. 'Good luck.'

He walked away. Foolishly believing he would never see her again.

★　★　★

'She's not there.'

'Rosa?' Isabella clearly didn't want to believe it.

'Yes. Rosa's not there with the nuns.'

'Are you certain?'

'Yes. I inspected every single girl.'

'Let me go and look at — '

'I know where she is. One of the girls told me.'

221

'Where?'

Isabella's arm was pressed tight against his, jostled close to him by the crowd that was craning forward to view the Balilla youth brigade that was marching past, legs snapping straight, rifles precisely angled on the shoulder. A shout of 'Bravo!' raced through the throng.

'In the refectory of the convent. It seems she is being watched over only by Sister Bernadetta, one of the novices, so — '

'Falco! What the hell have you been doing?' Chairman Grassi slapped a hand on Roberto's shoulder. 'Get down to the Mussolini gateway, damn you.'

Roberto moved in front of Isabella, his broad shoulders obscuring her from the chairman's gaze.

'Il Duce isn't due to arrive for another half-hour,' Roberto pointed out crisply.

'Get down there now, for Christ's sake.' The chairman's heavy features were flushed and Roberto suspected he'd already been busy calming his nerves with a grappa or two. 'His car could turn up here early.'

At that, Roberto laughed, a harsh sound. 'Generalissimo Benito Mussolini always chooses to be late, as everyone knows. He likes to make people wait.'

'The gateway,' Grassi snapped. 'Now!'

Roberto didn't argue. He walked Grassi down the road. Away from Isabella.

19

Isabella ran. She wasn't good at it. Even when she strained every muscle and sinew, it came out lopsided and threatened to tip her over. It shamed her. That she couldn't do what even a child could do with ease. She never attempted it in public. Never. But now she was running in full view of everyone.

As she drew near the convent, the streets became deserted and the roads oddly silent of traffic. Everyone was crammed on to the parade route, so she took advantage of it and pushed her precarious gait even harder, ignoring the white-hot ball of fire that had lodged at the base of her spine. Above her the sky was a lazy blue and the red-roofed houses seemed to preen themselves in the sunshine. Mussolini was going to be proud of his fine new town. He had sunk so much money into the place that he could not afford for anything to go wrong but in some way that Isabella didn't yet understand, Rosa had slipped into one of the unwanted cracks.

She fretted as she ran because she had not had the chance to thank Roberto in front of Grassi for the information about Rosa being in the convent. He had been forced to return to work with his camera but she couldn't stop herself from imagining him running alongside her now, his long lean legs eating up the pavements, his warm voice urging her on. The difference it would have made.

Yet it shocked her. That she needed him. Wanted him. She had not needed or wanted anyone running alongside her for ten long years. So why now?

* * *

A beam of sunlight latched on to the great iron cross on the wall above the arched doorway of the convent, turning it to gold. A good omen? Isabella decided to take it as such. She stood in front of the small hatched grille, catching her breath, heaving air back into her lungs and waiting for the zigzag lightning bolts of pain down her right leg to subside. She flexed it, nagged it to behave, then rang the bell.

Five minutes passed. She pressed the bell every thirty seconds after that. Eventually, reluctantly, the hatch in the door slid open.

'Yes?'

Two timid black eyes gazed out at her from a swarthy face, held tightly in place by a bone-white wimple.

'*Buongiorno*, sister. I have been sent by Mother Domenica with a message for Sister Bernadetta.'

'Oh.' She blinked slowly, like a cat waking up. 'I was at prayer.'

'I'm sorry to disturb your prayers, sister, but it's urgent that I speak with Sister Bernadetta.'

The timid eyes became more fearful. 'You can give me the message. I'll pass it on to her.'

'No, I'm sorry but Mother Domenica made me promise to deliver it myself.' Isabella shook her head, as if disappointed in the young nun. 'We wouldn't want to disobey the Reverend Mother, would we?'

The thick eyebrows behind the grille shot up. 'No.'

'Good. So please let me in.' Isabella smiled encouragingly.

'The Reverend Mother ordered me not to open the door to anyone while she was away.'

'She meant to strangers. I am not a stranger to her, I promise you.'

'But you are a stranger to me, so . . . ' The hatch started to close.

'Very well, sister. I shall go back and report your action to Mother Domenica immediately.' She started to march back down the path, cursing the limp which diminished the effect.

'No, wait.'

A key turned in the lock and a bolt shot back, allowing the heavy oak door to open.

'You'd better come in.'

★ ★ ★

The convent was cool. But its corridors were elegant with speckled marble tiles on the floors and high ceilings where there was room for spirits to whisper and prayers to accumulate. The young novice glided ahead of Isabella and stopped at an arched door of exquisitely grained walnut that bore a wooden tablet with the word REFECTORY carved into it.

225

'She's in here,' the nun informed Isabella. 'I'll let you go in on your own.' She scurried away, eager to be gone, black shoes tapping on the floor as she fled back to her prayers.

Isabella knocked on the door. No answer. She let a minute tick past then knocked again.

'Rosa, are you there?'

No answer.

After her third knock remained unanswered, she called again. 'Rosa?'

A faint sound seeped under the door, unmistakably a child's voice. It lay between Isabella and the door and she stepped over it without hesitation to swing the door open.

★ ★ ★

Rosa saw the door leap wide and the architect step into the room, up on her toes and hands out in front of her as if expecting a fight. Rosa felt a greyness ripple through her mind, fogging her thoughts because suddenly she realised there *was* a God. She had prayed. Hour after hour. And this time He had answered her prayers. Like Daniel in the lions' den, she was delivered. Happiness flowed out of her in the tears that poured down her cheeks.

Thank you, God. *Grazie, grazie, Dio.*

She never cried. Never whimpered. However hard the nuns smacked her knuckles with their rulers. But here, in front of the architect, all those unshed tears came at once.

'Rosa!'

Isabella Berotti hurried across the room. She

was wearing dark colours, a coat and headscarf, the same as Rosa's mother always did, but there the similarity ended, because Mamma never wore an expression on her face that came even close to the concern on the architect's. But she halted abruptly halfway across the room and Rosa heard her intake of breath, as loud as the wind in the chimney. She was staring, blue eyes frozen wide, at the other figure in the room.

Rosa and Sister Bernadetta were seated at opposite ends of a long refectory table with nothing but emptiness between them, an emptiness so solid that Sister Bernadetta had rested her head on it. The nun was young with a soft unhealthy sheen to her skin. She lay slumped forward with her cheek on the oak surface, her wire spectacles crooked on her nose and a little puddle of spittle gathering under her crumpled mouth. She was snoring loudly.

'She's drunk,' Rosa whispered.

On its side lay an empty wine bottle and the smell of it leaked into the room.

Suddenly the architect came close and her hand shot out towards Rosa's face. Instinctively Rosa flinched, ready for the slap that would knock her head back, but instead the fingers wiped the tears from her cheeks. She had forgotten she was crying, forgotten what it was like not to be slapped for no reason, forgotten most of all what it was like to be touched with affection and kindness. Something melted inside her. She didn't know what it was but it was running thick and sweet in her veins. She started to tremble and couldn't make it stop.

'Rosa, don't be frightened,' Isabella Berotti said firmly, as if the motionless figure at the other end of the table were nothing more than a scarecrow.

Her arms wrapped around Rosa who caught the scent of the outdoors on her skin and could smell sunshine in her hair where it had unravelled from the scarf. It's what her father always smelled of when he twirled her high in the air as if she were as weightless as a feather. That and black tobacco. Mamma had forever smelled of the bitter lemons she squeezed into hot water at breakfast.

'Come, let's leave here,' Isabella Berotti announced.

'I can't.'

'Don't be frightened, little one. I won't let any of them harm you or — '

'No. I can't.'

Rosa pointed to her foot. It was chained to the table leg. The architect's face didn't alter. Yet in some invisible way it did. It was as if a light had been turned off inside her.

'Good God,' she hissed, 'you are not a dog.'

Shame swamped Rosa and her cheeks burned. She had not thought of it like that.

'Where's the key, Rosa?'

'There.' She pointed.

It hung on a leather thong looped loosely around Sister Bernadetta's pale wrist that lay motionless on the table. At once Isabella Berotti moved down to the other end of the refectory table, her feet swift and silent on the wooden boards. She paused beside Sister Bernadetta, staring down at the key and at the nun's limp hand, and in that moment Rosa forgot how to breathe.

Don't.

Please don't.

Sister Bernadetta will wake. She will snatch away the key and she will flee to the chapel with it as an offering to God in penance for her sins. I will be chained here for ever.

Don't.

Or they will lock me in the —

Her mind froze as the architect's fingers reached out and hovered no more than a hair's breadth from the key. Her eyes flicked for a second to Rosa and there was no fear in her clear blue gaze. Only determination. Rosa shook her head violently.

Don't. She mouthed the word.

But the architect hooked a finger around the leather thong on the pale wrist and, working slowly and smoothly, she started to ease it over the sturdy bones of the nun's hand. Rosa watched, unable to look away. She didn't dare blink or breathe or believe it could be done, and when Sister Bernadetta suddenly moaned and curled her hands around her head as though warding off some imaginary blow, a silvery string of saliva stretched from Rosa's lips and she was convinced the end had come. If she'd had anything in her stomach, she would have vomited it up right there on the table.

But no.

Sister Bernadetta slept on. Her eyelids fluttered, nothing more, and the architect's finger remained hooked around the leather strap. She didn't let it escape. She kept her eyes on the nun's slack features as a barrage of snores started up again. With a steady hand Isabella Berotti edged the leather strap over the knuckles and very gently she lifted the nun's hand the merest fraction off the table, just enough to allow the thong to slide underneath it.

Abruptly the key was free.

Rosa started to breathe again. Isabella immediately tiptoed back, a smile on her face, and crouched beside Rosa's foot. But the smile turned to a frown as she turned the key, unravelled the chain from around her ankle and saw the blood glistening on the metal. Rosa took no notice of it. Her heart was hammering as she let her hand rest as light as a raindrop on the back of her rescuer, on the dark warm wool of her coat. Isabella looked up at Rosa and gave her a smile that wasn't really a smile. Was she angry? Had that touch broken some unspoken rule?

Panic rolled like a wave through her mind. But she jumped to her feet and obediently followed Isabella Berotti out of the room. Like a dog.

★ ★ ★

Isabella had never owned a pet. No cat, no dog, no bird in a cage. She had never loved something small and defenceless. Only her unborn child. So she didn't know which words to say, what tone of voice to use, how much to ask, which things to leave unsaid. What would hurt? What wouldn't. She wanted to run her hands over Rosa, inside

230

and out, to seek out the pain. Then she'd know. She'd know what to do and say to help this girl. She'd know what to touch and what to leave alone.

She took hold of Rosa's small hand. She knew from Roberto's photographs that the front door of the convent was kept locked and bolted, so using the mental map that his pictures had provided, she navigated her way to the convent kitchen and from there to a storeroom with a side door, which was left unlocked for deliveries, to the courtyard outside. She led Rosa to an area behind the chapel where a patch of land had been dug over and planted with winter vegetables; the odour of its loamy black soil hung ripe and musty in the fresh autumn air.

Only then did she allow herself to pause for breath. Beside her the small pointed face looked pale and uncertain under the brutally cropped fuzz of black curls.

'Why did they cut your hair off?' Isabella asked gently.

'I was bad.'

'Bad? No, Rosa, no. It's Mother Domenica who is behaving badly.'

What kind of person would do such a thing to a child?

Rosa's fingers clung fiercely to Isabella's but she wasn't crying any more. Isabella abandoned words, in case they were the wrong ones, and she drew the girl over to a long stone shed where it was clear that garden equipment was stored. A wooden ladder was propped inside against its dusty window, just as Roberto's photograph had shown. At least she could do something right and get Rosa out of here.

Around the convent rose a four metre wall. Isabella hoped the ladder was long enough to reach, but if not, she was sure Rosa would be good at scrabbling to the top. She had that look about her, with thin spidery arms and legs as if she had a long history of escaping through windows and clambering over walls. Isabella unbolted the shed door and yanked it open.

'Right, Rosa, let's get that ladder out.'

The child reacted as though Isabella had slapped her. She leapt backwards, snatching her hand from the one encircling hers, and stared at Isabella with wide shocked eyes.

'Why?'

'Why what?' Isabella asked.

'Why the ladder?'

'To get you out of here.'

The girl moved back the way they'd come. 'No.'

'Is it the ladder, the height of it? Is that what scares you?'

'No.'

'Once we get to the top, we can haul up the ladder and drop it down the other side. Rosa, I won't just abandon you on the street, I promise. I'll find you a good home away from Bellina.'

The child's eyes turned dull and flat, her cheeks more pinched. 'No.'

'But for now,' Isabella continued, 'you can stay

with me and my father. Until we sort out something permanent that you're happy with. My father is a doctor, so he knows more about . . . '

A tear slid on a solitary track down Rosa's pale cheek. 'No. I want to stay here.'

'What? Why would you want to remain in this . . . ?'

'Because my father will come for me here.'

Isabella didn't move. 'Rosa, why did you lie to me? Why tell me that he was dead?'

Just then a flock of birds cut through the clear blue sky above their heads and swept low over the amber roof of the convent, preparing to flee this place and head south for the winter. Rosa's troubled eyes tracked their flight as if yearning to follow.

'Rosa?' Isabella prompted.

The girl hung her head and yet her small chin set in a stubborn line.

'Rosa, why lie to *me*? To Chairman Grassi, I can understand. To Colonnello Sepe, yes, definitely. But why to me?'

Still no answer. Isabella stepped close to Rosa, conscious of the loneliness that the girl wore like a cloak, and said gently, 'Come and stay with me and we will find your papa.' She offered a smile. 'We can talk architecture and you can tell me to shut up when I go on about it too much because I — '

'He is a good man.'

Such adult words from such young lips.

'I'm sure he is, Rosa.' Their gaze met as the girl raised her head. 'Is he a fugitive?'

A nod.

'Did he commit a crime?'

'He hates Benito Mussolini.' Rosa spat expertly onto the raw earth at the mention of the name.

'Is that why Grassi keeps you here?'

'Yes. I am the bait.'

'All the more reason for you to come with me now. Quickly, let's get the ladder before anyone — '

The child's small hand seized Isabella's arm. 'Ask me, Signora Berotti, whatever is it you want to know. Then go.'

Isabella wanted to swallow the questions that crowded on her tongue and offer the child nothing more than a kiss on her cheek. But they forced their way out between her lips and refused to be silenced.

'You are right, Rosa, I do have questions. I want to know' — she was speaking fast because the words had waited for this moment too long to miss it — 'who killed my husband, Luigi Berotti, in Milan. Your mother mentioned him to me and said the Party knows who killed him. Why would she think that?'

'I don't know. She didn't tell me anything.'

'Did your papa know Luigi Berotti?'

'No.'

'Did your mamma know him?'

She saw Rosa tread carefully. 'No.'

There was a silence. Just the wind rustling between the tall chimneys. Neither spoke. Isabella ignored the lie and wrapped an arm around Rosa's paper-thin shoulders, drawing her close. 'Oh, Rosa,' she said and held her tight. She kissed the top of her head. They stayed like that, locked together for a long time, until the other novice nun in white came and found them. She led the child away.

20

Roberto was nowhere to be found. The parade was over and the crowds had dispersed by the time Isabella returned to the centre of town. The green and white flags fluttered everywhere, draped from windows in a riot of patriotic fervour, and only in one back street did she find the bunting shredded in the gutter like yesterday's newspaper. Someone would be made to pay for it.

It was Friday but the day had been declared a public holiday for most, so that as Mussolini toured the construction sites, the pumping stations, the flour mill and the great canal that bore his name, there would be no shortage of the populace to cheer and salute the arrival of their glorious leader. But Isabella did not feel herself part of that populace, not after what she'd seen today. She needed to work.

It was her opiate of choice. Not morphine. Not cocaine. Not alcohol or tobacco. But work. It was what she reached for when the pain grew too much. That's why this project was perfect for her because the architectural office was open all hours of the day and night, as they fought to meet deadlines, and when she was feeling bad she had been known to work seventy-two hours straight without a break.

A workhorse, her father called her. A stubborn workhorse.

Isabella thought of Roberto and the way his hands had caressed and soothed the muscular flanks of the workhorse at the station. The way he had whispered in its ear.

A workhorse. She could live with that. What she couldn't live with was Rosa in that convent.

⋆　⋆　⋆

Isabella had learned to blank out voices. Like she blanked out faces. When she was working she saw no one, heard nothing, spoke to no colleagues. If they thought her unsociable, that was their problem, not hers, because she enjoyed losing herself in her drawing and measuring, sliding her rule up the board in a smooth and satisfying ritual, shutting out the world. Existence was reduced to black lines on tracing paper and if she didn't like what she'd done one day, she could tear it up the next and no one was offended. No one was hurt.

When she recalled the formal distant look in Roberto's grey eyes this morning and the trembling mouth of Rosa as she sat chained to a chair, she would have given one of her fingers to be able to tear up today.

'*Pronto*, Isabella, *pronto*! Didn't you hear?'

Isabella looked up from her drawing board. Around her, people were fussing and talking excitedly. But then it took very little to get an Italian man excited. Arms were waved and voices raised.

'What is it?' she asked around the pencil between her teeth, only half listening.

'Didn't you hear the message from Dottore Martino?'

Instantly she was alert. 'No. What message?'

'Il Duce himself is on his way here.'

'Here? To this building?'

'To this office.' The draftsman was grinning ear to ear. 'Holy Mother of God, this is our lucky day.'

Lucky day?

That was not how it felt to Isabella.

★　★　★

'So,' Mussolini's arrogant voice boomed out of his broad barrel chest, 'this is where the real work of Bellina is done.'

He strutted into the spacious architectural office as if the air itself belonged to him. His proud chest entered the room first, followed by his heavy chin and jowls which were thrust forward to carve out a destiny for Italy. He was wearing a dark military uniform with a flash of medals and knee-high black boots that gleamed like polished metal and seemed to stride with a willpower of their own.

'Show me,' he declared, 'what goes on here, Martino.'

Only Mussolini could reduce the great Dottore Architetto Martino to a mere 'Martino'. Immediately he was escorted around the office while every worker in the room stood beside his drawing board with teeth chattering. He peered at a few of the designs, commented on some, ignored others and the air seemed to grow

238

brighter in whatever part of the room he was standing.

He didn't need to speak. His presence was enough. It made every other person seem bland, colourless and utterly insignificant in comparison. Isabella could *not* look away. Her gaze, along with everyone else's, was fixed on the figure of Il Duce with his powerful domed forehead, and for the first time she understood how he had come to power in 1922 as the youngest prime minister in Italy's history. That was before he became greedy and banished all opposition parties. He'd declared himself dictator — Il Duce — his hands dripping with blood, and suppressed civil liberties with ruthless determination. She knew all this, knew the cost that Italy was paying, yet still the excitement he brought into the room set her pulse racing.

He prowled the room the way a lion prowls its territory, owning it, placing his mark on it, and Isabella thought he had not noticed her. But when Dottore Martino was in the middle of explaining the intricacies of the grand drawing for a new hotel, Mussolini stretched out a muscular arm and pointed across the room.

'Who,' he demanded, 'is that in the corner?'

Without waiting for a reply he strode over to where Isabella stood next to her board. She felt her mouth go dry and wished she was wearing her vivid green dress instead of the drab brown skirt and high-necked blouse that was her usual fare at work to discourage wandering hands.

'Who are you?' the head of all Italy asked her.

'Isabella Berotti.'

'And what are you doing here?'

'I work here, Duce. I am an architect.'

He gave a bark of laughter so loud it made her jump. 'Go home and make babies for your country, Isabella Berotti. Leave this work to men.'

She could have slapped his face right there. The urge to do so raged through her and she clamped her hands together to prevent them breaking loose. She cursed herself for the colour that flooded her cheeks and let everyone see her outraged soul.

'I am a qualified architect, Duce. I worked hard to become one and am as good at the job as any man here. Ask Dottore Architetto Martino.'

Dottore Martino started to say something but was silenced by an abrupt wave of his leader's hand.

'That is impossible,' Il Duce declared. 'Go home to your husband, signora, where you belong, and make fine Italian babies to swell our workforce.'

She could have smiled submissively and said, 'Yes, Duce', because that was all that he wanted to hear. She could have lowered her eyes demurely in front of the most powerful man in Italy and maybe then she would have kept her job. But instead she looked directly into his domineering black eyes and spoke the truth.

'I cannot have children, Duce. My husband was shot dead after he took part in your March on Rome and I was wounded. If he hadn't marched beside you in 1922, he would still be my husband and I would have a house full of *bambini*. But instead I serve my country by creating beautiful buildings for the workers of Italy to live in. It is not impossible, Duce, for a woman to have a good brain.'

Silence took root in the room. No one spoke. No one breathed. A few mouths risked curving into a smile in anticipation of the outcome. Dottore Martino's cheeks drained of colour and Isabella realised he was seeing his own imminent dismissal in disgrace for hiring her.

'What was your husband's name?' Mussolini demanded.

'Luigi Berotti.'

'Ah, I remember him. He was one of my 'flying wedge' team in the early days. A good and loyal man.'

'Yes, Duce.'

He laughed good-naturedly and throughout the room great gulps of air could be heard being dragged into lungs, and Dottore Martino's heart started to beat again.

'So what was he doing,' Mussolini continued, 'a good Fascisti boy like Luigi, marrying a girl who thinks she can do a man's job?'

This time Isabella clamped her teeth on her tongue and smiled mutely.

Mussolini laughed uproariously, pleased with his victory, and all around her Isabella heard the sounds of male amusement. Il Duce placed a heavy hand on her shoulder, as though adding her to his possessions, and his forefinger lightly stroked the side of her neck.

'Are you one of my good Fascisti too, Isabella?'

'Yes, Duce.'

'Well said. Be disciplined, Isabella. Discipline and hard work are the linchpins of our country's economic recovery. I *will* make it happen.' He turned to the eager faces of the men at their drawing boards. 'Discipline! Hard work! This is our constructive force, is it not, signori?'

'Bravo! Bravo!'

The shouts came on cue and the applause seemed spontaneous. Immediately Mussolini lost interest in Isabella and released his grip on her. Around him arms were raised in the Fascist salute. He gazed with solemn satisfaction at the mesmerised audience, then accepted the salute, jabbing his arm upwards and backwards, before striding from the room without a word.

But the image of his uncompromising black stare remained behind. Watching over each one of them.

* * *

'Signora Berotti.'

'Yes, dottore?'

Dottore Martino caught her as she emerged from the washroom and his expression was tight, his spectacles like flat sheets of ice.

'In my office. Now.'

'Yes, dottore.'

She followed him into his office and he closed the door firmly behind her. Isabella braced herself. She knew what was coming. Had been expecting it. You don't turn Dottore Architetto Martino's cheeks chalk-white without receiving a reprimand and he was known for requiring a high degree of obedience and loyalty at all times. One of the older architects had been suspended from work for a month for complaining to a junior that the tracing paper supplied was poor quality. The junior had received a promotion. That's how things worked here. If you had any sense, you kept your mouth shut.

Why hadn't she kept her mouth shut?

'Signora Berotti, you have let me down.'

Martino placed himself behind his desk, as far from her as he could. His office was plain and functional. No frills. Architectural drawings pinned to the wall, a schedule plan on a blackboard, two drawing boards, and dominating the room was a display of miniature architectural models depicting the whole town built to scale on a table that occupied half the room. His desk was as orderly as the man himself.

'I apologise, dottore.'

'You don't answer back to Mussolini, you foolish girl. Don't you know that? Are you stupid? *Dio dannato*! Do I have to teach you every-thing?' His hand slammed down on the desk.

'Dottore, I did not mean to make trouble, but what he said was wrong.'

'Dear God, listen to the girl. Since when is it your job to decide on whether what Il Duce says is right or wrong?'

'Surely it is the job of all of us Italians.'

'No! No! It is not. You are here to design and draw buildings. Nothing more. Do you hear me?'

'Yes, dottore.'

243

'I don't want to know your thoughts on anything else. You are a woman.' His eyes blazed with anger behind his spectacles. 'I took you on. I trusted you. And this . . . ' his fist slammed again on the desk, 'is how you repay me. Mussolini could have taken my job from me for hiring such a . . . ' He pulled himself up short and wiped a hand across his mouth. 'You are a woman,' he growled, 'I should have known better.'

Every voice in her head urged her to protest, to say that she was no less a person because she was a woman, but she forced down her howls of rage and focused on one of the drawings pinned to the wall. It was one of hers.

'Thank you for employing me, dottore.' She gestured towards the drawing. 'I hope you have been satisfied with my work.'

She knew this was the end. She stood there, mortified, and waited for the inevitable. He was going to sack her from her job. She was about to lose everything she'd worked day and night for. On one man's passing whim.

'Your work is excellent, damn it,' Martino snapped. He drew in a slow breath and struggled to calm himself. 'Signora, there is to be a celebration party tonight for the great honour of having Mussolini staying in our town. It is to be held at seven thirty at the Constantine Hotel. Be there. Il Duce has requested your presence. Your escort will be Signor Francolini.' He stared at her with a look of disgust. 'It seems that you have pleased our leader.'

Her jaw dropped open and hope squirmed

into life, hot and painful at the base of her stomach.

'Now get out of here,' Martino ordered.

'Yes, dottore.'

He didn't look at her. He looked at the door. 'When you come in tomorrow morning, I want you to collect your belongings and your pay, and leave.'

Isabella froze.

'You're fired, Signora Berotti.'

★ ★ ★

'I don't like it, Isabella.'

'Papa, I have no choice. I have been ordered to attend.'

'You could refuse. You have no job to lose.'

'But Dottore Martino has. I couldn't do that to him.'

Her father was pacing the room, touching each piece of dark furniture as he passed it, seeking comfort from his dead wife who had spent years polishing it, as if he could find her fingerprints still there.

'Martino has forfeited any right to your loyalty, *cara mia*. You owe him nothing.'

'That's not true. I owe him much.'

Isabella walked over to the cabinet in the corner, poured them both a glass of red wine and handed one to her father. 'Don't fret so, Papa. Nothing will happen.'

It was the wrong thing to say. Her father's face crumpled in despair. 'Of course something will happen. Everyone knows that Benito Mussolini cannot keep his hands off a pretty woman. You're not fool enough to think he invited you to the party because he appreciates the finer points of your architecture, are you?' He knocked back his wine and hurled the empty glass at the door where it shattered into a thousand pieces that flew through the air in a rainbow of fear.

'Papa, look at me.'

He dragged his eyes heavily up from the glittering fragments on the floor and looked at her. Sorrowfully at first but then with sudden alertness. He almost smiled.

'You see, Papa. Who would want me? I am wearing my widow's weeds. Remember this dress? I wore it for five years after Luigi died. It smells of death.'

The dress was black and old, with full sleeves, a high collar and a long row of jet beads that fastened down the front. Her hair was raked back severely from her face and gathered in a black lace net at the back of her head.

Her father nodded. 'I remember it.'

'No jewellery. No painted nails. No lipstick. Mussolini won't even look at me twice.' She chuckled at her father to show how groundless his fears were. 'I'll just stand in a corner all evening and then come home.'

'I'll pick you up from the Constantine Hotel at ten o'clock sharp.'

'You certainly will not, Papa. Dottore Martino has arranged a car. I'm not a child, I am a grown woman and I don't need my father to — '

He strode over, crunching the slivers of glass underfoot, and embraced her fiercely, spilling a splash of her wine on her dress. She was unused to such displays of affection from him and she was deeply touched by it.

'You need your father to look after you,' he insisted, his voice thick. When he eventually released her, he was calmer. 'Who is this Signor Francolini anyway?'

'Just a colleague. No one special.'

'Tell him I will flay the skin off him strip by strip if he dare let anything happen to my daughter.'

'I'll tell him that.'

'Don't take it so lightly, Isabella. Il Duce is twenty years older than you and wants — '

'Papa, I am in mourning for my career. I will stink of decay and despair. No man will touch me because they will be afraid of catching whatever contamination I'm carrying.' She drank down her wine and let none of the tremors that were churning their way through her show in her hand. 'Now let me get this mess cleared up.'

But her father took hold of her upper arm, anchoring her to him, and gripped so tight that it hurt. 'Don't be so sure, Isabella. Why would a man bother to look at your drab clothes when he can look at your beautiful face?'

21

A corsage. An exquisite orchid. The translucent colour of a full moon, pale and silvery. That's what Davide Francolini pinned on Isabella. So what was the point of the sombre dress if he transformed it into a velvet night sky with his gift of a sublime flower? She didn't thank him for it but couldn't bring herself to reject it.

'Tonight is a business arrangement,' she pointed out.

'Of course.'

He smiled at her, his honey-coloured eyes amused by the boundaries she was laying down, but he passed no comment on her appearance and led her towards the ballroom of the hotel with a gentlemanly courtesy that she had to admit was appealing.

'You received my note?' she asked.

'I did indeed. There was no need for it.'

'Certainly there was. I wanted to thank you.'

She had not seen hide nor hair of him since Chairman Grassi's office. She'd wanted to thank him for his help that day but it was almost as if he didn't want to be seen talking with her, so she had not intruded and had left a note for him with Grassi's secretary instead.

'Did the meeting turn out as you'd hoped?'

'Not exactly.'

She gave a small shrug as though it were unimportant. That was one of the perils of living under a Fascist regime, you never knew whom you could trust. But he had risked Grassi's displeasure for her and for that she was grateful. She would have liked to ask why, why he had stuck his neck out, but you didn't ask such questions. In case the answers were too dangerous to know.

She caught his shrewd gaze, so as they entered the ballroom she slid her arm through his and he laughed, pleasantly surprised. Davide Francolini looked good in an evening suit. He possessed the slim build and narrow hips that could wear it effortlessly and look graceful as he escorted her into the crowded room. She was nervous. If Mussolini did turn his greedy eyes her way, she didn't want him to assume she was easy game.

'This isn't my favourite kind of event, Signora Berotti,' Francolini commented, 'but let's do Dottore Architetto Martino proud. You never know, he might even grant us the weekend off, if we're lucky.'

He had no idea that she'd been fired.

She wanted to shout at him. At Martino. At Mussolini. Shout that it was all wrong. Unfair. Unjust. Shout and tear off her corsage. But she didn't let her smile slip even a millimetre and asked, 'What would you do with a weekend off?'

He didn't hesitate. 'That's easy. I'd head straight up into the mountains, where the air is free of this wretched building dust. There are tall green trees and dense undergrowth where wild boar hide, instead of this stark landscape of barren earth.' Suddenly he turned his head to her and drew her closer. 'You should come with me. I'll show you places that — '

Isabella was smiling up at him, astonished by this intimate invitation, when a flashbulb exploded in their faces and she blinked, blinded for a moment. But even in that second of blindness her heart turned over because she knew exactly who would have pressed the trigger on the flash.

Roberto was standing there, unsmiling, wielding his camera. Isabella wanted to snatch her hand from where it lay on Davide Francolini's arm, but he had wrapped his own around it and was holding it in place. She wanted to step forward to touch Roberto's lips and tilt their corners into a smile. To laugh with him at the way his broad shoulders sat uneasily in his black dinner jacket which was too stiff for a man who liked to move freely. She wanted to tell him she had searched for him. Banged on his green front door. But all she'd found was the woman in the red dress prowling his street.

Where were you, Roberto? Tell me.

'Good evening, Signor Falco.' She gave him a wide smile to show she was pleased to see him. 'You've been busy today.'

'I'll be busy tonight as well.'

He didn't step out of their path the way a photographer should. 'I hope you also had a busy day that was successful.'

'Thank you. I did.'

He nodded, his gaze intent on hers. 'Enjoy your evening, signora.'

So polite. But there was something in his eyes, dark and angry, and she didn't know if it was

250

meant for her or for Grassi or for the evening's event itself.

'I'd like a word with you later, if you have a moment,' she said pleasantly.

'Of course, Signora Berotti.'

Briefly his eyes skimmed over Francolini, but others were arriving behind them. Roberto stepped aside. Isabella walked past him, her shoulder almost touching him, but his attention was already on his camera and the next guests.

★ ★ ★

'Dance?'

'No, thank you, Davide. I don't.' She gestured to her foot.

'Of course. I'm sorry.'

'No need to be sorry. It gives me an excuse to avoid the crush on the dance floor and,' she laughed to cover his moment of awkwardness, 'to watch others making a fool of themselves up there.'

'Is that what you think the dancers do?'

'Make fools of themselves?'

'Yes.'

'Of course they do. Half of them are like elephants on the floor and the other half can't keep their hands off each other.'

Davide Francolini regarded her with amusement. 'No cynicism then?'

Isabella laughed. 'None at all.'

She sipped her glass of prosecco spumante. It was her third. If she had just one more she reckoned the pain would stop. They were seated at a round table for ten people but the others were off on the dance floor. The ballroom was magnificent, Isabella had to admit that. It was a triumph of modernist design and a bottomless purse. The walls were an exquisite array of handsome white marble from Calacatta with dramatic grey veining, inlaid with black obsidian in bold geometric stripes. At one end a mural had been painted in angular cubist style depicting a group of Maremmana cattle being herded by men on horseback across the freshly drained grassland and in the background Isabella's own tower soared up towards the sky, pure virgin white.

Over the rim of her glass Isabella stared at the dancers in their finery. Diamonds flashed in the brilliant lights of the chandeliers and beaded gowns shimmered and rippled like sunlight on water. She used to love to dance. She and Luigi used to dance anywhere that there was music — in bars, on table tops, at weddings, even once at a funeral. But not now. The idea appalled her. She was a donkey now and had to stick to what donkeys are good at — work. Leave the dancing to the high-stepping ponies. But it made the soles of her feet itch, just to watch.

She finished her drink and turned to face Davide instead. He was smoking a small cigar, his expression sombre, as though his thoughts were far away. She couldn't see Roberto in the crowd but knew he must be somewhere in the room because every now and again she saw a camera flash light up a table.

'Did you fix the crack in the apartment in Via

252

Corelli?' she asked David suddenly.

'Yes, I did.'

'Were you able to discover why it occurred?'

'Poor plaster.'

'Oh.'

'It looks good as new now.'

'Are you sure?'

'Yes, I'm sure.' He patted her wrist. Nothing much, nothing for her to object to. A brief touch of skin. 'Don't worry.'

But she did worry. It could be poor plaster. Or bad brickwork or sandy cement underneath. Or worse. Far worse. Bad foundations. She had to trust him.

'I'll keep an eye on it,' she commented.

'No need. It's been repaired.'

She nodded. 'Good.' There was a pause, its awkwardness hidden by the sound of the band striking up 'Vicni sul Mar'. Isabella placed her glass down on the table and said self-consciously, 'I was grateful for your help. If ever I can repay the favour, just ask.'

He smiled slowly, in no hurry, and stubbed out his cigar. 'Thank you, Isabella. I will remember that.' There was a burst of laughter from the next table and he waited for it to subside before he pushed back a lock of his soft brown hair and said casually, 'Maybe we could drive up into the mountains one Sunday.'

But before Isabella could reply, a man in elaborate uniform suddenly materialised at her elbow. A tightness crept up her throat.

'Signora Berotti, Il Duce requests the pleasure of your company at his table.'

'You will dance with me,' Mussolini announced as soon as Isabella sat down in the chair next to his.

He was looking resplendent in a glaringly white uniform adorned with sash and medals. Like a Roman caesar, she thought, uncompromising in the force of his personality which again condemned the rest of his table companions to the shade. Chairman Grassi was there she noticed and, to her horror, Colonnello Sepe was seated immediately on her right, but it was the three women who stared hard at her, their eyes cold and bright behind their smiles. She was an interloper. Usurping the attention from them during their one moment in the sun.

'I don't dance, Duce,' she said quietly.

If she made no sound, no amusing chatter, he would grow bored and discard her in favour of one of the glamorous females panting to sink their painted nails in his back.

'Why not?' he demanded. 'Every Italian should dance.'

'Because I am lame.' His black eyes widened dramatically. 'I was wounded and I limp,' she elaborated. Very nearly added *And I have leprosy*, but decided even he wouldn't swallow that one.

'Ah yes.' He leaned close to her, eyes scouring hers, his breath sickly with the stink of brandy. 'You were Luigi Berotti's wife.'

'The day my husband was shot in Milan, I was shot too. I don't know who the murderer was. Neither do the police, it seems.'

He slid an arm along the back of her chair, coiling it around her shoulders, and let his scowl slide past her to Colonnello Sepe.

'Is that true, Sepe?'

'I know none of the details, Duce. It was the Milan police who dealt with the case.'

A roar of displeasure bellowed in Isabella's ear. 'Luigi Berotti was one of my loyal Fascisti and deserves better than this.' His eyes flicked hungrily over Isabella and she looked away in time to see the other women at the table lick their lips. 'His wife deserves better than this.'

'Yes, Duce.'

'Then we must give her better.' As quickly as it came the dark pall of anger vanished, and just as a tenor launched himself into the anguished '*Dicitencello Vuie*' song on stage, Mussolini's voice softened to a purr. 'You see, little one, I, Benito Mussolini, care about each and every one of my faithful followers.'

Isabella's breathing grew shallow. 'Duce, my husband fought hard for the Fascist cause and the imprint he made on my own life is still there. He was a warrior. If you can discover who cut off his young life, please tell me.' Seconds slid by in a noisy silence between them. 'Please,' she said again.

Mussolini leaned his bulky frame back in his chair, the glare of the chandeliers rebounding off his gleaming scalp like darts of lightning as he quietly contemplated her for a full minute. She didn't like the shrewdness of his narrowed eyes or his awareness of her need. This man was good at wrapping his fist around a person's naked soul.

'My dear Isabella,' he said without lowering his voice a jot, 'I can remove that beautiful orchid of yours if you think it will make you less noticeable. That's what you want, isn't it?'

Sepe at her shoulder uttered a snort of scorn but she didn't look round, didn't risk dropping her eyes from Il Duce's.

'That's why you're wearing those hideous clothes, I assume,' he continued. 'Isn't it?'

'Yes, Duce, it is. I want people to respect the memory of my husband.'

He released a bark of laughter and her entire body jumped when he rested his hand on hers. For ten seconds she stared at it, then took her hand away. She realised she didn't know what to say to him or how to act, if she was to drag out of him what she wanted to hear. He reached forward and unpinned the orchid, his fingers fumbling with the material of her dress, his wrists brushed against her breast. She knew this man believed he was beyond all rules.

He tossed the bruised bloom on to the table and listened for a nostalgic moment with his head on one side to the final verse of 'Dicitencello Vuie':

I want you so much, I want you so very
    much,
This bond between us will nevcr break!

'Now,' he touched a finger to her hot cheek, 'signora, let us go somewhere quiet and private to discuss the killer you seek.'

22

It was like being in a cage with a lion. Nothing less. He didn't need to roar or snarl. Just his presence was danger enough. He prowled around her where she stood in the centre of the small smoking room, an immense portrait of himself looking dynamic on horseback looming over her in case she managed to forget the power of her Duce. It was that power she wanted now. To work for her. Not against. A power that could drain marshes that defeated even Napoleon, the power of a man who didn't recognise the word 'no'.

Isabella spoke first, briskly and in a strictly businesslike tone. 'My husband, Luigi, marched on Rome with you in October 1922. He was helping you establish the foundations that became the Fascist government and he died for it. He was shot by someone in Milan the next day, someone who also crippled me, though I was not involved in the march in any way. I am asking you for justice, Duce. It is only justice that you should find out who the killer was. I was told by someone who is now dead that the Fascist Party knows who the killer is.' She drew a deep breath. 'He may be a Socialist or a Communist. Or any one of the enemies of the Fascisti.'

He circled her. A flash of white in front and then behind her, unnerving her. Shoulders back, chest out, and always that cynical expression that came naturally to his face. She had a sense of an arrogant man who despised and manipulated people, who sought out their weaknesses and was master of how to corrupt souls — even the pope's. She knew he had started out as a Socialist. At the age of twenty-nine he had been editor of the Socialist Party's daily paper, *Avanti*. But he'd turned on them in 1914 and was labelled Judas by the working classes because he had thrown in his lot with the middle-class youth.

He mobilised them. Energised them. Turned them into his 'flying wedge' and set them on the workers who were rebelling against bad working conditions and subsistence wages. His National Fascist Party spilled blood ruthlessly in the streets and yes, Isabella was acutely aware that Luigi might well have deserved an enemy or two. At the time, wildly in love, she'd known nothing about what he did, entrenched in her youthful ignorance, but now she was wiser. Warier. She regarded the man in front of her as lethal. The beat of her heart was violent.

'What I want to know, Duce, is what went on during that October day ten years ago in the Fascist Year 1 of the New Era. What happened and why?' She stood straight as he circled her and she gave no hint of her fear. 'I need to know what you can do to help me.'

He halted abruptly in front of her. 'The bigger question, Signora Berotti, is what *you* can do for *me*?'

She pretended to misunderstand. 'I will do all

I can to make Bellina the finest town in all Italy, to the glory of Il Duce.'

His laugh was like a slap, harsh and scornful. 'Don't play games, *cara mia*, not with me.'

He reached behind her head and yanked off the lace net, so that her hair broke free and cascaded around her shoulders. Mussolini twisted a hank of its dark curls around his fist and pulled her face closer to his. He was no taller than she was, and up close she could see the bad state of his skin and the sensuous curve of his upper lip. His pupils were black and huge with desire. She made herself stop pulling away from him and let her body go soft, but before she could even draw breath his lips were on hers.

Greedy lips. Selfish. Demanding. Lips that gave nothing and took everything. She crushed her urge to bite through one of them and suffered in silence the brandy-slickness of them devouring her own. His hands fumbled for the buttons at her neck and started to undo each one with impatience, a grumble sounding inside his chest when one resisted his fingers. His breath came hot and repellent on her cheek. She wanted to spit in his face. To lift her knee to ward off the press of his body, to rid herself of the smell of him, perfumed and cloying as it crawled up her nostrils.

When he reached the sixth button, that was enough. She pulled away from him but his hands still tugged at her drab dress, ripping off a button as he tried to haul her back.

'No,' she said sharply.

He kept one hand attached to the front of her

dress but stood still, breathing hard. His eyes narrowed to dark slits. 'What *stupid* game are you playing? With your ugly dress and your big sad blue eyes that make every man in the room want to give you something to smile about?'

Isabella shut her ears to his words. 'Tell me, Duce, when my Luigi was one of the *squadristi*, who was the head of his cohort?'

The *Fasci di Combattimenti*, the official term for the Blackshirts, made use of the structure of Ancient Rome for its military divisions rather than follow the ranks of the Italian army. The groups were termed cohorts.

'Why in the name of Christ Almighty would I remember a thing like that?'

'Because you are Benito Mussolini, *Comandante General* of the Blackshirts. Because you are known to be intelligent and to remember details that other men forget. So yes, I think you will remember; I am asking you for his name.'

He exhaled fiercely. He bunched the fist that had been mauling her buttons and for one sick moment Isabella believed he was going to knock her to the floor. Maybe he *was* intending to do that, but at the last second when the decision was balanced on a knife-edge, he thumped his fist against his thigh instead with a great bark of laughter.

'You bargain well, Isabella Berotti. I like your clever tongue, so I will admit you are right. I do remember things others forget and it serves me well. You want his name?'

'I do.'

He touched a finger to her lips and traced

their full outline. She didn't open her mouth and bite his finger off but she did raise her hand and remove it.

'So what is his name?'

'It is Pietro Luciani.'

'And where is he now?'

'In Rome. At the Ministry of the Interior.'

'*Grazie.*'

'Enough questions.'

She stepped back nimbly before he could wrap a possessive arm around her. Her pulse was pounding.

'Duce,' she said softly, 'leave me alone. I am honoured by your attention but you have fifty women out there who would gladly beg for your kisses. You don't need mine. In memory of my husband, out of respect for his death, let me walk out of here to — '

'Isabella!' His arm snapped out and encircled her waist. 'I don't want one of those fifty women, I want you.' He pulled her tight against him and she could feel the hardness of him in his white uniform, but she jabbed an elbow into his bulky ribs just as his lips sought her neck.

'No, don't . . . '

His heavy grip shifted to her throat, forcing back her head.

'You have your answers,' he said roughly.

'Duce, you and I want the same thing.'

He smiled, his black eyes triumphant, a sheen of sweat on his bald scalp, and started to ease the pressure of his fingers on her throat. She kept her eyes fixed on his, not letting her fear settle on her face.

'You and I both want this town constructed well and constructed fast. I am part of the team of architects.' She squeezed the words out past his fingers. 'They will not like it if they think I am being singled out for attention by our Duce. It will cause jealousies and disrupt the efficiency of — '

'That,' he said, dragging her face close to his by her neck, 'is not true. However' — abruptly he released her and she staggered, whooping air down her sore throat — 'I choose not to take the risk.' He jutted his broad chin at her with a sly smile on his lips. 'You would make a good politician. I like your cleverness, Signora Berotti. I'm sure Dottore Martino does too. I begin to see why he hired you.' He laughed, a dull anger hovering around his eyes like purple shadows. 'You've got what you came for.'

'And the business of my husband's death? I would be grateful if you would let me know what — '

'Enough! Your gratitude is worth nothing to me. Get out of here, girl.'

'Girl'. She had been demoted from Signora Berotti to 'girl'. She wanted to think he had a conscience about the death of the man he had captivated with his eloquence and indomitable will, she wanted to believe the shadows on his face were sorrow. But she wasn't fooled. Mussolini was a man without scruple. Or remorse.

She didn't wait there for an apology. She left the room in a hurry and only when she was outside in the marbled corridor did she see how

262

much she was shaking.

⋆ ⋆ ⋆

'Isabella?'

Isabella found Roberto. Or to be more accurate, he found her. In a place she never thought to see him. She had slipped quickly to the hotel's ladies' powder room to tidy herself and to avoid gossiping tongues and eyes that would cast sideways glances at her and her buttons. She knew what she had done. She knew her lips were soured and her skin dirtied, but there was no need for others to know. Especially Roberto.

She scoured her hands and her face, washed her lips and even her teeth and tongue with scalding water. But the sourness wouldn't wash off. The dirt remained, sticking to her worse than a plague of leeches. She did up her dress buttons, ignoring the one that was missing, and plaited her hair in a thick braid that hung down her back. Maybe people wouldn't remember the lace hairnet. *Maybe*. Maybe they wouldn't remember that she used to be clean.

She refused to look in the mirror. Couldn't bear to see the person who might look out at her. Instead she turned her back on it and locked herself in one of the cubicles, leaning against the wall with her eyes closed. But on the inside of her eyelids the images crawled — of arrogant greedy hands and a mouth that would devour her, teeth that would crunch on her bones. *Big sad blue eyes*, that's what Il Duce had said, but whose eyes in Italy were not sad now?

'Isabella?'

Roberto's voice. His fist banged on the cubicle door. 'Are you in there?'

Isabella flexed her fingers to make sure they were no longer trembling and unlocked the door.

'Isabella, are you all right?'

He stood in front of her, incongruous in his dark masculine jacket in the powder-puff pink room, his heavy brows drawn together. She wanted to touch the cleanness of him.

'Of course I'm all right,' she said and gave a smile. It was meant to be a smile but by the look of his face maybe it didn't come out right.

'Isabella.' This time he said her name in a soft crooning voice that made her want to cry. 'Was it worth it?'

'I don't know what you mean.'

'I mean . . . ' But he stopped and stared at her neck. An angry flush seeped up into his cheeks.

For the first time she looked in the mirror above the washbasins and the face framed within it made her shudder. She saw wide blue eyes that were flat and secretive under thick black lashes, and skin that was bone white. Stiff and frozen. *That's not me*, she wanted to say, *those aren't my eyes, Roberto. The mirror is lying*. Then she noticed the marks on this other person's long neck, a purple discolouration each side of her throat. She lifted a finger to them in disbelief. They were hot. Pulsing. She covered them with her hand and the stranger in the mirror did the same.

Before she could speak, Roberto stepped forward and folded her into his arms, and the warmth of them sent a tremor escaping from her chill bones. She buried her face into the lapel of his jacket and breathed in the mothball smell of it.

'I'm all right,' she mumbled.

'I know.' He kissed her hair, not once but twice. 'I know.'

And that was when she pressed her forehead hard against his chest, so hard it hurt, and said, 'I've lost my job.'

* ★ *

He drove her home in his Fiat, his wool scarf wrapped tight around her neck. She told him about Rosa at the convent and about Mussolini's visit to her office, but she made no mention of what went on with Mussolini in the smoking room. Roberto didn't question her except to ask who her escort was.

'That was Davide Francolini, a colleague. We were both ordered to attend by Dottore Martino. Nothing more.' She wanted him to be clear on that. *Nothing more.*

She had returned to her table just to say a polite goodbye to Davide and found him deep in conversation with Grassi who had regarded her with suspicion.

'I trust you enjoyed your evening, signora.' His mouth narrowed into a thin line. 'Did you get what you wanted?'

'What I want is information, Chairman Grassi,

as you well know. Il Duce himself said it is what I deserve.'

He had inspected her coldly. 'Signora, I'm sure Il Duce gave you exactly what you deserve.'

'Grassi, no need for that.' Davide Francolini bristled with annoyance and rose to his feet. 'Let me escort you home, Isabella.'

'Thank you, but no, I have a car waiting for me.' She'd smiled gratefully but did not risk looking again at Grassi in case she caused another scene and got herself fired a second time by Martino.

Roberto parked the car outside her apartment block and shut off the engine but neither of them made any move to climb out. Moonlight etched a silver filigree on the tall iron gates that let into the courtyard but didn't quite find its way inside the car. Isabella liked it that way; she didn't want Roberto seeing that thin woman in the mirror with the haunted eyes.

'So,' Roberto swivelled in the driving seat so that he was facing her in the darkness, 'you've had an eventful day.'

The simplicity of the comment made her laugh. It came from a place that felt dry and empty. 'That's true.'

'I'm sorry about your job, Isabella.'

'I'll find another one.'

'Not like this one.'

'No. You're right. Not like this one. It is a unique project to work on and I've been honoured to do so, though at the moment I'm worried that something is going wrong.'

'What do you mean?'

'I'm not sure. But cracks are appearing in buildings. Drainpipes are coming adrift. Stones are breaking. Accidents happening. Inferior materials are being used. Someone is cutting corners.'

'Have you reported this?'

'Not officially, no. But,' she shrugged as though indifferent, 'it's not my business any more, is it?'

'How can Bellina not be your business, Isabella? When you love it so much.'

'Well, I must learn to live without it. There must be someone else out there willing to take on a female architect.'

'But it would have to be in some other town in Italy.'

'Yes.' She paused. 'In some other town.'

The enormity of that statement sat in the car with them. Isabella could feel its cold breath on her cheek.

'Isabella, what was it about your husband that made someone want to kill him?'

It was as if Roberto had reached into her chest with no warning and squeezed her heart.

'Why him?' he persisted. 'Out of all the people who marched on Rome that day ten years ago, why Luigi Berotti?'

'I don't know.' Isabella shook her head, sending her dark plait leaping on to her shoulder. 'I don't know, and that's what gnaws at me when I close my eyes. Was it random? Was he just someone in a black shirt? Or was he targeted? And why me? Why shoot me? I've been through every single reason I can think of year after year and still I don't know.' She drew a quick breath to silence her words. 'I don't know, Roberto.'

'Then it's time we found out.'

She lightly touched the side of his thigh in the darkness. 'I'm going to Rome.'

She felt the shock ripple through him, a small jolt under her fingers.

'I found out tonight,' she explained, 'that the man who was the leader of my husband's Blackshirt unit is now working in Rome. In the Ministry of the Interior.'

He wrapped his hand around her fingers. For a while he said nothing, just rubbed his thumb gently over her knuckles, his eyes hidden in the shadows.

'So,' he murmured, 'tonight was worth it to you after all.'

'Stop it, Roberto,' she said. 'Stop it.'

She leaned forward and kissed his mouth. A firm angry kiss that lasted no more than a second, but when she tried to pull away, his hand cradled the back of her head and his lips came down on hers with an intensity that stopped her heart. He kissed her again and again, rapid and fierce, as though seeking to eradicate the memory of any kisses that had taken place behind the closed door of the hotel's smoking room. Heat coursed through her body, pumping her blood through her veins, hot and strident.

She had a longing to slip her fingers inside his stiff jacket, to undo the studs of his shirt and slide the palms of her hands over the hard muscles of his chest, to mingle her skin with his.

She wanted to inhale the warm scent of him deep into her lungs. She'd existed through ten years of need denied. Ten years of wanting no one, of touching no man. Wanting no man to touch her. And now Roberto had turned her world upside down so that she felt empty and cold when she was away from him, as if there was a hole in her that she'd never noticed before.

So when he drew back his head and murmured something, she didn't hear because she had turned sick at the thought of leaving him, abandoning Bellina to work and live elsewhere. She buried hcr face in his neck, feeling the pulse there like the kick of a horse, aware of his breath dragging in and out of his throat.

'I could always work in Francesca's bakery instead,' shc whispered, and he laughed. She loved that about him, the way he laughed at the things she said. She twisted her head, tracing in the darkness the strong line of his jaw with her hand, as though the weight of it was something she could carry away with her to consider later. 'What did you say earlier?'

He pressed his lips to her forehead, trailed kisses along the fine arch of her eyebrow. 'I said I'd come with you.'

'Where?'

She thought he meant to her apartment door in the courtyard, like before.

'To Rome,' he said.

'No, Roberto!'

What good was love, if it came to this? To

269

pushing him away because she couldn't bear him to get hurt.

★ ★ ★

'What happened, Isabella?'
  'Nothing, Papa.'
  'You spoke to Mussolini?'
  'Yes.'
  'And . . . ?'
  'I told you. Nothing happened.'
Isabella started to head towards her bedroom but her father stepped into her path. He was tall and intimidating in his floor-length wine-stained robe and his spectacles were pushed up into his ruffled grey hair as if he'd been raking his hands through it. It was past midnight and she could imagine him pacing back and forth behind the door for the past hour, waiting for her return. She was careful to keep Roberto's scarf in place around her neck and had an excuse ready for losing her mother's lace hairnet.
  'Isabella, don't lie to me. You're no good at it.'
  'I'm not lying, Papa.'
  'Did you dance with him?'
  'No, of course not. I don't dance and anyway I was at a different table with the other architects. Mussolini had much more glamorous women to amuse him, ones with painted nails and laughs that could crack a wine glass.'
He didn't smile. He came closer, looming over her, and lifted her chin so that he could peer short-sightedly into her eyes.
  'Something happened,' he said gravely.

Isabella could feel a flush staining her cheeks and her lips still burning with the taste of Roberto.

'I met someone, a man I like.'

It was as though she'd flicked a switch in him. He beamed at her, seized her by the shoulders and kissed both her cheeks flamboyantly.

'Ah, my Isabella, at last! You have unearthed that heart of yours that you buried with that no-good husband of yours. Come,' he drew her into the living room, 'let us drink to this new friend who has the power to raise Lazarus.' His chuckle of delight boomed through the apartment.

'It's late, Papa, I'm tired.'

'No, *cara mia*, today is a special day. We must celebrate it.'

'Papa, I lost my job today.'

'*Merda*, that is nothing compared to this joy in my heart.' He poured them both a full glass of wine and thrust one at Isabella. '*Salute*! Your mother would be happy.'

Tear sprang to Isabella's eyes at the mention of her mother. It was just one step too far today.

'*Salute*, Papa.'

'What's his name, this man who makes my daughter's eyes shine?'

'Roberto. He's a photographer.'

'A photographer? Hah! I suppose it will have to do. Not a Blackshirt this time, thank God.' He smiled at her, his moustache twitching with delight, and raised his glass. 'To Roberto!'

Isabella touched her glass to his. 'To Roberto.'

271

23

The office was silent. It was Saturday morning, early. The day had dawned with an empty blue sky, so clear and brittle it looked as if it would crack if anyone dared touch it. Isabella kept her mind fixed on what lay ahead, not on what skulked behind her. Sometimes the past seemed to her to be a giant mantrap with iron teeth that could snap your bones if you didn't watch where you put your feet.

She had brushed her hair till it shone, pulled on her brightest dress and brightest smile and strode into the office with a cheerful '*Buongiorno*' for the receptionist. Only a handful of the draughtsmen were yet at their boards, so she nodded a cheery good morning and was gathering up her personal belongings, throwing the ruler, sharpener and her favourite drawing pens into her shoulder bag, when Dottore Martino's secretary, Maria, strolled across the room with an envelope in her hand. Her face was shiny, she was excited about something.

'For you, Isabella.'

'*Grazie.*'

It would be her official notice and final pay cheque. Isabella almost didn't open it there. It was the kind of reading you kept for the privacy of your own room, so that no one else could see the turning of your hopes to ash in your mouth or the way your eyes go dead behind the smile. But Maria started chattering on about how thrilled she was that Mussolini had smiled at her when he came to the office yesterday — 'A proper smile from Il Duce just for me!' — and how she couldn't wait for the big rally at midday today in the field that was being turned into a sports arena.

'It is a privilege,' she enthused, her hands dancing through the air, 'to have our great leader here among us, addressing us at the rally. *Un grande uomo.* A great man in our midst. A man of history. I can't wait to view him again, so proud and . . . '

Isabella had stopped listening. Her restless fingers had slit open the envelope. There was no cheque inside. One folded sheet of paper, that was all.

'I hope Dottore Martino lets us leave early,' the secretary was saying eagerly, 'so that we can get there first and choose good places to . . . '

Isabella could think of nothing worse on earth at this moment than to rush to a propaganda rally to be close to Mussolini when he delivered his speech. She flicked out the sheet of paper, her eyes reluctant to read the words of dismissal. To her surprise she saw that there were only three handwritten lines.

Signora Isabella Berotti,
I am pleased to inform you that I am withdrawing your dismissal.
It seems I need you more than I thought I did.

It was signed *Alberto Martino* in a quick impatient scrawl.

Withdrawing your dismissal.

It took an effort to drag air into her lungs. Suddenly everything smelled different. The world smelled alive again, it smelled of busy people and of damp earth and freshly baked bread. Of cement. Of coffee. Of salt and tears. Isabella sensed something cramped unfurl inside her, so that she had to give a cough as she sought to work out exactly what had happened to reverse her employer's decision.

Who was responsible? Mussolini himself? Hit by remorse or driven by loyalty to Luigi? Or Davide Francolini? Did her escort discover last night that she'd been fired from her job and did he put pressure on Martino?

She had no idea. But her hand was trembling with relief as she carefully put each pen, one by one, back in its place.

★ ★ ★

The church of St Michael was bare. Unadorned and unpretentious. Isabella liked it at once, the moment she pushed open its heavy door. Its colours were soft and seemed to float on the scent of incense. The pews and the altar were of honey-toned woods and modern design, the kind of place where she could imagine prayers lingering, unwilling to abandon this cool restful space. The exception was the vivid sapphire-blue gown of the Madonna that glowed in the recess of a side chapel where a handful of votive candles flickered, remembering the souls of the departed. Isabella walked over and lit one for Luigi.

'*Dio vi benedica,*' a quiet voice murmured at her shoulder. 'God bless you, signora, in your time of need.'

It was the priest. A tall shapeless shadow in his black robe. She had last seen him in the police station the day all this had started and she remembered his kindness to Rosa, the firmness of his words.

'Thank you, Father Benedict.'

'A time of quiet reflection at the start of the day benefits us all. Especially on a day like today when the battle cry of Il Duce will soon resound in our ears.' He stepped backwards, melting into the muted light that filtered like amber oil through the stained-glass windows.

'Father, one moment of your time, please.'

He halted and she approached him. He gave no sign of recognising her.

'Father, do you know what happened to Sister Consolata?'

'She was transferred to another convent.' He spoke as though words were things to be measured out with care, not used to excess.

'Do you know why? And who made the decision? Was it Chairman Grassi?'

'I don't know the answer to that. But the church makes these decisions within its spiritual realm, not politicians, I assure you, Signora Berotti.'

So he knew exactly who she was.

'Was it because of Rosa Bianchi?'

His dark eyes had something of old leather about them, as if they had seen things that eyes were not meant to see, but they softened at the mention of the child's name. To Isabella's surprise, he nodded.

'I believe it could have been,' he said. 'She is important to them.'

'I'm worried about her. They are treating her like a prisoner. Why? Why is she so important to them? Is it because of her father? Have you spoken to her?'

'Signora, you ask too many questions. It is not always wise. You think I do not see what goes on in that place in God's name.'

The priest glanced quickly around the body of his church, mindful that somebody might have slipped unnoticed into one of the pews. But no, at this hour the pews were empty of morning worshippers.

'Why do you come to me?' he asked in a low tone.

'I am not permitted to see Rosa but I know she needs help. I thought that you, as the town's priest, would be able to enter the convent and — '

'That's the only reason you came here?'

'Yes.'

'No one told you to come?'

'No.'

Isabella studied his long sallow face and had a sense of coming close to something important, but it was so intangible that she didn't know where to look. The air in the church seemed to grow milky around them, thick with secrets that she had not expected to find in the house of God.

'Father,' Isabella pronounced his title sharply, 'who is Rosa Bianchi's father?'

For a long moment there was nothing but silence in the church and during the silence the priest's eyes scrutised her face.

'How should I know, signora?'

He was lying. And he was no better at it than she was.

'Will he be coming for Rosa?' Isabella asked. 'It's what she believes and also what Grassi seems to believe.' A thought suddenly struck her and she was appalled that it hadn't occurred to her before. 'Has Allegra Bianchi been buried yet?'

'Yes.'

'Where?'

'In our cemetery in sacred ground. Some say a suicide should be cast into outer darkness and denied hallowed ground, but I believe she is one of God's beloved children, despite her mortal sin.'

'Was Rosa there at the funeral?'

'Yes, of course.'

'But it didn't draw her father into the open? Colonnello Sepe must have been watching for him but I have heard of no arrest, so I assume he didn't come.'

This time the slightest of smiles released the tension around his mouth. 'Apparently not.'

Suddenly Isabella lost patience with the wall of secrets that blocked her path in every direction. Without warning she grasped a handful of the front of his cassock, gripping it tight enough to bind him to her.

'Father Benedict,' she said fiercely, 'please tell me the truth. I feel that you know more than you are saying.'

She could smell mothballs on him and a musky scent that made her think of the moist dark earth of funerals.

'Signora Berotti, you are too quick to jump to conclusions.' He sighed in a priestly manner. 'What is it you are so eager to know?'

'I want to find the man who killed my husband.'

Father Benedict's eyes widened with surprise. 'What makes you think that I know anything about that?'

'My father has told me that you used to work with him years ago at the hospital in Milan.'

'That is true.' He quietly extricated his robe from her fingers. 'But it was a long time ago. A lot has changed since then.'

'My husband was killed in Milan ten years ago, and Rosa's mother mentioned it to me here in Bellina before she took her own life. Somewhere there is a connection, I feel sure of it, but no one will speak out.'

'Is that your only interest in the child?' He regarded her sadly. 'Because you believe that she will lead you to what you want to know.'

'No.' But the question stung. She found herself wondering how much of it was true. 'I am of course concerned for the child's welfare too. She has lost her mother and I know how that feels.'

He smiled kindly. 'I used to see you sometimes as a child, trailing behind your father like a lost lamb. You don't remember me but I remember you. Even then you were different from other little girls.'

Isabella felt the warmth of his memories bridging the gap between them. 'Help me,' she said softly. 'Help me now. Tell me what you know.'

'I'm not the one you should be asking.'

She frowned. 'What do you mean?'

'No one has ever thought to come to me before to ask about what happened ten years ago. But you're right, there is a connection.'

Isabella felt the truth so close she could almost grasp it in her hand. 'What is it? Please, Father, I need to know.'

'In that case, Signora Berotti, I suggest you talk to your own father. He is the one who nursed your husband's killer back to health.'

★ ★ ★

Isabella threw open the door of the new Bellina hospital, a place she had helped to design. So she knew its layout, its corridors and its wards. She had drawn with fine pencils the floorplan of its operating theatres. But understanding a building was not the same as understanding the people within it. And living with her father was not the same as knowing the person inside his skin.

'Dr Cantini is busy, I'm afraid.'

Isabella limped hurriedly past his secretary without breaking stride. Through the outer office to the door of the inner sanctum. No doors were stopping her now and she jerked it open so hard that it bounced back against the wall with a bang that made her father leap to his feet. He was behind his desk and wearing his doctor-face. Not the one he showed patients which was all smiles and chuckles. This was his face of concern and worry when he was studying their files and working out what treatment to give.

'Papa!'

'I'm sorry, Doctor, but I couldn't stop your daughter marching straight in like this with no — '

Dr Cantini took one look at his daughter's face and held up a hand. 'Enough, Carla, it's all right. Shut the door after you.' But his eyes didn't leave Isabella's and he threw the pen in his hand down on the desk with a clatter the moment the door closed. 'What is it, Isabella? What has — ?'

'Liar!'

His dark brows swooped down and his cheeks flared the deep plum red that Isabella knew from experience was the forerunner of rage.

'All these years I believed you. All these years I thought you had tried to help me.' She stormed over to his desk and slammed both hands down on its surface. 'You lied! You told me there was a manhunt. That while I was in hospital, fighting for my life and then learning to walk again with operation after operation, the police had worked hard to find the killer of my husband or even his identity, but no clues were found. No evidence. He escaped.' Her voice was colliding with the walls, crashing against the windows. 'That's what you told me, Papa.'

'It's the truth, but you — '

'You lied! You lied!'

'Isabella, stop this at once!'

'That's why you ordered me to stay away from Rosa, isn't it? In case I learned the real truth. That's why you were so pleased about Roberto last night because you thought I would now forget about the killing and about Rosa and just get on with life.'

'Isabella, you are wrong.'

'No, I am not.'

'Sit down. Stop this shouting. At once.'

His voice was the one he used on negligent junior doctors, the one that had always been able to turn Isabella's knees to water. But not this time.

'I know the truth.'

She ignored the fact that he came striding towards her from behind his desk, ignored the chair he pointed to with his long forefinger. Ignored the 'Sit!' As though she were a dog.

'You nursed the man who shot Luigi. The killer who put a bullet in me.'

Her father froze. Hands mid-air. All colour leached from his face. And in that fraction of a second, Isabella knew that anything more he said would be a lie. She couldn't trust him.

'Isabella, that is a wicked thing to say.' His voice came out hoarse as if something hard and dry had stuck in his throat. 'It is grossly untrue. How could you ever begin to think such a thing? You mean the world to me — don't you know that, *cara mia*? I would never nurse any man who deliberately harmed you.'

'Swear it!'

'What?'

'Swear on Mamma's grave. That you did no such thing.'

He didn't hesitate. 'I swear it on your dear mother's grave.'

Nothing moved in the cold office. Not a breath. Not an eyelash. Not the beat of a heart. Isabella did everything in her power to disbelieve him, but she couldn't. She couldn't. He had loved her mother more than his own life and would never swear on her grave if it weren't true.

Would he? Damn his soul? No.

She walked over to the chair and collapsed on to it, breathing heavily as if she'd been running hard. Her father remained for several seconds standing stiffly in the centre of the room, then came over and placed himself beside her chair. Gently he rested a hand on her shoulder.

'Who told you such a terrible lie?'

'The priest.'

'Father Benedict?'

She nodded. She felt his hand jump, startled, and then return to its place.

'Father Benedict and I were friends in Milan,' he explained quietly. 'He used to bring comfort and the last rites to my dying patients and I used to patch up the congregation in his rough neighbourhood after knife stabbings and bottle fights. They were common outside the bars.' She felt, rather than saw, the resigned shrug he gave.

'You know what we Italians are like. All hot temper and points of honour.'

'But what reason would he have to lie to me?'

'To him it's not a lie. He believes what he told you. But he's wrong, I promise you.'

'It doesn't make sense, Papa.'

'The day Luigi was shot, a policeman was in the marketplace. He fired shots at the window where he thought the gunfire had come from, but no one was found there.'

'You've never told me this before.'

'There was no reason to. I was out of my mind with worry about you, but two days later one of Mussolini's henchmen came to my home at night in secret. He asked me to remove a bullet from his shoulder. I did so.'

Isabella lifted her head. She studied her father's face. He was staring down at his wedding ring. Remembering. His expression was tight. Was he listening for the rustle of truth weaving in and out of his words?

'Why in secret?' Isabella asked. 'What was he afraid of?'

'He'd had a run-in with some rebel Socialists who were raging against Mussolini's takeover of power. He'd been throwing his Fascist weight around as usual, provoking trouble, getting them riled up.'

'Why you? Why come to you?'

'I was known as a medic who could keep his mouth shut. He didn't want Mussolini to know he'd been fool enough to get himself shot.'

'And the priest?'

'Father Benedict caught me treating him and

got it into his head that this was the gunman who killed Luigi.'

'Why?'

'The man was feverish and loose-tongued enough to mutter about killing a man and his wife. But Isabella, it wasn't Luigi he shot. It wasn't you. The bullets in you and Luigi didn't come from a police gun. Hell, I've removed enough of them in my time to know exactly what they look like.'

Slowly Isabella rose to her feet. She thought hard before asking the next question that was sliding off her tongue. 'Who was that man? The one injured, the Fascist you helped.'

'It doesn't matter. It's not important.'

'It matters to me, Papa. Tell me.'

He drew himself up to his full height, his presence expanding to fill the room. 'It was Alberto Grassi.'

'Chairman Grassi?' It was the last name Isabella had expected.

'Yes.' Her father moved with heavy steps towards the door. 'Now forget I ever told you.'

His hand reached for the door handle but before he could grasp it Isabella made a strange hissing sound that escaped from her lips without warning. The room seemed suddenly too hot, her father's eyes too narrow, the secrets too big.

'That's why, isn't it?' she said in a low voice. 'That's why I have my job.'

His eyes flickered but he made no comment.

'In payment to you. That's why Dottore Martino employs me.'

Who do you trust? How do you know?

Isabella returned to the office. Tried to work. Failed. Her head would not stay still. Her eyes kept seeing again the priest's fiery eyes and her ears kept hearing again her father's sincere voice, *I swear it on your dear mother's grave.*

We all keep secrets. We hide our secrets from each other. From ourselves. But how do we know when the time has come to undo the locks on the secrets?

It was a relief when at eleven o'clock the office was emptied and coaches arrived to trundle every employee out to the arena field where the rally was to be held at noon. It was good to be out in the open, in the sunshine under a lofty blue sky that looked as if it had been swept clean for Mussolini's visit. Where shadows and secrets couldn't crawl up on her unnoticed. Isabella breathed more easily and felt the tight band around her chest loosen.

The field was a mass of colour and movement, a cauldron of noise and crowds and excitement. Isabella stood on tiptoe on the top step of the coach and surveyed the scene before her, section by section. Row after row of flags leapt back and forth impatiently in the breeze, the green, white and red flag of Italy alternating with the bold and dramatic flag of the Fascist Party. The Fascist flag looked to Isabella as if it wore jackboots. It bore a golden *fasces*, the ancient Roman symbol of authority, on a dominant black background. It made a harsh statement that no one could ignore. Luigi had told her that black was the official colour used by the Blackshirt militia as a reminder of the Italian Arditi soldiers for whom it represented death and an unswerving willingness to sacrifice self in combat for the cause.

Yes, I hear you, Duce, you and your flags. Isabella removed her gaze from the banners. The individual becomes a trivial cog in the vast Fascist machine. Dispensable. Replaceable. But I am not a cog. I am an architect, a good one too. Is that not so, Dottore Martino?

Isabella smiled as her eyes dissected the field as efficiently as they would a drawing on her board, roaming over every corner of it. Seeking. Scanning. Hunting down. Right now she was searching among the thousands of scarves and hats and caps for a mop of chaotic chestnut hair. A tall straight figure. A pair of shoulders that a Maremmana bull would envy. The smile stayed. Waiting for Roberto to come and claim it.

24

Roberto shinned up the wall. It was easier than climbing a mast and he'd done plenty of those. But not for a few years, he had to admit. His leg muscles felt rusty. Too many hours spent in his darkroom. The moment his feet hit hard ground he raced across the thirty metre stretch of open land and pulled up only when he was swallowed by a patch of dense shade at the base of the convent's squat tower.

The place felt deserted. The air was dry and dusty. No birdsong. Just a silent wood pigeon watching him from an elbow of stone that jutted out at the top of the building. A breeze was stirring up the surface of the bare black earth, raising the scents of the loamy marshland forests it had so recently cradled. He felt the brickwork warm against his back. The convent rose three storeys above him, a harsh angular design that wasn't to his taste, but he approved of the clever mix of brick and stone. It gave it a warmth, a friendliness that belied what went on behind the shuttered windows. His instinct was to get inside and throw open all the doors and windows, to let the stench of cruelty and hypocrisy pour out and to allow sunlight to flood the dark secretive corners. But that wasn't why he was here.

He had chosen his spot. It was up ahead, in the shadow of a stone porch that looked unused, judging by the pile of logs stacked within it. It was the place he would pick to break in if he had to. There were glass panes running down beside the door, tall as a man and easy to break unseen. A quick crack with a rock. Or the butt of a gun. Definitely the place to pick. If he had to.

He was hoping he wouldn't have to.

Over his shoulder hung a battered old leather satchel with the Leica tucked inside. He had abandoned his tripod and equipment case with his Graflex into the safekeeping of one of the LUCE cine-camera crew who had turned up at the rally field to film the big event. He gritted his teeth at the thought. He hated to trust others. He'd learned that much since getting thrown in prison — you trust yourself. Only yourself. But today he'd had no choice.

He ducked tight against the wall and raced towards the disused porch through a blaze of sunlight, cursing the nakedness of his position. But no one shouted. No black-robed nun stuck a hand out of a window to grab his shoulder. He hit the darkness and crouched down in the dank corner on the far side of the porch. A nest of red beetles clambered over his shoe; he brushed them off and scanned the high outer wall thirty metres distant. Nothing moved.

He swore at the wall. Time was something he couldn't afford to let trickle through his fingers and he wasn't good at watching walls. With a grunt of annoyance he settled down to wait.

★　★　★

The man was fast. A flutter of movement. A flash of blond hair caught in the sunlight. And then it was gone. No sound. He was over the wall and already out of Roberto's line of sight.

So he was good.

Had he seen Roberto arrive earlier? Did he know exactly where he had merged into the darkness beyond the porch door?

Was he that good?

Roberto couldn't see into the porch itself because he was hidden behind its stone sides and he heard no footsteps on the gravel path that skirted the convent. But the man was betrayed by his shadow which leapt out in front of Roberto. Had he taken three steps forward he could have stamped on it, pinned it to the ground.

There was one sharp snap, like someone cracking their knuckles. For ten seconds nothing more and then the delicate chink of glass. Roberto knew the glass was being removed enough to push a hand through to unlock the door.

He didn't breathe. Just stared unblinking right at the point where the figure would emerge if the man chose to stick his head around the wall of the porch to check that he was not being observed.

But he didn't.

The hinges of the door creaked faintly and then there was the sound of a latch as it swung shut again. The man was inside.

★ ★ ★

How long?

How long did he need? This man.

How long before he found his daughter?

Roberto gave him five minutes. He might need more, he might need less, but this was a man who was used to finding what he wanted. So five minutes. Enough. To search the premises and start a conversation. He would be preoccupied, his mind only half on the creak of a stair or the turn of a door handle, and he would not be expecting anyone hunting him down. Not here. Not today. The whole of Bellina would be on that rally field awaiting Mussolini and his strident speech. He was banking on that.

So was Roberto. That's why he was here, convinced that Rosa's father would not be able to resist the lure of his daughter alone in a deserted convent. The problem was: is that what Grassi and Colonnello Sepe had worked out too? Had they put their two brains together and come to the same conclusion or could they not see beyond Mussolini and the circus around him?

Roberto took his chance. He pushed open the porch door.

★　★　★

It was like sailing through rocks. Jagged ridges that wanted to rip out the bottom of your boat. That's what this felt like, the same kick of adrenalin in the gut each time he opened a new door. To be found here by Colonnello Sepe would mean serious consequences. To be found here by the man with blond hair and feet more silent than a leopard's would mean a gun in his face or a knife at his throat. That's how men like this stayed alive.

Roberto searched the ground floor. He moved quickly and noiselessly. Refectory, kitchen, classrooms, corridors, offices, lavatories. All empty. Not even a novice nun to stand in his way.

So. The man was upstairs. Or he was in the chapel.

The Reverend Mother would never shut Rosa in the chapel. Surely. Roberto tasted a bitterness in his mouth. There was no knowing what that woman would or wouldn't do, but he made his choice. The stairs. On his right lay a sweeping curved staircase of pale oak that struck Roberto as designed to dwarf the children, underlining their insignificance in this sinful world. He took the stairs carefully, alert for any sound, any creak of a floorboard, any murmur of voices from under a door.

It was a risk. But one Roberto knew he needed to take because he had to get to this man before Isabella did. Now that she'd set herself on this hunt, she wouldn't stop, he knew she wouldn't, and when she eventually cornered the man in some dark alley she would sink her teeth into him like a wildcat and never let go. She would get hurt. So yes, this was a risk but a risk he had to take. She'd lived through one bullet. She was unlikely to live through another. And he couldn't bear that.

The corridor at the top of the stairs was long and brown-painted, with dismal grey linoleum on the floor. A wooden crucifix hung on the wall and under it someone had placed a posy of wild flowers in a tin can, the delicate splash of colour creating a bright little moment of hope as he padded past. He stopped at each door along the corridor, leaning his head close to listen for the slightest scrape of sound, slowing his heartbeat so that he could hear more than its pounding.

It was as he crept towards the door at the very end that he heard something. A scratch. Like a cat at a door. Then a faint flutter. Fingertips brushing against wood. He placed his cheek against the door and felt the vibration, no more than the ripple of a butterfly's wing. Slowly he released his breath.

'Rosa?' he whispered into the silence.

No answer.

'Rosa?'

For half a minute he kept his ear pressed to the door, his eyes fixed on the stretch of corridor along which he'd come, on the flowers. On the top stair.

'Yes.'

The word was so slight it was barely a word, but Roberto's ears caught it. His hand slid down, curling around the big brass doorknob, and it was only then that he noticed the iron key tucked into the lock under the knob. Without hesitation he turned it and opened the door, ready to spring aside if an attack came from within. But there was no attack.

A silence greeted him. A silence that felt strange to Roberto, almost as though it were underwater. It was the greenness of the walls in the long thin room, the dimness of the light with the shutters half closed, and the two rows of metal beds covered in brown blankets. The air felt thick and unused, as the light from the corridor tumbled in ahead of him and he saw a pair of black eyes huge with fear in a small stark white face.

'Rosa!'

That was when he made his mistake. One split second's error. All he saw was the child. All he heard was her quick intake of breath. All he felt was the need to free her from the wretched chain on her leg, and a surge of anger at the woman with the lips that closed on wormwood and who called herself a daughter of Christ. He missed the furtive footstep behind him and the catch in the child's throat as she opened her mouth into a wide silent 'O' of shock.

A knife grazed his throat from behind, the cold sting of it sharp as a snake bite. His heart twisted in his chest and his hands rose to snatch the blade from his attacker.

'Damn you, if you move, I'll slit your throat wide open.'

The man's voice in his ear was calm. It was Roberto's own voice that bellowed with rage.

★   ★   ★

'Don't lie!'

'I'm not lying.' Roberto had himself back under control. 'I'm not spying on you for anybody. I'm a photographer.'

293

'It's true, Papa. I saw him. He photographed the school.'

'Then what the fuck are you doing hunting me down here?'

The man who asked the question was dangerous. Very dangerous. It wasn't that he looked panicked, far from it. His deep-set blue eyes were still and watchful, his breathing easy. He possessed the iron composure of a man who was untroubled by what he did, this casual use of a knife to slice his way to what he wanted. He smelled of violence, the way fireworks smell of gunpowder. His blond hair was swept back off his face, leaving the bones sharp and prominent, and he was standing with his back firmly to the wall for safety. The knife blade was thrust out in front of him and jabbing in Roberto's direction. But at least it was no longer jammed against his jugular.

'I came because I want to speak to Rosa,' Roberto informed him. 'She wouldn't leave here until she had seen you and — '

'You told him about me?' The man's words to his daughter were rough, but more disappointed than angry.

'No, Papa! I told him nothing.'

For the first time Rosa's father took his eyes off Roberto for half a second and glanced at his daughter. He gave her a flicker of a smile. 'It's all right, *piccolina*, I believe you.'

Roberto felt the tension in the room drop down a notch.

'Your name?' he asked the stranger in the brown suit.

'You don't need it. Any more than I need yours.' He coughed suddenly with a deep rattle in his lungs.

'Are you taking Rosa away?'

Her father said nothing at first, then shook his head a time or two.

'Papa, you must!'

Tears sprang to the girl's eyes and she fought to hold them back. As they trickled down her pale cheeks, she banged the flat of her hand against the brutally cropped hair and shook her shackled foot so fiercely that the metal tore a wide strip of skin off her ankle. It was a long chain that attached her to the bed nearest the door.

'Look at me, Papa, look at me,' she wailed. The look she gave him was feral, sharpened by hunger and need. 'I am worse than a dog. Take me with you!'

'No, my sweetheart, not yet.'

'I'll be good, Papa. I can be quiet as a dead person. No one will know I'm there. I'll say nothing, do nothing, except what you tell me.' Her thin voice was rising. 'Please, Papa, please? Take me with you.' She seized the chain in one hand and rattled it ferociously, so that it sounded to Roberto like the walking dead, and her sharp upper teeth sank into her lower lip to stop it trembling.

'Whatever your name is,' Roberto said in a flat voice, 'don't leave your child here. For God's sake, get her out. She doesn't deserve this. Now is your chance while the nuns are gone.'

'No,' the man said, 'not today.'

'She needs you.'

'I move around too much.'

'I can move too, Papa. I did with Mamma.' Her wide expressive eyes clung to a scrap of hope.

'No.' Her father turned his face from her, his cheeks rigid. 'Not today.' The knife started to lower.

'Mamma never wanted me. But . . . ' Rosa was shaking uncontrollably. 'I thought you did.'

It was like watching a cliff face crack open. The man fell to his knees in front of his daughter and wrapped his arms around her, moulding her small frame to his, ignoring Roberto's presence completely.

'Of course I want you, my Rosa. Of course I will come for you, *mia bella*, but not today.' He crooned soft comfort in her ear and Roberto caught the words, 'Today I have work to do.'

Roberto left them together. He placed a package from his satchel on the foot of the child's bed: a panini with caciotta cheese and *melone*, then he walked rapidly out of the melancholy dormitory before he could no longer resist the urge to seize hold of the knife and hack apart the lock on the chain.

* * *

How does a man leave the daughter he loves in a place like this? Answer: because he loves his 'work' more. It sickened Roberto. Yet he waited at the top of the stairs beside the wild flowers, waited to see how the crack in the man could be pinned together.

He was clearly an insurgent. A revolutionary. A Socialist or a Communist. It didn't matter which. They were all marked with the same death sentence hanging like the sword of Mussolini over their heads. Was it the child's safety he was thinking about when he refused to take her? Or his own?

He watched the man emerge from the room, turn the key in the lock and leave it in place. Roberto felt sorrow for the abandoned child and moved quickly away down the wide staircase to the outside world. Her father followed, but the force of the sunlight seemed to unsettle him and he stepped immediately into the dark shadow of the porch. He paused, aware that there were things that had to be said.

'Thank you,' he muttered to Roberto. '*Grazie*.'

'For what?'

'For helping my daughter. She told me about you and the architect.'

'That's not why I'm here.'

'I know, *fotografo*. So what are you really doing, falling over my footprints?'

'I came to find you.'

The man nodded and the knife reappeared in his hand. 'Why?'

'What do you know about Luigi Berotti's death?'

'Who wants to know?'

'His widow.'

'His widow?' The blue eyes settled with a flicker of surprise on Roberto, on the bootlace of blood at his throat. 'I thought she was dead.'

'You thought wrong.'

'It was a long time ago.'

'Not to her.'

Abruptly the man's eyes blazed. 'It's a fight for freedom. For the freedom of Italy itself. Can't you see that? Some people get hurt. It is a necessary sacrifice of the weak.'

Roberto had an urge to rip his tongue out. 'She was innocent, damn you!'

'No one is innocent. Everyone must choose. She chose a Blackshirt.'

The truth of the statement hit Roberto in the gut. It was the slippery thought that came to stalk him in the middle of the night and slid uninvited into his mind when he touched Isabella's creamy skin or watched the way she would throw him a smile with a little toss of her head. As if to say, *See, I remember how to laugh. I haven't lost that.*

She chose a Blackshirt.

'She was young,' he said.

'That is no excuse. We were all young and we all made our choices.'

Roberto could hear the righteous fury, the conviction that everything was to be sacrificed to the cause. Everything and everyone.

'Did you pull the trigger on the bullet that killed Luigi Berotti?' he demanded.

The man started to raise the knife. A warning. 'It doesn't matter who pulled the trigger. The destruction of Mussolini's brutal Fascist regime is the final goal. *That's* what matters.'

His eyes were shining with blind fervour. Roberto could feel it rising like heat from him. This was why he was so dangerous. This man saw one path ahead, only one, as straight as an arrow, and he would trample to dust the flesh and blood of anyone who stepped in his way. Is that what Isabella had unwittingly done in Milan? Did she blunder into his path that day?

'It is because of you that your daughter is chained up. Yet you leave her.'

'That's none of your business. Stay out of it. I will return for Rosa when the time is right.'

'Take her now. This may be your only chance and the child is lonely. She has lost her mother.'

It was the wrong thing to say. Instantly the eyes narrowed and the knife shot out so that the point of the blade pinned itself to the tip of Roberto's jaw.

'What is it you want from me, *fotografo*?' The question came out as a low hiss.

'I want you to speak to Signora Berotti.'

'Why should I do that?'

'Because if you do, I will make sure that Rosa is properly cared for if you don't come back.'

The man's mouth spasmed.

'A life for a life,' Roberto stated flatly, as if he were striking a bargain for the sale of horsemeat. 'Isabella Berotti lost her life because of you. Every night she relives that moment in the marketplace, minute by minute.' He raised his hand and firmly pushed the blade to one side. 'Speak to her. Give her back her life.'

The blue eyes grew cloudy and for the first time uncertain. 'How do I know I can trust you?'

'You are a man accustomed to taking risks. Speak to Isabella Berotti. Then — and only then — I will swear to see that your daughter will be

299

cared for in a decent place. If you fail to return.'

He saw the man's gaze roam up to the upper floor's windows.

'A life for a life,' Roberto murmured again.

The blond head nodded once. Sharp and decisive.

'Agreed.'

'And let me tell you this, father of Rosa. Next time you put a knife to my throat I will break your arm.'

The man gave a low private chuckle and slid the knife into a leather sheath inside his jacket. 'To seal our bond, *fotografo*, I will save your life. A life for a life, that's what you said.' He fixed his eyes on Roberto's face.

'What the hell do you mean?' Roberto demanded.

'Don't go to the rally. Don't go to listen to Mussolini.'

'I am employed to photograph the occasion.'

The man gave the faintest of shrugs. 'Then die.'

Roberto froze. It took three seconds for the reality to hit him. He spun around and raced towards the high stone wall. His heart kicking hard enough to crack a rib. Inside his head he was screaming, *Isabella*.

25

Where was she?

Where?

Roberto's fleeting flicker of hope that he could find her fast was snuffed out the moment he set foot inside the rally arena. A heaving swarm of dark heads and thousands of excited faces were creating a low buzz that sounded like a million bees.

The field was a mass of colour. Flags and bunting were reaching out on the breeze, fluttering fretfully above bright Sunday-best dresses and flower-trimmed hats. The men presented a more sombre spectacle in their caps and jackets of greys and browns, the drabber of the species, but they were the ones who crowded closest around the central stage, elbowing their way to the front.

It was impossible to find her.

Fear slid as thick as oil down his throat and he kept telling himself that she might not be here, might be safe somewhere else. As he forced his way past a stall selling salami pizzas, the smell of tomatoes and garlic cooking almost convinced him that he was being a fool. That nothing would happen. How could there be danger in a place where something as normal as tomatoes and garlic were being prepared for a meal? Or where a chicken turned on a spit and a cauldron of pork and peppers simmered temptingly on a stove? Piles of fresh bread were heaped high and people were biting into the soft warm dough, a normal peaceful day.

Nothing could happen. Not here under a clear sheet of sapphire sky where even the birds seemed to be rising on thermals of excitement. This was a town that was trying its best to appear normal, to go about its business with a wide confident smile, yet behind the smile it was anything but normal. Roberto could feel the ripples under his feet — the uncertainty, the disquiet, the strangeness. As unstable and treacherous as the marshes it was built on.

He worked systematically. Slicing through the crowds in long straight rows, the way he'd taught Alessandro to drive his furrows across the field. He started from the back and worked his way forward towards the stage that looked gaudy in red, white and green flags, draped in readiness for Il Duce's arrival.

'Roberto!'

He turned quickly, but it was only one of the cameramen from LUCE.

'Here, Roberto, you'll be needing this. Mussolini is due any moment.'

'*Grazie*, Alfredo.'

The plump man with bad acne scars shifted the Graflex camera equipment case from his own shoulder to Roberto's and vanished back into the crowd, trailing electric cables and light meters. The energy was growing. Voices grew louder. A band struck up with a marching song and the press of bodies around the stage became ever denser, as if the populace of Bellina were trying to force itself into one solid mass with but one thought in its head: Il Duce.

Where are you, Isabella?

He searched for her vibrant face among faces that were drab, for hair that was long and wild, for a distinctive walk with a limp, for a neck held straight and erect. He moved fast, shouldering a path through the crush, using his height to look over heads.

There!

His heart hammered. A green dress. Her back to him, and her hair wound in a braid at the nape of her slender neck. He swung to his left to cut across to her but at that moment the band struck up with a deafening rendition of 'Giovinezza' and a long maroon Alfa Romeo swept across the field, sleek as a leopard.

'Isabella!' Roberta shouted at the top of his lungs, bellowing like a bull, barging aside the people in between him and the green dress.

She turned. It wasn't her. Roberto felt a jolt of disappointment, absurdly angry at the woman for not being Isabella. Applause exploded through the crowd and Roberto knew that Mussolini had stepped out of the car. He should be there, Graflex in hand, doing the job he was paid for. That was the deal with Grassi. But right now the only thought in Roberto's head was to find Isabella and get her off this rally field immediately.

The speeches started, effusive tinny words flying out of the loudspeakers positioned throughout the crowd, but Roberto paid little heed. Even when Il Duce himself strutted up to

303

the microphone and launched into one of his usual harangues as a forest of arms rose in the Fascist salute. Still Roberto furiously carved his furrows.

'It is the State which educates its citizens in civic virtue.' Mussolini's words from the platform boomed out across the citizens of Bellina. 'It is the State which gives them a consciousness of their mission and welds them into unity.'

Roberto moved more carefully.

Blackshirts were mingling with the crowd, watching faces, eyeing any bulges in jackets, suspicion bristling with every black-booted step they took. Roberto eased himself away from them and in doing so caught the flash of a profile. A line of cheek. It drew him in the direction of the platform. For the first time he glanced up and saw Mussolini in his familiar grandiose stance, chest out, head back and chin jutting forward at his audience, for all the world like the statue of a Roman emperor. He was clad in a black uniform and its message was not lost on the crowd.

'The time for Italy is now!'

Roars of approval greeted his words.

'On this Agro Pontino we will wage the great Battle for Grain.'

Another roar. Hands shot skywards. Roberto used the moment to force his shoulder towards the spot where he had seen the delicate line of cheek but it had vanished. His head twisted and turned, frustration making his movements rough when others sought to bar his way.

'Believe, people of Bellina!' the loudspeaker crackled above his head.

The crowds swayed forward, chanting their allegiance, 'Il Duce! Il Duce!' And in the moment in which they drew their collective breath, Roberto heard something, a sound he didn't expect to hear. A familiar Gipsy four-cylinder engine. A low-pitched distinctive growl.

'Obey, people of Bellina!' Mussolini declared.

Roberto caught sight of a face only a few paces ahead right near the stage and instantly he recognised it.

'Fight, people of Bellina!'

He surged towards it, brushing aside those in his way, because it was Isabella's escort at the dinner last night, the construction manager with the look of a man whose fight is against himself. Roberto seized his slight shoulder. As he did so, the sound of the engine came again, louder this time. Nearer. Above them. Roberto let his eyes flick up and picked out a small light aircraft that was glinting like a sword-tip in the sunshine and approaching fast.

'Do you know where Signora . . . ?'

But at that same second he saw her because she heard his voice and turned to smile at him. She was standing on the far side of the construction manager, half hidden behind a towering Blackshirt who had also turned at the sound of someone not attending spellbound to Mussolini's speech. Roberto side-stepped the two men and took hold of Isabella's wrist. She looked surprised. But she also looked different. There was something dark and cloudy at the

305

back of her blue eyes that hadn't been there yesterday and he noticed the pale scarf she was wearing to conceal the bruising on her neck. He could sense a new tension in her as he moved closer.

'Isabella, come with me.'

'Now?'

'Yes, right now.'

Something about the way he said it unsettled her. She swung her head around, searching for danger. She saw none, but gripped his hand.

'Where are we going?' she asked quickly.

'Anywhere but here.'

Her eyes flared with alarm but she had the sense not to ask questions, not here where a hundred ears could be listening. The blare of the loudspeakers ceased briefly as Mussolini drew breath and surveyed the thousands of Fascist salutes with grim satisfaction. Roberto took that moment to edge away from the group Isabella was with and he drew her with him.

'Isabella?'

It was that colleague of hers, the one who looked at her with more than professional interest.

'It's an emergency, Davide. I have to leave.'

'Now?'

'Yes, now.'

'Don't. It's not wise.'

He reached out to hold her in place but she slid behind the broad backside of a toothless grandmother who was displaying a rictus grin of rapture for the benefit of the prowling Blackshirts. Isabella escaped.

To hell with it. Thousands of people. Too little space. Bodies jammed together. Attached to Isabella, Roberto's progress slowed, squeezing the two of them through gaps too small for one. Tempers flared. A punch was thrown in his ribs but he ploughed relentlessly on and nothing would make him release his grip on her hand.

All the time the engine's growl grew louder. Heads were starting to lift, eyes raking the empty sky until they found the tiny aircraft streaking directly in line with the field. Roberto didn't waste time looking up. He knew exactly what it was they were up against from his one earlier glance. A Caproni, the two-seater biplane nicknamed the Caproncino because it was so small. But big enough to create a blazing inferno. If it crashed.

'Roberto,' Isabella's voice scarcely made it to him over a burst of applause, 'what is — '

'Halt!' Two burly Blackshirts with swarthy faces and matching moustaches stepped in front of Roberto, truncheons already in their fists. One placed the tip of it in the centre of Roberto's chest and leaned his weight into it. 'Where do you think you are going? It is a betrayal of Il Duce. Get back to . . . '

Roberto knew the point had come that made him fear for Isabella. He brandished his camera case at the Blackshirts.

'Step aside,' he snapped. '*Pronto*! I am the official photographer appointed by Chairman Grassi and I must return to my car to fetch more film for Il Duce's departure.' He could hear the Caproncino. So close. Circling now.

'No, no one leaves. You remain here.'

Roberto looked at Isabella's face. 'Let the signora go to fetch it,' he said sternly. 'She is my — '

' — wife,' Isabella stated, and clutched at the arm of one of the Blackshirts, stumbling as if in pain. He tried to pull away from her but she hung on and whimpered at him, 'I'm pregnant. Help me. *Per favore*. I'm bleeding . . . '

The Blackshirt recoiled with an expression of disgust and this time she let him go. 'Get out of here,' he ordered smartly and, using his truncheon freely on the throng of bodies, he carved a path for their exit.

'*Grazie*,' Isabella murmured.

'Run!' Roberto hissed at her.

The crowd was thinning here. They moved faster. Blackshirts were staring up into the sky as the aeroplane climbed higher and higher above the field, a tiny leaf spiralling up into the blue. He saw Isabella look up as she ran and for the first time register where the noise was coming from. The plane flipped over high above and Isabella's jaw dropped open as it dawned on her what was about to happen.

She jerked to a halt.

'No, Isabella!'

Roberto forced her forward but she dug her heels into the ground with a strength that surprised him and wrenched herself out of his grip. She started to push her way back into the crowd.

'No, Isabella, don't. It's too late.'

She turned to him, her face twisted in anguish. 'No,' she whispered, shaking her head, 'no, no, don't say that. It's not too late to warn — '

The plane came screeching out of the sky. Nose first, it roared vertically downward straight as an arrow, tearing through the flimsy layers of air above the spectators' heads. Rushing at its target — the square platform that flaunted its presence with the boastful red, white and green flags. And at the black and gold banner that declared the Fascist grip on the rally.

The stampede started. Roberto knew it was coming, he could sense their fear in the air before they knew it themselves. He was already loping towards the perimeter of the field, his arm clamped around Isabella, pinning her to him. Her feet scarcely touched the ground and he could feel her heart pounding as thousands of feet came storming across the field behind them. A wild panic sent people charging from the aeroplane's path, screams and cries lacerating the air.

Roberto had seen panic before. Knew what it did to people. It made them forget that they were human in their fight to survive. He risked a glance over his shoulder and was sickened to his core by what he saw. In the wave of panic the weak were being trampled in the crush. He yanked a terrified child from in front of the onrush of feet and pressed it sobbing into the arms of its father, but nothing could hold back the tide.

Suddenly the shrill screams were obliterated,

as the impact of the plane made the ground shudder under Roberto's feet. Tremors raced through the ancient marshland far below. He tightened his hold on Isabella and together they swung around to see the fuel tanks burst into flames. Fire leapt hungrily over the crumpled fuselage and the little Caproncino exploded with a deafening roar.

* * *

Roberto couldn't hear right. He was crouched at the side of a man on the ground whose leg was shattered. The bones had come adrift, sticking out at the wrong angles, and the skin on one side of his face was burned to a glassy blistered shine. His lips were moving. But Roberto heard only a dull whirr of sound. Was it the man? Or was it him?

He was holding the unknown man's hand, sorrow making them cling to each other as they stared out at the carnage around them. The lips kept moving and it dawned on Roberto that the word that they were mouthing over and over was *sigaretta*. He rummaged in his camera case, found half a pack, lit one and set it between the wounded man's blue lips.

'You'll be all right, my friend,' he reassured him. 'The doctors are here. They'll get you to hospital where you'll be fixed up.'

The man nodded and forced a smile. His teeth were broken. A nurse descended and summoned stretcher-bearers who whisked him away to wait in the queue for ambulances. Roberto rose to his

310

feet, breathing fiercely. It was hard not to hate. When he saw all the suffering strewn around him, it was hard not to harbour the bitter hatred that was lodged in his chest tight up against his breastbone. The stage and the flimsy biplane that had both been constructed of wood and canvas had been totally incinerated and he could see the Gipsy engine, mangled and twisted, sprawled off to one side of the blackened mess, having barrelled through the crowd in a storm of shrieking whirling metal.

Cries of pain. Howls of grief. They littered the field. Bandages fluttered and blood seeped into the earth. People rushed to help and to offer comfort. To hold a hand. And behind each act of kindness Roberto knew there lay the silent guilty thought: *Thanks be to God that it was you and not me.*

★ ★ ★

How could one man do this?

The question clawed at Roberto's mind, and he moved over to where Isabella was working, tying a tourniquet on a man's arm. Just the sight of her calm, dry-eyed face and the swift efficient manner in which she twisted and knotted the rubber tubing around his bicep made him recall his own profession.

Quickly he put the Graflex to work. He had to record this day of infamy and it was easier, always easier, to look at it through the glazed indifference of his camera lens than through his own eyes. But when his stomach had had all it could take, he returned to check on Isabella. A great swath of the skirt of her green dress was torn away, a bandage for somebody, and she was kneeling on the ground talking with a tall man who wore spectacles and carried a stethoscope around his neck. He was dealing with a woman's stomach wound and his hands, like Isabella's, were swift and efficient, not afraid of handling shredded flesh.

Roberto had no intention of disturbing her at work, but it was as if Isabella could sense him, as if she could smell his skin or hear his heartbeat, because she immediately lifted her head and looked for him. It was one of those moments that would weave itself into the fabric of who he was. That fraction of a second before she remembered that there were others around, that a doctor was close to her elbow. That infinitesimal moment.

As she rose to her feet her blue eyes widened, warm and beautiful, and she looked at him as though there was no one else on the face of the earth she wanted to be looking at right now. He wanted to tell her that when he thought she was about to die on the rally field, he knew a part of him would die too, the part of him that mattered. But now was not the moment.

'I'm all right, Roberto,' she said at once.

Her hair was scraped back from her face and tied out of the way with a bootlace. She reached up and touched it, and he knew that what she really wanted to do was touch him.

'Roberto?' The doctor's head shot up from where he was tending the woman on the ground.

312

'Is this *the* Roberto, Isabella?'

'Yes, Papa. This is Roberto.'

Her father? Yes, he could see it now. The eyes. Their directness.

'I've heard things,' Roberto told them, 'as I've been going around the field with my camera.' His eyes travelled to the carabinieri patrolling past them and the brigade of Blackshirts spread out in force across the field.

'What is it, Roberto?'

'Mussolini escaped. Alive.'

He described for them the conflicting reports of the assassination attempt — that Il Duce was unhurt, that he'd lost a leg, that he was alive but wounded by a piece of flying metal that had sliced open his cheek to the bone. Isabella listened, her face intent, her eyes on his.

'Mussolini is alive?' she whispered.

'Yes.' He nodded grimly.

'Mussolini is alive? The plane didn't kill him?'

'It's true. The suicide plan failed to kill him.'

She stood mute, her eyes huge and unblinking. For a split second her face started to crumple and then grew livid with rage.

'You mean,' she shouted, as she swung an arm in a wide arc to indicate what looked like a battlefield around them, 'that this was for nothing? All this. For nothing?'

'Not for nothing, Isabella,' Roberto replied quietly. 'We will all pay for this.'

26

'Water?' A rasping cry rattled down the hospital ward. '*Acqua, per favore.*'

Isabella limped up to the far end with a jug of water, poured some into a glass and sat down with the patient to help him drink it. He was a young man running a fever. Sweat clogged his hair and stung his eyes. One of his lungs had been punctured.

'Try to rest,' she murmured and held his trembling hand as he lay back on his sweat-stained pillow with a sigh that seemed to drag the life out of him. He let his eyes fall shut.

'Talk to me,' he muttered through parched lips.

So she talked. About the only thing she knew. Her architecture. She told him the story of the disputes it took to settle whether the police station should be allowed a small tower of its own, and she told it in such a way that he smiled and flashed his fine white teeth at her. When he finally drifted into sleep she stayed with him, as though somehow her presence was a weapon against his fever.

It was dark now. Yet the muted edges of night failed to bring silence to the ward where the moans and sobs and murmurs of comfort continued as each hour shuffled past. Isabella was so weary that her bones felt ready to crack but she didn't close her eyes. The images from the rally today were too vivid, stuck like burrs on the inside of her head, and when she heard footsteps approaching the bed, she swung around, a smile leaping to her face in the hope that it might be Roberto. It was her father.

'Isabella, what the devil are you doing still here? I thought you'd gone long ago.' He spoke in a loud whisper. 'Take yourself off home and get some sleep.'

'I don't need sleep, Papa.'

'I'm the doctor, Isabella, and I'm ordering you to get some sleep.' He rummaged in the capacious pocket of his jacket, pulled out a bottle of tablets and tipped two in her palm. 'Go home, take these, and I'll see you tomorrow.'

'Aren't you coming?'

'No. I'll be spending the night here.'

'Oh, Papa.'

'Go.'

Isabella's hand closed over the tablets. There was a time not so long ago when she hadn't been past begging for these, anything to block out the crippling images whirring inside her head. A white powdery pill that had the power to block out the sound of her back splitting and to rid her of the vision of her husband's dead doll's eyes. She had welcomed the physical pain because when it was all-consuming it meant she could think of nothing else.

But not now. She slipped the tablets back into her father's hand. 'I'll go,' she said, 'but I won't use these. Give them to someone who needs them.'

'I thought that someone was you.'

315

'Not any more.' She smiled up at him in the dim light thrown by the lamp on the central table in the ward and kissed his cheek. 'Maybe you should take them yourself.'

'Pah! I never take tablets.'

She laughed softly at the irony of it. But her gaze settled on the rows of beds packed together so tightly and the smile drained out of her. 'What will happen?' she asked under her breath.

'None of us knows.'

'The pilot is dead. So no one can prove why he did it.'

'Colonnello Sepe is not going to need proof,' her father pointed out with a cold twitch of his mouth that people who didn't know better would have taken for a smile. 'Go home, *cara mia*, and don't leave the house tomorrow. Keep off the streets. Take a taxi home. Speak to no one.'

★　★　★

There were no taxis outside the hospital at this hour. It was late at night and the town was holding its breath after the horrors of the day. Isabella knew it wasn't over, not yet. The moon picked out patches of mist slinking like stray dogs in the gutters, and behind the shutters of the houses and apartments lives were being stitched back together.

She would walk home. She needed to feel the wind in her face and to let the night air dispel some of the things she'd seen in the hospital tonight. But she knew where her feet would lead her, even if she pointed them towards home, so she decided not to fight it. The house with the green door was some distance from the hospital but it didn't matter. That's where she would be heading and it wasn't just a courteous need to thank Roberto.

It was a craving.

★ ★ ★

Isabella strode quickly through the hospital gates, her leg dragging more than usual because of tiredness. She looked across the road. She didn't know why. Something pulled inside her, something drew her eyes to the dark spot opposite where two buildings almost met. There was a polite gap between them, a narrow alleyway going nowhere, and that was where Isabella's eyes looked tonight.

He was there. In the black mouth of the gap, staring out at the hospital frontage, stood Roberto. And then he was running across the empty street towards her, great leaping strides that brought him to her side in a rush of energy that swept aside her exhaustion and brought a wave of cool night air to clear the turmoil in her head.

She felt a sharp single thud of her heart and then his hand wound around the back of her neck and drew her to him. He kissed her and she could taste on his lips the heat of the words he wasn't saying and smell the darkroom chemicals on his skin. Her exhaustion fell away and in its place surged a desire to walk to

Rome and back with this man.

'Isabella,' he murmured against her lips, 'it's time for me to drive you home.'

★   ★   ★

She sat Roberto at one end of the sofa and herself at the other. A chasm of space between them. It had to be like that. If she sat any closer she would not be able to stop herself reaching out and touching him, and if she touched him, all the questions she needed to ask would vanish from her head.

She sat in silence for a full minute while he inspected the room. He took his time. The heavy furniture, the photograph of her mother, the gramophone and the ranks of records. The shelves groaning under stacks of medical books. A sketch of herself when she was about five years old drawn by her mother, her hair a mass of unruly dark curls even then. He looked at it intently and passed no comment, but the muscles of his face seemed to relax as if he felt at home here. She had poured him a drink but it sat untouched on the table.

'How did you know?' she asked bluntly.

His gaze abandoned the sketch of her childhood face and fixed on her adult one. 'How did I know what?'

'What was going to happen at the rally.'

'I didn't. All I learned was that it was not a wise place to be today. Safer to steer clear of it.'

'Yet you came there. For me.'

He didn't smile. 'Of course I did. Did you think I wouldn't?'

'Thank you, Roberto.' A pulse was beating in her throat. She licked her dry lips. 'If you had not come for me I would have been killed or maimed. That's certain, so thank you. This is the second time you've . . . '

He frowned, his heavy brows drawing together and she could see he was uncomfortable with her thanks, just as he'd been when he'd saved her from the horse.

'What about your friend from your office, the one who was standing with you? What happened to him?'

'Davide Francolini, you mean? I saw him at the hospital. He's a lucky man and should be thanking you too. When he saw you rush me away from there, he realised something was wrong and started to leave, but he got caught by the stampede and has a dislocated shoulder.'

'Better than dead.'

'That's what he said.'

'He has a nose for survival, that man.'

But Isabella knew what Roberto was doing and she would not let him distract her. 'How did you know that trouble was coming?'

She saw his features tighten, his body grow tense. Whatever it was, he didn't want to tell her. She could sense his mind whirring, working out how much he needed to tell her of whatever it was he was hiding from her.

'Roberto.' She said his name sharply, and it sounded harsh to her ears. She didn't mean it to be harsh. 'Roberto, who told you that the rally field would be dangerous? And why don't you want to tell me?'

He smiled, but it was stretched too tight. 'Because you will be angry and I fear what you will do when you're angry.'

She waited in silence for a name.

'Rosa's father told me there would be trouble.'

'What?'

'Rosa's father. I saw him today and spoke with him.'

'What do you mean?'

Roberto's words were so incredible that they would not go into Isabella's head, but it penetrated slowly that he wasn't lying to her or teasing her. He meant what he said.

'Where did you see him?' In her eagerness she shuffled further along the padded seat, her body creeping closer to him, whether she liked it or not. 'When?'

'Today. At the convent.'

'How did you know he'd be there?'

'I didn't. I guessed. It made sense. He'd take the chance to see his daughter while everyone else was in thrall to Mussolini. He couldn't be sure everyone would turn out to welcome Il Duce to Bellina when he arrived in the cavalcade, but the whole town was expected to be there for his speech at the rally.'

She shuddered, uncertain whether it was anger at him or herself. 'What was he like, this man who deserts his child?'

'A dangerous man. All he can see is the goal. To rid Italy of Mussolini. Everything else is sacrificed to that end. Even his daughter.'

320

'Including me.'

'Including you.'

He told her the details of his meeting with the rebel, and how he had neither confirmed nor denied that he was responsible for Luigi Berotti's death and the crippling of Isabella herself. So this killer of her husband had been so close she could have spat in his face, if she'd known where to look. The thought sent a tremor of hatred through her, so strong it made her teeth chatter.

'I've informed the police,' he said, but when he saw the surprise on her face, he asked, 'Isn't that what you want? For him to be arrested and thrown into gaol?'

'What I want is to tear his heart out.'

'Isabella,' Roberto shook his head, 'we don't know this man's name. Or even if he was the one who killed your husband. All we can be sure of is that he was involved in the plot to assassinate Mussolini today. He knew it was coming and warned me away.'

'But he knows, doesn't he, about the shooting in Milan?'

'Oh yes, he knows all right. I made it clear that you need to speak to him. He thought you were dead.' Roberto gave an odd little snort of laughter. 'He's probably hoping the police will get to him first.'

His laugh caught Isabella by surprise and her heartbeat slowed a fraction. Her mind cleared, but she did what she had promised herself she would not do. She laid her fingers on Roberto's arm. She stared at them, pale wilful creatures on the dark material of his jacket. When had she

321

moved so close to him?

Isabella dipped her head so that her thick hair fell between them. 'Sometimes I can go a whole day without thinking about him once. Sometimes. And those are the good days. But I can never go a whole night without that man stalking my dreams. I wake screaming every time the shots are fired again. There's a hole in me, Roberto. Not just in my back. In me.'

'Isabella,' Roberto murmured in a voice she hadn't heard before.

This was the voice that had whispered in the horse's ear when it was spooked, and she felt it trickle now, sweet and comforting, into her own ear. Her fingers relaxed their grip on his sleeve. She felt the warmth of his hand as he cupped her head and drew it to his chest where she buried her face against him. She inhaled the scent of him safe inside her and knew that the tremors wouldn't strike today, not with his scent so strong.

'Isabella, that's why we'll find him again and next time you'll speak to him face to face.' Tenderly he brushed her hair back and kissed her forehead. 'He will be coming back to the convent. For Rosa.'

'You think he'll risk it?'

'Yes, I do.' He slid one hand to his jacket pocket and extracted something. 'Look at these.'

He placed in her hand two photographs. One was of a high wall and Isabella recognised it at once as the convent wall. On top of it lay the figure of a man as he scrambled over it. Too far away to be clear. Blurred features. Fair hair. A sense of determination caught in the frozen action of his limbs. Isabella didn't breathe, didn't blink in case he vanished. The second photograph was taken in a corridor and it was a picture that turned her heart over.

'See?' Roberto prompted.

Isabella saw. At the end of the corridor stood a tall slight figure in a shabby suit that had a long tear in the jacket, so that one of its lapels hung loose. At the moment that the photograph was taken he was bending over to turn a key in a door. His hair had fallen forward but still his face was clearly visible. It wasn't the face Isabella had expected.

It was fine-featured and intelligent-looking, the kind of intellectual face that belonged in a university. Except for the hard cliff-edge cheekbones. And the knife that was visible where his torn jacket fell forward. The small hairs on the back of Isabella's neck rose like the hackles on a dog.

★　★　★

Isabella woke. How could she have fallen asleep?

She had slept without dreams of any kind. Her body felt rested and warm, her mind loose and elastic. Slowly she let her eyes drift open.

'Roberto!'

She was stretched out on the sofa, her head propped on a cushion on Roberto's lap and his arm was wrapped around her shoulders. In shock, she sat herself upright instantly.

'Roberto, I'm sorry.'

She was a mess. Her skirt, with the strips torn out of it for bandages on the rally field, had ridden up over her legs, revealing her thigh. She pulled it down and ran both hands through the tangled nest of her hair.

'Sorry,' she said again. 'Damn it, I don't know how that happened.'

'You were exhausted. You'd seen too many horrors. You needed rest, Isabella.'

His voice lodged in her mind. It was different. The rhythms of it had altered. As though something had changed inside him while he watched her sleep. There was a new caged energy about him. The earlier tension that had compressed his mouth into a hard line when he was showing her the photographs was gone and there was a shine to his eyes that made it impossible for her to look away.

'What is it, Roberto?'

He was regarding her intently. 'Tell me about Luigi,' he said. 'What kind of man was he?'

'My husband?'

'Yes. You never talk about him.'

She didn't mean to shrug, but she did it anyway. She wasn't comfortable talking about Luigi. 'Oh, you know, very Italian. Full of big gestures and sure of his place in the world.'

'And what place was that?'

'One where he was in control.'

There was a moment, a flicker of time, when she knew he was about to ask the unaskable and she felt something she thought was dead stir and grunt inside her. The air in the room seemed to slacken, so that the gap between them barely existed.

'Did he ever hurt you?'

The question he should not ask.

'Why do you think that?' she said, annoyed.

'In your sleep. You were fighting someone off.'

She swallowed carefully. 'Everyone hurts others at some time, people we love. We all do it.'

He put his hands on either side of her face and kissed her lips. Not fierce or possessive. It was a firm decisive kiss and Isabella knew she needed to tell him more.

'He was a big man,' she elaborated. 'Sometimes he didn't know his own strength.'

'Every man knows his own strength.'

Isabella lifted Roberto's hand and placed a kiss in the centre of its broad callused palm, a hand with a touch as soft as a breeze on a horse's hide.

'I was young when I married Luigi, young and dazzled by the splendour of him in his dramatic uniform. I was swept up in the passion of his great plans for the future of Italy, powered by the grandiose rhetoric of Mussolini.' She shook her head, remembering those heady days in Milan. 'Luigi was a man of action, Roberto. I had been brought up in a house of ideas and ideals, where principles mattered more than practicalities. Suddenly with Luigi I saw how Italy could really reform and become strong again if we took action. I was stupid enough to believe Mussolini's promises.'

Isabella stretched her arms wide as though to wrap them around the whole world. 'I was captivated. Can you understand that?'

'Foolish,' Roberto muttered, but his hands closed around one of hers.

'Weren't you ever foolish when you were young?' she demanded.

Roberto laughed and drew her close. She could feel the ripple of his laughter still vibrating in his chest.

'I once tried to swim from Sorrento right across the Bay of Naples,' he confessed with a dog-eared smile. He brushed his lips along the smooth line of her cheek. 'I was so arrogant I believed nothing could defeat me.'

'Did it?'

'Oh yes. I almost drowned long before I reached Napoli. Treacherous currents.' He chuckled, a rich throaty sound. 'I learned my lesson.'

'I learned mine too, Roberto.'

A silence slid into the room and settled on the sofa. Isabella could hear her own heartbeat.

'What did you learn, Isabella?'

'When I came out of hospital I learned to take control of my own life. I swore never to give it up to someone else ever again.'

His gaze on her face was solemn and thoughtful. 'I admire what you've done, Isabella. There can't be more than three or four female architects in the whole of Italy. That must have taken sheer guts, to stand up to a daily battle against our male prejudices against women in jobs of this kind. You must be tougher than you look.'

She scowled at him. 'I am tough.' She ignored his sudden smile in case it tempted her to lay her head back down on the cushion. 'Tough enough,' she continued, 'to go to Rome.'

'No, Isabella, don't — '

'To drag information out of the man whose name Mussolini gave me. He was Luigi's commander in the Blackshirts. It's the only way I can find out what was going on ten years ago.'

Roberto's eyes flicked sharply across her face.

'I came to a decision while you slept,' he announced.

'Yes?'

This was it. Isabella knew that whatever it was, it wasn't going to be what she wanted to hear. Roberto had stepped into danger too often for her already and the weight of that knowledge pressed hard on a soft spot inside her that wanted to wrestle him to the ground and keep him safe.

'It's about Rosa.'

She rested a finger on his mouth, tracing the sharply defined curves of his lips, and whispered, 'No.'

'Isabella, I — '

She silenced him with a kiss. Soft at first, no more than a light brush of her lips along his, to keep the words from tumbling out, but as she entwined her arms around his neck, the kiss became fierce and hungry. Her body pressed itself against his, and she was losing all sense of self in his scent and warmth. She felt things clicking into place inside her. Where had it come from, this overwhelming need for this man, this precious ability to love again that she thought she'd lost?

From him. From Roberto himself. A gift that he had given her. A deep sigh of happiness escaped her. It was beyond her comprehension.

His hands caressed her throat, her breast, sending heat spiralling through her veins and a pulse kicked into life in her groin that she had thought was dead and buried. She rubbed her smooth sleepy cheek against the bristle on his jaw and heard his breath rumble deep in his throat when her hand slid inside his shirt and found the hard lean muscles of his chest.

Her hair fell thick and wild over him and he swept it up in his hand, a tangled hank of it, and tipped her head back, so that his lips could claim her long throat.

'Isabella,' Roberto murmured, exhaling the words in soft puffs of warm air over her pale skin. 'I want us to remove Rosa from the convent tomorrow. You can keep her here with you, so that when her father comes for her, he will be forced to speak with you.'

Her hand tightened on his chest like the bite of a horse. 'Roberto — '

'And I will go to Rome to question the man who was Luigi's commander.'

There it was. His decision. The heavy furniture seemed to press closer, waiting for a response. Isabella opened her mouth to say she could not risk him again, he was too much a part of her now, woven into the heart of her.

The crash on the front door ricocheted through the apartment. No knock. No ringing of the bell. Just the splintering crash resonating in the silent room and then boots in the hall.

Roberto leapt to his feet as five men in carabinieri uniform burst through the door into Dr Cantini's living room. The air seemed to vibrate around them. Fear burrowed into Isabella's chest, driving the breath from her lungs.

'Signora Berotti,' declared the leading police officer, the one with his heavy chin thrown forward and the bicorn hat worn like a weapon on his head, 'you are under arrest.'

'No,' Roberto said firmly. 'There is some mistake, officer. Signora Berotti is not — '

'Shut your mouth before I shut it for you. Who are you?'

'I am Roberto Falco, photographer for the town of Bellina. I work for Chairman Grassi and I shall be reporting you to him for incompetence and wilful misconduct if you do not leave this house at once.'

The aggression in the officer's eyes faltered. Isabella could see him calculating inwardly, but only until his sharp gaze fixed once more on her and then he marched forward. She had staggered to her feet. Struck dumb. But she stood straight and made no sound when he seized her wrist with a grip that nearly wrenched her arm from its socket.

Instantly Roberto smashed his fist into the man's face with the full weight of his body behind it.

'No!' she screamed, as a barrage of blows fell on him, driving him to the floor.

'Come, bitch,' the officer snarled through a bloodied lip.

She was handcuffed and dragged to the door.

'On what charge?' Roberto bellowed. A gun was pointed at his head.

'Treachery.'

'Roberto,' Isabella cried out.

'Isabella, it's a mistake. Don't worry. I'll go to Grassi.'

She nodded stiffly.

'Don't be afraid.'

But when she was shut alone in total darkness in the back of the police van outside, silent terror descended on her mind.

27

The cell was clean. It was new. It was cold.

Isabella sat for three hours on the edge of the hard bed without moving. Eyes straight ahead. Spine rigid. If she moved, she feared she would fall off a cliff into a chasm. Her thoughts were spiky. Jagged. She kept remembering the colleague of her father, Dr Pavese, the one who vanished one day and was replaced without a word. She pictured a new architect walking up to her drawing board, using her drawing pens, sharpening her pencils. The others in the office would notice. They'd look. But would they ask, 'Where's Isabella?' Would they demand an answer from Dottore Martino?

Of course not.

No questions. Not if you didn't want Blackshirts' boots in your bedroom at two o'clock in the morning.

Treachery.

The word burned, each letter branded into her brain. Treachery got you shot in front of a firing squad. Or hanged. Or beaten to death in your cell. Her eyes, the only part of her that still moved, scoured the cold tiles on the floor for bloodstains but found none. She breathed, but only just.

Treachery.

What had she done to deserve that word?

Did rejecting Il Duce's greedy lips count as

treachery? Or speaking to a rebel's child? Or pointing out a crack in a house? Or binding up the wound of a farmer who wasn't a farmer?

Dear God, where was the line between treachery and reality?

Roberto had once warned her that she must guard not only her words but also her thoughts from scrutiny.

Who had listened to her thoughts?

Anger came. It drove the chills from her veins and forced her to stride back and forth across the small space, her heart hammering to break loose. She wanted them to come for her, to start the questions. She wanted to see their faces and look directly into their lying eyes. These people. They had wrenched control of her life from her hands and she had to take it back.

Hours ticked past. The cell grew smaller and the air became too thick to breathe. The silence hurt her ears and loneliness twisted itself into a tight knot in her stomach. There was nothing here except a narrow bed and a galvanised bucket and the stink of her own fear on her skin. Life stripped of its outer layers, the way she'd seen a rabbit carcass flayed of its skin, hanging red and raw from a hook.

But Roberto was here. With her. She invited him in and he came willingly. The sublime sound of his laughter demolished the fear inside her head and she heard again the promise in his voice when he said, *It's a mistake. Don't worry.*

She stared at the blank wall and refused to blink.

'I want a lawyer.'

'All in good time, Signora Berotti.'

'Colonnello Sepe, I want a lawyer now.'

The policeman's thin lips pulled into a sour line of displeasure. 'We are not here to deal with what *you* want, signora.'

'Then why am I here?'

'To answer the charge of treachery to the State of Italy and to Il Duce as the representative of this country.'

Isabella's heart lurched and she kept her hands linked together in the handcuffs on her lap, so that they would not shake.

'I am baffled, Colonnello. I have never done anything against my country. On the contrary, I — '

'Do not lie!' His hand slammed down on the desk, but his voice grew as soft as oil. 'It will get you nowhere.'

Isabella wanted to run. To batter the door down. To leave this room. She could see in his dead eyes that she had already been tried and condemned in his mind. This was a formality, that was all. He was seated behind a metal desk in a chilly room, a poster on the wall of Il Duce on the famous balcony of the Venezia Palace as he addressed the crowds of Rome. It was the kind of grey-painted room where a person could lose their soul. Another officer sat silent in the corner, and the manilla file in front of Colonnello Sepe looked alarmingly thick.

She sat upright on the hard chair and refused

to drop her gaze. 'What proof do you have, Colonnello, that I ever — '

'You are not here to ask questions,' he snapped. 'You are here to answer them.'

Isabella said nothing. She waited in silence for more from the hawkish face before her, and saw a faint flash of pleasure flare the nostrils of his long pointed nose.

'You are charged,' he said, 'with treason. You were running from the rally field long before anyone knew the aeroplane's intention was to attack.' He placed one hand on top of the other on his desk, a small bony tower. 'Why was that, Signora Berotti?'

Isabella's mouth was dry as dust. No words emerged. If she told the truth, she would be placing Roberto on this chair with these handcuffs biting into the strong bones of his wrists.

'It is clear,' the carabiniere continued, 'that you knew what was about to happen and yet you warned no one. You were willing for Mussolini to die and that is treason.'

'No.'

'You have shown undue attention and care to the daughter of a known traitor.'

'That was because her mother — '

'You were present on a farm when the tenant was revealed to be an instrument of deception.'

'Instrument of deception?'

'Yes.'

Isabella's mind was spinning. Something was clawing up her throat, trying to get out.

'And,' Sepe said, releasing his hands, palms up

like a conjuror, 'cracks have been appearing in a building in your charge. You are sabotaging the very construction of our town.'

He sat back in his chair, the skin on his forehead so tight it looked as though it might split. His eyes narrowed, observing her, and there was a gleam of satisfaction in them. Was this revenge for last time, when she had stood in the way of his questioning of Rosa?

'So, signora. What do you have to say for yourself?'

'I am innocent.'

He snorted his disgust. 'The cracks?'

Only one person could have told him about the cracks. 'They are the result of cost-cutting during the construction process,' she said. 'Either the cement contains too much sand or the foundations were not dug deep enough. Neither of those is my responsibility.'

He jotted something down on a lined pad in front of him. 'The farmer?'

'I was visiting him for the first time. I knew nothing about his farming skills.'

'So why were you there?'

She hesitated. A fatal error, she was aware. 'To look at one of the homesteads from an architectural standpoint, now that they are occupied.'

Were her words too thin? Too weightless? Was her breathing too fast?

'And the girl called Rosa? I have seen for myself your attachment to that traitor's child, so don't deny it.'

'Her mother gave her to me to look after.'

'Why would she do that?'

'I don't know.'

I don't know. I don't know.

This time the fleshless man in the dark uniform let a silence grow in the room, a silence that was as heavy and viscous as the mud in which her feet were trapped. They both knew what was coming next.

'Why did you run from the rally?'

This time she was ready for him.

'I was feeling ill. I wanted to get away before I was sick.'

'Liar!'

'No, it's true. I was — '

'Liar!'

She shook her head.

'Signora, you left Il Duce and his loyal supporters to die on that field while you fled like the treacherous coward you are.' Scorn and disgust rippled through his words. 'Who told you about the plane?'

'No one.'

Colonnello Sepe stood up abruptly, knocking back his chair.

'Who are you working with against Il Duce?'

'No one. I am not — '

'The truth, signora. I *will* have the truth.'

'I am telling the truth.'

Why did he not mention Roberto? Or Davide Francolini? If he knew so much about her, he must know she was with them on the rally field. She was breathing too fast, but she was aware of Sepe's every tiny expression, each flick of an eyelid, each tightening of a muscle, the way his

336

pitch-black pupils contracted and expanded as he breathed. She saw it coming, his need to strip away another layer of her defences, but there was nothing she could do to stop it.

He walked forward until he was standing right next to her in her chair at the front of the desk. She could smell his aftershave, something spicy and sharp, and the cloying scent of his hair oil. It took all her willpower not to flinch away from him. Without comment he seized her right wrist and laid it flat on the desk, dragging the other hand with it in the handcuffs. His grip was like steel.

'Now, signora, let us have the truth from you.'

From his holster he withdrew his gun but held it by its muzzle, raising it in the air above her fingers like a hammer.

'I imagine you need your hands to be very precise in your line of work, don't you, signora?'

'Yes.'

'So you need full use of your fingers?'

'Yes.'

Her fingers spasmed on the desk.

'Who told you that the aeroplane was coming to crash into the platform?'

'No one.'

A sigh spilled out of him. A pretence. As if he didn't enjoy his work.

'One last time. Who told you?'

'No one.'

The gun came down.

28

'Get out of my car.'

'Not yet.'

'Falco, damn you, get out of my car right now or I'll have you thrown out.' Two spots of livid colour appeared high on Chairman Grassi's cheeks.

They were seated in the rear of the chairman's sleek black motor car, a long unmistakable Lancia Dilambda that cruised the streets of Bellina every Sunday morning to inspect progress in the town and assess the behaviour of the inhabitants, like a shark patrolling its waters. A muscular uniformed chauffeur sat up front in the driving seat, suitably separated from his passengers in the elegant limousine by a glass partition. Nonetheless, Roberto kept his voice low. He had waited on the street corner in the chill wind that whistled up Via San Michele and as soon as the chairman's car slowed at the crossroads on its usual route, he had stepped into the road, pulled open the rear door and swung himself onto the seat before Grassi could voice his objection. They faced each other from opposite ends of the long leather seat, hackles raised.

Roberto placed a photograph face down on the patch of cream leather between them.

'What the hell is this? Grassi demanded. 'What are you playing at?'

'It's not a game, chairman.'

Grassi snatched up the photograph. He was a man used to dealing with surprises. Each day he handled unpleasantness and he was skilled at maintaining his composure, his slate-grey eyes revealing nothing. But his jaw dropped open. He scowled at the picture.

'Where did you get this?'

'I took it myself. That's what you pay me for.'

'It's Marchini.'

'Right first time.'

Roberto saw the moment when the Fascist Party's chairman let his anger trickle out through his rigid fingers and in its place seeped the realisation of what the photograph meant. Grassi started to chuckle, a thick unpleasant sound that rose to a roar of laughter. He reached over and slapped Roberto heavily on the knee.

'*Bene, bene*,' he said boisterously, 'you've done well, Falco.' But the deep grooves on each side of his mouth hardened and the laughter was cut off short. 'This isn't enough,' he growled. 'This proves nothing.'

A smile that didn't even attempt to reach Roberto's eyes pinned itself to his face. 'There are more.'

Grassi nodded to himself, satisfied. 'Alberto Marchini will regret this day, the perverted bastard.' He flicked the photograph into Roberto's lap with disgust.

Signor Marchini was Chairman Grassi's chief assistant in the Party headquarters and was extremely efficient at his job, industrious and painstaking. He was a slender man in his forties, tall and elegant, who wore finely styled suits and possessed a soft pink complexion that belied the sharpness of his mind. He had come up through the ranks with Grassi from the early Milan days, but the trouble with having an assistant who had been with you so many years was that he knew you too well. He'd seen your mistakes. Your weaknesses. He knew where the black corners were hidden in your heart. You were at his mercy and someone like Grassi would writhe in the cold hours of the night at that thought.

Roberto was relying on it.

'Where did you take the picture?'

'On one of his trips to Party headquarters in Rome.'

The photograph showed Alberto Marchini wearing a brassiere on his naked chest. Not any old brassiere, nothing so banal. This one was a stripper's brassiere of shimmering gold, with holes cut out. His nipples peeked through, painted some dark colour that didn't show up in the black and white photograph, but which Roberto recalled all too well had been a shocking deep Chinese carmine. It had looked obscene. The man's paper-white skin. The tawdry brassiere. His nipples glistening and coated in thick layers of red lipstick.

'Who are they?' Grassi jabbed a finger at the two young women with bottle-blonde hair and flesh spilling out of their tight clothes, one on each side of him, holding him up on his feet.

'They were just cheap bar girls who worked the club. They had no idea who he was.'

'*Bene*!'

The photograph was taken in a narrow dark street at the back of a nightclub in one of Rome's seedier districts. Roberto had needed to use a flash but Marchini was too drunk to notice and the girls didn't care. His button flies hung open in the picture. It wouldn't have mattered much, not really, if it had been anyone other than Marchini. But he, of all men, had set himself above what he vigorously condemned as degeneracy. He was an avid churchgoer, a self-proclaimed moral man with a wife and six offspring, whom he held up as moral examples for the rest of the town. Daily he cursed the depravity and debauchery of the modern Italian male and urged them on to the path of sobriety and piety. His face was blurred, as if it had somehow melted in the heat of his own debauchery.

Roberto felt sorry for Marchini. Truly sorry. But nowhere near as sorry as he was feeling for Isabella right now.

'There are more,' he said again. 'More revealing ones.'

'Show me.'

The church bells started to peal at that moment and if Roberto had believed in such things, he might have taken it as warning. But he didn't. So he shook his head, as the car purred past the hospital where the wounded from the rally field fought for life, and he gave the chairman a level stare.

'No,' he said.

'Don't be a fool, damn you. Give them to me.'

But even as he held out a hand for them,

341

Roberto could see understanding dawn in the distrustful grey eyes. The chairman slumped back against the cream leather with a snort of annoyance.

'What is it you want, Falco?'

'Isabella Berotti out of the police cell.'

'What?'

'You ordered Colonnello Sepe to arrest her.'

'What the police do is their affair, not mine.'

Roberto leaned closer and could see the tiny muscle at the side of Grassi's eye jump and twitch. Not a good sign. He didn't waste time.

'Release Signora Berotti and the rest of the photographs will be yours. You'll be able to make Alberto Marchini jump to your tune for as long as you like.'

Chairman Grassi stared out of the window, thinking hard, his teeth clamped together. After a full minute's silence he turned his head.

'So, Falco, you have become one of us. You are like Marchini. Feet of clay. No room for you on the moral heights any more.' He gave Roberto a slow insinuating smile. 'You use what you have to in order to get what you want.' He laughed softly. 'As dirty as the rest of us now.'

'I've learned from an expert.' Roberto nodded at Grassi.

Abruptly the chairman sat up, straightened his camel overcoat and black felt trilby, patting a hand on his bulky chest as though to reassure himself of who he was.

'That girl is a bloody nuisance to me, Falco.'

Roberto held out his hand, hovering over the cream leather in invitation. 'The photographs will be in your hands the moment she is released.'

'To hell with you.'

'Agreed?'

'Yes. Agreed.' He shook Roberto's hand and it was all Roberto could do to stop himself slapping the soft clinging flesh away.

'We use what we have to,' Roberto said quietly.

The chairman laughed loudly, goading him, but Roberto banged on the glass partition.

'Stop here,' he ordered.

The car drifted to a halt outside the elegantly curved station building and Roberto opened the door, but instead of climbing out he swung round to Grassi.

'Leave Signora Berotti out of this. She knows nothing about the man you are hunting. Don't be a fool, don't waste your time on her.'

The chairman suddenly shuddered and dragged a hand slowly down over his face, as though trying to rearrange whatever thoughts were in his head.

'Mussolini wants heads on a platter,' he snapped. 'He's demanding bodies hanging in the streets. And if I don't bring him the traitor who plotted this assassination attempt, he will make sure that mine will be one of those bodies.'

Roberto slapped the photograph face down on the seat between them. 'If you live by lies, Grassi, you die by lies. You should know that by now.'

He stepped out of the car.

'Falco!'

He slammed the door.

The window rolled down. 'She's involved,

Falco. You know it and I know it. We'll be watching her.' He uttered a deep humourless chuckle. 'Perhaps that pretty head of hers on a platter will satisfy Mussolini's thirst for blood.'

As Roberto strode away, the chairman's voice chased after him. 'Don't forget the photographs, Falco.'

As dirty as the rest of us now.

29

Isabella sat still. If she didn't move, it didn't hurt as much. Not her right hand which was cradled in her lap, but everything. Everything that ached inside her. She knew without a doubt that Colonnello Sepe intended to throw her to the dogs of war, to let her be torn limb from limb. Roberto was right. The town of Bellina was going to pay and the price was to be in blood.

She threaded through her mind each of the questions that Sepe had asked and thought carefully about each answer she had given, and every time she came up against the same brick wall. Why had he not once mentioned Roberto? Why?

There were witnesses. Others must have seen him racing her away from the rally. Davide Francolini certainly did. She felt the hairs on her neck rise at the thought of Davide. He had reported her. He had to be the one who implied that the cracks in the building were her fault. That was enough to lose her her job. At the very least.

So why?

Her thoughts shredded each other as they chased through her head and she could feel the pain in her damaged hand throbbing in time with them. But physical pain was an old familiar foe that she'd learned to vanquish years ago; it held no fears for her. It strutted through her nerve-endings on a daily basis and she knew how to shut it away in a special compartment of her brain. At night it could still sink its teeth in and catch her unawares, but at night she was alone and there was no one to see her face or look into her eyes.

Finally she rose to her feet, her eyes too frightened to close because of what they might see in the darkness inside her head. Where once there had been the bright vista of a future and of boundless ambition, now there was nothing. An aching nothingness. Because there would be no future, no ambitions. It was all over. Here in this wretched cell, it all ended. A faint moan slithered around the tiled walls and it took her a full minute to realise it had come from her own mouth. She stepped up to the hefty metal door and pressed her burning cheek hard against its cold surface until it made her teeth ache.

'Roberto,' she murmured. 'What are you doing? Did you put me here?'

The second the words skimmed past her lips, she wanted to snatch them back, to deny them air to breathe. She hated the treacherous whisper and hated herself for the betrayal. Yet she came back to it again and again — why was she the only one arrested?

It was as she stood there moulded against the door that a sudden thought stabbed into her mind, as silent and as lethal as an assassin's blade.

What if he was arrested too?

Visions of truncheons descending on his broad back and crashing down on his unprotected skull flared in her head and she felt her stomach turn. She vomited on to the white tiles of the floor, too late to reach the bucket, and felt as if her innards had been wrenched out by feral claws.

'Roberto,' she whispered.

She heard his laugh. In her head she heard his laugh, clear and enticing.

'Roberto,' she howled.

He had dragged her out of the safe numb state that she had wrapped around herself like a shell, he had cracked it wide open and brought her gasping into his warm, sensitive and passionate world, but she had not been prepared for this version of love. For the craving in her body for him. For the violence of it. For the way it could stop her heart.

* * *

Colonnello Sepe stood in the cell doorway, the heel of one black boot drumming on the floor. He had thrown open the metal door with such force that it slammed back against the wall, cracking a row of tiles. Isabella had the feeling that he had hoped to catch her behind it.

'Signora Berotti, it has been decided that you can leave.'

She stood her ground in the middle of the floor. 'It has been decided by whom?'

'That is not important.'

'It is to me.'

He stared down at the spray of vomit spread out in front of her and wrinkled his nose in disgust. The silver braid on his bicorn hat and the gaudy display of medals on his bird-like chest did not distract Isabella from an awareness of the anger in him. Whoever had made this decision, it certainly wasn't him.

Relief started small, just a trickle through her veins, but within seconds it was a torrent raging through her, deafening her ears.

'Was it my father, Dr Cantini? she asked. 'Was it his request for my release that — '

'Get out!'

'I knew he would not stand for your — '

'Get out!'

Isabella hesitated no longer. As she strode past him his sharp hawk's nose thrust forward as if it could barely resist tearing strips of skin off her.

Don't limp. She raised her damaged hand and rested it on her chest, but it was her leg she was cursing. Don't you dare limp.

*　*　*

The van spilled Isabella on to the pavement outside the apartment block where she lived. She had been bundled like laundry into the black van waiting in the yard at the rear of the police station and then dumped with no explanation or even any attempt at politeness.

She was surprised by the sky. It was a vast swath of lilac, shot through by vivid slashes of gold and an astonishing deep purple as the sun slid into the sea to the west of the plain. Isabella had no idea it was so late in the day. Her jailers had removed her watch and there was no window in the cell, so her only sense of time had been the one that existed in her head. As she walked into the courtyard of the apartment her elongated shadow hobbled ahead of her as though in a hurry to get indoors.

When she unlocked the door she found the rooms silent and eerily lit by pools of misty lilac light from outside, but no lamps were on in the apartment.

'Papa?' she said softly.

She didn't shout. She could hear a distinct clicking sound and knew immediately what it was — a gramophone record had come to the end and was still turning. Quickly she hurried into the living room.

'Papa?' she said again.

Her father was slumped with his head on the table. His spectacles had fallen off his nose and hung crookedly from one ear, and gripped in one hand was the photograph of his wife. Isabella hurried to his side and her fingers felt for his pulse, the way she'd seen him do a thousand times to his patients. His skin was warm, not ice cold. She touched his slack unshaven cheek and was greeted with a contented snore. She laughed. It burst from her in a loud rush of relief, as the tension she'd been holding so tight inside suddenly broke free, and she shook her father's shoulder. He grunted, startled, and fought to open his eyes a slit.

'Papa!'

Clearly he'd been working at the hospital day and night as he struggled to put bones and body parts back together, but Isabella could not let him sleep now. She needed to thank him. Had to

349

press her cheek to his, had to let him know how grateful she was for the fact that he must have begged Grassi on bended knee to release his daughter.

'*Grazie*,' she said simply.

He blinked as he came back to life and pushed himself up on his elbows. His face was creased with exhaustion.

'Isabella! Where on earth have you been? I've been worried. Don't you know there's a curfew?'

'A curfew?'

'Yes, no one's allowed on the streets after dark.' He put on his spectacles and inspected her with a frown. 'You don't look good. What have you been doing?'

He didn't know. Her father had been at the hospital for the last twenty-four hours and had no idea that his daughter had been in a prison cell. Quickly she poured him a drink and placed it in front of him without answering his question.

'Papa, you must go to bed. You need sleep.'

He reached for the wine.

'How bad is it at the hospital?' she asked.

'Bad enough.' He drank half the wine.

'I'm so sorry.'

'I thought you might have come back there today to help.'

'I couldn't, Papa. Not today.'

Something in her voice gave her away. He pushed himself to his feet and examined her with a professional medical gaze. She saw it dawn on his weary brain that she was still in the same torn green dress as yesterday, but his gaze fixed on her swollen hand.

'What happened, Isabella?'

'I was arrested.'

A groan escaped him, but that was all. He fetched his medical bag, sat her down and gently examined her hand, then bandaged it with quick efficient care.

'Your forefinger is broken in two places,' he announced. 'Several of the metacarpals of your hand could be broken too. I suspect they are but it's impossible to be certain without an X-ray because of the swelling.' He gave her a couple of tablets for the pain.

'Thank you, Papa.'

His cheeks were a dangerous crimson but he didn't raise his voice. 'Who did this?'

'I'm sure they're arresting a lot of people. It was bound to happen.' She gave him a tight smile. 'I'm one of the lucky ones — I've been released.'

'Did they arrest you because of Rosa?'

'Partly. But you know what they're like, Papa. They don't need a reason.'

Dr Cantini knocked back the last of his wine and gently folded his arms around his daughter, holding her tight. He smelled of medicines and blood and pain. Isabella knew he needed to come home to rest, not to find more pain waiting for him in a torn green dress. She kissed his rough cheek.

'Papa, I am glad you are my father.'

He blinked and pulled his head back to look at her with surprise. His blue eyes were embarrassed.

'Good,' he said gruffly.

'Now go to bed.'

She walked him to his bedroom door and he shook his head in despair. 'If someone doesn't fight back, there's no hope for Italy. That pilot sacrificed himself and others yesterday, but if he'd succeeded . . . just think of it, Isabella. An Italy without Mussolini.' With a deep sigh he kissed her forehead. 'Take care of your hand. *Buonanotte*. Sleep well.'

'Thank you, Papa. I'm all right.'

As soon as his door closed, Isabella tore off her dress one-handed and pulled on a jumper and skirt. She snatched her coat from the hall and bolted out into the night under the last dregs of the lilac sky.

★　★　★

The green door opened the moment she knocked. Had he been standing there? Hour after hour, waiting for her?

Did he know she would come?

Roberto drew her in and held her close without a word. Held her so close, it was as if he were trying to fuse her body to his, and all she could hear was the violent beating of his heart. She could feel his hand stroking her hair, pushing back its dark tangles from her face. She was acutely aware of the lightness of his touch, of the heaviness of his breath. All thought of everything else vanished into oblivion, and for a long time they stood there in the dimly lit hallway until, bit by bit, the world slowly came back to her. Fragile at first, but growing more solid with each breath she took.

She lifted her head from his shoulder. 'Thank you, Roberto,' she whispered against his lips.

Reluctantly his arms unwound and he stepped back to look at her. In the shadows it seemed as if his features had shifted, their lines altered in some indefinable way in the last eighteen hours, and she wondered whether hers had done the same.

'What did they do to you?' His voice was flat.

'Nothing much. Asked some questions.'

His eyes rested on the bandage on her hand. He said nothing but his mouth tightened and he examined her face intently, watching every flicker of an eyelid. She wanted to stretch her good hand across the short space and touch him again, but he walked over to the door and opened it a crack.

'I'm glad you came,' he said. 'Now I'll drive you home quickly before it is totally dark. There's a curfew.'

Her heart was crashing around her chest, appalled by his dismissal of her.

'No, Roberto.'

He hugged her fiercely. Briefly. 'We must be quick,' he said and opened the door.

'No, Roberto.' She kicked the door shut. 'I will stay.'

The silent rage that he had been holding back suddenly flooded the hall, thickening the air, and she felt the full force of it.

'You should not have to pay with your hand for — ' he started, but she placed her bandaged fingers over his lips.

'Don't, Roberto. My hand will heal. Forget these men.'

'Look at you, Isabella. Look at what they've done to you.' He was cradling her hand but staring at her face, not at the bandages.

'They can't hurt me, Roberto. Only you can hurt me.'

He lifted her hand swaddled in the bandages to his lips and kissed it, as though saying goodbye.

'I am staying,' she stated.

Immediately his strong arm encircled her waist and his eyes were full of the hunger she had been waiting for. 'Say it again, Isabella.'

'I am staying.'

30

Desire breathed through her lips. It seeped from her skin. It wove itself into the sounds that came out of her mouth, into the laughter and the moans and the strange unfamiliar whimpers of pleasure that she didn't recognise as her own.

The objects in the room vanished into a vague veiled world that held no meaning for her, because all that existed right now was this. Him and her. Roberto and Isabella. Everywhere he touched her he left a fingerprint on her skin, and everywhere her lips caressed him the taste of him unleashed something fierce inside her.

When he led her upstairs she unfastened his shirt buttons with no thought but her need to touch him, to slide her hands over the broad muscles of his chest and feel the dense bristle of dark hairs and the strong unyielding cage of his ribs. He kissed her as though he would consume her. The breath tearing in and out of her throat was hot, as his hands drew her body tight against his, her breasts crushed to his naked chest. She was not prepared for the way parts of her seemed to leap into life, parts that had been numb and cold, untouched for so long.

She had arched against him, her wounded hand propped on his shoulder, when she felt Roberto's fingertips slide under her jumper. He found the delicate curves of her back and brushed softly over her skin until they were melting into each other, and a powerful ache for him almost blinded her mind to what was happening.

'No, Roberto.' She twisted away out of his arms. 'Not my back.'

'I won't hurt it, I promise.'

'No. It's . . . ' She stopped.

'It's what?'

When she didn't answer, he moved closer again, towering over her, and for one fleeting second she remembered Luigi doing the same.

'I know it's scarred, Isabella.'

'It's . . . ' She took a breath and felt colour flood her cheeks. 'It's ugly.'

'Nothing about you is ugly, Isabella. Now show me.'

She froze.

His gaze fixed on her face. She could see a pulse flickering at the base of his throat.

'What is it, Isabella? Do you think I won't understand, is that it? That a blemish in your creamy skin will repulse me and send me screaming down the stairs.' He dragged a hand through her hair as if he would drag the idea out of her head if he could. 'Do you think so little of me?'

Isabella shook her head. Mute.

'What then?'

Her words were hard to push out. 'The scars on my back *are* ugly, believe me, they are. But it's the scars inside that I'm afraid you'll see.'

'Oh, Isabella, I won't — '

'Don't.' She pushed his hand away. 'I changed after the shooting, Roberto. I fought my way

356

back through operation after operation, then battled tooth and claw for a place at the university of Rome to study architecture. No one wanted me. Because I was a woman. But I wasn't going to lie down and let them deny me it. I showed them what a woman can do.'

A slow grin crept across his face. 'I bet you did.'

'But I had to protect myself, Roberto. I had to construct high walls. Not just in my buildings, but in myself. They are too deep. Chasms inside me. Irreparable. So I keep them hidden.' She turned her head away. 'If I allowed you to see them,' she muttered in a low voice that was heavy with regret, 'you would be *behind* my defence wall. I would be . . . exposed.'

'Isabella, look at me.'

At first, she refused. If she let her eyes feast on this man, she would not be able to look away. But he waited patiently, minute after minute, and finally she turned.

He was smiling at her. She wanted him to stop.

'Isabella, the first time I saw you, you had a blasted chicken stuck under your arm and an ancient *vecchia* clinging to you for dear life, almost toppling you over. All around there was noise and confusion and the greyness of uncertainty. Fear was stamped on everyone's face. But you, with your chicken and your old woman and your smile, were like a shaft of sunlight on that station platform.' He let his words drift across the space that divided them. 'I loved you then, Isabella, and I love you now.'

Slowly, deliberately, without hesitation, she lifted the hem of her sweater with her good hand and pulled it over her head.

* * *

She didn't know it would be like this. So — she struggled for a word that came close — so *awakening*.

As if everything had been asleep. The nerves of her skin, the blood in her veins, the thoughts in her head. It was as though the old Isabella had been sleepwalking through her life. Suddenly she understood clearly why her father's eyes had always looked at her with such concern and why he fussed over her as if she were still an invalid in need of help.

She had been half dead and didn't even know it.

New sounds came from her. New whispers and sighs, new moans and cries. Strange undreamed-of tastes in her mouth, wild contortions of her heart. Roberto's kisses and caresses breathed new life into her. She discovered a salty scent to him as if he were some powerful creature who had risen from the sea and she craved what she could smell under his skin. She found scars on him, marks that life had engraved on him, and she kissed them, as he kissed hers.

She brushed her lips hungrily across his chest and downwards over his hard flat stomach, getting to know his body, each bone and muscle of it, her heartbeat thudding in her ears. An ache flared throughout her and she rubbed her skin

358

against his in a pulsating rhythm, melting her flesh into his, moulding perfectly together.

'Roberto.'

She whispered his name. Greedily.

His hand swept up her pale thigh, and his lips on her breast sent this new rapacious blood of hers coursing through her veins. Limbs entangled, fused to each other. And as she felt the weight of him on her, moving against her, and the strength of him inside her, her moans broke free and he kissed her mouth to devour them.

When they both finally shuddered, gripping each other, they subsided with gasps together. Roberto laid his head on her naked shoulder, his broad back glistening with sweat, and laced his fingers with hers, holding her close.

'Isabella,' he murmured into the hollow of her neck, his breath burning her skin, 'don't go to Rome.'

She kissed his hair in place of an answer. She would sleep with Roberto's arms around her and know that no dreams would dare come for her tonight.

★   ★   ★

Dawn slid through the slats of the shutters, casting a ladder of gold across Roberto's chest where he lay beside her in the bed. Isabella was up on her good elbow, watching him sleep on his back. She adored watching him. The soft fullness of his lips, the long straight nose. The rapid movements of his eyes beneath large eyelids

359

fringed with lashes that glinted gold in the dawn light. She leaned down so that his breath brushed her lips and it took all her willpower not to kiss him.

She had woken with the warmth of him on her skin and the scent of him in her nostrils, and the knowledge that it would be dangerously easy to forget the world outside this room. No Grassi or Sepe. No enemies or friends. Not even Rosa or her father. Yet when she smiled down at Roberto like this, all the good reasons for keeping a sharp watch on them vanished from her head. So she forced herself to look away, and only then could she leave his bed.

★ ★ ★

'No, Isabella.'

'I've told you, Roberto. It's no good. Pietro Luciani will tell me things about when he was Luigi's brigade leader that he would never tell an outsider. To him I am the good Fascist widow, still grieving ten years later and still needing answers to the question of why my husband died.'

'I don't like it.'

Isabella wrapped her arm around his neck, her body flush with his. 'I have to go.' She kissed his lips and could taste his anger there. 'I am going to inform Dottore Martino that I will be travelling to Rome today to inspect the quarry that is one of our main suppliers of stone. I want to check on the quality of their stock.'

'What about your hand?'

'Don't, Roberto,' she said softly and placed the flat of her left hand on the centre of his chest. She could feel his heart drumming like one of the marsh pumps. 'Don't look for excuses. My hand will be no trouble. Papa will give me some pills for the pain, and anyway,' she smiled up at him, 'I'm left-handed, so I can manage.'

'If they decide you are out to make trouble, they won't give a damn whether you're left or right-handed.'

'It's the only way, Roberto.'

They were standing by the bedroom door. He had positioned himself between her and it. She knew he would lock her in if he had to and she could think of nothing she would prefer, but she was going to Rome to meet with Luigi's brigade leader. She knew that Roberto was only wanting to keep her safe, so she hooked two fingers inside his white shirt between the buttons and said, 'Come with me.'

His hand closed over hers, gently trapping it. 'You stay here. I know that you are fretting about the child. Try to see Rosa. I'll go to Rome to speak to Luciani for you.'

'Roberto, you and I both know he won't tell you anything. But we can go together — it's less than an hour by train — and we can try to get Rosa out of the convent as soon as we're back.' She felt a need to see the girl again, not just to find out more about her father, but because she needed to wrap an arm around her again, to make sure the child was not breaking into pieces.

But Isabella could see Roberto's fear, a dark

wing at the back of his eyes, and she knew it was for her.

'What did Grassi say?' she asked.

'That they will be watching you.'

She rested her forehead against Roberto's chest so that he wouldn't see her face. 'Why me?'

'They think you have some connection with Rosa's father. I swore to Grassi that you don't even know him, but,' she felt a rumble in his chest, 'he chooses not to believe me.'

'Come with me.'

He rested his chin on the top of her head. 'I'll come.'

'Thank you.'

'But we'd better not be seen together. We'll catch separate trains.'

'Why?'

'Because I work for Grassi. At the moment he is willing to give me information. But if he thought I was consorting with the enemy . . . ' He pressed his lips against her hair. 'You, my love, have become the enemy. He would feel it necessary to remove you. Just like he removed Rosa.'

'The enemy'? How did she become 'the enemy'?

'We'll travel on separate trains,' she said flatly.

He cupped her head in his hand and tilted it backwards so that he could see her face. For a long quiet moment when the room and the bed and her coat on the floor ceased to exist, he examined every light and shadow in her eyes.

'I want you to be afraid,' he said sternly. 'Because if you're afraid, you'll be careful. But

I'll be there. All the time I'll be there with you. I'm serious, Isabella. What are you smiling at?'

'How can I look at you and not smile?'

His dark brows swooped down and he scowled at her, but his hand caressed her cheek. 'They released you once, Isabella. Be very careful. They won't release you so easily a second time.'

The memory of the dead-white tiles on the cell wall and of Colonnello Sepe with the gun butt in his hand lurched into her head. Quickly her unbandaged fingers started to fasten the shirt buttons.

31

Italy came to Isabella. Bit by bit, kilometre by kilometre, it came back to her. With its lush greenery, its beautiful ancient villages tumbling over the sides of hills or sprawling in shady valleys. Through the train window the Italy that Isabella had loved all her life burst upon her with a force that she had not expected, because she had forgotten how much she was missing it.

Vineyards and orchards were scooped up for a few tantalising seconds and left behind. And trees, so many trees, so many shades of green shimmering after the morning's rain shower, vivid emeralds and dusky olives mingling with the darker hues of autumn. In Bellina there were no trees yet, no really thick trunks and towering greenery. Thousands of young saplings had been planted, especially feathery eucalyptus to line the roads and soak up the underlying water from the soil, but it would take years before the plain of the Pontine Marshes would look anything like wooded again.

Isabella stared transfixed at the rows of tall elegant cypresses that so casually littered the landscape and the silvery stands of birches. She had been born and raised in the city of Milan with its industrial smoke and dirt engrained in her pores, but like all Italians she loved the countryside, loved its abundance. She had felt starved of its ever-changing scenery. She missed its undulating hills and fertile valleys, its unexpected ridges and buckles, instead of the billiard-smooth table of the Agro Pontino divided into rigid bare rectangles.

As the train rattled through the stations and wheezed its way nearer to Rome, Isabella felt a kick of excitement. A tightness in her chest. Here she would find answers. Here she would meet the man who knew far more about Luigi than she did, who would be able to point a finger at his killer.

Able to point a finger, yes. But would he be willing to?

She was wearing a stylish black dress and black fitted coat that she knew suited her slender figure, but she had barely worn them. When she came out of hospital she had draped herself in shapeless black garments that meant no man would look at her. Her father had given her this dress and coat and she had smiled her thanks but pushed them to the back of her wardrobe and stuck with her unattractive outer shell. It had felt safer. But now . . .

Now was different.

Now she was entering Rome, the centre of the world.

Here she would meet Roberto.

★   ★   ★

She was careful. Just as Roberto had warned her to be. She took a taxi from the railway station to the Trevi Fountain, as though she were just one of the many tourists who mingled there all year

365

round. She had always thought the vast fountain was intensely ugly, far too baroque for her taste, so she didn't linger, but climbed out of the taxi and crossed the street, one of her favourites. It was lined with small shops in the classical style and an abundance of wrought-iron balconies. The last of the summer geraniums spilled over in a riot of scarlet overhead, while Isabella ambled along doing a decent imitation of window-shopping.

The sky had cleared and the sun was picking out the scrollwork on the brass tables scattered over the pavement when she reached the pretty square of Piazza San Silvestro. She wandered into the small *ristorante* on the corner and, without stopping, walked right through to the kitchens and out the back, ignoring the waiter's puzzled questions. From there she made her way quickly up to Via Sistina where she jumped into another taxi.

'The Ministry of the Interior, *per favore*.'

She peered out of the rear window at the vehicles behind as the car barged its way through the crush of traffic and swung past the Fontana del Tritone in Piazza Barberini — yet another grandiose baroque fountain by the seventeenth-century sculptor Bernini. She sank down in the rear seat, keeping her head low. She was sure she'd make a good spy.

★　★　★

'Signor Luciani, please.'
'Do you have an appointment?'

366

'No.'

'*Minister* Luciani is an extremely busy man. He has meetings all day today, I'm sorry.'

The woman didn't look sorry. She looked pleased at being the one to lay down the law. She had fine blonde hair that she wore in tight waves in rows over her head, like the rungs of a ladder, and almost transparent skin that would burn easily in the sun. Her fingernails were painted red and were very pointed, like claws dipped in blood.

'Will you tell him that the widow of Luigi Berotti is here to speak to him?' Isabella said.

The woman eyed her through long theatrical eyelashes, her curiosity roused. 'He is due to finish his meeting any minute now. I'll inform him that you're here.'

'*Grazie.*'

Isabella returned to her plush red seat and tried not to look impatient. Not for one second did she take her eyes off the blonde behind the desk in the reception chamber and that was how she caught her speaking softly into the telephone, rolling her eyes flirtatiously with whoever was on the other end. Isabella rose to her feet and walked briskly back to the desk. The woman looked up, startled.

Isabella smiled. It was the kind of smile that had nothing to do with being friendly. 'Please inform Minister Luciani that I am the personal architectural adviser to Il Duce in the spectacular new town, Bellina, and that it was Il Duce himself who gave me the minister's name.' She nodded smartly and returned to her seat.

Two minutes. That's all it took for the woman to come over, her high heels clicking on the polished marble floor. Only two minutes for Isabella to sit as if she had no concern other than to admire the elaborate plaster decorations that Manfredo Manfredi had designed into his buildings for the Italian government. Her heartbeat was as noisy as the woman's heels.

'Minister Luciani regrets that he is unable to see you this morning.' Her gaze dwelt on Isabella's bandage. 'But he can spare you a few minutes this afternoon.'

Isabella rose to her feet. She tried not to let her relief leak out. 'At what time?'

'At two o'clock.'

'Please give the minister my thanks.'

She walked across the expanse of polished floor in her black coat, black flat shoes and small black beret tilted at an angle. For once she didn't try to hide her limp. She was the widow of a Fascist hero.

★   ★   ★

Isabella found herself a café and chose a seat at a pavement table tucked in a corner away from the bustle and ceaseless flow of Rome's inhabitants. She loved Rome. Loved its noise and its vigour, the blaring of its car horns and the delicious aromas of pasta cooked with herb sauces and spicy sausages that drifted from doorways and small *ristorante* kitchens. The women were slender and fashionable; the men in their stylish suits flashed their dark eyes at each other and took themselves too seriously, which made her laugh.

Isabella ordered a tisane for herself. She wanted a glass of wine but needed a clear head. Without appearing to, she studied the people who passed the café, seeking a face that appeared twice or a pair of eyes that intruded beyond the normal indifference to the city-dwellers around them.

She saw nothing to arouse her suspicions. She sipped her hot tisane, took one of her father's pills and felt the muscles of her ribs relax a notch so that she could breathe more easily. She looked down at her left hand. How could skin retain memory? She uncurled her fingers and smiled at her palm as if she could still see the kisses that lay in its centre. She lifted it to her own lips and felt the warmth of him still cradled there.

Are you in Rome yet, Roberto?

She sat at the table for an hour, alert and watchful, till her tisane grew cold and clouds swung in from the east, bringing an odd kind of white light to the street that drained it of colour. Or was that in her mind? The brightness inside her head was so strong that everything else retreated into a veiled blandness. Around her, people were minding their own business and drinking their coffee, cigarette smoke weaving from table to table, while the road snarled up with dusty trucks and cars. A grey cat skulked against the wall.

She ordered herself an espresso and a cinnamon roll. Not that she was hungry. Her stomach was too tense for food but she wanted something to do with her fingers, something to pick at. It was when the stout waiter in his small black waistcoat placed her order and a glass of water in front of her that a man dodged across the road, setting horns blaring, and headed straight for Isabella's pavement table. He had long ginger hair that Titian would have been proud of and a black overcoat that showed it off.

'*Buongiorno*, signora. May I join you?'

He pulled out a seat and beamed down at her. He was good-looking in an arty way, about thirty years old, and Isabella had no idea whether this was a random pick-up or if he was someone who had come looking for her.

'No,' she said politely, 'you may not.'

He sat down.

'Please leave,' she insisted firmly.

'Ah, signora, I was passing and saw you here, too beautiful to be alone, so I said to myself, Marco, you cannot walk on without . . . '

A random pick-up, damn it. Isabella took her coffee and moved to another table. This one was more in the open, more exposed. She didn't like it. He followed her.

'*Bella* signora, what have you done to your poor hand? Don't look so — '

'If you don't go away, I will throw this coffee over you.'

His eyes widened with surprise but his smile broadened and he started to pull out a chair to sit on. '*Per favore.*'

'No! *Va via!*'

He flashed his white teeth at her.

Isabella tossed her coffee over the front of his

blue shirt. He leapt back, startled, but then burst out laughing. 'I adore a woman with spirit,' he said and made to sit down, but a large hand swept forward from nowhere. It gripped his black collar and yanked him a metre away from her table.

'*Bastardo*, leave the lady in peace.'

'Get your hands off me, you . . . '

But Isabella heard nothing. No words. Just the thud of her heart. Roberto was there. Standing before her in a long raincoat the colour of sand and a chocolate-brown fedora that gave him a harder city edge. Suddenly she caught a new glimpse of him — not a professional photographer or a muscular fisherman or a gentle farmer who could calm an animal's fear. This was the man who had spent five years in prison and who knew how to make other men turn and walk away when he chose.

It was the first time she'd seen him use the powerful large-boned structure of his body as a weapon rather than a source of comfort and help. How could she have missed seeing it? How threatening those muscles could be. She looked at the ginger-haired man's face and knew he would walk away and be glad his limbs were in one piece.

Roberto released his grip on the collar.

'*Merda!*' The man shook his shoulders and straightened his coat but failed to retrieve his composure. Without a glance at Isabella he walked back across the street, only turning when he was at a safe distance to shout '*Bastardo*' at Roberto.

Roberto paid him as much attention as he would a fly. His solemn grey eyes regarded Isabella with a stillness that silenced the words on her tongue. With the courteous gesture of a total stranger, he raised his hat to her.

'I wish you good day, signora.'

'*Grazie.*'

He walked away. She wanted to summon him back to her, but she sat mute in her chair and let only her eyes follow him to the corner of the street where he turned and vanished from sight.

How had he found her?

She rapidly scanned the crowded pavement. If it was so easy for him, who else had found her?

32

The Ministry of the Interior was housed in the Palazzo del Viminale on the Viminal Hill, the smallest of the seven hills of Rome. It was the strategic centre of executive power, constructed in 1914 to be close to the Quirinale.

Isabella crossed the newly built square with its fountain in front of the palazzo, and even though her mind was focused on the meeting she was about to enter with the government minister, her professional eye could not help admiring the giant spiral volutes that decorated the parapets of the wide steps up to the Viminale's grand entrance. Pigeons drifted up to the high roof on thermals of intrigue and political manoeuvring that rose from inside the building, even thicker than the cigar smoke that fogged its hundreds of chambers.

Manfredi, the designer, had drawn his inspiration from Greek and Roman architecture to create majestic external frontals. Isabella could see their appeal, but they annoyed her with their lack of modern perspectives. She hoped the minds inside were not as rooted in the past as the building itself. She had a theory that if you immersed yourself day after day in an environment that hankered after the past, your thoughts would get stuck there too. That's why she loved Bellina so much. It opened up a whole new future, not just for Bellina and its inhabitants but for the whole of Italy. And for herself. She knew that the only way forward for her was to walk away from the past, to put what happened in Milan behind her. Yet still it held her in its iron grip.

Luigi was part of the past. That's where he belonged. So why was his shadow here today, striding up the steps beside her, laughing at her limp?

'Va via!' she said for the second time that day. 'Go away.'

★ ★ ★

Minister Pietro Luciani's office was not as grand as she had expected, but was still a beautiful frescoed room for someone who was only a junior member of the government. With such high ceilings and elaborate oak panelling, it was no wonder that his opinion of himself had soared to fill the space.

'Buongiorno, Signora Berotti.' He pronounced his words ponderously, as if they were full of significance.

'Thank you for seeing me today, Minister.'

'Your husband Luigi Berotti was a fine young man, a member of the Fascisti, and he was committed to ridding Italy of its plague of Communists with their strikes and their pay demands, and Socialists who wanted to bring this country to its knees. I was proud to have him in my brigade.'

Isabella nodded. She didn't remind him that Mussolini had once been an ardent Socialist who had edited the Socialist magazine *Avanti*. She could tell that Luciani was the kind of man who would not take well to such comments, especially coming from a woman. He had spiky grey hair and a permanent tilt to his mouth that had frozen halfway between a sneer and a smile, but his eyes were large and warm, as if they belonged to someone else.

'My belated commiserations to you, signora. Your husband's death was a tragic loss to us all. What is it that you want from me?'

This man wasn't wasting time. Each minute of his day would be accounted for, she was sure. She wouldn't have long.

'I'm here because I want to know the real reason my husband was killed and why I was targeted too. Why shoot me? It doesn't make sense. At the time I was told by the police that it was a political attack against the Blackshirts by an unknown — '

'Whatever the police told you will be true. I know nothing more.'

She let the words lie there, unchallenged, on the desk between them.

'Was Luigi involved in something?'

'The Blackshirts were always involved in something, Signora Berotti. Back then we were fighting against the corruption of those in power and against the treachery of the militant left wing who would have brought Italy to its knees if it hadn't been for Mussolini. Il Duce and his Fascist Party saved our nation.'

'I know all this,' Isabella pointed out demurely. She rested her damaged hand with its

375

gleaming white bandages on the funereal black of the arm of her coat. To remind him. Of the cost she had paid. She lowered her lashes.

'Can you help me, Minister? *Per favore.*'

'I told you, I know nothing more. It was a long time ago.'

'Maybe a file you can look at? A memorandum that might tell — '

Luciani stood up abruptly. 'That's all, signora. I'm sorry I can't help you further.'

'Can't?' she murmured. 'Or won't?'

A silence shifted nervously around the room. Isabella looked pointedly at a portrait of Mussolini striking a magnificent pose and she smiled at it as if they were friends.

'Minister,' she turned a sceptical look on Luciani, 'let me remind you who it was who gave me your name. It was Il Duce himself. He passed your name to me as someone he assured me would help. Do you want me to go back to him with a report that you did nothing? That you were too busy here in your fine office to remember a fallen comrade who marched at Mussolini's side. Is that what you want?'

Minister Luciani removed a cigar from the cedar box on his desk top and took his time lighting it. He eyed Isabella through the thick veil of smoke as though he hoped she would disappear.

'There is someone,' he said.

'Someone?'

'Who might know.'

Isabella felt the blood pound in her damaged hand, a sharp unexpected warning. Suddenly the information was coming too easily.

'His name?'

'Giorgio Andretti.'

Her eyes widened. It rang a dim bell. Luigi had spoken that name.

'Where can I find him?'

Luciani retreated into his cigar. His eyes narrowed against the lie he was about to say. 'I know nothing more that can help you, but Andretti might.'

'He was in the same Blackshirt brigade with my husband, wasn't he?'

'Yes, that's right.' He paced up and down, waving his cigar around like a fly swat, except it was Isabella he wanted to swat away. 'He works in a warehouse now. A foreman, married with five children.'

It struck her that this was a lot of information to know off the cuff like that, and she realised he had come well prepared for her questions. That's why he was a minister and Andretti was only a foreman. But her sense of unease was growing with every puff of his cigar. Why was this respected minister so eager to slough off responsibility for passing on any information? What was he hiding behind his smokescreen?

'How can I get in touch with him?' she asked.

'If you wish it I will arrange a meeting. Just you and Andretti. Nine o'clock tomorrow morning at Caffè Greco. You know it?'

She nodded. Everyone knew Caffè Greco, it was one of the finest and certainly the oldest cafés in Rome. But he had said it too fast, too glib on the tip of his tongue, and it dawned on

Isabella that he had already arranged the meeting with Andretti. It was all set up. He was that sure of her. He didn't even ask if she could make it.

'Thank you, Minister.'

She heard the smallest sigh of relief escape him. If she caused trouble anywhere along the line, it wasn't going to be his fault. He strutted over to the door and flung it open.

'Good day, Signora Berotti. Again my commiserations to you.'

His eyes and his mouth together managed a smile that was almost convincing. He could afford to be generous now. He'd washed his hands of her.

*   *   *

A fine gritty dust crept between Isabella's teeth and under her eyelids the moment she climbed down the steep steps into the stone quarry. The meeting with Luciani had left her jumpy. Wary. A feeling that she was being manipulated. But the second her foot touched the sunken floor gouged out of the solid rock of the quarry and her eyes feasted on the veins and pores within the rockface itself, she felt a sense of calm. It was always like that.

Sound changed in a quarry. It had nowhere to go. So it reverberated off the sheer cliffs and rebounded right back at you, growing heavier in the process, as if weighed down by the dust. The sky seemed to draw closer, the thin white clouds forming a tight lid over the quarry, creating a

378

barren world that was cut off from the green landscape above. Isabella could imagine how a person who worked here day after day, year after year, surrounded by a netherworld that was halfway to the bowels of the earth, could forget the reality of life in the city. Here, deep within this timeless arena of ancient rock, you could forget that there were rules. You might be tempted to make up your own.

She made her way towards a long black shed that sat with its back against a wall of travertine but before she reached it a lorry piled with stone chippings ground its gears and slewed across her path. A man leapt out of the cab, indifferent to the storm of dust he had stirred up around them, but Isabella was still coughing when he greeted her with a wide grin.

'*Bella* signora, you brighten up this dirty old hole in the ground but,' he wagged a thick finger at her, 'you should not be here.'

He was a middle-aged man with grizzled black hair and moustache embedded with rock dust and a belly that declared a serious penchant for pasta and parmesan.

'I am Signora Berotti.'

He scooped up her good hand in his grubby paw and kissed the back of it. 'My pleasure, *bella* signora.' He waved an expansive arm at the workmen drilling and hammering and at the ramp where lorries were struggling to ascend the slope with their loads, and flashed his tobacco-stained teeth at her. 'This is no place for a beautiful woman. I am Gaetan Orrico, manager of this quarry.'

'Well, Signor Orrico, I am an architect, so I am accustomed to quarries.' She smiled pleasantly enough. 'I've come from Bellina to speak to you.'

It was as though she had snipped the strings that held up his broad smile. It collapsed instantly and the laughter drained from his eyes.

'I said I'd pay up.' He said the words harshly, and glanced around to ensure no one was within earshot. 'I told him that. He can trust me.'

Isabella blinked. '*Scusi?*'

'You're from Martino's architectural office, right?'

'Yes, I am.'

He shook his head, his lower lip pouting like a child's. 'You didn't need to come.'

'Yes, I did. I have some serious questions to ask.'

He glanced at her unbandaged hand, as if he would take back his kiss if he could, and stomped off to the shed that was his office.

★ ★ ★

'So?' Isabella shut the door firmly behind her. 'What is going on?'

She could sense his nerves. He stood in front of her, shoulders hunched, chewing on his moustache.

'Tell him I said I'd pay up. He'll get his share,' Orrico stated, but now his tone was belligerent.

The office and desk were orderly but something was clearly wrong. Isabella could smell it. She looked at the pile of paperwork on his desk and wondered what was being hidden

380

under the columns of numbers. The fact that he'd mistaken her for the messenger of someone to whom he owed money depressed her because it stank of corruption. Someone was demanding his share of a payout from this man.

A payout in return for what?

'I see,' she said.

'Make sure you tell him.'

She nodded. She needed a name. 'The stone you're supplying is substandard.'

'You're not here to complain about that, are you? Of course it's bloody substandard. How else does he think he'll get his rake-off?'

'There have been cracks in the buildings.' Isabella took a risk. 'Dottore Architetto Martino isn't happy.'

His eyes suddenly narrowed. 'How do I know you're who you say you are? Since when has Martino employed a female architect?' He stepped nearer, wary of her now. 'You don't look like an architect.'

She laughed in his face. 'What does an architect look like?'

He eyed her up and down, enjoying the moment. '*Merda*, not like you, that's certain.'

From her shoulder bag, careful not to jar her hand, Isabella extracted a verification card that stated she was employed as an architect by Dottore Martino. It wasn't the first time she'd been asked to produce it.

'Here.' She handed it to him.

He raised it close to his face and peered at it intently. 'Isabella.' He looked sideways at her and gave her a sour smile. 'Not a nice business you're in, Isabella, not nice at all.'

'I am in the business of building houses.'

He tossed her card back at her. 'Houses with faulty stone and cheap mortar with too much sand and foundations that are not dug deep enough. That kind of business.' He gave a grunt of scornful laughter. 'That kind of house.'

'Let's settle this,' she said sharply. 'Payment is expected.'

'Tell him I don't like dealing with his messenger. How do I know I can trust you? Make sure that next time he comes himself.'

'I'll tell him.'

He turned away with a shrug to his desk drawer and pulled out a manilla envelope. He opened it up and removed a thick handful of lira banknotes from inside, tucking them with satisfaction back into the drawer and leaving only a small number of them in the envelope. He sealed it and held it stiffly across his desk to Isabella.

'If he wants the rest of it, he'll damn well have to come and get it in person. I don't deal with messengers.' He treated her to an openly lecherous smile. 'Not even pretty ones.'

Isabella snatched the envelope from his hand and walked out of the shed — she could stand no more. It was only when she was fighting her way up the steep climb of the quarry steps that she allowed herself to glance down at the front of the envelope. In large unruly handwriting was scrawled the single name: *Francolini*.

Francolini?

No, Davide, no. How could you do this? This

betrayal. How could you knife Bellina in the back like a filthy assassin?

When she emerged from the quarry into the green world above, her eyes were still fixed with fury on the name, willing it to transform into a different one that she didn't know. Which is why she dropped her guard. She didn't hear the footsteps behind her, didn't notice the shadow until too late. By then a hand had clamped over her mouth and a hiss sounded in her ear.

She whirled around to see a man's face framed by a thatch of ginger hair that Titian would have been proud of.

33

She will come.

Patience. She will come.

But each time Roberto breathed in, it felt as though the air had to drag itself through wet muslin to reach his lungs.

She will come because she promised. And Isabella is a woman of her word. Unless . . .

He refused to contemplate 'unless'. But he didn't trust Grassi and knew that the chairman's reach was long and stealthy. If Grassi had decided to tighten his grip, Isabella could already be on her knees in some stinking prison cell that Roberto could not prise her out of so easily this time.

The sound of a prayer drifted to him. The scent of candles and wet raincoats. They mingled in the sombre light within the circular and ornate body of the church of Santa Maria dei Miracoli. He stood in deep shadow in one of the niches and waited.

And waited.

★ ★ ★

She came. Limping badly. Her black coat was buttoned up to the neck, her beret rolled into a tube and sticking out of her pocket.

Roberto didn't move. He remained in shadow, waiting to see whether anyone had hurried off the Piazza del Popolo and followed her into the church. But he could make out no one shifting uneasily between the side chapels or lighting votive candles with a hand that was unsteady and unaccustomed to the task.

Isabella looked around the church, her gaze flicking over the few figures sitting silently in the pews who in the dim light looked like statues themselves. She glanced up at the richly decorated cupola above and then took a seat on one of the front benches, cradling her hand to her chest. Roberto was surprised that she turned her back on the door. It made her vulnerable. It was as if she were shutting herself away from whatever was on the other side of it. Her face was solemn and seemed to be focused on gazing straight ahead at the ornate altar with its black marble pillars and gold-framed image of the Virgin Mary. There was something fragile about Isabella, in the way she sat. In the set of her shoulders, something he hadn't seen in her before, and it pained him to see it now.

In the hushed atmosphere he moved quietly. He sat in the pew behind her in silence, letting her rest in peace, guarding her back. He sat there so long that it was growing dark outside and only then did Isabella tip her head back slightly, looking up at the powerful gold cross that soared above the altar.

'Did you think,' she murmured in a low voice meant for Roberto's ears alone, 'that I didn't know you were there?'

Roberto smiled softly. 'Of course you knew.'

She could hear his heartbeat as clearly as he heard hers.

★ ★ ★

Picking their way through the darker streets of Rome, they headed for the Tiber river, the *Fiume Tèvere*, and Roberto felt a rush of relief. The centre of Rome was left behind. They crossed on the Garibaldi bridge, its lights glittering in the swirling black depths of the river like stars that had slipped down from the night sky by mistake.

A fine drizzle felt soft and warm on their faces and he walked with his arm around Isabella's waist, his pace trimmed to match hers. She spoke little. She told him about the meeting arranged for tomorrow morning and that her visit to the quarry had been interesting. But that was it. Something had closed down inside her. He cursed whatever it was that had driven her back in on herself where the nightmares stalked.

He wrapped a scarf around her arm and fastened it like a sling. She didn't object but she didn't welcome it either. He could smell the rain in her hair. Once over the bridge into the district of Trastevere, he breathed easier. Here was a maze of narrow streets that twisted and turned on themselves, a place where artists and thieves knew they could find a meal and a bed or a damp cellar to hide in.

'Here we'll be safe,' he assured her.

She nodded. Her shoulder against his felt weightless.

'Isabella.'

She turned her head to him. The blue lamp outside a smoky bar spilled its melancholy light over her as though there were bruises under her skin that had been hidden till now. Her face looked flat and drawn.

'Tomorrow you'll learn more from this fellow Blackshirt about your husband and why you were shot. Things will become clearer. You will feel better.'

'You think so?'

'Yes. Tomorrow will change things.'

She looked away. At a rat slinking along the gutter. 'Today has already done that.'

★ ★ ★

'Anything more?'

'No. *Grazie.*'

'Sure?'

'Yes. It smells good.'

The waitress, with long dark-blonde hair and wide-set cornflower-blue eyes, grinned at Roberto. 'It tastes good too.' She gestured at the two dishes of pork in a steaming spicy sauce of tomatoes and capers that she had placed on the table.

Roberto smiled at her. 'Are you English?'

'Of course I am. You're a sharp one, aren't you? I came to Rome on holiday and . . . ' She slid an affectionate glance across the tables of the tiny restaurant to where a young slim-hipped waiter was taking an order for an *aperitivo*. 'Well, I stayed.' She cast a look at Isabella's tense face and her bandaged hand, and asked quietly, 'Do you need anything, signora? An aspirin perhaps?'

Isabella looked up, surprised. 'No, I'm all right. But thank you, that's kind of you.' She smiled at the girl. 'You must like it here in Rome.'

'*Si*! Italian men are much more romantic than Englishmen.'

'Hah!' Roberto uttered a snort of laughter.

The girl tossed her hair with a grin. 'It's true.'

'Just remember, don't believe a word they say,' Isabella commented lightly but her smile grew stiff and tight around the edges.

Roberto felt an uneasy chill. What did she mean by that? He studied her face by the flickering light of the candle overflowing in the neck of a wine bottle on the table, but she had pulled the shutters down too securely and he could fathom nothing. It was a mistake. He shouldn't have brought her here. The place was full of people having a good time, drinking, talking and laughing.

'Enjoy your meal,' the waitress urged. 'If you need any more wine, signore, just give me a shout. My name is Issie.'

'Thank you.'

The moment she had moved away, Roberto reached across the table and cut up the pork on Isabella's plate into bite-size pieces. 'There, try that. It should be easier to eat one-handed.'

During the meal he talked to her. He

chattered about the photographs he'd taken in the city today at the Campo dei Fiori market, but she uttered no comment and he had no idea what twists and turns were spiralling inside her head. So he filled in the silences by making a show of enjoying his meal. She chased her food around her plate with a fork, but none of it reached her mouth. Every now and again she gave a small shake of her head that tumbled long tendrils of her dark hair over her cheeks, and he wondered what it was she was denying with each shake of her head.

The minutes ticked past slowly and a man in a gondolier costume sang 'O sole mio', accompanied by an enthusiastic accordion. The waitress cleared their plates, replacing them with tiny cups of fierce black coffee and a crisp almond *biscotti*.

'You didn't enjoy your meal, signora?'

'I wasn't hungry after all, I'm afraid.'

The girl shrugged and drifted away to lean her shoulder like a young whippet against the slim-hipped waiter who was watching his *padrone* play *briscola* with one of the customers. Roberto sat back in his chair. He drank the last of his wine and allowed a silence to build to the point where Isabella was forced to look straight at him. Her eyes were slate-grey instead of blue, as if someone had thrown a handful of grit in them while she was at that damned quarry of hers.

'Isabella, why do you find it easy to talk to the waitress but not to me?' Even he could hear the restrained anger in his voice and he clipped it out before it did damage. 'Don't shut yourself away, Isabella. I'm here to — '

'To what? To help? Or to spy on me?'

She saw his reaction. Saw the dark regret that shadowed his face. Without a word she rose from her chair and walked out into the night.

34

There was a roaring in Isabella's ears. A raging. A screaming that she knew was coming from the part of her that refused to accept that Roberto had betrayed her.

Yet she stood silent in the room. It was a room that didn't deserve to watch the destruction of love, a room that was small and humble. Roberto had found it earlier in a Trastevere *pensione* and booked it for them to spend the night together, but now the double bed with its spotless linen seemed to taunt her. She couldn't look at it.

Instead she looked at Roberto. He was still wearing his wet hat and raincoat as if he didn't expect to stay. She longed to go to him and press the warmth of her body against his, begging him to tell her that she was wrong.

'I love you,' she stated simply.

He stepped towards her but she shook her head. He seemed too big for this flimsy room, its ceiling scarcely higher than his head.

'But today,' she continued, 'I was informed that you have been working for Grassi all this time.'

'You know I work for Grassi.'

'I don't mean as Bellina's official photographer. I mean as his spy. The reason you kept close to me was to find out more about Rosa's father.'

'Isabella.' The way he said her name, as though

it tasted sweet on his lips, made her forget the fire that burned in her leg from walking too many of Rome's streets. 'I keep close to you, as you put it, for one reason only. Because I love you.'

She closed her eyes against hot sudden tears.

'Who told you otherwise?' he demanded.

'It was the man who tried to sit at my table this morning, the one with ginger hair and the high opinion of himself. He found me again. He tracked me to the quarry.'

She heard his breath come hard. 'Who is he?'

'His name is Luca Peppe. He is one of Rosa's father's men, the ones who launched the attack to assassinate Mussolini with the biplane.'

She looked at him with a straight gaze and saw him sway, actually sway backwards the way he would if she'd punched him in the chest. She could feel their connection tearing at the edges.

'What did he say?' Roberto asked sharply.

'He told me that you are a spy for Chairman Grassi, building up dossiers on the people in the town, so that every rule they break or indiscretion they commit is preserved on your photographic paper. Grassi uses this information to force his will on the people of Bellina and to manipulate the employees who work for him. Luca Peppe insisted that's how you got me out of prison, by throwing Grassi's deputy to the dogs. It's the reason you avoided arrest after the rally.'

'And you believed him?' he demanded.

'Yes.'

'Do you have so little trust in me?'

The taste of bile in Isabella's mouth was so strong she needed to spit it out. 'Roberto, why would Grassi arrest me for fleeing from the rally but not you? I couldn't understand it at the time. It only made sense when Peppe revealed that you were in Grassi's pocket.'

She wanted Roberto to deny it, to shout his innocence at her, but he didn't. 'Why would Grassi know about cracks in my building on Via Corelli when you were the only one I'd told? At first I thought it must be Davide Francolini who had accused me — he knew about the cracks and he was on the rally field — but it wasn't, was it? It was you. Why would Grassi release me from prison when you asked him to? And why did the Blackshirts turn up at Caldarone's farm not long after you and I went out there? It all came from you, didn't it? Tell me, Roberto, that it's not true what Luca Peppe said? Tell me it is all a lie.'

'I can't do that, Isabella. Because it's all true.' His face was rigid, the words brittle.

His voice died abruptly and part of Isabella died with it. It left cold air between them. She shivered but gave no other outward sign of what his words did to her. His eyes didn't blink. He was watching her intently. Outside, everything grew still and quiet, the street noises ceased, the buzz of the traffic in the narrow road, the woman berating her husband from a balcony. It fell silent and she felt as though her heart had stopped beating. Why should it want to beat when its reason for doing so had been stolen from her?

Yet still she had a thirst for him, a need, a raging hunger that she'd felt for no other man

393

and she knew she could not walk out of this room, any more than she could walk out of her skin. So she stepped closer to him, removed the wet brown fedora from his head and eased his raincoat from his wide shoulders with one hand.

He had betrayed her.

How can you betray someone you love?

You can't. If you betray a person, you cannot love them.

It was as simple as that.

There was an ache in her chest, as though a piece of glass had lodged itself between her ribs. 'Sit down, Roberto.'

'You're the one who needs to sit, Isabella.'

'Please sit.' She gestured at the bed. There were no chairs in the room.

For a few seconds she thought he would refuse, as he stood there tall and silent, filling the room with sadness. But then he did as she asked and sat on the edge of the bed, its flowered counterpane in sharp contrast to his dark city suit.

'Roberto, explain it to me. I know you do not possess a treacherous heart. You are not a person who would ruthlessly pocket Grassi's gold in exchange for information. You are not that kind of man, I am certain. So what is going on? What have you done?'

She stood in front of the shuttered window, her left arm wrapped around the sling. The scarf he'd used still smelled of him and she hugged it close.

'I need to know,' she said. 'The truth.'

'The truth?' He gave a faint shake of his head.

394

'We all have our own version of the truth.'

'If you love me, why are you spying on me for Chairman Grassi?'

Slowly he extended his long legs in front of him, as though stretching out this thing she was calling truth.

'I'll tell you,' he said, his gaze on her face, 'what happened six years ago. I was a photographer in Sorrento and Naples. I loved what I was doing and was putting together a series of photographic studies for an exhibition. I had found a sponsor who was excited about my work and the exhibition was going to be an exposition of the sea in all its moods. I'd go out in my father's fishing boat in all weathers to capture the pictures I wanted. It was hard and dangerous at times but . . . '

Isabella listened. Fascinated. There was something in his voice, a tail-end of the excitement he had felt in those days.

'What happened?' she asked.

'To earn a crust while I was scouring the sea with my camera, I took photographs of tourists. You know the sort. A quick snap while they're at dinner and I return an hour later to sell the romantic moment to them preserved for ever as a photograph. Not exactly creative genius, but I made a living out of it.'

He fell silent.

She didn't hurry him.

'Then one evening I took the photograph that destroyed my life.'

'What was it?'

'I was doing the usual trawl of the restaurants

in the town square in Sorrento and there was a small grey man at a table eating mussels, sauce glistening on his chin. He looked like a nobody, but with him was the most beautiful blonde, a pampered and petted young woman wearing too much make-up. She couldn't keep her hands off him. I thought it strange but took my photograph anyway.' He shrugged, a hard angular movement of his shoulders. 'That was it. I was arrested on the spot. My camera destroyed. My studio and darkroom burned to the ground with all my photographs for the exhibition. That was the end.'

In two strides she was beside him, seated on the gaily coloured cover. She didn't touch him.

'Why, Roberto? Who was the man?'

'He was — ' He stopped himself. 'No, I'll not name him, it's safer for you not to know. But it turned out that he was one of Mussolini's chief sidekicks.'

'And the young woman?'

'She was Mussolini's current mistress at that time. She was spreading her favours too wide, it turned out.'

'Oh, Roberto. But surely the man had destroyed the photograph? He didn't have to destroy you.'

He turned and smiled at her, a crooked tilt of his mouth that made Isabella's heart falter. 'No, he didn't trust me not to go to Mussolini even without the photograph, so he trumped up the charge of blackmail. Claimed I was trying to extort money.' Again he gave that sharp sinewy shrug. 'Don't look like that, Isabella.' He touched her chin, a tender little tweak. 'I survived. As you can see.'

'Five years? Was that the prison sentence?'

'No, ten years.'

Her eyes widened. Outside, the wind had risen and the whole world seemed to be raining.

'Ten years?' she breathed.

'Yes.'

'But you only served five.'

'Yes.'

'Why only five years?'

'Only? Only?' He clenched his lips into a hard ironic line. 'Five years inside one of Mussolini's labour prisons for something you didn't do is never 'only', Isabella.'

'I know, Roberto,' she whispered.

He gently stroked her bandaged hand. 'But five is better than ten.'

'How did you get out?'

'How do you think?'

'Grassi.'

'Exactly.'

She leaned the weight of her shoulder against him.

'That bastard came to me,' Roberto continued, 'and offered me a deal. To work for him. Or rot in that hell for another five years. A simple choice.'

Isabella felt a shudder pass through him.

'So I took it,' he said. 'If it wasn't me, it would have been someone else doing the job. At least I could ensure that . . . ' He frowned, drawing his brows together, and released a small groan of disgust.

'Ensure that what?'

His foot drummed on the floor. 'I tell myself that I ensure that some get away. Like the Caldarone family. Because I know who is in danger, I can prepare them ahead of time. Like I was teaching Gabriele and Alessandro to handle a plough. I warn them to give them a breathing space to escape. But not all succeed. I am not blind, Isabella, I know I have bought my freedom at the cost of others. And it disgusts me.'

*　*　*

It was said. The truth. It lay broken on the floor and Isabella had to bend down and pick it up. How could she know what decision she would have made in his place?

'Listen to me, Roberto — you are right when you say that if you didn't help Grassi, he would have found someone else to do the job, and that person might not be so considerate. But — '

But betrayal . . .

A long silence took hold of the room. Neither wanted to unearth more words, afraid of what they might find, of what they might feel.

'This is an evil system, Isabella, that has Italy by the throat,' Roberto said quietly. 'That forces its people into such choices. Mussolini has banned all political opposition and crushed all freedom of the press, so it is no wonder that men like Rosa's father turn to violence. They see no peaceful option. Mussolini and his Blackshirts are driving us to be people we never wanted to be.'

'And did you spy on me?'

It was asked. The question fell into the silence and could not be taken back.

Roberto turned his face to her, a rapid movement that left no room for lies. 'Yes.'

She nodded, letting the word sink into her mind.

'Isabella, I promise you that I did nothing that would harm you. Grassi was convinced you were connected with Rosa's father in some way. I did everything I could to convince him that he was a fool to believe such nonsense but he is not a man who listens. He wanted to arrest you at once after you went to see Rosa at the convent, but I persuaded him to wait. To let me coax the truth out of you, when all the time I was trying to keep you safe.'

Slowly Isabella began to stroke the back of his neck, to soothe the hard muscles bunched there, drawing the anger out of him.

'Roberto, you never did anything but help me. You saved me time and again. I know that. I'm not blind either.'

She tipped her head forward and buried her face in his neck and the familiar masculine scent of him set her body aching with love for him. If Roberto had betrayed her, he had also saved her, just as he'd saved the Caldarone family and who knows how many others? He was good and decent inside, a fine honest man who was tearing himself apart.

She lifted her head and gently kissed his lips, soothing, murmuring, whispering to him. His arms curled around her and he lovingly pressed his lips to hers. She longed to keep him like this, tight against her body, fused to her, safe from Mussolini's savage world. She drew him back on to the bed cover, their limbs entwined. The scent of him and the heat of their bodies bound them together, skin to skin, as they peeled off their clothes and he took care not to jolt her damaged hand.

Their loving was leisurely this time, as if they were trying to convince themselves they had all the time in the world to explore each other's passions and desires. Their hands and lips caressed and lingered, until a moan broke free from his lips as they teased desire to breaking point. Isabella felt her bones grow soft and yearning under his kisses. For this one moment, the city of Rome vanished. Nothing existed outside this room with its bright bedcover in this precious sliver of time. There was just this. Just him and just her, together.

35

Giorgio Andretti was not what Isabella expected. He struck her as only a year or two older than Luigi would have been, probably in his mid-thirties now, but he looked much more. Grey streaked his brown hair and his eyes were sunk deep in a layer of fat as though trying to hide. But his smile was a girl's smile, soft and uncertain, and Isabella wondered how this man had ever been a Blackshirt.

'Good morning, Signora Berotti.'

He rose from his red velvet chair in the Caffè Greco with a courtesy that sat awkwardly on his large fleshy figure, his belly as fat and loose as a sow's.

'Good morning, Signor Andretti. Thank you for taking the time to see me.'

He chuckled, sending a ripple through his numerous chins, and waved her to the chair opposite him at the small oval marble table. 'I don't take the credit, signora. I was given no choice.'

Isabella was startled by his honesty. It made a refreshing change in this maze of lies and deceit that Italians now had to hide behind for their own safety. This wasn't a man who wanted to pretend that he was something he wasn't. For the first time she began to believe that here in this elegant café, tucked away on the Via dei Condotti at the bottom of the Spanish steps, she might actually find answers.

'*Allora*,' he said, 'you are Luigi's pretty widow.' The small eyes inspected her as she took a seat and he smiled, a genuine smile that made her respond with one of her own. 'A black widow spider with a serious bite, I suspect,' he laughed.

'I can bite,' she said lightly, 'when I have to.'

'And are you on the hunt for someone to bite today?'

'Of course not. I'm here just to ask a few questions about the work that my husband did with you before he died.'

'I didn't think you had come because of my handsome good looks.'

He ran a stubby hand over his lifeless brown hair and laughed at himself, but there was something achingly sad in the gesture.

'Let's order some cake and coffee,' he added. 'We can't come to Greco's and not do so, especially when Pietro Luciani is paying.' He waved a hand at a waiter and ordered cake for them both, ignoring her 'Just espresso for me'.

The café was a warren of elegant rooms that flowed into each other through arches, frequented in the past by the likes of Goethe, Byron and Liszt. The walls were covered right up to the ceiling with old oil paintings in gilt frames that gave the place an amber sheen that was oddly relaxing. But Isabella could not afford to relax.

They each waited for the other to make the first move. She kept her voice low, aware of other coffee drinkers around them, and asked politely, 'What kind of work do you do now?'

'I work in a factory. Not on the factory floor. I

wouldn't last ten minutes there. I work in the office, buried in ledgers. We make ball bearings.'

'Useful.'

For the first time his smile grew thin. 'It doesn't hurt anybody.'

'Is that what you did before? With Luigi. Hurt people?'

'Sometimes.'

'Tell me about it, please. What was it that my husband did that I was too stupid to realise at the time?'

Andretti leaned back in his chair, making it creak dangerously, and took his time lighting a cigarette. When he finally looked at her again, it was through a veil of smoke that turned his skin grey.

'We were Fascisti, Signora Berotti. We were passionate, Luigi and I. We believed.' He exhaled a sigh and whispered, 'We were fools.'

'As Blackshirts, what did you do in Milan?'

The coffee arrived and Isabella waited with impatience while Andretti scooped up a mouthful of apple cake on his fork. He paused with it hovering on the verge of his lips, looked at her face and reluctantly placed it back on the plate.

'I eat,' he said, 'to bury the person I was back then.'

'You won't succeed,' she said quietly.

'I know.'

They both sipped their coffee and his eyelids quivered. When he put down his cup, she could see he was ready. Her mouth was suddenly dry.

'Very well, signora. These are the facts. We all

403

believed in Mussolini. He was going to build a new Italy for us, tossing aside the old decadent ways, ridding us of poverty and corruption, driving out the chaos of nation states that refused to cooperate with each other. Italy would become great again. We were the laughing stock of Europe and he promised us a way to stand tall again.'

Isabella nodded. 'I know this is what Luigi believed.'

'So we set about bringing Benito Mussolini to power.'

'How?'

'By force.'

He looked longingly down at his cake but kept his fingers away from it. Around them the noise and laughter in the café seemed to fade.

'Of course Mussolini held meetings to gather the faithful. He is a great orator. But the background work was done by us, the Blackshirts. We *persuaded*,' he lingered on the word, 'people to sign up to become members of the Fascist Party. We went into factories where Socialists and Communists — the scum of the earth — were stirring up strikes and we *persuaded*,' again the emphasis on that word, 'them to stop.'

'How did you persuade them?'

'How do you think?' He jabbed his cigarette into the onyx ashtray, grinding the life out of it.

'You used force?'

'Yes.'

'Truncheons?'

'Yes. And worse.' His gaze rested on her bandage. 'What happened to your hand?'

'It had an argument with a gun butt.'

A flush crept up his ivory white neck and spread from chin to chin. He continued quietly, 'We went into people's houses, into their shops. We beat anyone who stood against us till they whimpered on the ground for mercy.'

She shuddered. Thinking of Luigi in his fine black uniform that she had admired so blindly. Guilt swept over her, hot and liquid in her stomach, because she knew she had been complicit in her husband's sins by not asking what she should have been asking. She hung her head, letting her hair sweep forward to hide her shame. Andretti took the opportunity to attack his cake.

'If you were all 'persuading' like that,' she asked after a pool of silence had flowed across their table, 'why was Luigi the one who was killed? Why was he singled out? And why attack me?'

The apple cake vanished. Just crumbs on a plate.

'May I?' he asked, and pointed at her chocolate truffle torte which she hadn't touched.

She nodded.

'I don't know why he was killed,' he said quickly, reaching for her plate.

'You're lying, Signor Andretti.'

He shovelled torte into his mouth, its dark brown crumbs tumbling down the black waistcoat stretched to bursting point across his chest. He didn't meet her eyes and Isabella knew

405

there was more he was keeping from her.

'Tell me, signore,' she pushed him harder, 'did you ever talk with Luigi about what you were both doing? About the savagery of it? The immorality of it?'

Andretti laughed, a quick flash of unpleasant sound that turned Isabella's stomach.

'Of course we didn't talk about it.'

'Why not?'

Abruptly he leaned as far forward as his belly would allow. 'Because, Signora Berotti, your husband loved what he was doing. His eyes would light up when he swung that truncheon and he never wanted it to stop. It made him come alive.' He blinked slowly, remembering. 'To hurt someone.'

Isabella remembered the blows. When the grappa got the better of him. The bolt of pain. The degradation. The kisses and apologies and promises the next morning. She remembered only too well, but never had she let a word of it pass her lips. She finished her coffee, a shot of something to drown the memory.

'What is it that Luigi did?' she asked.

He stared at her. So lost. She could see it in his eyes. She stretched out her fingers and laid them on his hand where it lay on the table, soft and fleshy and impotent. She couldn't imagine it wielding a truncheon, breaking bones or cracking skulls.

'I'm sorry,' she said. 'I'm sorry for you. And for Italy. And for all those people that my husband terrorised.' A tear slipped down her cheek and she brushed it away angrily on the

406

bandage, but it didn't brush away the ache that scorched a path down her flesh. 'I'm so sorry.'

Andretti spread his bulky arms in a futile gesture of despair. 'It is too late to be sorry.'

'So please help me. It's not too late for that. Tell me what Luigi did to get himself killed. Something that you and the other Blackshirts didn't do. It can't hurt him now, but it will help me. And maybe it will help you too.'

'It wasn't his fault,' he insisted suddenly. 'Don't think badly of him. He didn't mean to . . . ' He hesitated.

'To what?'

Andretti gripped her hand. 'One night we had a purge on known Communists. A large unit of us marched from house to house, knocking on doors, dragging people out into the street so that others could see what would happen to anyone who stood against the Fascisti.'

He tried to light another cigarette but his hand was shaking so badly that Isabella had to hold his lighter steady for him, and whatever horrors he had taken part in in the past, she couldn't find it in her heart to hate a man so wracked with guilt for the wrongs he'd committed. But atonement was beyond her power to grant him. She waited until he had smoked half the cigarette and then asked again.

'What did Luigi do that no one else did?'

'Signora, you are a lovely lady. You are free of him. Don't ask for more.'

'I am *not* free of him. I can't forget . . . '

She stopped. Their eyes held each other and gently this man who was trying to hide himself inside his layers of fat breathed out a soft sugary breath.

'Very well.' A sad smile tugged at his full lips. 'I tell you because you were his wife and you, of all people, deserve to know, but I warn you that you are your own worst enemy.'

'I very much doubt that, Signor Andretti.'

He lowered his voice to a whisper. 'Luigi was all fired up after our purge of the Communists. He was like a rat catcher who couldn't get enough rats to satisfy his thirst for their blood, eyes wild with it. So when one of the poor bastards screamed that he would betray a whole nest of the Communists if Luigi would leave him alone, your husband listened.'

There was sweat on Andretti's brow, though the café was not hot, and he wiped his palms jerkily on his knees, at the same time signalling for a waiter.

'Two cognacs, *per favore*,' he barked.

'*Si*, signore.'

Neither spoke. They sat in silence until the glasses were placed in front of them, the amber liquid gleaming under the lights. Andretti drank his straight down and wiped his mouth on the back of his hand with a grunt of satisfaction.

'Go on,' Isabella murmured.

'There *was* a nest of them. Of Communist scum gathered in a meeting house to escape our purge. Your Luigi went over there and set fire to it. Most of them fled under cover of the smoke, but two were burned to death.'

Isabella picked up her drink, swallowed a slug of cognac and felt it hit her stomach with a

408

punch that deadened the sickness that threatened to erupt.

'That's not all,' he told her.

She let her breath out in a thin fragile thread. 'What happened?'

'Afterwards. When the building was nothing but ash and stone, that was when we learned that upstairs in the attic were hiding twelve wives and four children.'

A cry tore from Isabella. Heads turned but she didn't see them. 'Did they live?'

'What do you think?'

'Did none survive? Not one?'

'None.'

She seized her cognac and drank it down. To burn away the screams she could hear in her head.

'But he was never charged, was he?'

'No. It was called an accident. A fallen candle. Communists proving to be their own destroyers. No one can trust a Communist, that's what we said to each other.'

'But it was Luigi.'

'Yes.'

She lowered her head in her hand so that he would not see her face and her shoulders trembled violently.

He put a hand on her bowed head and kindly stroked her hair. 'From that moment on, the men who escaped the smoke that night formed a tight group that became fanatical about the need to destroy Mussolini's regime. They fought violence with violence and their leader became a man to be feared. He stood out because of his blond hair and so should have been easy to capture. But he wasn't. He was quick and cunning and melted through our fingers. Like trying to catch a ghost. He eluded us every time.'

Isabella lifted her head from her hand. 'What was his name?'

For a second the words could not push past Andretti's lips but finally they trickled on to the table between them.

'Carlo Olivera.'

36

She looked ill. When Isabella walked out of the Caffè Greco into the Rome morning sunlight, it was as if she had a fever. Her wide blue eyes were too bright. Her skin was flushed except for the patch around her mouth where it was a dull leaden grey that reminded Roberto of the colour of the sea when readying itself for a storm.

He felt a pulse of anger. At the man inside the café who had done this to her. And at the husband, the brash black-shirted husband who had dragged her into this nightmare that she was fighting so hard to break out of.

Immediately Roberto went to her side. Her hand had fallen from the makeshift sling, so he gently retied it and drew her other arm through his. As they walked, she told him the information that Giorgio Andretti had given her and it was hard, appallingly hard, not to heap his rage and disgust on Luigi Berotti's name. But he was her husband. And he was dead. He had paid the final price for his sins. Evil attracts evil to itself as surely as the moon draws the tide each day, and it was stalking the streets of Italy every day as long as Mussolini held power in his fist.

On the train Roberto sat Isabella beside a window, giving her room to breathe. To think. To find in her head the man she thought her husband to be and to fit him into the skin of this murdering bastard whose blood pumped faster

411

when he was brutalising others. Roberto could see the rise and fall of her chest, as laboured as if she were running.

Her thigh pressed along the length of his where they sat side by side in the smoky carriage. Her body needing him, needing the comfort that her mind refused to ask for. During the hour of the journey she stared with unfocused eyes at the beauty of Italy's green fields and shimmering poplars speeding past and yet for Roberto it was impossible not to imagine Luigi Berotti's hands claiming ownership of her slender body, his lips leaving the imprint of his kisses on every part of her creamy skin.

Ten years ago. He reminded himself with a rough shake that it was ten years ago and she had been only seventeen when she married him.

Don't judge her, Roberto. Don't judge her. Any harsher than you judge yourself.

He turned to her and kissed her hair. He breathed her deep inside him as if by doing so he could inhale the pain, removing all trace of it from her, and in its place leave the solidity, the certainty, the calmness she craved.

Her hand sought his, sliding her fingers between his, and together they waited for Bellina to come closer.

★   ★   ★

Dark blue uniforms. A red stripe down the side of the trousers. A white bandolier across the chest. The carabinieri were out in force. The sight of the dark wall of them standing to

412

attention on the Bellina railway station platform alarmed Roberto, but he turned his back on them, helped Isabella off the train and set off towards the exit gate with no sign of agitation. His aim was to get her out of here as fast as possible.

'Signor Roberto Falco?'

Colonnello Sepe stood before him. The thin face and brilliantined hair looked deceptively ordinary and innocent in the warm autumn sunshine. Except for the gun on his hip. That didn't look innocent.

'Yes?'

'You are under arrest, Signor Falco.'

Beside him Isabella uttered a cry.

'On what charge?' Roberto demanded.

'On the charge of sexually maltreating a child.'

'What! Don't be absurd.'

Isabella stepped in front of him, placing herself between him and Sepe. 'There's been a mistake,' she said firmly.

'Roberto Falco,' Sepe continued, 'do you deny that you kissed one of the girls at the convent? Gisella Sevona, to be exact.'

'Of course he didn't,' Isabella responded. 'This is a lie that someone is — ' But she glanced over her shoulder at Roberto's face and the words died on her lips. 'Roberto,' she whispered. 'No.'

'It wasn't like that,' Roberto said stiffly. 'It was nothing more than — '

'You did kiss this Gisella?'

'Yes. But it was as a friend, nothing more. I kissed her forehead.'

Colonnello Sepe gave a signal to the wall of uniforms which immediately surrounded them. 'You had only just met the child,' he pointed out with disgust. 'So don't call her your *friend*, Falco.'

The handcuffs closed over his wrists. Isabella was wrenched away from him. The black doors of the arrest vehicle slammed shut.

★　★　★

The girl stood immobile. Trembling.

Her cheeks were flaming. Her eyes clung to the floor of terracotta tiles in one of the interrogation rooms at the police station. On each side she was flanked by Mother Domenica and Sister Agatha, but her head seemed too heavy for her because it hung down low.

'Gisella, repeat what you told me,' Mother Domenica commanded, her white neck stretched taut as a swan.

'He kissed me,' the girl muttered to her feet.

'Say it again.'

'Signor Falco kissed me.'

'By force?'

'Yes.'

'Gisella,' Roberto stated flatly, 'that's not true.'

'Silence, photographer,' Mother Superior hissed. 'Silence. What you did was an abomination.' Her colourless eyes flared with righteousness. 'Our Lord Jesus tells us, 'Whosoever shall offend one of these little ones which believe in me, it were better for him that a millstone were hanged about his neck, and that he were drowned in the depth

414

of the sea.' You hear those words, photographer? Drowned in the sea. Even that is too good for your damned soul.'

The woman was a distraction. She wasn't the one with the key to the handcuffs or with the prison cell waiting to slam shut on him. He switched his attention to Colonnello Sepe and felt his heart clench tight. The policeman had him condemned and convicted already. The dark eyes were bored. They wanted the girl to fall into hysterics, to crumple to the floor, to sob out her accusation and demand that her violator be hanged.

Instead she hunched in silent miscry before him.

'Look at me, Gisella,' Roberto said quietly, and her furtive gaze sneaked up at him out of the corner of her eye. 'Tell the truth to them. You know and I know what really happened. I only kissed your forehead because you begged me.' His glance flicked around the sterile room and over the uniforms of the policemen and the nuns. 'But I know you're frightened. It's all right, I understand, I'm not angry with you. But please tell them the truth.'

The girl in grey spoke to her shoes. 'I did tell the truth.'

'Condemned out of his own mouth,' Mother Domenica stated with satisfaction. 'He admits he kissed her.' She waved an arm at him like a great bat's wing, and as it whispered through the air he saw a gleam of triumph leap into her eyes. 'He will pay for his sins.'

'And you will pay for yours, Mother

415

Domenica,' Roberto said angrily. 'You are the one who has forced that child into this situation, but who is forcing you? Who is behind your venom?'

'I am appointed by God to protect these innocent children.' She raised the metal crucifix that hung on a chain around her neck and thrust it towards him in a dramatic gesture. 'Be gone, the devil is within you.'

'We are each our own devil and make this world our hell,' Roberto said harshly. 'Even you.'

'Enough! Colonnello Sepe, remove this man. You've heard enough from his own lips.'

The policeman regarded her with dislike. 'I do not require you to tell me my job, Mother Domenica.' He nodded at the two carabinieri standing to attention by the door and they stepped forward to seize Roberto's elbow. He turned on Sepe.

'Tell Grassi this will not work. He may have something on that nun over there, but he has nothing on me. This is dangerous. Dangerous to him.' His words filled the small silent room, banging on the walls. 'Tell him that from me.'

'Take the prisoner to the cells.'

37

Isabella ran into the street with the green door, her lopsided gait jarring at this speed but her mind was oblivious to all else.

You are under arrest, Signor Falco.

Colonnello Sepe's voice. His words. The sour tone of voice. The pleasure he took in his work. They all reverberated through her mind. And Roberto's *It wasn't like that*. Of course it wasn't like *that*. Whatever reason he had for kissing the convent girl's forehead, it was an innocent one, Isabella had no doubt. It was being twisted into something abominable, but by whom?

That's what she was here to find out. She raced towards the small huddle of women gathered on the pavement across the road from the house where Roberto lived. The woman in the red dress was there, though not in red today, and her dark eyes were bright and excited. She watched Isabella approach and without a word she extended her arm and pointed a long painted finger at the green door opposite. It was hanging off its hinges.

'What happened?'

'They came.' The woman shrugged.

'The Blackshirts?'

'Yes. They didn't even wait for old Signora Russomanno, who lives downstairs, to open the door. They just knocked it down and barged straight in.' She cocked her head on one side and

417

gave Isabella a speculative stare. 'What has he done?'

'Nothing. It's a mistake.'

A harsh laugh broke from the woman, revealing a chipped front tooth. 'That's what they all say.'

'In this case it's true.'

The woman smiled thinly. 'You want a glass of wine?' She shrugged again. 'You don't look good.'

'*Grazie*. But no. I have to find something.'

'In there?' She nodded up at Roberto's rooms.

'Yes.'

'Pah! You're too late.'

'What do you mean?'

'Go take a look.'

★　★　★

It would be here. Something would be here.

Isabella stood in the middle of Roberto's room. It had been torn apart. They had relished their work, those Blackshirts, and done it thoroughly. The photographs were stripped from the walls and shredded like grey confetti on the floor, catching the sunlight and throwing dancing patterns of it on the ceiling. Every cupboard and every drawer had been ransacked and emptied, their contents tossed in a pile and hammered to pieces by their truncheons. Even the furniture. Broken wooden legs and splintered side panels jabbed up in the air at odd angles.

But the darkroom was the worst. The filing

cabinets of thousands and thousands of photographs had been spilled out all over the floor and his developing chemicals had been poured over them. Images had blackened, faces had melted. The stink was as rotten as the men who did the deed. The Graflex camera was smashed and it broke something inside Isabella. She couldn't bear to see all Roberto's work destroyed. Such brutal devastation, it hurt to look at it.

Her anger threatened to choke her as she crouched, frozen with rage, surrounded by the wreckage. She stirred the sodden heap, searching for anything, any clue, any sign, any glimmer of hope in the blackened mass that would tell her she was right. She had to be right, there had to be something here.

Where is it, Roberto? Your safety net. Your fallback. For when times get tough. Your insurance against Grassi.

Because she was certain he had one. Why Grassi would suddenly turn on Roberto like this when he had previously left him free to seek out information and feed it to him, she didn't know, but Roberto would be prepared. He would have known this day would come.

Where?

She picked her way around the apartment, hearing his laughter, seeing his hands holding up the camera to show her, its knobs and levers like extensions of his fingers, his handsome face lit up with a kind of deep commitment. Like a man showing off his lover.

Where, Roberto, where?

She stood immobile in the room for five full

minutes, her eyes searching. Her mind fighting its way through the chaos. Only then did she fling open the door and charge down the stairs with hair flying behind her.

How could she have been so stupid?

* * *

His car, his little black Fiat Balilla. It sat patiently under a tarpaulin in the blacksmith's yard. Roberto had told her that he'd tucked it away there yesterday before travelling to Rome because he didn't trust Grassi not to have him followed if the car was at the station. Roberto had once helped the blacksmith's brother when he fell foul of the law against foreign contraband — bringing foreign wine into the country instead of using Italian ones. So the blacksmith was happy to oblige with a corner of his yard occasionally.

Isabella pulled the tarpaulin off the car, seized the chrome handle and swung open the driver's door. No one in Bellina locked their cars, it was considered antisocial. She breathed in deeply, seeking his scent, but what greeted her was a faint ripple of the smell of his photographic chemicals — what was it he'd told her? Sodium thiosulfate, that was it. He must have carried it inside the car.

It made her smile. When she thought her mouth had forgotten how to do such a thing, it curved into the beginnings of a smile and she could feel Roberto watching her. The sensation was so strong that she turned and studied the yard around her with its iron tongs and chisels hung on hooks on the wall and the roar of the forge where the blacksmith was hammering inside his stone shed. Roberto wasn't here. Of course he wasn't. Her mind was jittery.

She began her search. Quick. Thorough. Unobtrusive. No sign of panic to anyone who glanced her way. Under the seat frames, in the pockets, behind the rug folded on the back shelf. She rummaged through everything and peered under the curve of the broad wheel arches.

Nothing.

Just a petrol can, a toolkit, a tyre lever and a tripod on the back seat. She moved faster, going through every part of the car. Her hands even explored the engine compartment, searching its oily corners and crannies.

Nothing.

Where, Roberto? Where? I know you. You won't leave your back uncovered.

She sat herself in the driving seat and sank her forehead on the steering wheel with a moan. What was she missing? What else was there to search?

With a sudden thought she sat up and looked above at the headlining, a beige cloth that was stretched taunt. She clambered on to her knees and her fingers skimmed it as attentively as she'd seen her father's fingers explore a patient's abdomen. But it was smooth and unruffled, nothing hiding behind it. Nevertheless, in desperation she removed a screwdriver from the toolkit and tore it open.

Only then did it occur to her to look under her

feet. The floor was covered with a thick rubberised black matting that was firmly stuck down, but using the screwdriver she prised up the edges and ripped it back in the driver's footwell and then in the passenger's.

Again, nothing.

She climbed into the rear, sank the tip of the tool under the matting once more and wrenched it free. And there it was. Gazing up at her as if to say 'What took you so long?' It was a brown envelope. She snatched it up, tore open the sealed flap and slid out exactly what she expected: a photograph.

She flipped it over to take a look at the front of the picture and her eyes widened with surprise. She felt a buzzing on her tongue as if she had bitten a live wire and it snapped something into life in her head that had been frozen since the moment she'd heard the words *You are under arrest, Signor Falco*.

She clutched the photograph to her chest, as though someone might snatch it away, and covered it possessively with her hands. Abruptly she started to laugh. A strange whooping sound that was wrenched up from deep inside her and set her limbs shaking. She sat in the back of Roberto's car and laughed till tears came rolling down her cheeks. Only when they finally ceased did she dare look at the photograph again.

It was a shot of Benito Mussolini himself. In all his finery. A pristine white uniform with a blaze of medals across his chest and his knee-high black boots gleaming like glass. He was in a large courtyard that Isabella didn't recognise, but the building behind was without question the Party headquarters in Bellina and the Fascist flag fluttered boastfully from above a doorway from which Mussolini had just emerged.

But Il Duce had missed his footing. Whether through drink or lack of attention, he had skidded off the step into the courtyard and the photograph showed him in mid-air, halfway to the cobbles. His hands were outstretched to break his fall and he looked like a fat white rabbit leaping through the air. Italy's leader looked absurd. His face was distorted with alarm, his mouth open wide in a shout.

But the clever part. The wondrous part. The miraculous part of this photograph lay somewhere else, because behind him, still in the shadow of the doorway, stood Chairman Grassi, clearly taken by surprise by his leader's stumble.

He was laughing.

*　*　*

The Blackshirts again. They blocked Isabella's path across the high-ceilinged marble reception hall of the Party headquarters, but this time she brandished her envelope under their noses.

'Chairman Grassi needs to see this,' she told them firmly. 'I promise you he will have you shot if you don't let me through to show him what's in here.'

They hesitated. One held out a hand. 'Let me have it. I will make sure he sees it.'

'No. The chairman will want to speak to me.'

'That is not possible. You have no appointment.'

'That's true, but I have an important message for him. It is from Mussolini himself and Il Duce will not be pleased if you get in his way.'

The Blackshirt laughed. He was young and handsome and did not take kindly to being threatened by a woman. He sneered at Isabella openly. 'Why would Mussolini bother with a cripple like you?' He started to walk away.

'Because I am Signora Berotti, an important architect in this town.'

He turned and looked at her uncertainly.

'I dined with Il Duce,' she informed him. 'I sat at his table and I have his private ear. That is why. You would be wise to listen to me. You will suffer, I promise you, if you do not take me to see Chairman Grassi immediately.'

'I don't believe you.'

But the one with the bullet-shaped head and the patronising manner looked uneasy. He decided to cover his back. 'I will speak to Deputy Marchini. Wait here.' His eyes flicked over her figure appreciatively, lingering on her breasts. 'The chairman might like some amusement in his morning.'

She restrained from slapping him. 'Be quick,' she said. '*Pronto.*'

He marched away, deliberately slowing his step, but returned exactly four minutes later at speed with Grassi's deputy, Signor Marchini, at his side.

Marchini offered no greeting. He looked agitated. 'I am told you have a message from Il

424

Duce for Chairman Grassi.'

'That is true.'

He looked at the envelope in her hand. 'I will convey it to him.'

'No, Deputy Marchini. Il Duce was adamant. I must deliver it myself.' She treated him to the faintest of smiles. 'I'm sure you recall that I enjoyed the pleasure of our great leader's company during the celebration at the Constantine Hotel.'

Marchini's neat well-groomed features looked increasingly unhappy. He took a grip on her upper arm and walked her down the corridor with a curt 'The chairman will see you for two minutes. Keep it brief. He is in the middle of a meeting which he has adjourned. This is a bad time, I warn you. What with the aeroplane crashing on the rally and now this new attack by the Communist insurgents yesterday, the chairman is — '

'What attack?' She pulled her arm free.

The deputy scowled at her. 'Just watch what the hell you say in there.'

They'd reached the office and he knocked on the door, opened it, ushered her in and withdrew. Grassi was seated behind his desk signing papers. He didn't even bother to look up.

'Be quick, signora. I am busy.'

She placed herself in front of his desk and stood there in silence.

'Well?' he barked.

'When I have your full attention, I have something to show you, chairman. I think you will find it interesting.'

His pen paused. His fleshy lips tightened. Reluctantly his eyes rose to hers. 'I am told you have a message from Il Duce but I assume this is really about Signor Falco's arrest. That is not my business. Go and talk to the police. You're wasting my time.' His eyes were travelling back to his documents when he caught sight of the envelope in her hand.

Isabella didn't exactly hear his intake of breath — he was too good for that — but she saw his chest lift and there was a faint hitch in the rhythm of his breathing.

'What now?' he snapped.

She placed the brown envelope on her side of the desk and kept her good hand on it.

'What was the Communist attack yesterday?'

He ran his fingers over his carefully waxed caesar-style hair, as if to hold his thoughts together by physical force. His round eyes half-closed while he worked out whether to tell her or not. She inched the envelope a fraction in his direction.

'Your friend Carlo Olivera chose yesterday evening to come for his daughter. There was gunfire. Colonnello Sepe and his men were ready for him and cornered him in the shunting yard.'

'He's not my friend.'

He rolled his eyes as though she'd made a joke. 'He was shot.'

Oh, Rosa. Bellina has brought you nothing but sorrow and shame. I am so sorry.

'Now get out of my office,' he ordered.

'First, look at this.' She placed the envelope

426

under his nose on the desk. 'Then, Chairman Grassi, we shall talk. About you and Il Duce.'

★ ★ ★

An hour Isabella waited and still Roberto didn't come. She had no idea how many times she looked out of the windows of his apartment above the green door, scanning the street below, but it was too many. It wasn't until the afternoon that it suddenly dawned on her that he would not be released until after dark, when the curfew kept people off the streets. When there was nothing but the wind and the town's proud new buildings to watch him.

She did what she could with the mess in his rooms. She borrowed hessian sacks from Signora Russomanno, the elderly woman downstairs, and crammed as much of the destruction as she could inside them. As she scrubbed the darkroom from floor to ceiling to remove the chemicals that had been flung around it with venom, she cursed Grassi and swore to carve his heart out if he didn't keep to his word. He had taken one look at the photograph and his lips turned a chalky white that he sought to disguise by lighting himself a cigar. But she saw the flame as he held it to the tip, the way it shook, and she knew that he knew that he had nowhere to run.

'Get out,' he said, and they were both surprised by the gruffness of his voice. As if it hadn't been used for a long while. 'Get out and don't come back.' He tore the photograph into a hundred pieces, returned the pieces to the envelope and slid it into his inside jacket pocket. 'Leave.'

'Chairman, you don't imagine that that was the only print of it, do you?'

'His studio was destroyed.'

She nodded. 'Of course that was why. You ordered it to get rid of anything he may have on you. But Roberto Falco is not so foolish.' She gave him a cold smile to hide the lie that was coming. 'Trust me. That photograph is with someone in Rome who will be delivering it to Il Duce in person if he doesn't hear from Roberto before tomorrow.'

She turned and walked back to the door. As she gripped the handle, she glanced back over her shoulder at the heavy figure hunched inside his grey cloud of tobacco smoke. His face was that of a man who was sharpening his knife.

'Chairman, one more thing. Please arrange for me to take Rosa Bianchi out of the convent for a few hours today, maybe even overnight.' She unleashed the smile once more and pinned it on her face. 'You may not believe me, Chairman Grassi. You may decide that I am lying. But can you take that risk?'

★ ★ ★

Isabella found Davide Francolini crawling out from under a stone. An archway at the sports stadium had tumbled down on him, catching his shoulder, and though the damage to him was slight — some bruising and a gash to the side of his head — the damage to his pride was considerable. Isabella walked into the stadium just as he was brushing aside the offers of assistance from his workmen. It struck her as divine retribution. An eye for an eye. As you sow, so shall you reap. Use mortar that is mixed with too much sand and you will pay the price.

'Signor Francolini,' she said with no preamble, 'a word in private, if you please.'

He was in an ill temper after the accident, rubbing blood off his cheek, and did not pay the attention he should have to the tone of her voice.

'What is it, Signora Berotti? Can't we deal with it later? I'm busy here.'

'No.'

Realisation stirred in him then, some vague awareness that something wasn't right. He ordered two workmen to set about clearing away the broken stonework and walked Isabella to a small office within the stadium. It had unplastered walls and electric wires protruding from them with naked tips. There was a metal table in the centre of the room and a telephone, but little else. By the time they entered, his manners had improved.

'It's good to see you again, Isabella,' he smiled. 'But I'm surprised to find you so far out of town. I thought your work was in the centre.'

'I came to find you.'

'I'd like to think that is a good sign,' he laughed lightly, 'but looking at your face I think I'd be mistaken. What's wrong?'

'This is wrong.'

Isabella threw the envelope containing Orrico's money on the table.

Francolini didn't pick it up. He regarded it through narrowed eyes, then turned them on Isabella. 'What is that?'

'A present from Signor Gaetan Orrico. I believe you know him.'

'Yes. I work with him sometimes.' Still he didn't move.

'As manager of one of the main quarries supplying us with stone, he must work with you constantly.'

'Isabella, what is this about?'

'It's about you taking bribes and cutting costs so tightly that buildings are cracking and drainpipes are falling off and arches are tumbling down. That's what this is about.'

For the first time he approached the table. 'He's lying.'

'There's the envelope and that's your name on it.'

He leaned over and picked it up. Instantly a frown darkened his face and Isabella knew he had expected the envelope to be heavier.

'Orrico kept most of the payment in his drawer. He said he doesn't like dealing with messengers. He mistook me for your messenger.'

'Bloody fool.'

'So you admit he's passing you bribes.'

'No. I admit nothing. The man is probably annoyed because I gave the latest contract to a different quarry in an attempt to improve quality. So he's trying to make trouble for me.'

She could prove nothing. She knew that.

'Signor Francolini, I have come to tell you this.' She moved closer, her eyes fixed on his. 'I will be checking and double-checking everything you do from now on. I will be keeping notes on everything that goes wrong, every little slip, every crack and crumble. I will send in the surveyors to examine the depth of foundations and to poke around in the corners that are unseen.'

'Isabella, for God's sake, this is — '

'I will not let you destroy this town for the sake of your own greed.'

'Greed?' He was stung by the word. 'This has nothing to do with greed.'

'What is it then?' Her anger slipped out and she had to reel it back in. 'What are you trying to do to this beautiful town?'

'Beautiful?' The word exploded from him. 'Beautiful? This is an abomination of a place. Can't you see it, Isabella? It is based on lies and pretence with its fake Roman architecture and its fake farms. Pretending to be an ideal community when it is constructed on stinking lies. It is built on foul marshland and will one day sink back into it.'

'Don't,' she said firmly. 'Don't destroy what you do not understand.'

He turned away from her, a tremor twisting his mouth. 'I understand only too well the evil that is this town. This is not Italy.' He threw an arm out towards the small square window. 'Italy is up there in the mountains. Built on solid foundations, on ancient rock. Not on lies.'

'Signor Francolini, what you say is treachery and would get you shot if I report it.'

His caramel eyes studied her as he slowly regained control. 'No one would believe you, Isabella.'

'You're wrong. Many are questioning the accidents.' Isabella could not bear to breathe the same air as this man any longer and headed towards the door. 'I have warned you.'

'Who are you to warn me?'

'I am an architect. And I *will* see this town built.' She opened the door and left.

38

'No.'

'You have to stop.'

'No,' Rosa said adamantly.

'You have to.'

'No, Carmela.'

'You will go to hell.'

'There's no such place as hell.'

Carmela crossed herself fervently. 'Holy Mother of God forgive you, Rosa Bianchi.'

'I'm not Rosa Bianchi any more.'

The cropped ginger head bent down to Rosa's level. 'Who are you then?'

'I am Rosa Olivera.'

'That's your father's name.'

'Well, now it's mine.'

Carmela dropped her voice to a whisper. 'But he is a Communist traitor, Rosa. You don't want people to know that — '

'I want the whole world to know that I am Carlo Olivera's daughter. That way they'll be afraid of me. They won't dare treat me bad.'

Carmela rubbed her pale sandy eyelashes and thought long and hard about that. 'Rosa,' she said gently, 'Mother Domenica told you he's dead. That they shot him last night when — '

Rosa clamped a hand over her tall friend's mouth. 'Don't say it,' she hissed. 'Mother Domenica is an evil liar who sups with the devil.'

Carmela crossed herself again and murmured

a Hail Mary, but didn't contradict Rosa's statement. 'But Rosa, you have to stop.'

'No.'

They were hiding in the chapel under a row of spare habits at the back that smelled of women and of God. Rosa had broken into the box that contained the sacramental wafers and she was gorging on them as if they were sweets instead of unleavened bread.

'I have to eat,' she informed Carmela, 'to make myself strong.'

'Why?'

'I need to go up into the mountains.'

★   ★   ★

They had to eat in silence. Not real silence, because Sister Agatha was reading aloud from the Bible about Samson while the rows of girls in grey bowed their heads and consumed their bowls of thin broth at the long refectory tables. Rosa had noticed before that Sister Agatha had a liking for Samson and often chose to read out verses from his adventurous life. Rosa liked the way he went around smiting lions and Philistines but she wasn't so sure of the way he set fire to three hundred foxes, turning their tails into torches.

They had just reached the exciting part where Samson walks away with the massive gates of the city of Gaza, when Mother Domenica strutted into the room and Sister Agatha stopped mid-sentence. All the girls rose to their feet. Rosa stared down at her bowl. It was still half full. She was tempted to snatch it up and drink it quickly because she had an awful dread that whatever the Mother Superior was here for, it wasn't good. Not for Rosa.

She heard the rapid tap-tap of footsteps approaching and heard the rustle of heavy black material. She didn't look up.

A hand landed on her shoulder, fingers digging in with spite. 'Come with me, Rosa Bianchi.'

Beside her Carmela drew a startled breath and turned worried eyes on her friend. The empty box of communion wafers rose to haunt them.

★   ★   ★

The men in purple robes were staring down at her again. She followed the Mother Superior into the room, dragging her feet, afraid of drowning in the cupboard with the pool of darkness, but the nun stepped aside to reveal another person in the room.

'Hello, Rosa.'

Rosa wanted to say hello. She wanted to run forward, to fling her arms around the slender figure standing in the middle of the room, her back turned to the purple men. But something had gone wrong. It was the architect. The same one as before, of course it was. The same wild and lawless hair, the same elegant way of standing, but her face was different. It wasn't the face that had walked with her through the streets of Bellina before. It had changed.

Rosa could see right inside it. The shutters had gone. And what she saw made her heart beat faster because what she saw was a way out of here. Rosa's tongue had so much to say that it stuck to the roof of her mouth and all she could do was nod.

'How are you?' The gentle smile was still the same, but she carried her arm in a sling.

'Answer Signora Berotti, girl.'

'I'm well.'

'I'm glad to hear it.'

Rosa clamped her lips tight together to stop all the things she wanted to say spilling into the room and filling it right up to its high ceiling, so only a little clutch of words escaped her.

'Are you here to take me away?'

'Indeed I am, Rosa. I have permission to take you out just until tomorrow. Are you pleased?'

Rosa nodded.

'Thank the signora,' Mother Domenica commanded.

'Thank you.'

But before the nun could say more, the architect seized hold of Rosa's hand and marched her out of the room. Down the corridor without a glance to her right or left, and out into the courtyard where a vast blue sky seemed to be stretched so tight that it looked ready to split.

'Wait!'

Isabella Berotti came to a halt. 'What is it?'

'Is my father hurt? I heard guns last night.' She gripped the hand in hers hard. 'Is he?'

'That, my dear Rosa, is what you and I are going to find out.'

* * *

The architect's house was empty. She seemed surprised. She walked around the rooms calling 'Papa!' but no one answered. The tall man with the glasses and the noisy laugh wasn't there and Rosa could see that this was a problem, though she didn't know why. Rosa stood quietly by the gramophone without actually touching it, though she wanted to, and waited for the architect to stop whisking through the house as if she were moving on hot coals. Something was wrong.

'Is it me?' Rosa asked.

'Is what you?'

'The problem.'

'Oh no, Rosa, it's not you.' The architect bent forward and ruffled what was left of Rosa's cropped curls. 'You and I are working together now. Don't forget that. I've heard reports that shots were fired last night.'

'At Papa?'

The architect crouched down and sat on her heels. Rosa wanted to touch her face but didn't dare.

'Yes, Rosa, I'm sorry but I think so. You and I have to find him before the carabinieri do.'

'That's why they've let me out with you, isn't it? So they can follow us.'

'Yes, I think it is. You're very clever, Rosa. You see everything.'

'So we have to leave them behind.'

'Exactly.'

Rosa didn't ask how. Not yet.

'Signora Berotti, what's wrong?'

Her beautiful blue eyes filled with tears which scared Rosa more than any words. She twined her arms around the architect's neck and hugged her tight.

★ ★ ★

They waited upstairs, Rosa and Signora Berotti, in a house that she said belonged to the photographer. Rosa was distressed by the sight of it, everything broken and sacks piled in the corner full of ugly shapes that bulged out the sides. She could not imagine what kind of wild man the photographer must be to live in such a place, but Isabella Berotti explained that the Blackshirts had come calling yesterday when he was in Rome, and then it made sense. Rosa understood about Blackshirts.

She spat on the floor the way her mother always did whenever she heard the word 'Blackshirts', and the architect laughed, though Rosa wasn't sure why. They didn't talk much. Isabella Berotti tried at first but she was no good at it. She kept looking out of the window, clutching the sill till her knuckles turned white and murmuring words under her breath.

'I'm waiting for Signor Faldo to come, Rosa, and I'm frightened that he won't.'

She stood awkwardly and shifted her weight from foot to foot as though in pain. Her ankles were thin but her calves had muscles Rosa could see, hard muscles she used to keep her legs in balance, and Rosa wondered how she would

438

manage in the mountains. Especially with her arm in a sling.

At one point Signora Berotti came over to her and from her pocket drew a brass crucifix. Rosa knew it at once. It was her mother's, the one she had placed on the table in the piazza just before she died. Rosa cradled it between her hands and lowered her lips to its warm surface. She sat on the floor because there was nowhere else to sit, head bowed, tears dripping on to her fingers as she fought against the pain in her chest.

A gentle hand stroked the back of her neck and the architect sat beside her, murmuring soft words until the tears stopped. Then she found her some flat focaccia bread that tasted of herbs and a chunk of crumbly cheese from the kitchen. Rosa remembered not to cram it into her mouth.

'Thank you.'

'You'll have to thank Roberto Falco when he arrives.'

'When is he coming?'

'When it's dark.'

But the way she said it wasn't right. To Rosa it sounded like a lie she was trying to make herself believe.

'Signora, how will we get to your home if it's dark? There is a curfew.'

The architect bent down and kissed Rosa's head of tight curls and Rosa could feel the warmth of the kiss. 'I'm not planning on going home tonight.' She returned to the window but kept the light switched off. 'We have other places to go.' She smiled at Rosa in a way that only her father ever smiled at her.

The photographer arrived in silence.

The street was empty, nothing moved, but between Rosa's blinks he suddenly stood in the doorway. In the darkness of the apartment he looked like a man with no face, just a shape with wide shoulders that filled the room and a way of moving that made her want to sit on his big shoulders and feel safe. She was too old for that, much too old at nine years. But she could remember what it felt like to ride on her father's shoulders and a silly childish longing for it made her murmur a soft greeting.

The architect went to him, she flew across the room. Weightless in the air. Rosa did not know how it happened but the two separate shapes met with a small explosion of sound, as though the air fled from both of them as their bodies came together. The architect's one good arm wrapped around the man's strong neck and their heads merged, pressed tight against each other, as though any gap might steal their souls.

Rosa whispered a Hail Mary under her breath to say thank you to God, though she had her doubts about whether He was responsible. It seemed to Rosa that the architect had done this, the architect and the photographer together.

She crouched on the floor, wide-eyed in the darkness. Rosa had never seen this before, a man and a woman become so much a part of each other that their edges blurred as they held each other. She heard their breath, the warm twist of air that snaked across the room. She edged

440

closer to them, shuffling on her knees over the floor because she suddenly needed to make the gap smaller, so that she could put out a hand and touch them. To discover what love felt like on her skin.

39

They set off long before dawn. Roberto said little, except to offer instructions and to keep Rosa tight against his side, so that she presented no target to any watchers.

It was Isabella's idea to use the attics.

'They are constructed in threes,' she explained. 'The attics of all three houses run into each other, with only a low wall inside the roof dividing them up. If we could get up into the attic, we could move along and climb out into the house two doors down.'

Roberto kissed her lips. 'You, *cara mia*, are a genius. They will be watching the door and windows of my house, but if we move quickly while it's still dark and come out of the back of the house three doors away, we should stand a chance.'

'Your neighbours might object,' she pointed out.

'I'll take that chance. The ones three doors down are elderly. They won't hear a thing.'

But they did.

'Signor Falco!'

The old couple stood on their landing in their nightshirts, their faces crumpled from sleep. Their eyes were wide with shock at seeing their neighbour and two strangers descend from their attic in the middle of the night.

'Say nothing, *per favore*,' Roberto said to

442

them cheerfully. 'Sorry to wake you.'

The man opened his mouth to shout his annoyance but his wife laid her hand on his arm to restrain him. 'Look, Leonardo, look at the poor child. You're frightening her.' She smiled sweetly at Rosa and flapped her hands at her as though shooing a puppy from her door. 'Off you go. Be good.'

'Not much chance of that at this hour,' the old man grumbled, but he stood back to let them pass. As they slipped noiselessly down the stairs he called out, 'Whatever it is you've done, Falco, they'll come after you. They are like hounds when they have the scent of blood and they'll tear that child to bits without blinking an eye. Think about it.' His voice was rising. 'Think about it. Don't be a stubborn fool. You can't win.'

Isabella lifted her head as she hurried to the bottom of the stairs and looked up at the old couple above. 'If nobody does anything, nothing will ever change.' She pointed straight at the front door. 'Tell them out there not to be stubborn fools when they come banging on your door. See if they listen.'

Unexpectedly the old man started to laugh, a wheezy rattle of a laugh that sounded loud in the silence. 'Get out of here,' he chuckled, and went stumbling back to bed.

The three of them climbed out the rear window. Under cover of darkness they retrieved Roberto's car from the blacksmith's yard.

★ ★ ★

The road into the Lepini mountains zigzagged back and forth up the forested slopes, taking its time. These were ancient hunchbacked mountains that had no need to hurry. Dawn had painted the eastern slopes golden, turning the tree trunks to bronze and the leaves to gilded fluttering creatures that rippled to escape in the morning breeze.

The sounds of the forest drifted to Isabella inside the car, noises that she was unaccustomed to, its sighs and murmurs, its sudden startling cracks and creaks. The bark of some wild animal echoed between the dense trunks and she had no idea which direction it came from. It unnerved her. She could sense the forest's desire to close around them, to swallow them whole in its relentless greenness. She could smell its breath, damp and earthy. She wrapped a scarf around her nose.

But the view as they climbed higher was breathtaking. Like a gift from the mountains it stretched out below them, the Agro Pontino, the vast plain that had once been the impenetrable wooded Pontine Marshes. Barren now and pockmarked by the gigantic yellow Tosi digging machinery, the fields would rise again green and fertile next spring and for many springs to come, to become the breadbasket of Rome.

Roberto had opened his driver's window and was inhaling great gusts of clean mountain air deep into his lungs as if he could not rid himself of the stench of the cells fast enough. He could feel her gaze on him and turned to her but he didn't smile. His eyes were solemn, a dark prison grey, and she knew he didn't want her to make this journey into the mountains; he'd wanted to come alone.

Behind them on the rear bench sat Rosa, her young face brimming with excitement, her limbs free at last from the rigidity that had turned them stiff and spiky since entering the convent and it gave Isabella pleasure to see it. She could taste the child's anticipation as sweet as honey in the air.

'He's here,' Rosa said quickly. 'I know Papa will be here. It's where Mamma took me to see him. In Sermoneta.'

★   ★   ★

Sermoneta hovered on the edge of a cliff. Poised as if to fly. It was a crooked little medieval town that had been hewn out of the rock itself, two hundred and eighty metres high above the Pontine Plain to keep a watch out for marauders.

There had been plenty of those over the centuries, including Spanish and French troops, which was why the town boasted massive fortified stone walls and the impressive Caetani Castle. It was constructed in the fourteenth century with watchtowers built on high rocks to keep invaders at bay.

Isabella had never been here before. At any other time she would have been enchanted by the ancient beauty of the narrow streets and medieval stone houses, turned to amber by the morning sun while others hung back in the blackest shade that looked as old as the castle

445

itself. But not today. Today they were relying on Rosa's word. Carlo Olivera would be here. Rosa was certain. She could pick out the house, she told them over and over, as though she feared they would not believe her. She knew the trails in the mountains better than the wild boar.

'Mamma brought me to Sermoneta many times.' Her black eyes stared up at them, willing them to trust her.

So they had driven without headlights for much of the way, following the twisting silver ribbon of the road by moonlight, alert for any sound of a car behind them. But they saw no sign of pursuit and all three of them breathed more easily as the dark broken back of the mountains loomed closer. Dawn had spilled over the plain and a pearly mist rose from the canals, creeping on its belly up the first slopes of the Lepini mountains. Roberto parked the car hidden from sight deep under trees, well away from the stone walls of Sermoneta, and they sat in it, waiting and listening.

When they were certain the approach road was quiet, they climbed out of the car and started up the incline to the ancient Porta Annibaldi, the arched gateway through the massive walls into the heart of the town. A flower seller crouched in its heavy shade, an aged woman in black skirts and headscarf with creases cobwebbing her cheeks and the kind of voice that is the prerogative of the very deaf. It cut through the quiet morning air, as she talked to someone just out of sight on the other side of the archway.

446

'You are bad for business,' the old woman yowled at the other person. 'Go away! *Va via!*'

The walls were too thick to hear the reply, but Roberto took hold of Rosa's hand as they approached the shadow of the archway.

Isabella smiled at him. 'You're too jumpy. It's just a flower seller having an argument with — '

A man stepped out from the far side of the arch as though he heard their footsteps, though Isabella was sure they had been silent. The sight of the dark uniform and the bicorn hat with the silver braid stopped her heartbeat, but she stood squarely in front of him and didn't give ground.

'Good morning, Colonnello Sepe. You are out early.'

Sepe's thin features were taut with suspicion. 'You also, Signora Berotti and Signor Falco. Very early for a stroll.'

He covered himself well, but he was surprised to find them in Sermoneta. Isabella could see his unease at this unexpected complication and she knew then that he hadn't followed Roberto's car. He was here ahead of them. Sepe bent down to Rosa, seeking out their weakest point, and curved his narrow figure over her as though poised to strike.

'And you, Rosa Bianchi. What are you doing here? Have you come to find your father?'

'No,' Roberto intervened. 'No, she came with us to get her out of the town for a — '

'I asked the girl, Falco. Not you. Tell me, child of a traitor, why you have come to Sermoneta?'

'Papa is *not* a traitor.'

447

'Carlo Olivera is a traitor to his country and to his king and to the new world that Il Duce is building, so that Italy will be proud and powerful once more. Men like your father are scum and should be poisoned like rats in a drain.' He gave a sour smile. 'Is that not so, Falco? The offspring of rats should be hung up by their tails and fed to the crows.'

None of them saw it coming. Isabella was facing the wrong way, looking at Roberto, frightened that he would be provoked into retaliation against the police colonel. She could see the muscles in his neck tightening as Sepe goaded them, caught the flash of anger in his eyes that turned them from grey to a dull bruised purple and she was stretching a hand out to brush his elbow in warning.

But it was the child who attacked. She flew at Sepe with a feral shriek, leaping up at his thin jeering face. Clawing at his eyes like a wild cat. Sinking her small sharp teeth into the hollow flesh of his cheek and hanging there, while blood spurted down her face and drained into his black jacket where it glistened darkly.

Sepe's gloved hand smacked her away with a roar and the girl flew backwards through the air. She slammed into the stone wall with a crack to the back of her head and slithered to the earth with no sound. Not even a cry of shock.

'Rosa!'

But the child was already up on her feet when ten carabinieri charged into the archway at the sound of their colonel's roar of anguish. She was off and running, ducking and dodging to avoid their grasping hands, twisting and turning, never letting her small feet stay still for a second.

'Catch her!' Sepe roared.

But it was like ordering his men to catch a weasel. She was too quick, too sharp, too sure of where she was heading. She vanished down a narrow cobbled side street no wider than a handcart, scampered up a set of stone steps and leapfrogged over a low wall. Isabella tried to keep up but lost her.

'Isabella.'

Roberto was at her side.

'Now, *pronto*! It's the moment to walk away, Isabella. We'll find Rosa.' He drew Isabella's arm through his, holding it tight. 'Or more likely, she will find us when she's ready.'

He steered her swiftly into a shadowed alleyway that led towards the outer defence wall but they were too late. The carabinieri were fanning out, scouring the tiny cobbled streets, moving swiftly from one to another. Roberto pulled Isabella deeper into the alley where it was overhung with tendrils of ivy and elder branches which hid them from view. They halted, their backs pressed against the ancient wall, listening hard. They could hear the clatter of boots, the shouts of the police as they searched. The rattle of rifles broke the still morning air and sent a wave of starlings sweeping in spirals up to the top of the square cathedral tower.

Isabella leaned her shoulder against Roberto's. Her heart was thudding and she could feel its echo vibrating through him.

'They're close, Roberto. Sepe will take us both

for questioning. He will want revenge after what Rosa just did to him. Right in front of his men.' She paused, shrugged and gave him a lopsided smile. She couldn't bring herself to say more.

'I know, Isabella. We've slipped through Sepe's fingers too often. He won't let us go again.'

'Why are they here? Why are the carabinieri in Sermoneta in such force? They were here before us, so they didn't follow us.' She caught the slam of a door somewhere and the sound of angry male voices.

'They must have heard that Carlo Olivera is holed up here.'

'But how?'

They looked at each other, the same thought beating a path through their heads: Rosa. Who else had Rosa told about her father's secret hideout?

For one brief moment Isabella tipped her forehead against Roberto's cheek. 'Treachery is everywhere in Mussolini's Italy,' she whispered. 'If anything happens to me, I want you to flee somewhere safe where — '

'Don't, Isabella.' He placed two fingers on her lips. 'I won't let anything happen to you.'

But even as Roberto spoke, one of the carabinieri patrols marched into the far end of their alleyway and started to work its way down towards them. Rifle butts rammed into a wooden window box on a sill that was flaunting the last of its scarlet geraniums, and smashed it to splinters just for the hell of it. These men were looking for a fight. Isabella gripped Roberto's hand and together they moved fast. Tight against the wall, no more than shadows skimming through deeper shadow. The alley twisted at the end, a sudden dog-leg, past an ancient stone terrace of houses with doors that opened on to the cobbles. But all were closed tight. Word was out in Sermoneta. Close your doors. Fasten your shutters. Keep off the streets if you want to keep your skull in one piece today.

Isabella could taste the fear thick as grease on the back of her tongue and she forced her legs to run at Roberto's pace. But as they darted around the corner of the dog-leg he glanced over his shoulder, saw her face and his own expression clouded with a sudden bleakness. She cursed herself for letting the pain stamp itself on her features and when he abruptly slowed, she said furiously, 'Run! Run! Don't . . . '

But her words withered and died on her lips as she saw what lay ahead.

'What is it, Isabella?'

He swung around and saw what she saw. A blank stone wall. It was ten metres high, a section of the massive defences of the town. It blocked the end of the sunless alleyway and allowed no exit. It threw its shadow like a shield over the narrow houses crammed together under its protection. There was no way over the wall.

Trapped like rats in a pipe.

Isabella knew this was the end. The boots were marching closer and a shudder ran through her, so strong it felt as if her bones were cracking. Not because of the cell that awaited her. Not because of the bullet that this time would steal her life. But because it was the end of her life with Roberto. She didn't look at the wall that was ending everything or at the dark uniforms swinging into view at the dog-leg twist in the road. She looked only at Roberto's face. At the strong decent lines of it, at the softness of his mouth, at the deep anger that was etching creases into his brow. Creases that she wanted to banish with a touch of her fingers.

She loved him fiercely and the thought of losing him drove all other thoughts from her head. She spun around and turned on the uniforms with a savagery that ripped through her. She started to race back up the alley towards them. Blood was rushing through her ears, pounding through her broken hand, searing her nerve-ends with its heat.

If she was going to die, she would do it in the street *with* Roberto, not alone *without* him, not knowing whether he was alive or dead. She opened her mouth to utter a cry of fury but before any sound emerged, Roberto's hand clamped over her mouth and for no more than a second she was lifted off her feet and turned to face an old battered door that she was charging past. It stood open a crack. One dark eye and a tense young mouth could be seen in the shadows, a male hand stretched out and beckoning.

Before Isabella could switch her mind into working out whether this was a trap laid for them, Roberto stepped through the doorway and half-pushed half-carried her in front of him. He kicked the door shut behind him and their young rescuer slammed a metal bar into brackets across it. Then in the gloom of the darkened hallway he turned to face them. A thin bony face with a flattened nose.

It was Alessandro Caldarone.

40

'Come!'

Already fists were hammering on the front door.

'Come!' Alessandro hissed again.

It was the son of the would-be farmer, Gabriele Caldarone, the family that Roberto had helped flee to the mountains when their charade of farming life was discovered.

'Alessandro?' Roberto clapped him on the shoulder, his hand swallowing the boy's slight bones. '*Grazie.*'

'Come!' Alessandro said for the third time, even more urgently than before. He turned and dodged down the unlit passageway, beckoning them to follow.

They did so without questions. This was not the time to doubt him. They heard a panel of the front door crack open and a voice bellow through it, but they didn't stop, didn't dare lose a second. Isabella hurried after the boy, Roberto behind her, covering her back. The house was narrow but rose three storeys high, with rough whitewashed walls inside. Alessandro scampered up a flight of bare wooden stairs and Isabella groped her way up them in the gloom.

'Upstairs?' she whispered.

It felt all wrong. They would be trapped up there.

'Are you sure, Alessandro?' Roberto questioned as he loped up behind her.

'Hurry!' the boy hissed.

With a crash, a panel of the front door smashed to the ground, and Alessandro leapt forward with alarm as he raced up another flight of stairs.

'Quickly!'

On the second landing he turned into a room at the back of the house that lay in almost complete darkness. Isabella kept up with him, Roberto at her side, but he didn't take her arm and she loved him for that. She knew her limp was bad right now, but she couldn't bear to be carried. The room was empty of furniture.

'Alessandro,' Roberto said in an urgent voice, 'this room is a dead end. What the hell are we doing in here? There's no way out.'

'It's a safe room.'

'How is this room safe?' Roberto was already heading back to the door and for the first time Isabella saw a gun in his hand.

'No, Roberto, don't, it's — '

'Look,' Alessandro said quickly. 'Here.'

The walls of the room were rough plastered, pitted with indentations and grooves where the trowel had spread the mix on the surface. Alessandro swiftly snatched up a long, thin metal skewer that lay in a basket of logs as though discarded and ran his fingertips over a section of the end wall which was blank and windowless. Even in the semi-darkness the boy showed no hesitation, though his hand shook as he lifted the point of the spike to touch the wall. It had a rough knob on the thicker end and a small hook on its tip which he inserted into a tiny hole, one of many in the plasterwork. He pushed it far in and twisted it with both hands. There was a distinct click.

Downstairs the metal bar across the door clattered to the flagstones. They were in.

Isabella felt the vibrations of them ripple through the house as the carabinieri charged into the hallway, she heard their shouts, and her heart was clawing at her chest. Roberto remained calm. A stillness seemed to wrap itself around his broad shoulders as he closed the door of the room and turned to Isabella with his face half-buried in the shadows.

'I love you,' he said softly. Then he pointed his gun at the door and waited. She went to him.

'In here! Before they come. Be quick!' Alessandro was swinging open a metre-wide section of wall at the corner, that swivelled on a hinge to reveal a hidden gap.

Boots echoed on the first staircase. They were coming.

'Get in,' Alessandro urged.

Isabella moved fast. She hurried over to the open hole in the wall and climbed in.

'Come quickly, Roberto. And you, Alessandro.'

The boots were pounding up the second staircase. The voices rose up to the landing ahead of them, and there was an eagerness to them, a keenness. Like hounds delirious with the scent of prey. It sent chills through Isabella. Alessandro scrambled into the narrow gap behind the wall and only when they were both in

456

did Roberto follow them. He pulled the section of wall closed behind him.

'Lock it!'

Alessandro grasped a metal handle that was on the inside, twisted it and they all heard a lock click into place. Each of them held their breath. Inside the dark space lay the smell of fear. As though the stones themselves were impregnated with it from all the men and women who had stood like this. Not blinking. Not breathing. Hearts drumming in their chests. Listening. To every creak and every footstep. Mouths dry as dust, blackness filling their world. The kind of fear that strips the soul.

Roberto's arm wrapped around Isabella and they stood in silence.

★ ★ ★

'They're here. They have to be. The bastards are hiding somewhere.'

'*Capitano*, we've searched every room. There's no one here.'

'Damn you, Vizzini, search them again!'

'There's nowhere for them to hide.'

'Find them, you lazy *bastardo*, or my fist will find your head.'

'Yes, sir.'

Footsteps prowled. A fist thumped the walls. An arm's length from Isabella's throat, she heard the captain of the search party growl with frustration. He stood still, listening as intently as they were listening. She could feel his mind pushing against the walls.

'Now.'

Roberto whispered the word in Alessandro's
ear, the first word spoken in over an hour.

Fear and darkness alter the mind, they break
down the scaffolding of thoughts, and leave
damage and disruption behind. Fear alters
perception. For a moment, before Alessandro
swung the section of wall open, Isabella believed
she was in hospital again, unable to open her
eyes however hard she tried. In a world of pain
and blackness. But she felt Roberto's hand on
hers and it brought her back to the secret hole in
the safe room and she nodded to him, as if he
could see her. At last the carabinieri had gone.

A crack of light splintered the darkness and
Isabella caught a glint of the gun in Roberto's
hand. As the wall swung open, she knew this was
not the Roberto from the farm, this was a man
who would use a gun if he had to, and if he put
it in her hand, she would use it too. That
knowledge frightened her. But that's what
violence did to a person. It had bred something
in her that she didn't know was there.

Roberto stepped out first, blinking in the dim
light. He held a finger to his lips and gestured for
them to remain where they were. He crossed to
the door and left the room on silent feet. Isabella
immediately picked up the long metal spike that
had opened the secret hiding place and stood in
the doorway with it clutched in her hand like a
dagger. But he returned and she said nothing.
Not showing what those two minutes cost her.

She turned to the young boy whose face was grey in the shadows, sweat beading at his temples.

'Alessandro.' She spoke in a whisper, though the house was empty. 'Thank you.' She walked over and kissed his young cheek. 'Thank you for saving us. You are brave.'

He blushed. Even sick with fear, he could blush. 'I was sent to find you. We have safe houses scattered through the town, but the carabinieri are too stupid to know.'

'That *capitano* knew,' Roberto pointed out. 'That's why he stayed.'

He offered his hand to Alessandro. 'You have courage, young man. I thank you for it.'

The boy smiled shyly as he shook Roberto's hand. 'I stayed,' he told them. 'To help Carlo Olivera and his followers fight back. Papa and the girls have gone south.' His hand slid to a knife in a leather sheath under his jacket and as he touched it, his manner seemed to stiffen, his muscles to harden. Isabella grieved for the young boy who wanted to be a farmer but who was forced to swap the plough for the knife. Eventually the knife would become a gun. That's how killers are made.

'Who sent you to find us?' Roberto asked.

'Carlo. He's — '

Footsteps on the stairs, soft secretive ones. Quick furtive sounds. Roberto stepped smoothly to one side of the door, Alessandro took the other side, Isabella remained where she was, visible as a distraction to the gaze of whoever emerged. She waited without a flicker of movement. Just a pulse at her throat.

Abruptly the intruder appeared out of the gloom on the landing. A thin small face. It was Rosa.

She grinned at Isabella and beckoned. 'Come, signora.'

★   ★   ★

Rosa had the nose of a rat for where the patrols of carabinieri were searching. She crept up the steep climb towards the castle and then instantly dipped down again and doubled back on herself. Avoiding the dark uniforms by no more than a few paces around a corner, by a sliver of a shadow.

Isabella saw a different Rosa. It was as though she had shed a skin along with her grey uniform. She was now wearing a loose smock of coarse cloth and she moved with the freedom of a small woodland creature, certain of her step. She squeezed Roberto into niches that almost cracked his shoulders, and tucked Isabella under arches of stone steps until danger passed.

They succeeded in crossing the town and entered a small street that basked in sunlight, the wind swirling through the washing that hung on lines stretched across it, shirts and sheets that fluttered like ghosts who had lost their way.

'Here,' Rosa pointed.

It was another of the red-tiled medieval houses with its stone walls gilded by the sun, its doors low and its windows shuttered and small.

'Rosa.' Roberto's voice was careful.

'Yes?'

'Did you tell anyone else that your father was up here in Sermoneta? Colonnello Sepe was here before we were.'

Rosa shook her head but her eyes grew huge and anxious. She was once more the silent child who had first sat at Isabella's table in the Piazza del Popolo.

'What is it, Rosa?' Isabella asked. She took Rosa's hand in hers. 'Who did you tell?'

The girl's face crumpled. 'I didn't mean to.'

'It's all right. Your papa will know you didn't mean to.' She squeezed the small hand that had curled into a tight ball inside her own. 'Who was it?'

'Carmela.'

'Who is Carmela?'

'My friend at school.'

Isabella and Roberto exchanged a look. So Sepe was interrogating children now. How many of them had he terrified? How many had nightmares of men in uniforms and of women in black habits? Isabella crushed her anger and approached the front door with Roberto. She hated to see the gun in his hand. Don't, Roberto, don't forget who you are.

Rosa darted forward in front of them and rattled out a prearranged knock on the door, her knuckles beating a rhythmic tattoo on the bleached wood. Isabella stood beside Roberto, ready to slip inside, but even she was unprepared for the face that scrutinised them when the door swung open. It possessed a mane of ginger hair and a quick sharp stare. At once Isabella recognised the man who had accosted her in Rome: Luca Peppe.

He smiled in recognition but the smile didn't even attempt to travel from his mouth to his eyes. He didn't trust her. But neither did she trust him.

'I've come with Rosa to see Carlo Olivera,' she stated.

She was exposed here standing out in the street for any of the patrols to spot. The autumn warmth from the sun felt too fragile to drive the chill from her spine and she was grateful for Roberto's solid presence beside her. He was regarding the man at the door with deep suspicion. Peppe was taken by surprise when Roberto abruptly shouldered his way forward into the narrow hallway and checked behind the door. No one was waiting there with a knife for their backs.

'Rosa,' Peppe said as if Roberto and Isabella were not there, 'he's asking for you. Get in quickly.'

Rosa shot past them, her dark head disappearing down to the end of the passage. The house felt cold, and from the rough old walls seeped the dank smell of a place that was unlived in, a sadness adrift in the air.

'Is Carlo Olivera here?' Roberto demanded.

'He is.'

Peppe shut the door quickly behind them and led them towards the room at the far end of the hall, down several steps. Over his shoulder he glanced at Isabella. 'I don't know why you're here or why he's fool enough to let you come, but don't think I won't be watching every move you make.'

His eyes shifted to Roberto who seemed to fill the narrow space. Peppe was about to say more but a voice from within the room made him change his mind and he pushed open the door.

Isabella's mouth went dry. To confront the man who had put a bullet in her back and ended her husband's life, that was why she was here. But the moment did not come alone. It brought the past with it, hurtling along the passage with a howl, and she wanted to reach out and seize it by the throat. To choke the life out of it. To hear its last desperate breath, its death rattle. To know there would be no more nightmares, no more sweat and tears each night. After she'd entered this room, she would be able to say to Roberto, *Look at me. My scars have gone. I don't have to hide any more.*

But first she had to take that step, to face the man who had killed her husband and crippled her. She didn't hesitate but walked into the room, eyes wide open. The room had been turned into a makeshift bedroom, dominated by a handsomely carved wooden bedstead, but it must have at one time been a dining room because a table and chairs were pushed against the wall out of the way. The walls were rough-plastered and white-washed, with a framed picture of the Madonna hung in pride of place.

A man lay on the bed, a man with blond hair matted with dried blood and intense blue eyes that fixed on her with a brilliance that glittered

463

with fever. The man was the one in the photograph that Roberto took at the convent, the Communist who called himself Carlo Olivera, the one Isabella had sworn on Luigi's grave to kill.

She approached the bed that was crumpled and stained with blood, and saw the gun he clutched in his hand that was lying weak and trembling at his side.

'We meet at last,' she said fiercely.

Another man with his back to her was bending over a medical bag on the other side of the bed and he swung round quickly at the sound of her voice. Isabella stared, aghast, at the tall bespectacled doctor.

It was her father.

41

Roberto could smell the sickness. The room stank of it. Of sickness and pain. And blood. He had once walked into a barn full of goats that had been savaged by a rabid dog and it had smelled like this. He stepped away from the ginger-haired escort, whose eyes never left the spot where Roberto's gun was now concealed under his jacket, and took a position with his back to the wall, alert and watchful. Isabella's father put down the syringe he was holding and stalked around the bed to stand in front of his daughter.

'Don't, Isabella, don't look so shocked.' He peered over his spectacles at her with stern disapproval. 'What are you doing here? Get out now. This . . . ' he waved a hand at the ashen figure on the bed, 'is no place for you.'

Isabella seemed to shake herself, her hair rippling back to life before she did. As though for a split second something had stopped working inside her.

'You knew, Papa. All this time you knew, didn't you, that it was Carlo Olivera and where he was hiding? You knew and you never told me. Why? Why keep it from me?'

Dr Cantini frowned at her. 'You'd been through enough. I wanted you to forget.'

Her eyes flashed angrily at both men. 'Did you really think I could forget?' She moved closer to

465

the bed. 'I understand your hatred of my husband,' she said to Olivera, 'but did you think that you could kill him and maim me and I would *forget?*' She placed her hand on the mattress beside him and stared down into the fierce blue eyes, bending over him. Blocking his sight. Filling his mind with the person who had come for vengeance.

He knew it. Roberto could see it in his eyes. Just as clearly as Roberto knew it himself. Yet he didn't cry out. They both saw her slide her left hand into the sling that supported her right arm and let her fingers steal around the knife that they were certain lay there, though they couldn't see it. She had hidden it well.

'Signora Berotti,' Carlo Olivera whispered, as his ice-blue eyes scrutinised her face, 'you are hating the wrong person. All that rage. Tearing you apart. When the person you should be hating is Benito Mussolini.' He spat out a thick jet of blood-streaked spittle, as though the name burned his tongue. 'He is the one you should be saving an assassin's blade for. Not me.'

'Mussolini is not the killer who pulled the trigger that destroyed my life, Signor Olivera. You are!'

Peppe stepped towards her but Roberto blocked his path.

With a great effort Olivera pushed himself to sit upright, forcing Isabella back. His shirt hung open to reveal a thick pad of bandages across his chest, fresh scarlet stains flowering across them with the movement.

'Don't, Carlo,' Dr Cantini groaned. 'For

God's sake, what is the point of my patching you up if you — '

But Olivera brushed aside the objections with a sharp twist of one shoulder. He was propping himself up on one hand and Roberto could see the force of will keeping him there. His lips had turned grey and sweat pooled in the hollow of his throat. This was not a man who listened to others telling him what to do. The Communist leaned his face close to Isabella's, their eyes fixed on each other. Her slender body was quivering and a low-pitched sound was coming from her, vibrating the air between them.

'I let you come here today,' Olivera told her, 'because you were kind to my daughter when she needed me and I couldn't be there. You have helped her, so now I help you.'

He glanced away to Rosa who was on her knees on the floor on the far side of the bed in an attitude of fervent prayer. Her eyes tight shut, her small hands clasped around her mother's crucifix, her lips moving in silent prayer.

'Come here, Rosa.'

Instantly she was beside him, her head tucked against his bandaged ribs. He stroked her cropped curls for a moment, but without warning he suddenly wrapped his fingers hard around the hand in Isabella's sling. It must have hurt but she gave no sign of it, and Roberto could sense her father's concern as intense as his own, but both knew better than to intervene. This was between them, Olivera and Isabella. Roberto fought down the desire to rip her away

467

from the man's grasp.

'Signora Berotti,' Olivera said with an odd smile that sat crookedly on his lean face, 'you do not have it in you to kill. Look at my eyes, look hard. Yes, you see, don't you, what is destroyed in a person each time a trigger is pulled. I am willing to pay that price for my country. But it is not in you, you don't have what it takes to kill.' His eyes flicked over to Roberto. 'Unlike your big friend over there who does.'

'You mistake me, signore,' Isabella said quietly.

Roberto saw it then. What he had not until now believed. In the darkening of her eyes. He saw that the Communist was wrong. No warning. No hesitation. No doubting herself. The knife was in her hand and the blade was pinned against Olivera's throat.

The air had become solid. No one breathed. No one moved. The child whimpered. Olivera's blue eyes turned the colour of death as the reality of his mistake drained all certainty from them.

'Isabella,' Roberto said softly.

That was all. Just her name. To call her back. But she didn't hear. She was somewhere he couldn't reach her and he knew it was almost too late. He moved towards her.

'No, Roberto.'

A trickle of blood slid down the Communist's throat. His eyes didn't leave hers.

'For God's sake, Carlo,' her father shouted, 'tell her. Tell her the truth. I won't see her hang for you.' He turned to his daughter and his face was suddenly ten years older, the flesh hanging from his cheekbones. 'Tell Isabella the truth or I will.'

Isabella blinked. The blade froze. 'What truth?'

Olivera let himself breathe. 'I did not kill your husband. I was not the one who pulled the trigger to fire the bullets that took his life and wounded you.'

A shake of her head. A tightening of her mouth. 'You're lying.'

'No, he's not,' her father insisted.

'Who then? If it wasn't you, who was it?'

The silence in the room was only broken by the moan of the child. She lifted her head from her father's side and tears rolled down her cheeks.

'It was Mamma.'

Isabella dropped the knife.

Olivera nodded. 'It was my wife. Allegra Bianchi.'

42

'It's not true.'

The words faded as soon as they fell from Isabella's lips. She knew she was holding on to something that no longer existed, like clinging to a ghost. The rage and hatred that had solidified around her heart for so many years seemed to crack open and she could feel her blood flowing hot and vital through her veins. No longer thick and heavy, no longer sterile and sluggish. But her mind struggled to grasp what was happening.

'Why? Why would Allegra Bianchi try to kill me and then bring me her child?'

Nothing made sense.

The small room with the stink of blood in it suddenly felt too crowded for her thoughts, as they twisted around each other, seeking a way to understand what was going on. Why had Carlo Olivera allowed her to come so close? He was wounded and sick. In danger and in desperate need of help. So why let her, of all people, inside the house? Was it in return for her father's care, a payment for his medical treatment? For his silence? All this time, year after year, for a decade her father had known Luigi's killer was Allegra Bianchi.

Yet he had kept it a secret.

Why?

She felt the question roaring inside her.

What reason did the troubled woman with the

wild hair and the angry eyes have for wanting to kill Luigi and herself?

The people in the attic?

The thought flashed into Isabella's mind. Was that it? Did someone close to her die in the fire that Luigi started in the Communist meeting house? The one Giorgio Andretti had told her about.

She spun around to Roberto. He was the only one she could trust in this maze of lies and secrets, and she found him right behind her, guarding her back.

'Isabella,' he said urgently. 'Leave now. Walk away from this — '

The door of the room burst open and Alessandro rushed into the sickroom. He flung himself to the bedside of Carlo Olivera, panting hard, eyes wide with panic.

'They're here! The Blackshirts are here. They're marching up the street. Someone in the town has betrayed us, Carlo.'

* * *

Roberto was the first to react.

He seized Isabella's shoulder. 'We leave right now. If you stay, you will be shot for helping a traitor.' His tone was clear and decisive, his grey eyes were on her face.

Carlo Olivera was swinging himself off the bed, but he buckled as soon as his feet hit the floor.

'*Merda!*'

Isabella fought down her fear. She saw her

471

father and the ginger-haired Peppe leap to support him on each side, as Rosa grabbed the gun from under his pillow. Isabella snatched up her knife from the floor and followed Roberto to the door. She pressed herself to his side, making no sound. Out in the street she could hear the steady beat of Blackshirt boots. Shouts snapped through the bright morning air, edging closer.

'It's too late to run, Isabella,' Roberto said in a low murmur. 'We'll have to fight.' They both knew what the outcome would be. He pulled his gun from under his jacket and Isabella wanted to claw it from his hand.

'No,' she whispered, wrapping her arm around his to hamper it. 'Don't.'

He touched her face, a brief heart-stopping touch. Then he unwound her arm from his and stood behind the door, drawing her to his far side.

'Isabella!'

It was her father's voice, urgent and low.

'This way!'

Peppe and Alessandro were prising up one of the flagstones from the floor, while her father held Olivera on his feet, though he swayed with the effort. Instantly Roberto strode over and lifted the stone clear of the floor. Underneath lay a black hole with metal rungs set into the rock. Isabella was staring into the mouth of a tunnel and its meaning made her almost double up with a fierce pain that cut through her like a knife blade. It was relief.

They might live.

The tunnel lay in absolute darkness.

It closed around them as suffocating as soot. It smelled of things unseen and of ancient footsteps and it contained the kind of stale air that had been breathed by too many others. Centuries old, it had been hewn through solid rock, a secret escape line when invaders came calling and Sermoneta's defences failed to keep them at bay.

The town had learned the hard way that you keep a back door open at all times in case the wolves come howling at the front. The minds of the people of Sermoneta were as tortuous as its streets and Isabella breathed a blessing on their forethought as she hurried through the tunnel, bent over to avoid the low ceiling. It felt like a tomb.

The darkness was pressing on her chest. In front of her, Alessandro led the way. She couldn't see him but she could hear his breath, ragged and erratic, as though he stopped breathing for long moments. For a young boy who was clearly terrified, she admired the courage of his fight against the Fascist regime. Behind her scrambled Rosa, holding Isabella's hand, her small fingers clamped tight as if she thought the darkness would swallow her whole if she let go. Small wordless sounds came from her whenever Isabella murmured softly to reassure her.

Following the child were Roberto and Carlo Olivera, a black two-headed monster, because

Roberto was carrying the Communist on his back. The tunnel was so low and so narrow that he was bent double with Olivera's head slumped on his shoulder, but somehow he was forcing his way forward. He snorted like a bull each time he cracked his skull on the rocks but otherwise remained silent.

It was her father behind them who spoke quietly to Olivera at intervals, checking on him, offering him pills to chew on for the pain, but Olivera just grunted in reply. In the rear Luca Peppe called instructions to Alessandro in the lead.

'One more corner and then we can use the torches. I think there's no one following. They haven't found the tunnel, but watch your step, Alessandro, because it drops down steeply after the bend.'

The darkness inside Isabella's head was growing denser, like winter fog. She discarded her sling and drew Rosa tighter to her, twisting round to brush her hand over the child's cheek, and she felt the small teeth chattering.

'I won't let go of you,' she whispered. 'Don't be frightened, we're safe here.'

Her foot stepped on something soft, unnerving her, and she realised it must be a dead rat. She led Rosa past it. Once around the next bend a torch sprang into life in Alessandro's hand, a pencil-thin line of dancing light like a split in the blackness, and she heard Rosa's smothered sob of relief.

'Roberto,' Isabella murmured, 'there are steps here. Take care.'

He gave a harsh grunt, readjusted the burden on his bent back, and after a second added, 'If I fall, you'll make a soft landing for us.'

She laughed, a strange unexpected sound that trickled through the tunnel and she wondered when these walls had last heard a laugh. Maybe never. Cries of alarm and the scurrying of frightened feet were the only noises that an escape tunnel heard.

The steps were steep and seemed to have no end. They descended into the darkness inside the bowels of the mountain, rough and treacherous, slimy with water that oozed from the walls. Isabella kept a tight hold on Rosa, aware of the bleak terror in the child, but Rosa possessed her father's courage and made no sound. Isabella loved her brave heart and the way she stared the leaping shadows in the face.

Abruptly the steps came to a halt and a passageway curved away to the right. There was no sign that the tunnel had ended but suddenly Alessandro was pushing his shoulder against a barrier that began to shift and tumble. Daylight leapt through the gaps, blinding the small group. Pure sunlight washed over them as Alessandro tore down the barrier of branches and Isabella drew in great lungfuls of clean fresh air.

The world had turned green. A thousand shades of green, emerald and lime and dark olive, mingled with the yellows and browns of autumn and the heavy musty smell of damp earth. Trees offered their trunks and their canopies for shelter, and the sense of safety under them felt like something solid and warm inside her. Isabella saw the same relief flooding Rosa's dark eyes but when she turned to Roberto, the brightness of the moment faded.

'What is it?' she said at once.

He shook his head. The strain of carrying Olivera through the cramped tunnel was etched on his face, its muscles taut and smeared with blood. He placed the Communist down on a patch of shaded grass where her father tended him, and Peppe was moving forward stealthily through the trees ahead.

'What is it?' she asked again.

She put a hand on his chest and felt each heavy beat of his heart. Over his shoulder was slung a rifle, presumably Olivera's, and it sent a shiver through her.

'It was too easy,' he said.

'Easy? You call that easy?'

He drew her against his chest and held her there, but his eyes scanned the gaps between the trees to the forested valley below. 'They know we're here.'

★ ★ ★

'Isabella, do you need something?' Her father tapped his medical bag, the old scuffed leather one that was as much a part of him as his spectacles and moustache.

'No, *grazie*.'

He peered into her face. 'Are you all right?'

She gave him a smile. 'I'm more all right than Carlo Olivera is. How bad is he?'

'Bad enough.'

'He should be in hospital.'

'That would be a death warrant, so what's the point? Thank God for your Roberto's strong back. Olivera would never have made it this far on his own.'

The tunnel had emerged halfway down the side of a mountain, surrounded by forested slopes in every direction and overlooking a verdant valley far below. Shadows slid from mountain to mountain like thieves on the run and grey rock ledges rose from the greenery as though trying to keep watch, their skin wrinkled and ancient. It was a world that was alien to Isabella, one that made her uneasy because there was always something unknown hidden in a forest. Something that laid its fingers on your soul.

'You should have told me, Papa.'

'How could I? You were unhappy enough. It was easier to lay the shooting at the door of a known Communist insurgent.'

'Why did she do it?'

'I don't know.'

'You're lying, Papa.'

He sighed and walked back to his patient.

★   ★   ★

They know we're here.

Roberto's words drummed in Isabella's head and made the hairs rise on the back of her neck, ice cold. Her eyes darted from tree to tree. From rock to rock. Searching for a face, the glint of a rifle barrel, the movement of a shadow.

They kept away from the bumpy track that ran along the hollow of the valley, and forged a path between the trees. It was harder going, especially on Roberto with the chalk-faced Communist on his back, but it was safer. Rosa trotted alongside her father, her hand resting on his thigh, her teeth clenched together in distress. They walked fast, up over the next ridge and down into a further wooded valley that was smaller and steeper. More secretive. No one spoke.

For an hour the silence held them in its grip. The only sound was the splash of a heron as it took off among the reeds, rising into the air on the morning thermals and arcing off down the valley. Isabella was jumpy. She started at the rustle of branches brushing against each other in the wind and trod carefully over the carpet of autumn leaves under her feet. The forest was decaying, wet and lush, roots tangling, the earth was dark and muddy. The world was becoming quieter.

Only Roberto's breath behind her remained constant. She listened to the rhythm of it, step by step. She offered to carry the rifle for him but he gave her a bleak smile and declined to relinquish it. That told her too much. She kept her eyes scouring the mountainside on the opposite slope across the valley — it was the obvious place from which to launch an attack — but nothing moved. Beyond it lay the blur of further mountains.

She tried to hold back the anger that was growing in her each time she looked behind at the burden on Roberto's back. She wanted to throw Olivera's broken figure to the earth and make Roberto run. Run on those long legs of his to somewhere safe and uncharted. Somewhere too far away for Mussolini to stretch his grasping fingers and steal Roberto's life. She wasn't willing to exchange Roberto for anyone else's life, however hard they were fighting for Italy's salvation.

She was selfish when it came to Roberto. No one else could have him. He was hers to love and to spend the rest of her life with, talking far into the night about fishing or horses or building a fine new school or . . . Anything. Just talking. Heads together on a pillow. Hands entwined, stroking each other's skin absent-mindedly while they discussed whatever it was that took their fancy at that moment. Committing to deep memory the feel of each other's fingertips.

She wouldn't let him go.

She wouldn't.

43

The shot, when it rang out across the valley, missed its target. It slammed into Roberto instead of into the Communist hunched on his back. The crack of the rifle shattered the silence and sent Roberto spinning to the ground, Olivera crashing down beside him.

Isabella heard the breath leave Roberto's lungs and the air seemed to fracture around her. It was ten years ago, all over again. The rifle shot. The birds rising in panic. The blood on the shirt. For years the images had crept under the covers at night with her and now they were here again in broad daylight.

She was struck mute with horror. *Roberto.* His name filled her head. *Roberto.*

She hurled herself to the ground at his side. His eyes were closed. Not staring doll's eyes like Luigi's. Grief howled like a pack of wild dogs in her ears and her mind became clumsy, but her hands worked with swift efficient movements, as she'd seen her father do a thousand times. She eased back his jacket to open the site of the wound at his collarbone and managed to start breathing again when she saw his eyelids flicker open.

'Papa!'

She summoned her father who was busy pressing a pad on to Olivera's chest to stop the bleeding.

'Papa, come here.'

He scurried over just as another bullet sent a spray of dark earth skittering over Olivera's cheek.

'Get under cover,' Roberto hissed sharply to Isabella. He tried to sit up, but Dr Cantini and Isabella took his arms and edged him back behind a broad fir tree that hid him from view from across the valley. 'Dottore,' he said, 'I'm all right. See to him.' He gestured at Olivera.

But Luca Peppe was already dragging his leader into the shelter of a tangle of bushes with Rosa, while Alessandro dodged behind a tree and took aim with Peppe's rifle. Dr Cantini took a look at Roberto's wound, probing with expert fingers.

'A scratch,' he announced with an encouraging smile.

'Papa! How bad is it really?'

'All right, the bullet has smashed your left clavicle, your collarbone. It is lodged inside there. I'll do what I can to stem the bleeding.' He worked quickly, before taping a pad over the area and tying Roberto's arm up in a sling.

The whole time Isabella's gaze was fixed on Roberto's face, following each flinch of his eyes or grimace of his mouth. She felt sick inside from the blood and the pain and the hatred. She wanted to take his hand in hers and walk him away from this valley of death.

'Help me up, Isabella.'

She didn't argue. She tucked her shoulder under Roberto's arm and eased him to his feet.

'Pass me the rifle.'

'No.'

'Isabella!'

'No. Isn't this enough?'

He gently held her chin in his hand and gave it a tiny shake. 'My love, there is no way out of here now for us. We die or we fight.'

'No. If we fight we'll die.'

He leaned forward and kissed her forehead tenderly. 'I won't let you die.'

For a long moment their eyes locked and then she turned and picked up the rifle.

'You can't fire it,' she said flatly. 'Not with a broken collarbone and a bullet inside you.'

'No,' he said in a soft voice, 'I can't.'

She looked down at her own bandaged right hand and at Roberto's patched left shoulder. She smiled oddly at him. 'Together we make one person,' she said.

'Yes, Isabella. Together we make one person.'

A shout of alarm from Alessandro jerked their attention back to the valley. 'There on the ridge. Look! It's the carabinieri.'

Peppe snatched his rifle from the boy and zigzagged forward through the trees. Two shots rang out from the mountainside across the valley but they snicked harmlessly into the trunk of a larch, spitting pieces of bark into the air. Isabella's pulse raced as she saw Peppe take aim and return fire.

'Isabella,' her father ordered, 'get down.'

But Isabella was off and running over to their right, step for step behind Roberto. Ducking behind bushes, swerving between trees, darting over fallen branches. The leaves under their feet silenced their footsteps; they kept low and in the shadows. Luck was on their side. The sun was behind their mountain, so their slopes were in shade, while it glared full in the face of the opposite side of the valley. A dark uniform stood out like a black cat in snow.

A smattering of shots was exchanged between Peppe and the carabinieri, and Isabella could see the uniforms spilling down from the higher slopes to the valley floor, though how they hoped to cross the open wetland there, she didn't know.

'Roberto, how did they find us?'

He grimaced. 'Informers must have told them about the tunnel. Nowhere is safe in Mussolini's State of Italy. He has poisoned the minds of Italians and no one can trust his neighbour any more. So Sepe has sent his forces to scour the hillsides for us.'

Still Roberto kept moving further down the valley and Isabella had to work hard to avoid tripping on the roots that writhed and twisted in her path. She knew what he was doing. Exactly as he must have done a thousand times when out hunting deer or wild boar in his forests at home. Outflanking them. She kept glancing across to the other side of the valley as she dodged behind trunks, dragging breath into her lungs, and bit by bit the far side of the rocky ridge came into view.

'There.' Roberto stopped dead and pointed.

Tucked down beside the ridge in the safety of its overhang were three uniformed figures. Even to Isabella it was clear that the middle one was thin and angular, with a wealth of silver braid adorning his jacket and bicorn hat as he

483

gesticulated at the others, issuing orders. It was Colonnello Sepe.

'Now,' Roberto whispered.

He raised the rifle in his right hand and tucked it tight against his shoulder. Isabella stood in front of him with the barrel resting on her shoulder, taking the weight of it, and with her left hand she steadied it as Roberto sighted along it. When he was satisfied, he said again, 'Now.'

He pulled the trigger. She felt the kick. The recoil. The crack of the rifle was so loud it made her ears ring, just like on that day in the Milan market, but Roberto kept an arm around her from behind, holding them both together.

The dark figure fell. Across the valley it looked small and insignificant, with other spiky figures fussing around it. Neither Roberto nor Isabella spoke, neither of them said the words, *We have killed a man between us*. Not out loud. Not for others to hear. But she could feel the shivers that gripped him at the thought of having taken a human life, and she knew neither of them would forget this day. She held him. Her cheek on his rough jacket, aware of the Communist's blood that had soaked into its fabric. In the same way that the Communist's hatred had soaked into her.

She stared in silence out across the valley, shocked by the calmness of her thoughts, by the certainty that she could kill again if she had to.

Is that what Luigi found? That the first time was hard but the second time came easier? And easier still the time after that. Isabella stood on the side of a windswept mountain and felt she

484

understood her husband just a little more than before.

'They'll go now,' Roberto told her. 'Without their leader, the carabinieri will have no stomach for the fight. They'll be frightened they will have to answer to someone for that bullet.'

But even as they watched, a column of Blackshirts came marching up the valley.

44

They hid in a cave. The mountainside was pockmarked with them, each one known to Olivera and Peppe, each one prepared with undergrowth spread over the entrance, water, straw and kindling hidden away inside. A man could hold out here for weeks.

The air in the cave was cool, the walls rough and glistening with moisture. Moss grew near the entrance like a green carpet but deeper inside the limestone rock there was a coppery taste in the air. As if the mountain breathed its ancient memories into the hollows within itself.

'Take this.'

Isabella was bathing Roberto's wound with iodine. Her fingers opened his mouth and placed one of her father's pills on his tongue. She could feel the heat building in him, the fire under his skin, and the jagged edges of the wound were looking raw and angry. She dropped a kiss on his dusty tangle of chestnut hair and rubbed her cheek across it. The bullet needed to come out but it was too dangerous for her father to attempt it here. She had to get him home.

She crossed over deeper into the cave to where her father was seated on the ground next to Carlo Olivera who was lying on a bed of straw. Rosa lay tight alongside him, her hair touching his jaw, the chain of her mother's crucifix wrapped around her wrist. Isabella crouched down beside them and could see plainly that Olivera didn't look good. His skin had changed from chalky white to a greyish-blue colour that didn't belong on skin, and deep lines of pain were gouging themselves down his cheeks. His eyes were closed and her father's brown coat lay over him.

'How is he?' she asked in a low murmur, resting a hand on her father's shoulder.

The cave altered sound. It buffed the edges off words, making them softer, absorbing them into its rock walls.

'He's not too bad,' her father said in his professionally cheerful tone, designed to give patients hope. 'He's had bad wounds before and come through them. I've patched him up more times than either of us can remember. He's tough. Isn't that so, Carlo?'

The Communist's mouth curved in a smile and his eyes dragged themselves open. 'You can't kill weeds.'

Rosa lifted her head to watch her father's face.

'We'll get you out of here tonight when it gets dark,' Dr Cantini assured him. 'Peppe is out there checking on the patrols. We'll fix you up, so you can make Mussolini curse your name for years to come.' He patted his friend's limp arm.

'You always were a rotten liar, Cantini.'

'Don't give up, my friend. Not yet.'

The muddy blue eyes of the Communist settled on Isabella's face and she could feel the force of them even now, the strength of will that had made him such a thorn in Mussolini's side.

'It is strange, Cantini, is it not' — his words came in short bursts between each laboured breath — 'that despite our friendship, our families have brought nothing but grief to each other.'

Isabella's father turned to look at her, his large head seeming unsteady, as though suddenly too heavy. 'My daughter has the courage of a lioness.'

Isabella blinked. Missed a breath. She had no idea. No idea that he thought such a thing.

'Papa, thank you.'

She kissed his cheek but he became gruff and businesslike.

'How is your Roberto doing?'

She would not be sidetracked. 'Tell me what happened. If I have courage, I can bear the truth. Why did Allegra Bianchi shoot Luigi and me? And why did she leap from my tower?'

Her father shook his head. 'Leave the past where it is, Isabella. Think of your future.' His eyes drifted to where Roberto was standing in the cave mouth, watching for movement among the trees beyond the barrier of branches. He was giving them privacy.

'No, Papa. I need to know . . .'

Before her father could refuse her again, Carlo Olivera raised a weak hand to silence him.

'She has a right to know,' he said softly.

'No, Carlo, she has no right to — '

'He was her husband.'

Her father's anger hardened his voice. 'That's why she does not need to be told.'

'Signor Olivera, I have helped you today. I am

488

asking you to help me now. Tell me why your wife shot us.'

'I'm sorry, old friend,' the Communist brushed his hand on her father's arm, 'but . . . ' A sudden cough ripped through his wounded chest and blood coloured his teeth.

'Don't talk.'

But her father's glare did not silence him.

'Rosa, go and see if Luca Peppe is in sight yet. He will know what the Blackshirts are doing.'

'No, Papa, let me stay.' The child's thin arms tightened around him.

'Go, Rosa.'

She gathered up her limbs and jumped to her feet. He waited until she was out of earshot before he continued.

'My wife shot your husband because of what he did.'

'You mean burning the building with people in the attic.' Isabella shuddered again at the image. 'That was — '

'No. Not that.'

'What then?'

'He came with his Blackshirt friend, Giorgio Andretti, to the house where my wife was living. They had found out where she was.' His lungs were starting to rattle as he spoke. 'They knew I was in Rome. Working with union men and organising strikes for better conditions. I was there for two months.'

'Did he interrogate her?'

Isabella pictured the truncheon in Luigi's strong fist. Heard in her head the crack of it on fragile bones.

489

'No. He raped her.'

Isabella made a small choking noise and her heart stopped dead.

'No, no. Not even Luigi would do such a — '

'He did it. With brute force. We never found out whether it was the only time he did that to the wife of a known rebel or . . . ' he fought for breath, 'or whether it was a method of intimidation used by his Blackshirt unit. No other women came forward. We will never know.'

A nerve jumped in his grey cheek and he looked away abruptly, as though Isabella's face was a reminder of her husband and what he had inflicted on Allegra.

'I'm sorry,' Isabella told him. 'I'm so sorry.' Her hands were shaking, and she clasped them together to hide their weakness.

How could she not have known? How could she not have seen it in Luigi? She had been too young and too blinded by his Blackshirt glamour. Sorrow for Allegra swept through her, but rage directed at herself drove her to bow her head in shame.

'Enough, Carlo. Rest your lungs.'

'Tell her.' The Communist would not be denied. 'Tell her the rest.'

45

Roberto wanted to go to her. To fold Isabella's trembling body in his arms and take her away from this cave. He had heard the Communist's words and they raised a black hatred in his heart for the man who could rise from Isabella's bed and tear another woman's life apart. Isabella's head hung down, hiding her face and her shame behind her hair. Her curls were as tangled and snarled as he knew her emotions must be.

She'd heard enough.

When the Communist said, 'Tell her the rest,' Roberto had moved closer to her, ready to snatch her away from the words that carried what they called the truth. *Truth?* Truth was never absolute. It was never finite. The truth was that this Communist was a killer, and now Roberto and Isabella had become killers. They all had their reasons for doing what they did, so who was to say that Allegra Bianchi was in the wrong when she pulled the trigger?

'Tell me, Papa. Tell me the rest.' Isabella didn't lift her head.

Her father said nothing for a long moment and then exhaled a harsh breath of resignation. 'Very well. Allegra took revenge by shooting Luigi. She tried to kill you too because she believed at that time that he must have told you what he'd done.' He shook his head in sorrow, and his gaze lingered on his daughter.

'Go on, Papa. I'm listening.'

'She had a bullet wound in her leg. A policeman had fired on her when she was fleeing the building that she'd used to ambush you and Luigi. She came to me. I patched her up.'

'You helped her? While I was almost dying in the hospital?'

'Yes.'

Roberto saw her flinch. But she said no more.

'She came to me again a month later,' Dr Cantini continued. 'She was pregnant. She asked me to terminate it.' The words seemed to stick on his tongue. 'It was Luigi's.'

Isabella's head shot up. Her eyes were huge and seemed to have sunk deep into her head.

'Did you do as she asked?'

'No.'

A silence, thick as fog, filled the cave.

'Rosa is that child?' Isabella whispered.

'Yes.'

'Rosa is Luigi's child.'

'Yes.'

Carlo Olivera raised his head from the straw. 'That's why she brought her to you.' His voice was raw with emotion. 'I love Rosa like my own child, but Allegra never forgave her for being his.'

Isabella did not move. Did not seem to breathe.

'The carabinieri were right on her heels,' Olivera explained, 'the day she came to Bellina. I can only guess that she'd had enough. Too many years on the run. Never having a home. Or knowing when the knock on the door would come to say I was dead.' He let his head fall back on the straw, the tendons in his neck taut. 'I did that to my wife.'

It was finished. Roberto would not let these two men rip the heart out of Isabella any more. He strode over, wrapped an arm around her and lifted her to her feet. She stood stiff and upright, but her shoulder pressed hard against his.

'You tried to make me stay away from Rosa, Papa.'

'Yes.'

'Why?'

Her father pushed himself to his feet and studied her intently. 'I didn't want you involved in any of this, because — '

'You were wrong,' Roberto interrupted. 'Isabella needed to know what had happened. You're a doctor, couldn't you see what it was doing to her? It was your duty as her father to tell her.'

Roberto took hold of Isabella's arm and walked her towards the veil of greenery that obscured the cave entrance. 'Let's find Rosa,' he said.

She turned her beautiful face to him. 'Yes, it's time to find Rosa.'

46

Carlo Olivera breathed his last just before sunset.

This time Isabella did not have to tell Rosa that her parent had died. The child was there, holding her father's hand. She buried her young face in his neck and wouldn't leave him. Her grief was silent and without tears, but she kept vigil at his side all through the long hours of the night. When Isabella took her hand well before dawn and led her away from him into the damp morning air, she whimpered once but no more.

In the darkness they silently retraced their steps across the mountains, listening carefully for any sounds, but there was no sign of any guards posted. They retrieved their cars from their hiding places and drove back down the winding roads, leaving the mountains and their secrets behind. The wide expanse of the Agro Pontino plain opened up ahead of them and Isabella was caught by surprise by the strength of her desire to return to it.

They had discussed the dangers of returning. Her father had argued against it, convinced that Roberto and Isabella would be arrested because of the fight in the mountains, but Roberto had pointed out that they were too far away across the valley to be seen during the exchange of shots and had been hidden too well among the shaded trees for anyone to identify them. They could have been any of Olivera's fighting force. The sooner they showed their faces in town, and continued with their work as normal, the better.

As they drove down on to the plain the sun rose behind them above the hunched back of the mountains and bathed the barren fields in a shimmering golden light. Suddenly Isabella could see what the plain would look like next summer when golden fields of wheat would cover the land, and she felt a fierce need to be there to see it happen.

She looked down at the shorn dark head tucked against her shoulder and she tightened her arm around Rosa's small shoulders. Allegra Bianchi had stolen so much from Isabella and it would take time for her to understand what drove Luigi and Allegra to do what they had done, to believe that they had the right to so much savagery. Yet Allegra had brought her a child.

This child.

She rested her cheek on the warm head and watched the tower of Bellina come closer.

★ ★ ★

'Surviving?'

'Yes. I'm good at that.' Roberto smiled up at Isabella as she bandaged his shoulder.

Her father had removed the bullet, watched with care by Isabella, and he'd stitched up the wound, accompanied by comments like 'It's only a scratch' and 'You'll be heaving pigs around again in no time'.

495

'Papa, he's a photographer.'

'*Was* a photographer,' Roberto corrected. 'What good is a photographer with no camera?'

She remembered the smashed pieces of his beloved Graflex and the confetti of photographs littering his darkroom floor. The police had taken his Leica from him when he was under arrest.

'You can start again. A new camera.'

He rose to his feet and lightly kissed her lips. 'We can both start again.'

She smiled at him but a sharp knock at the door startled them all. A stab of fear made her reach for Roberto for a second, before she broke free and walked quickly to answer it. She swung the door open, knowing the dark uniforms would be on the other side.

'Hello, stranger, where have you been keeping yourself?'

It was Francesca, her white-blonde hair gleaming like snow in the sunlight.

Isabella laughed with relief. 'I've been in Rome, looking at stone.'

'You and your stones! Here, I've brought you breakfast. You haven't been into the shop for a few days.'

She handed over a napkin wrapped around warm spicy rolls and Isabella kissed her on both cheeks.

'Thank you, Francesca. Come on in for coffee.'

'No, I can't now. More baking to do. But this evening I'll come round and you can tell me what you've been doing.'

Isabella smiled. 'Any news?'

Francesca's pale blue eyes opened wide. 'Haven't you heard?'

'No. What is it?'

'The chief of carabinieri was killed in a fight with Communists up in the mountains yesterday.'

Isabella didn't blink. She recalled the kick of the rifle on Roberto's shoulder and the weight of its barrel in her hand. The figure in its dark blue uniform slumping to the ground.

'But, listen,' Francesca waved her arms through the air, 'the big news is that Mussolini has had Chairman Grassi arrested. He has been transported to Rome for failing to find who was responsible for the aeroplane crash at the rally.'

'What?'

'It's true.' Francesca grinned. 'That bastard is having a taste of his own medicine.' She glanced at her watch. 'And I must get back to my oven.' She blew a kiss to Isabella and hurried away through the courtyard.

Isabella turned to look at Roberto and at her father, not quite able to believe what she'd just heard.

'They've gone.' The words reverberated quietly in the room. 'Sepe and Grassi have gone.'

'That is wonderful news,' her father exclaimed, and his tall figure seemed to uncurl, as if a heavy weight had lifted from his shoulders. 'Isabella,' he was packing his instruments away in his medical bag after cleaning and sterilising them, 'I might leave Bellina too.'

'No, Papa.' Isabella put a hand on his bag as if

that small action could hold him. 'Stay here with us.'

He shook his head in a tired gesture. 'I've never liked this town, you know that. It's too stark and modern for me.'

'Where will you go?'

'I want to go back to the old Italy, to the beautiful places I knew before. I'm thinking of returning to Milan. I can continue to help the rebels there.'

'Papa, I'll miss you. But if that's what you want . . .'

'It is. I only stayed here to watch over you, my daughter.' He smiled broadly at Roberto. 'But now you have someone else to do that. And you have Rosa. What will you do with her?'

'Adopt her, of course. She won't be going back to the convent.'

A sound from the doorway of the room drew Isabella's attention and she looked round to see Rosa standing there in her loose smock. Her eyes were fixed on Isabella's face.

'I thought you were asleep on my bed, Rosa.'

'I heard a knock.'

'It's all right, it was just a friend. She brought good news. Both Chairman Grassi and Colonnello Sepe have left Bellina for ever.'

A small moan escaped Rosa's pale lips and she ran across the room to Isabella. Isabella crouched down and encircled the child in her arms, holding her trembling body close. 'What is it, Rosa?'

'I don't ever want to go back there, but I'm frightened for Carmela.'

'Your friend at the convent?'

Rosa nodded. 'She's all on her own now.'

Isabella realised at that moment how great were the complexities that this child was bringing into her life, but she stroked her young cheek reassuringly. 'I don't know what the connection was between Chairman Grassi and the Reverend Mother, but now that he has gone her position is weakened. In future she will have to be more careful how she treats her pupils at the convent. Anyway, I will keep a watch on Carmela and we will invite her to visit us as often as you like.' She ruffled the cropped curls. 'If that's what you want?'

Rosa didn't speak for a long moment. Her dark eyes shone and she nodded again. 'Mamma was right,' she said solemnly. 'You are a good person.'

* * *

When Rosa finally fell asleep once more, Isabella walked with Roberto through the town in the amber light of early morning, heading for her architectural office. Back in the Piazza del Popolo, where it all began, she paused, gazing at the fine buildings around her. At last she could see a real future for Bellina. She was aware of Roberto standing close behind her and she leaned against him, feeling the strength of him at her back.

'We could leave too,' he said thoughtfully. 'Start again elsewhere, if that's what you want.'

'No, Roberto, this is where I want to be. Right

here. With you and Rosa. I love this town and I love my work in it. There's so much more I want to do here in Bellina, and there are the five other new towns that have yet to be built on the Agro Pontino.' She stretched a hand out in front of her. 'It is waiting for us to create the future we want.'

Roberto wrapped an arm around her. 'We don't know who will replace Grassi and Sepe, but let's believe that whoever it is, they will have the good of the town at heart. I'll order a new Graflex camera for myself,' he added and she could hear the enthusiasm in his voice, 'and continue to record the growth of the town in pictures. But this time it won't be for Grassi. It will be so that in the future when everything has changed, people will be able to look at them and know what it was like here. How we built a town for them.'

Isabella looked eastward, her eyes drawn to the ancient mountains in the distance. They lay in purple shadow and watched patiently over the golden plain below.

Why I Chose To Write About The Pontine Marshes

The moment I heard about the extraordinary feat of the draining of Italy's Pontine Marshes — the Agro Pontino — and the construction of the new towns in the 1930s, I knew I had found the perfect setting for my next book.

It was my husband who first drew my attention to this amazing project of Mussolini's Fascist regime and I became fascinated by it. The scheme was driven by a risky combination of idealistic vision to create a brave new world and pragmatic political expediency to silence the unrest among the veterans of the Great War and give them employment. But it was the engineering expertise and the bottomless coffers that made it possible. I think it is debatable whether anything but a totalitarian state could have forced through such a vast project at the time. In 1933, at the peak of the work, 124,000 men were employed on it.

Of course I had to go and take a look at the flat expanse of the Agro Pontino as it is now — naturally checking out the delicious local Carmenere and limoncello at the same time! — and it was an enthralling research trip. The wide open plain covers an extended rectangle about thirty miles long and roughly twenty miles wide, bordered by the coastline of the Tyrrhenian

Sea to the west and by the Lepini mountains to the east. It lies thirty miles SW of Rome, between the ancient towns of Cisterna in the north and Terracina in the south.

I started my research by reading all about the area and its history and quickly discovered what the problem was that caused the unhealthy swampland to form. Much of the land is below sea level and there is a quaternary dune that runs parallel to the coastline, preventing the mountain rivers from draining into the sea. So they pool and stagnate on the plain, and as a result these marshlands became an impenetrable forested malarial swamp. It was infested by dense black clouds of anopheles mosquitoes that had plagued this area for centuries. Even Nero and Napoleon and numerous Popes attempted to release the water by digging channels through the barrier dunes but no one succeeded.

Until Benito Mussolini.

His breathtaking ambition stormed through all obstacles.

How did he do it?
In 1930 the forest was cleared by a vast army of workmen, many of them veterans from the war. It's hard to imagine the logistics of this. The amount of timber that had to be hauled. The fires that had to burn day and night to consume the branches and stumps in the black volcanic earth. It must at times have felt like a scene out of hell.

The workmen lived in camps behind barbed wire, poorly fed and poorly paid. Many hundreds of them, maybe thousands, died from malaria and in accidents, but no records were kept of this. The sick and the dead were removed, so that the Great Scheme could claim it was untainted by failure. The workers then constructed over 10,000 miles of canals and trenches, as well as the essential pumping stations to keep the water flowing into the sea.

Once stripped of vegetation and drained of water, the barren plain was dug and furrowed by hundreds of giant tractors until it was ready to be farmed. Small blue homesteads sprouted up for farmers across the plain and five new towns were built during the years 1932–1939. The first was called Littoria, later renamed Latina, which was followed by Sabaudia, Pontinia, Aprilia and Pomezia.

Mussolini knew the value of propaganda. He employed LUCE Films to make regular newsreels of the Pontine Marshes to be shown in cinemas throughout Italy to demonstrate the success and power of Fascism. He made frequent trips to the area to be photographed in macho poses — shirtless with a shovel in his hand or driving a tractor or threshing wheat at harvest time. He loved to present himself as a man of the people and a lover of the land. But there was never any mention in the propaganda films of his Blackshirts or his secret police who backed up every decision he made.

Afterwards
In 1940 Italy entered World War II as an ally of Germany. The Agro Pontino and its new towns

would suffer for this when towards the end of 1943 American and British forces landed nearby to fight the German troops stationed at Anzio. Anzio lies on the edge of the Pontine plain and to gain access to the land a bombardment of the area was carried out by American forces. At the same time the Germans stopped the pumps and opened the dikes, flooding the marsh once again, causing devastation to the population and the agriculture. The Allies and the Germans found themselves fighting in a mosquito-infested bog.

The Battle of Anzio laid waste the area. Everything that Mussolini had accomplished was reversed. The towns were in ruins, the houses blown up, the marshes flooded, the canals filled in and the mosquitoes flourished. Malaria returned and the remaining population of the towns fled.

This struck me as immensely sad. It had been such an awesome achievement, but rescue came after the war ended in 1945. The major structures for water control were renovated, the Pontine plain was restored and the towns were rebuilt.

Now

I was anxious when I travelled to Latina, afraid that there would be nothing left to see of the grand buildings constructed in the 1930s. But what I saw on my research trip to the Agro Pontino warmed my heart. It is a green and flowering landscape. I saw flourishing towns and a wonderfully fertile plain where a wealth of fruit and grapes are cultivated. Particularly striking are the kiwi fruits. Mile after mile of tall graceful vines were fluttering in the warm breeze. They were introduced into Italy from New Zealand in the 1980s and Italy now produces 70% of the northern hemisphere's kiwis. A high percentage of them are grown on the Pontine plain.

And the towns? The wonderful Modernist buildings that my fictional heroine, Isabella, helped to create. What about them?

Though many of them were flattened by the wartime bombardment, fortunately many of them did survive and form a magnificent reminder of an era that has long past. In Latina in particular there is still much to see.

The town of Bellina in my book is, I must emphasise, a fictional town, a creation of my imagination for the purposes of my story. There were in reality only five new towns constructed, not six as I state in my story, but Bellina is loosely based on the impressive centre of Latina (originally Littoria). Dramatic, grandiose and beautiful, the buildings and town plan of Latina are a blend of Modernist and Rationalist styles, and form a tribute to the vision of Mussolini's great architects and to the people of Italy.

I would also like to point out to readers that the assassination attempt on Mussolini's life in *The Italian Wife* is fictional.

We do hope that you have enjoyed reading this large print book.

Did you know that all of our titles are available for purchase?

We publish a wide range of high quality large print books including:
Romances, Mysteries, Classics
General Fiction
Non Fiction and Westerns

Special interest titles available in large print are:
The Little Oxford Dictionary
Music Book
Song Book
Hymn Book
Service Book

Also available from us courtesy of Oxford University Press:
Young Readers' Dictionary
(large print edition)
Young Readers' Thesaurus
(large print edition)

For further information or a free brochure, please contact us at:
Ulverscroft Large Print Books Ltd.,
The Green, Bradgate Road, Anstey,
Leicester, LE7 7FU, England.
Tel: (00 44) 0116 236 4325
Fax: (00 44) 0116 234 0205

Other titles published by Ulverscroft:

WE'LL MEET AGAIN

Mary Nichols

1940: London is facing the full wrath of the Blitz. Amid the chaos, Sheila Phipps is orphaned after a devastating air raid claims her family and her home. Evacuated to Buckinghamshire to live with her aunt Constance, Sheila forms an unlikely friendship with Prudence Le Strange, working in the code-breaking unit at Bletchley Park. While their friendship grows stronger, the war subjects Sheila and Prue to fresh tragedies as, one by one, those they love are called away to distant battlefields, only to join the growing ranks of the missing, the captured and the dead. As the war escalates, the two friends find their lives increasingly complicated not only by the secrets of wartime, but by those the conflict begins to dredge up from the past . . .

THE YEAR I MET YOU

Cecelia Ahern

Jasmine knows two things. One, she loves her vulnerable sister unconditionally, and will fight to the death to protect her from anyone who upsets her. Two, she's only ever been good at one thing — her job helping business start-ups. So when she's sacked and put on gardening leave, Jasmine realises that she has nothing else to fill her life. Insomnia keeps her staring out of her bedroom window, and she finds herself watching the antics of her neighbour, shock jock Matt, with more than a casual eye. On New Year's Eve Matt is also forced to take a leave of absence from work, after one of his controversial chat shows goes too far; and as the year unfolds, through moonlit nights and suburban days, an unlikely friendship slowly starts to blossom . . .

TO HAVE AND TO HOLD

Helen Chandler

From the outside, Ella has the happy marriage, the cute kids and the comfortable home — yet inside she craves something more. But giving in to temptation will stir up a whole heap of trouble ... Imogen's relationship with Pete was once fun and carefree, but since they've become parents, everything is different. Then an accident proves the catalyst for a life-changing decision ... Fifteen-year-old Phoebe is miserable at home and at school. And now her dad, who was always her ally, seems completely distracted by something — or someone. Maybe it's time Phoebe took a stand, and took control of her own life ... As Ella, Imogen and Phoebe contemplate taking the biggest gamble of their lives, marriages, families and friendships hang in the balance. Should they take the leap, or do they risk losing everything?

THE BEACH HUT NEXT DOOR

Veronica Henry

Summer appeared from nowhere that year in Everdene; and for those lucky enough to own one of the beach huts, this was the summer of their dreams. For Elodie, returning to Everdene means reawakening the memories of one summer fifty years ago. A summer when everything changed . . . Vince and his brother are struggling to come to terms with the death of their father, but they have very different ways of coping . . . And for Jenna, determined to put the past behind her, the opportunity to become the 'Ice-Cream Girl' once again might just turn her life around. But this summer is not all sunshine and surf — as secrets unfold, and some lives are changed forever . . .